BLESSED
ASSURANCE

By Lyn Cote

BLESSED ASSURANCE

Coming Soon

THE TEXAS STAR OF DESTINY SERIES

BLESSED
ASSURANCE

Whispers of Love
Lost In His Love
Echoes of Mercy

LYN COTE

AVON
INSPIRE
An Imprint of HarperCollinsPublishers

Previously published by Broadman & Holman as three separate novels:
Whispers of Love copyright © 1999 by Lyn Cote
Lost In His Love copyright © 2000 by Lyn Cote
Echoes of Mercy copyright © 2000 by Lyn Cote

FIRST EDITION

Interior text designed by Diahann Sturge

Library of Congress Cataloging-in-Publication Data

Cote, Lyn.
   [Short stories Selections]
   Blessed assurance / Lyn Cote.—1st ed.
      p. cm.
   ISBN: 978-0-06-134994-2
   ISBN-10: 0-06-134994-1
   I. Title.
   PS3553.O76378B55   2007
   813'.54—dc22   2007005021

07 08 09 10 11   ✤/RRD   10 9 8 7 6 5 4 3 2 1

Blessed Assurance, Jesus is mine!
Oh, what a foretaste of glory divine!
Heir of salvation, purchase of God,
Born of His spirit, washed in His blood.

Perfect submission, perfect delight,
Visions of rapture now burst on my sight;
Angels descending bring from above
Echoes of Mercy, Whispers of love.

Perfect submission, all is at rest,
I in my Savior am happy and blest;
Watching and waiting, looking above,
Filled with His goodness, lost in His love.

From the hymn "Blessed Assurance" by Fanny Crosby

WHISPERS OF LOVE

Chapter 1

April 9, 1871

Would the baby live? He'd survived the night, thanks be to God. But would he finally keep liquids down today? The dark-skinned baby in Jessie's arms drew a deep, wonderful breath. She'd bathed the fevered child all night long. Trembling with fatigue, she wilted onto the old rocker.

Across from her in the gray glow of near dawn, she glanced at the outline of the baby's mother and father. They lay side by side on their narrow rope-bed in mutual exhaustion. Earlier, the mother, unwell herself, had nearly fainted and Jessie had forced her to lie down. Now, the way the black couple lay so close, so intimate, made her throat tighten. She looked away as if she'd intruded. She took a deep breath, steadying herself.

The grim dread that had oppressed her all night turned to cautious gratitude. *But I must get home now.* "Ruth," she called softly to the sleeping mother.

The young woman stirred and moaned, "My baby?"

"I think his fever may have broken."

Ruth stumbled to Jessie's side, lifting the child. With the inside of her wrist, Ruth tested her son's forehead. "You have the bestest way with sickness."

Aching, Jessie shuffled the few steps to the door and retrieved her black cape and bonnet from a nail. "Ruth, he's not out of danger yet." She fumbled with the ribbons of her black bonnet.

"Please, my husband will walk you home."

Jessie knew she must hurry home before her gossipy neighbors saw that she, a young widow, had spent a night away from home. And if a black man were seen accompanying her? Even worse. She shook her head. "Ruth, please don't give your baby anything but mother's milk. It's important. Promise me."

Cradling her baby son close, Ruth nodded. "God bless you, Mrs. Wagstaff."

After one last reminder to Ruth to heed her warning, Jessie shut the flimsy door behind her. She hurried north along the railroad tracks and then crossed them. Like the Continental Divide, the parallel black metal lines divided the freed slaves on one side of the railway from the Irish immigrants opposite them. Though the gray-brown shanties, thrown together from used lumber and tin, looked like heads bent in sadness, leaning close to each other as though sharing their sorrows, the two sides, both equally needy, never mixed. The scene always depressed her.

Jessie's long black skirt and petticoats swirled around her ankles, their weight growing with every step, slowing her down. Over the thud of her heels on the wooden Randolph Street Bridge, she heard the jingle of the harness bells and clattering hooves of the first morning bob-tail trolley. A stitch in her side, she hurried to the corner, flagging it down thankfully.

Lifting her skirts discreetly, she climbed up the steps. While she looked for a seat among the day-maids and workmen, the trolley jerked to a start. She stumbled, sat down abruptly, then moved to accommodate her modest bustle.

She would make it home now well before the gossips were up and snooping. Sighing, she closed her eyes, letting herself sway with the trolley's curious rhythm of going forward while rocking side to side. She snapped her eyes wide open. If she missed her stop, then needed to ride back, it would cost another penny and minutes she couldn't afford.

Blinking to keep her watering eyes open, she glimpsed the skyline of downtown. Dawn had come. The rising sun cast a rosy glow over the squared, ornate parapets of the limestone hotels. Her Will had called them imitation castles. Will's face surfaced in her memory, smiling as always, blond and blue-eyed. He whispered to her, "Come here, princess." He drew her into strong arms and his warm lips touched—

Ring! Startled awake, Jessie sat up straighter. With eyes now wide open, Jessie noted each northward street sign. At Ontario Street, she yanked the bell cord. Relief left her feeling hollow as she stepped down at the corner. Her pace quickened down the alleys so near home now, murky puddles wetting her shoes and cotton stockings.

Around the familiar, white frame houses, the lowing of a few cows and the clatter of a milk pail told her some people had already risen. She walked into heavy mist close to Lake Michigan; it concealed her.

Almost there. She began to breathe easier. From her alley shed, she heard the tut-tut of her hens. At last, through the grayness, she approached her back steps, an island in the surrounding fog.

Like a rag doll moved by unseen hands, she listened to the crunch-crunch rhythm of her shoes on the coal-cinder path. Longing for her first cup of coffee, she hurried to the first step.

"Jessie?" a sleep-filled voice muttered out of the mist.

A man's voice. A cold needle of shock jabbed her. She yelped.

"Jessie, Jessie Wagstaff?" the same voice asked.

Her eyes found the man, looming above her on the porch. But the slender stranger with dark hair and eyes, dressed in a well-cut black suit, did not appear threatening to her. Indeed, his startled reaction must have mirrored her own. "Who ... are you?" she stammered.

"Smith. I'm Lee Smith."

Heat flooded her. All her hurry and worry were for naught. Every neighborhood gossip must have heard her shout. She turned her aggravation on him full force. "Why are you on my porch at this hour?"

The man just gawked at her.

The door behind him hit the outside wall with a crack like a gunshot. Susan bolted toward the stranger, brandishing a broom. Outrage twisted her dark features. "Get! Get! You leave Mrs. Wagstaff alone!"

The man ducked just in time to avoid the swat aimed for his head.

Frozen with shock, Jessie merely watched as the man stumbled down the few steps to her side. "Susan!" Jessie finally shouted over her friend's stream of threats and captured the end of the broom, grabbing it away from Susan. "Stop! Please! I'm unharmed!"

Jessie glared at the stranger. "Sir, you have sixty seconds to persuade me that you have a lawful reason to be here before Susan and I run you off."

The stranger removed his now cockeyed hat. He began in a soothing tone, "I apologize. I didn't mean to alarm you. I must have dozed off while I waited for you—"

"I asked you a simple question." Jessie gripped the end of the broom as if it were her temper. "Answer it or I summon the police." Susan too scorched the man with her gaze.

"If this is the Wagstaff House, I am looking for a room."

"You want a *room*?" Jessie couldn't keep her voice low.

"This is a boardinghouse. I need a room—"

"It's only five A.M. Who would look for a room at this hour?"

"I'm so sorry, Mrs. Wagstaff. You are Mrs. Wagstaff, are you not?"

"Yes, I'm Mrs. Wagstaff," she admitted though would have much preferred to punch him. Susan began to mutter under her breath again, sounding like a locomotive building up a good head of steam.

"I arrived at the railway station downtown only about two hours ago," the man continued. "I asked directions and walked here—"

"Here? Why?" she demanded, her eyes narrowing. "Do I know you?"

"No, your boardinghouse was recommended by the conductor on my train."

Liar. "Chicago has over three hundred thousand people and you expect me to believe that some train conductor I don't know gave you my address."

"Well, he spoke highly of you." The man's irksome smile held.

The hooves of a fast-approaching horse clacked on the wooden street out front. A uniformed officer dismounted only a few feet from Jessie. "Police! What is the disturbance here?"

Jessie felt her face go red. Police and a strange man in her backyard at dawn. The gossips would have a heyday with this. Jessie deftly dropped the broom and swung to face the policeman. "Officer, I'm so sorry you were called. The fog hid Mr. Smith from my sight and he startled me."

"One of your neighbors heard and flagged me down. You're certain you do not need any assistance, madam?" The policeman glared at Smith.

"No, but thank you for coming so quickly, Officer. It does my heart good to know that such a minor disturbance brought such quick action. Thank you again," Jessie said as she linked her arm with Smith's and led him up the steps to the back door.

Astonished and so close to Jessie, Smith took a moment to really look at her. A young woman with ivory skin, dark, serious eyes, and soft, wavy brown hair; she'd changed little from the pretty girl on the worn daguerreotype he still carried in his pocket. Then over his shoulder he nodded civilly to the policeman as they stepped into a large kitchen. As soon as the door closed, Jessie dropped his arm as if he had leprosy.

With his hat still in one hand, he stood stiffly, conscious of being travel-worn, wishing he had delayed and taken time to have his suit freshly brushed and pressed. The two of them stood facing each other and listening to the officer's departure.

"He gone, Jess—Mrs. Wagstaff," Susan said.

Jessie released a deep sigh. "That takes care of that."

Lee's curiosity forced him to ask, "How did someone alert the police so quickly?"

"You think," the hired girl asked, "someone pulled the alarm on the corner?"

"No, not enough time." Jessie untied the strings of her dreary bonnet. "The person probably was heading for the alarm and saw the policeman down the street."

"Alarm?"

"Yes. You sound like you're from the East." Jesse propped her hands on her hips, giving him a disgusted look. "So we know you didn't expect to find that Chicago is up to date. We have alarm boxes every few blocks that are connected by wire to the nearest police and fire station." She turned her back on him. "Susan, who do you think flagged down the policeman?"

"Got to be that Mrs. O'Toole," Susan said.

Grimacing, Jessie nodded. "What would everyone do for diversion if we didn't live here?"

He detected only the barest touch of humor in the widow's tone. Then he found her disapproving gaze on him once more and he fought the urge to tug at his stiff white collar. He tried to come up with some reason to stop her from sending him right back out her door.

"I suppose you'll have to stay . . . for a while," Jessie grumbled. Her unwelcoming expression made him feel like a child who'd come to her table with dirty hands. "At least, till breakfast is finished. One of my nosy neighbors will certainly stop the officer and ask him about you. It would look suspicious if you were seen leaving too soon."

"Old biddies," Susan muttered.

Well, the old biddies had done him a favor. They'd got him inside and were keeping him there. Stifling a mocking grin at this irony, he bowed. "Thank you for your charming invitation. I am free for breakfast."

"Humph." Jessie walked away from him.

He bit back a retort while she took off her dowdy, threadbare bonnet, cape, and gloves.

A startling fact occurred to Lee. At five o'clock in the morning, the widow had been coming *up* the steps, not out of her door. Where had Mrs. Jessie Wagstaff been all night?

The girl was tying a red calico apron around herself when she put his thoughts into words. "Do you think they saw you was coming *in*, not stepping *out*?"

Jessie, donning a full white apron, shook her head at Susan. For a moment, Lee considered repeating the hired girl's question. However, he couldn't afford to antagonize Jessie any further.

"How Ruth's baby?" the girl asked.

"Better, but not out of the woods yet. I hope Ruth heeds my warning." Jessie motioned to Lee, directing him toward a long table beside the kitchen window. The stark white curtains that fluttered over it suited the sparsely adorned whitewashed room, and it all seemed to go with its cheerless mistress. She ordered, "You might as well sit."

With clenched teeth, he obeyed, balancing his hat on his knee. He hadn't known exactly what to expect from Mrs. Jessie Wagstaff, but it hadn't been this. How long did this woman think she could get by with treating him like a pesky bill collector?

Ignoring him, the two women went on with their obvious morning routine. *Fine. Just as long as breakfast is good and comes quick.* Susan picked up a milk pail and left by the back door. Jessie filled a wall-mounted coffee mill and began to crank it. The aroma of freshly ground coffee beans made his mouth water.

He got up his nerve to attempt to get a toehold here. "Do you have a room for rent?"

"I have no vacancy and even if I did, I never take in male boarders. A widow can't be too careful when it comes to gossip."

Her dismissive tone sparked his temper. "I want a room—not a widow," he snapped back.

She glared at him.

Suddenly he didn't like Jessie Wagstaff one bit. But he reminded himself that he didn't need to like her to achieve his goal. His long-delayed purpose for coming compelled him to swallow her rebuff. He reverted to his lifelong tactic. Charming nonchalance had always infuriated his family while giving them no opportunity to badger him. He gave her a practiced, languid smile and dusted the top of his hat with careless fingers. "I'm merely looking for a clean room and good food. You were recommended and—"

"Mother!" A young lad with tousled blond hair, still dressed in his white nightshirt, rushed through the curtained doorway into the kitchen. The sight of the boy caught Lee off guard. Her son—this was Lincoln.

As Jessie unhooked the jar of freshly ground coffee from the mill, the boy grasped her forearms and bounced on his bare toes. "There was a policeman and a horse. I saw them out of my window."

Jessie balanced the coffee jar to keep it from spilling. "Well, why not? Policemen often come down our street, Linc."

The boy dropped his hold on his mother and turned to Lee. "Who's this?"

Lee looked into the face of the boy—so new to him, yet so familiar. Without warning, the innocent face unleashed an avalanche of wrenching images inside Lee. Phantom cannon roared in his ears and the sweetly putrid smell of gangrenous flesh made him gag. Fighting the urge to retch, he clutched his hat brim with both hands.

Susan came in and set a heavy milk pail on the edge of the sink. "Mister, you be all right?"

He couldn't answer. He fought free of the haunting sensations. "I'm fine." Both women were staring at him. "I'm fine," he repeated, his voice firmer. "I'm Lee Smith." He stretched out his right hand and grasped the youngster's hand.

"Linc, Mr. Smith is staying for breakfast," Jessie said. "He is new in town and wanted to rent a room from us. But since we don't have any rooms available, he'll have to look elsewhere."

Linc moved closer to Lee. The boy's scent, a mix of cornstarch powder and soap, blotted out the lingering horror in Lee's memory.

"Mr. Smith, I wish you could stay," Linc said. "I'm the only boy here."

Unused to being around children, but touched by this sentiment, Lee clumsily stroked the boy's hair. "I'm happy I was able to meet you, Linc." *Poor kid—defenseless in a household of "skirts." Well, maybe I can to do something about that.*

Jessie came up behind the boy and turned him by the shoulders, then swatted him gently on the behind. "Young man, you need to get yourself ready for breakfast. You remember what happens today, don't you?"

"The game's today, isn't it?" Linc hopped up and down. "It's April ninth!"

Smiling, Jessie bent and kissed the bobbing head. "Yes, Linc, it is finally the ninth. Go mark it off on the calendar."

Beaming, Linc charged toward the calendar beside the pantry doorway. He lifted a pencil, dangling from a string, and marked a large "X" through the date.

His mother touched the boy's shoulder. "Get more wood, please. We barely have enough to finish heating the wash water and I need to start brewing the coffee."

Groaning, the boy padded back out of the room.

Jessie went to the sink and began filling the two large coffeepots with water.

"What game is Linc excited about?" Lee asked, searching her face.

"Today is the first exhibition game of the new Chicago White Stockings Baseball Club. My son is an avid supporter."

"Is he?" Lee grinned, cheered to see that she wasn't as stern with her son as with unwanted strangers at her door.

Jessie began spooning coffee into the pots. "Yes, he can tell you all about them and the new National Association of Professional Baseball Players." Lee liked the way her voice gentled as she spoke of her son.

"Five games they play with five other teams," said the hired girl, carrying a wire basket out the back door.

"Yes, would you like us to recite the names of the other teams, Mr. Smith?" Jessie surprised Lee by actually chuckling.

Emboldened by this, he took another chance and asked, "Thank you, no. But when do you think you might have a vacancy?"

"You are persistent, Mr. Smith. But *even* if I had a vacancy and even if I rented to males, I still would never rent to a stranger. I cannot, will not, rent you a room, Mr. Smith."

In Boston, it had all seemed so easy. She ran a boardinghouse. He'd rent a room from her. Behind grimly smiling lips, Lee gritted his teeth. *I'll get into your life one way or another, Jessie. I'm late but I'm here to stay.*

A young woman's voice from the other side of the curtain interrupted them, "Mrs. Wagstaff, is the wash water ready? Some of the boarders are complaining."

He watched Jessie grimace, but her voice did not betray this. "Please tell them it won't be long."

The young boarder murmured indistinctly and retreated.

Linc came into the kitchen, pulling his suspenders into place. Jessie motioned her son to the door. "Hurry, Linc, we're running late."

A querulous voice issuing from the hallway startled Lee. "How long is a body supposed to wait for a small pitcher of warm water?" A very old twisted-looking woman, leaning heavily on a gnarled wooden cane, made a good effort at stomping into the room. Common politeness made him rise.

"Why are you entertaining a man in this kitchen at this hour? Or is he peddling?"

"I'm not a peddler, ma'am," Lee cut in, holding back his temper.

The old prune ignored him and spoke to Jessie. "Is he another army comrade of Will's? I thought we were all done with that sort of chicanery. They start by making women believe they are army friends of their husbands and, in the end, the ninny women have bought worthless shares—"

"I'm not—" Lee began, but Jessie overrode him. "Miss Wright, Mr. Smith arrived this morning looking for lodging and employment. He is staying for breakfast."

"Humph. Too poor to buy his own breakfast . . ." she grumbled.

Linc brought in an armload of wood. Miss Wright scolded him, "You there, boy, why didn't you bring in enough wood last night?"

Bristling, Lee was impressed by Linc's composure while under attack. The boy carefully, but swiftly, loaded the wood into the stove.

The irritating old woman went on, "If his father were here, he would take a strap to this boy—"

"No, he wouldn't . . ." Lee and Jessie, who had spoken the same words at the same time, stopped and stared at each other.

"Humph!" the old woman declared. "Send that worthless black girl up with my water. I don't know why I put up with the inconvenience of living here. If only Margaret were still alive," Miss Wright continued her tirade, thumping her cane all the way down the hall.

"Why did you say that about my late husband?" Jessie asked him, eyeing him with fresh distrust.

Scrambling for a reason, he lied through all of his smiling white teeth, "No particular reason. I just don't like peevish old women. And before breakfast."

Susan entered with the wire basket now full of brown eggs. When she glanced darkly at the curtained doorway and grumbled to herself, Lee was certain Susan had heard every nasty word the unpleasant old woman had said.

Jessie shook her head. While Susan shot inquiring glances his way, Jessie never turned her eyes toward him. Her ability to ignore him completely grated on his tender nerves. Why couldn't he ignore the fact that she'd matured into an attractive woman? Why couldn't she have turned out to be a mousy, miss-ish widow who'd welcome a man at her door—just the kind of woman he'd expected and the kind he avoided? But Jessie Wagstaff was both pretty and a woman to be reckoned with. Not at all what he wanted.

Soon the aromas of bubbling coffee and sizzling bacon and eggs made Lee's stomach rumble. Finally, Jessie removed her white apron. At her nod, he followed her through the curtain into the long, narrow dining room. She carried a large tray, laden with a covered blue-and-white tureen filled with oatmeal and a matching platter of the bacon and eggs to the table.

Breakfast, at last.

Lee scanned the room. The rectangular table of dark walnut, though covered with a white oilcloth, stood out as a showpiece with its ornately carved legs. Three women sat around it, the old one with her cane, a middle-aged redhead, and a pretty young blonde. *This should prove interesting.*

He bowed to them. The young, stylish blonde nodded politely and looked away. The middle-aged redhead ogled him. Miss Wright scowled at him. He smiled his most aggravating smile at the old biddy.

Jessie supplied the introductions, "Mr. Smith, you have already met Miss Wright. This is Mrs. Bolt and Miss Greenleigh."

Mrs. Bolt, the redhead, simpered, "Your chair, I believe, is next to mine, sir."

Lee bowed to the ladies once more and sat down. Linc welcomed him with a grin. As Lee spread the crisply starched napkin across his lap, he heard the old lady sniff pointedly. He looked up. Everyone, except for the old woman and him, had their heads bowed for morning grace. *Scold me, will you?*

He waggled his forefinger as though chastising her. Then smiling inwardly, he folded his hands in his lap and lowered his head as Jessie prayed aloud. Afterward, Mrs. Bolt, who immediately informed him she was a war widow and taught eighth grade, kept him busy lying to each of her questions. Interspersed between the coy widow's chatter and Linc's occasional comments about the afternoon's game, the old spinster glowered at him. But overall, Jessie's silent, unwelcoming perusal discouraged him most. How would he break through the wall she surrounded herself with? Without telling her the truth?

The meal ended. Linc dashed upstairs to get his books. In bonnets and gloves, Miss Greenleigh and Mrs. Bolt departed to the local school where they both taught. The old woman, thumping her cane as though still scolding Lee, crossed the hall to the parlor. He and Jessie were left alone at the table.

"What kind of work will you be looking for in Chicago, Mr. Smith?" Jessie asked him in a cool tone, daunting him further.

"Clerking," he mumbled. *How did one go about finding a job in a strange city?*

"The McCormick Reaper plant is nearby at the corner of Rush and Erie. But there are many offices downtown or at the grain elevators along the river or the lumberyards—"

"Excuse me, Mr. Smith." Linc rushed in, saving Lee from more of this dismal information. "Mother, I'm ready for school." The boy halted beside her, his hair slicked back with water. "Remember—I'll be going to Drexel Park to see the White Stockings."

"Yes, and that's *after* school." Jessie tugged his earlobe.

"Aw, Mother." He headed out, calling over his shoulder, "Bye, Mr. Smith, I wish you were staying."

Touched in spite of himself, Lee called farewell. Linc wouldn't be hard to get close to. Lee stood up. "I'll be off now."

Jessie accompanied him to the front door, evidently to make sure he left the premises. At the bottom of the front steps, he looked up at her standing in the doorway of the simple white frame house. Again, he was struck by her young prettiness, which her serious expression couldn't hide. And he recalled the intriguing fact that she'd been coming home this morning at dawn. *Where had you been, Widow Wagstaff?* "Thank you for a fine breakfast."

"You're welcome. Please let me know how you get on, Mr. Smith." Her face wore a warning expression that did not match her polite words.

But the Widow Wagstaff would see him again and soon. He'd left his valise on her back porch.

Chapter 2

When Jessie returned to the dining room, Susan was still clearing the breakfast dishes. Jessie read the question on her friend's face. "Yes, he's gone."

"What that man come here for anyway, I want to know?"

Jessie shrugged her shoulders. But the stranger's presence, a crowing rooster among a brood of fluttery hens, had disturbed her.

"We'll probably never see him again." Even as she said the words, she thought Mr. Smith might prove to be the bad penny, always turning up. Her mind returned to Miss Wright's earlier comment about men who passed as army friends to fleece widows. Her husband had served, caring for the wounded. He'd had two friends, both named Smith—an ambulance driver and Dr. Smith, Will's best friend who died soon after Will in the final months of the war. So many Smiths in the world.

She pushed this weight aside and helped Susan. When they entered the kitchen, Susan set her stack of dishes down with an irritated thump.

Jessie pursed her lips. "You heard Miss Wright—"

"'Worthless black girl.' After the war, when I come north free, I think Chicago's gone to be my promised land. But I work here for more'n five years and I still that worthless black girl."

Coming to Susan's side, Jessie pressed her cheek to Susan's and tucked one arm around her friend's waist. "I know it's hard to forgive and forget again and again, but she's too old to change—"

"I don't 'spect her to change her ideas about all colored folks, just me. I work hard—"

"And I thank God for you everyday."

Susan laced her arm through Jessie's. "Don't you know I feel the same way?"

Jessie smiled. "Susan, I couldn't do all this work by myself and still have time to mother Linc."

"God bless me with you."

"We were both blessed. You needed work and a home and I needed help." Jessie drew away, feeling an unusual restlessness. That man wouldn't leave her mind.

"I got more'n a home here. I got a friend, who teach me how to think free."

Jessie looked lovingly around the simple kitchen. "I know what you mean. When I was twelve, coming to this house to be Margaret's hired girl set me free, too."

"I don't know how you turned out so sweet raised by such a hard-hearted step-daddy."

"How my mother can love someone as unlovable as my stepfather . . ." Jessie caught herself before saying more. Margaret wouldn't have liked what Jessie'd just said. "I hope Margaret taught me how to show my love to others."

Susan began rinsing dishes. "Margaret did a good job. Everybody know you got a big heart. And that's the trouble with you. I bet you didn't get two hours sleep last night."

Jessie yawned and stretched her arms overhead, wiggling out the kinks in her back. "'I can do all things through Christ who strengtheneth me.'"

"I know that, but do He want you doing everything?"

Jessie sighed and reached for a dishcloth.

Susan yanked it out of her hand. "Go nap. I can do these dishes alone."

"I'll help you then lay down."

"You go now or I'll do the shopping and you won't get to see your mama today."

Jessie gave Susan a crooked smile. "All right, *Miss* Susan."

With an oak basket on one arm, Jessie inched through the bustling crowd of women in bonnets at the Lake Street open market. The stalls were filled with farmers' rhubarb, eggs, and more.

"Mrs. Wagstaff, your boy need any pencils today?" The double amputee sat on a homemade wicker wheelchair at his regular spot on the corner.

"Yes, he goes through them like lightning." She gave him a penny and looked in the crowd for her mother's arrival.

He tossed the bright yellow pencil into her basket.

A cool breeze off the nearby Chicago River blew over them, making Jessie press a lavender-scented handkerchief to her nose. "That awful odor! Forgive me for mentioning it. How do you stand it all day?"

"My nose must get used to it."

"They can't fix the Chicago River soon enough for me," Jessie spoke through her handkerchief.

He pointed a yellow pencil at her like a teacher with a pointing stick. "Do you really think they can change a river's flow by digging a deep ditch?"

"We'll know that in July."

"Jessie."

She turned to greet her mother, a slender woman with the same dark hair and eyes and a handkerchief over her nose also. For a moment, Jessie hoped her mother would open her arms and pull her in for a quick hug. But, of course, her mother merely offered Jessie her hand. Hiram Huff had taught them never to show affection in public or private. Just thinking her stepfather's name sparked fire in her stomach. *God, free me from this anger,* she prayed silently.

Almost cringing, Jessie's mother spoke to the pencil–peddler. "My husband said this pencil broke because it's poorly made. He wants you to return it to your supplier." Her mother's face turned bright pink.

Jessie's resentment flamed up again. Only Hiram Huff would return a pencil to a crippled Union army veteran.

"I'll do that, ma'am. Tell your husband I stand behind my pencils." He gave her a new one.

Jessie thought fast. "Oh! Miss Greenleigh asked me to pick up two red pencils." She handed him a nickel. He tossed the pencils into her basket.

With parting nods to him, they walked away side by side.

"Thank you, dear," her mother murmured.

Jessie nodded. They both knew that Jessie had bought the red pencils out of kindness since Hiram Huff made his wife account for each penny. The breeze changed and they lowered their handkerchiefs.

"You look tired, Jessie. Have you been up late again nursing someone?"

After Susan's lecture on the same subject, Jessie changed topics. "I had an unexpected visitor this morning at dawn."

"At dawn? Who was it?"

"A stranger. He actually tried to make me believe some train conductor recommended my boardinghouse."

"Why would he choose your house if someone hadn't recommended you?"

"Just my luck." Jessie gave a half-smile. He continued to intrigue her. *Why?* Maybe it was merely the fact that the war had taken such a dreadful toll on the population of young men that no man under the age of forty had sat at her table for over five years. Maybe that made him keep popping into mind.

"But . . . please be careful."

"After meeting Miss Wright, I doubt he'll be back." Jessie firmly put the man out of her mind.

"How is Miss Wright, the poor woman?"

"Poor woman with a razor-sharp tongue. She sliced that stranger up like the bacon for breakfast."

Her mother shook her head. "Margaret loved Miss Wright so. You had the sweetest mother-in-law I've ever known."

"Yes, I did." Jessie looked away. Losing Margaret in the final months of the war less than a year after Will had died still had the power to hurt her.

How often she still yearned to lean her head on Margaret's soft bosom and listen to her voice soothe every problem with a prayer.

Jessie took a deep breath and felt her stays press against her ribs.

Then she heard it, the idle clang of a fire bell. With misgiving, she watched the shiny red, black, and brass fire wagon coming toward them. Her stepfather, in his highly starched blue fire-captain's uniform, hopped down from it; grim satisfaction on his square face.

"Hiram, I . . . ." Her mother pressed her hand to her heart. "You surprised me."

"I knew you'd be shopping about now and I wanted to have a word with your headstrong daughter."

"I don't need that word," Jessie muttered.

"Please." Her mother touched Jessie's sleeve.

"We already know, Esther, that your daughter doesn't have a teachable spirit."

"What is it you want to *teach* me, stepfather?" Jessie forced herself to speak politely for her mother's sake. Her mother suffered over any confrontation, however mild.

"A fellow fire captain of mine saw you leaving that shantytown at an ungodly hour this morning—again."

"A sick baby needed me." Jessie lifted her chin.

"Your actions reflect on us. No decent woman would go there at any time, but certainly not at night."

"The baby might have died—"

"This odd behavior will stop *now*. Esther, I'll be home late this evening." He tipped his hat and climbed back on the wagon.

His condemnation set a wildfire inside Jessie. She tried to call up some of the phrases that Margaret had taught her about loving those who persecute us in vain. In a low voice, Jessie said, "Mother, I am doing the work God has given me. No one will turn me from my purpose."

Painful crosscurrents of love and shame showed on her mother's face. "Daughter, will you come to Field & Leiter's with me?" Her mother blinked back tears.

Jessie was touched. Calling her "daughter" sounded like a commonplace. But in their unspoken code, using this term was an endearment that had slipped by her stepfather. Even now when Jessie no longer lived under her stepfather's roof, these brief daily shopping trips were the only way they saw each other regularly. "No, but I'll walk you there."

Jessie enjoyed strolling beside her mother through the streets crowded with shoppers. Then at the corner of Washington and State stood the five-story "marble palace" built by Potter Palmer. Its gala grand opening night had taken place two years ago. If Will had survived the war, he would have drawn her arm through his and escorted her like his princess through the aisles of exotic rugs, Balmoral petticoats, silks, and more. Instead, she'd only read about it in the *Trib*.

Her mother coaxed, "Won't you please come in this time. It's so cheery inside."

"There's no reason for me to look at what I can't afford." At her mother's crestfallen expression, Jessie said, "Linc and I are making ends meet, but I have to save for his future. I want Will's son to go as far in life as he is able."

"You're only in your twenties. I want you to enjoy life more while you can."

My joy died with Will. He'll never walk the marble floors of Palmer's Palace. "Mother, I'm going to my first baseball game today. What could be more fun than that?" Jessie was rewarded with a genuine smile from her mother.

"Then I won't keep you. I'm sure you have much to do, so you can make the game in time." With a wave, her mother walked through the door held open by a boy in a royal blue uniform with bright brass buttons. Stylishly dressed and still handsome, her mother looked exactly right walking into the elegant store.

Will had always said that Hiram Huff's only redeeming quality was that he always demanded his wife wear the very best. Which only proved what Will had believed was right; happiness didn't lay in finery. *I have Linc, a home, and Susan—God's given me all I need.*

Jessie hurried to the butcher. Out of the corner of her eye, the way a slender man in a dark suit moved, a kind of cocky nonchalance, caught her eye. It was Mr. Smith. That indefinable feeling zigzagged through her again. She pushed it away. She'd never see Smith's face at her door again. And woe to him if she did.

Lee wearied of roaming the unusual wooden sidewalks of downtown Chicago. In the main shopping district around State and Randolph, the streets and sidewalks were flush with each other. But a few blocks away, though the street and first floor of a business were even, often the entrance was by means of a staircase to the second floor. Why?

As he walked, several windows with signs saying "Help Wanted" had beckoned him, but crosscurrents inside him had kept him walking by. What did he really want to do while he set everything up? He'd planned to start by getting a room at Jessie's. But he'd failed at that. How could he get close to Jessie Wagstaff?

His stomach rumbled. Just ahead of him on the south side of the river was a tavern, "The Workman's Rest." Its sign also proclaimed "Free lunch with nickel beer." His mouth watered at the thought of a long draught of ale. But as he approached the double swinging doors, he paused. He shouldn't go in.

Two burly men crowded one on each side of Lee and carried him along with them into the tavern. One of them called out, "Pearl, brought you a new customer! He's wearing a suit!"

Lee halted, shocked at finding himself in the last place he wanted to be.

"He's welcome!" The woman behind the bar called back without taking her eyes from the two tankards of ale she was filling at the tap. She thumped them down on the bar, then wiped her fingers on her white apron. "Welcome to the Workman's Rest, stranger. I'm Pearl Flesher. Put her there." The woman thrust out her hand.

She was tall, blond, good-looking and thirtyish. Lee accepted her hand. "A pleasure, ma'am."

"A man with manners. What can I do for you, mister?"

Lee was stumped. He knew he was expected to say, "A beer, Pearl" but he couldn't.

"He wants a beer just like we do, Pearl," the workmen on both sides of him declared. "Come on, we can't waste our short lunch-time."

Lee cleared his dry throat. "Really, I would prefer a barley water." The words brought a stunned silence to the two workmen.

"Barley water!" one exploded.

"Yes, my stomach, you see." Neck on fire, Lee felt all eyes turned on him.

One of the men started to speak, but Pearl cut him off, "If he wants barley water, it'll be barley water. You jugheads could digest nails."

The men around him laughed and Lee felt intense relief. Soon he was having a congenial exchange with them as he sipped his barley water and enjoyed his thick sandwich of sliced sausage on fresh bread.

An older man farther down the bar pointed his pipe in Lee's direction. "You sound like you come from out East. What do you think of our Chicago?"

"It is truly a modern city—policemen, fire hydrants, gaslights on the street corners." Lee bowed with mock formality. "But why do some sidewalks here go up and down like hills?"

The old man took a draw on his pipe. "Chicago was built on a swamp. They couldn't do nothing about the land being so low and muddy so they shaved off a hill nearby and used it to fill up the main part of town—to make it level."

Lee paused with his glass to his lips. "They filled it in? With the buildings already there?"

"Pullman did that," Pearl broke in while she refilled a glass. "I seen it when I was a girl. He had a thousand men put large wooden screw lifts under the foundations."

The old man caught Lee's eye. "Like the Hotel Tremont. That Pullman fella, he blew a whistle and they'd all give one turn. Another whistle, another turn."

"You're kidding me," Lee said with a grin.

"No, he did it. With people staying in the hotel the whole time," Pearl cut in, "just like nothing was happening."

Lee shook his head. Though a row of small tables lined the wall, most of the men mingled around the bar. The conversation around him turned back to baseball and some wagering over the White Stockings' chances. Lee tried to come up with a way to get close to Jessie. In the homey-feeling tavern, a few posters announcing today's ball game were pinned on the back wall.

Lee stared at the posters and suddenly he pictured Jessie talking about her boy's interest in baseball. She'd actually smiled. *The son is the key to the mother. And baseball is the key to the boy.* Lee stood up straighter. "Where's the baseball field from here, Pearl?"

"Down by the lake, near the river," she answered. "You can't miss it."

The hour passed and the lunch crowd trickled out on their way to nearby factories. Finally, Lee handed Pearl a dime. "Keep the change."

"Thanks, mister. Come in for another barley water any time."

Lee tipped his hat and walked out, whistling. At last, he knew what to do.

That afternoon at Drexel Park, the breeze off Lake Michigan was brisk. From a block away, Lee sized up the park's wide open view of spring's early green lawn and the lake's white-capped blue waves, dazzling in the sun. Optimism had returned. He looked for the boy.

The first pitch of the baseball game had already taken place when he reached the field. No Linc. But school hours were still on; he saw only a few scruffy-looking truants among the men. While he waited for Linc to arrive, he leaned back against a sturdy elm and surveyed the Chicago White Stockings in their striking white cotton stockings and spanking white knickers, at their first exhibition game.

The crack of the bat uncorked a rush of undiluted nostalgia. How many impromptu baseball games had he played in the army? Days of waiting between battles and campaigns . . .

A wagon on the nearby street creaked loudly over a bump. A picture flashed from Lee's memory. A rough horse-drawn ambulance bumping over a rutted road and a steady trickle of scarlet blood spilling from inside the wagon bed onto the dust.

He shuttered his mind against the images. *I am alive and in Chicago. I have eight dollars in my pocket. It won't last very long, but I'll see to that soon.*

Lee turned back to the game. The batter had reached first base. Inning followed inning. At last, near the front of a wave of arriving schoolboys, Lee recognized Linc's blond head. Lee lifted his hat and motioned to Linc. The lad left the other boys behind, heading to him, unexpectedly warming Lee's heart.

"Mr. Smith," Linc exclaimed with a wide smile.

"Linc." Lee offered his hand and the two shared one quick, handshake. "It's the fourth inning."

Linc turned to watch. "I saw that hitter last year at a game. He always gets a run."

"The White Stockings need it. They're down by two." Standing beside Linc, Lee awaited the pitch, both their attention riveted on the man at bat. It came. The bat caught the ball with a satisfying crack. Lee joined the rising crescendo of shrill enthusiastic voices and bellows urging the runner to first base. The player made it with only a second to spare. A cheer surged through the onlookers. Lee found himself grinning.

In quick succession, two more White Stockings made it off the plate. With three men on base, the contagious excitement lifted Lee's spirits. Then the White Stockings' batter struck out. As though uttered by one voice, a moan went through the crowd.

Disgusted, Linc threw his hat to the ground. "Three men on base. How could he let that pitcher strike him out?" With a rueful nod, Lee retrieved the hat and replaced it on Linc's head.

With his hand on Linc's shoulder, Lee watched the game. In swift order, the White Stockings' pitcher struck out the first two batters, but the third opponent proved to be a challenge. As the pitcher took his time reassessing the batter, Lee idly scanned the crowd and caught sight of Jessie Wagstaff approaching. Why had she come?

A stiff black bonnet, completely without feather or ornament, covered her warm brown hair. Its black brim paled her rosy complexion. After six years, why did she still dress in deep mourning, totally in black with not even a touch of gray? Mourning clothes and her stiffly upright posture made her look older.

For a fraction of a second he envisioned the face and form of the girl his father had recently chosen for him to marry. She was a confection of creamy white skin, rosy lips, fluffy blond hair, and fluffy ideas. To Jessie's credit, he doubted she would ever have the kind of malleability his father had desired in a daughter-in-law.

Like a well-aimed dart, Jessie's dismayed glance of recognition pierced him. He bowed in her direction. Reading disapproval in the set of her chin, he prepared himself for a thorough jousting.

The bat cracked. Lee's glance darted back to the play. Foul ball. As Jessie reached them, the faint fragrance of lavender wafted from her. Perhaps inside the widow's armor, a soft, feminine woman still breathed.

Jessie stepped between Mr. Smith and her son, keeping her irritation out of her voice. This wasn't Linc's fault. But more exasperating was her own reaction at seeing this stranger again. She couldn't ignore the effect his gaze had on her.

"Lincoln, why didn't he run to base?"

"Hello, Mother. The ball went outside the boundaries of the bases. See?"

"I do." She glanced at Mr. Smith, but he said nothing. The player hit another ball that popped upward and was caught. Linc cheered as the hand-held score cards were changed. Jessie stepped behind Linc.

Mr. Smith said, "The White Stockings are back at bat now, ma'am."

She looked sideways at him, out of the seclusion of her severe bonnet. Was it by coincidence or design that this man kept appearing today? Worry pinched her and she prayed silently for wisdom. Why had this man popped up in their lives? And how could she get rid of him? "You're a baseball enthusiast, then?" She made her tone say clearly she wasn't pleased to find him here with her son.

"I am."

Jessie heard a man shout, "Three strikes!" When Linc groaned with disgust along with the rest of the audience, she asked, "What happened?"

Mr. Smith answered, "You're new to the game? I thought Linc would have instructed you in baseball."

His voice was meant to charm; she pursed her lips. "One of my neighbor's sons began bringing him to amateur games only at the end of last summer."

"I see."

Trying to ignore the man beside her, Jessie watched the game without further comment. Then she bent her head to read the face of her pendant watch. "Linc, I must be getting home."

"Yes, Mother."

Jessie smiled to herself at her son's complete concentration on the game, but remembering the stranger she added, "Come straight home, son."

"Yes, Mother."

"Supper will be at six as usual."

"Yes, mother."

"Make sure you come in quietly so Miss Wright won't scold you."

"Yes, Mother."

Even in the midst of her concern about this stranger, she swallowed her amusement at her son's sanguine personality, so like his father. Nothing spoiled his enjoyment of life. She turned to face Mr. Smith. "I will bid you good day." She emphasized her words, making "good day" mean "depart forever."

"Good day to you, Mrs. Wagstaff." He bowed slightly and rested his hand on Linc's shoulder. The boy looked up with a grin at him. Jessie walked away, fuming.

"He was at the game!" Jessie let the kitchen door slam behind her.

"That man?" Standing by the stove, Susan turned to face her.

"Yes, *that man.*" Jessie whipped off her bonnet and jerked it down onto the hook on the wall.

"He with Lincoln?"

"Yes." Impatiently Jessie tugged open her wrist buttons, folded up her sleeves, then reached for her apron. "I don't like it. He shows up this morning sitting on our porch at a time that no man should be anywhere but in bed."

"I'm agreeing with you." Susan turned the potato slices sizzling in the hot fat.

"I mean who is he?"

"And is he really a *Mistah Smith*?"

"Exactly. And why did he pick our door?"

"Xactly."

Jessie set a large gray stoneware bowl onto the table by the window. She reached into it with both hands and lifted a thick clutch of dandelion greens out of the cleansing salt water and laid them on a fresh white towel beside the bowl. Picking up a paring knife, she began to slice off the tough ends of the greens. How could she have felt a flush of giddiness at the sight of Mr. Smith? That man had flustered her twice in one day.

Susan's words sliced through Jessie's thoughts. "You keep using the knife that way and you gone to cut a finger into the greens."

Jessie sighed. She stilled her hands and slowly rolled her neck to loosen her muscles. "Seeing him there got my goat. I didn't want to leave Linc with him, but I couldn't bear to make Linc come home before the end of the game."

"He been counting the days till that game."

Jessie consciously relaxed her shoulder muscles and began to make the salad. "I suppose Linc will be safe enough in the crowd and he'll be home well before dark."

"God will take care of him."

"I know."

Susan shook her finger as though scolding a child. "But if that man comes 'round here one more time—"

"I will send him off with a bee in his ear!"

Jessie and Susan chuckled. Then Jessie lost herself in the flurry of preparing supper. When it was time for Jessie to carry the kettle of warm water to fill the washbasins in the boarders' rooms, she was surprised to find Mrs. Bolt waiting in the foyer.

"I'll take that up, Mrs. Wagstaff," Mrs. Bolt tittered. With a grin of anticipation on her face, the redhead hurried toward the stairs. Jessie cast a questioning glance at Miss Greenleigh, who had just come in the front door.

Miss Greenleigh, stylishly dressed as always, carefully pulled off tan kid gloves. "I believe she saw someone on our way home and is expecting company for dinner," the pretty blonde announced cryptically. Loosening the lavender ribbons on her fashionable bonnet, she went to join Miss Wright for their usual after-school chat in the parlor.

Jessie paused, then turned back to the kitchen. She never knew what Mrs. Bolt might do next.

Soon Jessie was crumbling bacon onto her dandelion salad. Linc burst through the back door. "We won! We won!"

Jessie turned to applaud the White Stockings' triumph. Her hands froze in midair.

"Good evening, Mrs. Wagstaff, Susan."

Jessie stared in disbelief. The last man on earth she wanted in her kitchen stood there with a "cat-in-the-cream" grin on his face.

Mr. Smith removed his hat and bowed to them. Jessie's hands itched to strangle him.

Chapter 3

"Mr. Smith!" Mrs. Bolt swished through the curtain. "I thought I heard your voice."

The redhead deigning to enter the kitchen? Jessie stared at her.

"Mother, I brought Mr. Smith home for supper," Lincoln said from the washbasin, where he was scrubbing his hands and face.

"Lincoln—"

"How thoughtful," coy Mrs. Bolt gushed. "Lincoln's such a dear boy. Here, Mrs. Wagstaff, I'll carry that bowl to the table and show Mr. Smith where to hang his hat." As though helping in the kitchen were an everyday occurrence, the schoolteacher picked up the bowl of pungent salad and led the grinning man through the curtain.

Jessie's mouth formed a perfect O.

"All done, Mother," Linc announced proudly, holding up his clean hands.

Jessie turned a stern face to her son, whose innocent eyes gazed up at her.

"Lincoln, why did you bring Mr. Smith home?"

"You said I could bring friends home for dinner if their mothers gave permission. Mr. Smith is my newest friend, but he's too old to ask his mother. Mother, he knows *everything* about baseball."

What could she say to that? Jessie pursed her lips. "We will talk later, Lincoln. Go take your seat." The boy nodded and happily hurried out. Jessie whipped off her apron, snagged it on a nail, tugged down her sleeves and, with two quick twists, buttoned the cuffs.

Bad enough Mr. Smith had returned, but he'd caught her with her face flushed from the heat of the stove, her clothing disheveled. Taking a deep breath, she smoothed her hair and pressed a wet cloth against her flaming cheeks.

Then she whispered to Susan, "He'd better enjoy supper. It'll be his last meal at my table."

"Amen to that."

Grimly resolute, Jessie headed to the dining room. Susan followed, carrying a tray with salad, fried potatoes, and pork chops.

Greeting all with a curt nod, Jessie sat down at the head of the table. After grace, Susan moved the steaming dishes from the dark, ornately carved sideboard to the table.

"Oh, dandelions! So early!" Miss Greenleigh smiled.

Grinning stiffly, Jessie eyed the unwelcome man wedged in between Linc and the Widow Bolt.

"Dandelions," Linc echoed, quiet dismay in his voice.

When the bowl came to Lee, he spooned a modest helping onto his plate, but only a dab onto Linc's. "Be brave," he murmured. "This too will pass."

"You're so good with children, Mr. Smith," Mrs. Bolt cooed.

Jessie frowned at the woman.

"Don't talk twaddle." Miss Wright glowered at the widow and the man. Mrs. Bolt flushed an alarming red.

Yet for once, Jessie silently agreed with the spinster.

Miss Greenleigh asked, "Were you successful in finding a position today, Mr. Smith?"

"I'm afraid not."

"I'm sure—" Mrs. Bolt began.

Miss Wright snorted in disgust. "Any fool can find a job in Chicago."

"I hope to prove you correct," Mr. Smith said.

The man's smooth flippancy set Jessie's teeth on edge. While Mrs. Bolt scowled at Miss Wright, Jessie observed Miss Greenleigh swallow a chuckle. If it weren't this particular man, she might find this exchange amusing also. Her fatigue was overwhelming her annoyance.

Stifling a yawn, Jessie lay the back of her hand to her forehead. The light from the oil lamp over the dining table hurt her eyes. Just as the long night before, the day had gone on and on—picking dandelions from several yards, doing the marketing.

As she accepted the platter of pork chops from Miss Greenleigh, Jessie's hands trembled. She tried to pass the platter on to Susan without taking a helping. Susan crossed her arms over her breast. Only when Jessie slid the smallest remaining chop onto her plate, did Susan accept the platter, then disappear through the muslin curtain. Jessie stared down at the food on her plate. A wave of dizziness made it impossible to eat.

"Mrs. Wagstaff, are you well?" Miss Greenleigh's soft voice roused Jessie.

"I'm just—"

Miss Wright thumped her cane on the floor making Jessie's nerves jump. "She's exhausted from staying up all hours."

Jessie stood up. "I'll be right back." Nauseated, she stumbled through the kitchen curtain. Her right temple pounded.

By dim lamplight, Susan sat at the kitchen window having her supper. "You don't look good." Rising, she hustled into the pantry. "I going to make you a cup of Margaret's chamomile tea."

While Susan bustled around the stove, Jessie sank into the chair at the table and rested her head on the nest of her folded arms.

She heard Susan pour the hissing water into the teapot and recalled her mother-in-law, showing her the different herbs and explaining each one's healing properties. *Jessie, dear, God has given us the cures for most illness, but never forget the best medicines are love and prayer.* Then she felt Margaret's gentle touch on her cheek.

Muted voices from the other room floated to Jessie as she sipped the heavily honeyed cup of chamomile. Gradually, the muscles in her neck loosened and she sighed. "Thank you. What would I do without you, my friend?"

Susan patted Jessie's hand. "What would I be doing without you?"

Jessie squeezed Susan's hand in response.

"Mother?" Linc peeped into the kitchen between the folds of the muslin curtain. "Are you all right?"

"I'll be in again soon." Jessie stood up and her son left the doorway. "I must go back, Susan."

"I'll be in soon with pie. Maybe that'll shut them up."

Half smiling, Jessie shook her head at Susan's saucy words. She straightened her shoulders. A rapping on the back door halted her.

"I'll get it." Susan opened the door.

Ruth with her son in a ragged blanket rushed past Susan. "You have to help us, Mrs. Wagstaff!"

Jessie flew to Ruth's side and lifted the baby from her arms. "He's burning up again." She saw with dread his dull eyes sunken in a tiny, drawn, emotionless face. Dismay squeezed her, nearly making her gasp. "Ruth! Wasn't he able to nurse today?"

Ruth pressed her folded hands to her mouth.

Ben stood beside his wife shaking his head. "Ruth's lost her milk, ma'am."

Jessie looked up, the terrible truth streaking through her like iced lightning. "Oh, no, I warned you. You promised me. At only nine months, he's not old enough to be given cow's milk."

Ruth trembled. "We didn't have anything else."

"I brought it home at lunch." Ben pulled his wife close and put his arm around her shoulders. "It was fresh and sweet. We warmed it. What else could we do? Let him starve?"

"What is all this?" Miss Wright demanded as she struggled to walk into the kitchen.

Jessie stiffened and gave Susan the baby. "Miss Wright, there's no need for you—"

"You people are going to be the death of this woman." She gestured toward Jessie. "She can't work all day and take care of you all night."

Like a mother hen gathering her chicks with her wings, Jessie with open arms crossed the room to intercept the older woman. "There's no need for you to trouble yourself."

Miss Wright resisted her. "If Margaret were still alive, she would put a stop—"

The mention of Will's late mother intensified Jessie's resistance. How could this Miss Wright twist memories of Margaret to suit her needs? Margaret would never have turned anyone who needed help from her door. But Margaret had loved this woman. Instead of shouting, Jessie gritted her teeth. "Miss Wright, this doesn't concern you." She placed her hand under the older woman's elbow to urge her out of the room.

Miss Wright pulled away. "I'm not a child. I don't need to be led around like one. I see the toll this nursing is taking on you. What if you contract an illness and are carried away before your time? Who will be left to raise your son?"

Jessie froze. Her heart stilled.

"Do you want to see your son in an orphanage? Your stepfather would never let your mother take Lincoln in."

"Mrs. Wagstaff!" Susan called out.

Jessie swung back to the table. The baby began gagging violently. Jessie scooped him up. "Convulsions!"

Ruth moaned and dropped to her knees.

"It's the fever." Jessie held the baby close and tried to think. The baby was dangerously near death. This thought almost paralyzed her. *God, help me. They're counting on me. But what can I do?*

An overwhelming urge to seek aid came over her. "I need help."

"Just tell us what to do." Susan took hold of Jessie's arm.

"This baby needs a doctor," Miss Wright snapped.

Ben shouted in an agonized tone, "No doctor I know will take colored folk."

"Take the child to the charity hospital on Kinzie," Miss Wright urged. "It's less than a mile away."

"Yes," Jessie said. "Ruth, get my hat and cape." Without waiting, Jessie hurried out the back door, carrying the still quivering child.

Miss Wright called after her, "You can't keep on doing this!"

Through the deep twilight, Jessie rushed out to the wooden sidewalk, Ben and Ruth behind her.

Heart pounding, Jessie didn't stop until she burst through the double doors at the old hospital. The child in her arms went limp. "Help me—please!"

A matron rose near an old, scarred table with a feeble lamp. "Your servants will have to leave, ma'am."

"What?" Jessie gasped, catching her breath. "I need a doctor. This baby's had convulsions—"

The matron peered into the blanket. "This baby's colored!"

"I need a doctor." Jessie pushed past the woman.

"Ma'am! Stop!" The matron seized Jessie's arm.

Still trembling, Jessie wrenched away. "I don't know who you are, but I'm not leaving until I see a doctor."

The matron swelled with indignation. "If these colored people don't leave now, I will summon the police."

Jessie stood taller. "Call the police. If you send this sick child away and he dies, you'll be liable for murder."

The matron turned an ugly red.

"What is the problem?" a cool voice asked. An imposing man in a long black frock coat stepped out of the shadows.

Jessie hurried toward him. "Are you a doctor? Help me. This baby's dying!" She thrust the child toward him.

The man briefly stared into her face, then bowed. "Dr. Gooden."

At Jessie's elbow, the matron burst out, "Coloreds aren't allowed in this hospital."

The doctor spoke to Jessie alone, "The parents may wait outside. No one could object to the infant, but . . ."

Jessie pivoted. "Ruth and Ben, I'll see that everything possible is done."

Ben tugged Ruth toward the door obviously against her will. The sight nearly broke Jessie's heart, but the baby's life was all that mattered now.

The doctor touched Jessie's sleeve. "Come."

Jessie hurried beside the doctor down the dimly lit passage.

"What is your name, please?"

"Mrs. Wagstaff." She trotted after him, keeping up with his longer stride.

"The child has been sick, how long?" he said in a voice that held the barest hint of an accent.

"He began to be feverish at night over a week ago."

"Diarrhea?"

"Yes." Jessie turned the corner.

"The mother stopped nursing, isn't that it?"

"Yes, I warned them not to use cow's milk with a baby this young—"

"It is most likely milk fever, that you know. A mother loses her milk in the warmer part of the year before a child is a year old or more, so she gives the child cow's milk . . ." He lifted his hands in a gesture that said, "What can be done?"

"I know," she said desperately.

The baby jerked in her arms and began gagging again. "He's started again!" *Oh, God, I don't know what to do!*

The doctor sprinted the last few feet into a small examining room. Jessie ran to keep up with him. He paused, just long enough to turn up the gas lamp on the wall. "Lay the child on the table." He hurried to a bowl and ewer in the corner and washed his hands.

Within seconds, he was turning the child to its side. He probed the quivering child with deft fingers, checking for pulse and temperature, and listening to the heart with his stethoscope.

"Isn't there anything we can do?" Jessie twisted her hands together.

"You will you act as my nurse?"

"I'll do whatever you tell me to." *Father God, bless this doctor. How could I face telling Ruth her baby's gone?*

"We start with an alcohol bath."

Soon Jessie was sponging down the naked baby with the cool, pungent alcohol. The child went limp again, but his appearance terrified her even more. His little jaw hung slack and under his dark skin, an ashen undertone. "I feel so helpless," Jessie whispered.

"I know."

The empathy in his voice made Jessie study the man who stood across from her in the stark room. He was tall like Will. He was blond with blue eyes like Will only much darker blue. *If only Will had been spared.* She sucked in the familiar vacant feeling.

The doctor leaned over the table, studying the child. "I ask myself over and over—what is the cause? The cure?"

In spite of the dire situation, for just a moment, Jessie was thrilled to have him speak to her as though she were an equal.

He went on, speaking forcefully as though he thought his words could subdue the child's disease. "What is in cow's milk that is not in mother's milk? Older children drink cow's milk without bad effect—why? I need to know the answers."

She looked at him wonder-struck. "I've felt that way myself."

"I thought so." His gaze connected with hers, then dropped back to the baby.

"What are you going to try?"

"We will introduce a mild salicin—"

"Salicin?"

"A powder from willow bark in boiled water. To lower the fever."

"What do you want me to do?" *God, help this doctor do what is right.*

"Spoon this solution into his mouth."

Jessie obeyed, drawing strength from the doctor's firm voice. Minutes crawled by. Spoonfuls of the treated water trickled into the baby. Finally, the small vial was empty. "He hasn't gone into convulsions again."

"I promise you nothing. I could be doing exactly the thing that is wrong."

His honest words shocked her. She had never heard a doctor admit to not knowing something. Though he offered her no comfort, she felt an easing of tension. She watched the small chest taking in and letting out tiny breaths.

"Sit. I must make rounds. If you need me, just step into the corridor and call."

Nodding, Jessie focused again on the infant in her arms. The doctor's footsteps faded down the hallway. The night minutes ticked away, measured by the ponderous clock in the hall. Her vigil stretched on.

"Mrs. Wagstaff, feel his brow," the doctor said.

Jessie roused herself. "I must have been dozing."

She touched the baby's forehead. "He seems cooler."

Dr. Gooden stood across from her. "It's after dawn, did you know?"

Little Ben looked up at Jessie. "That isn't important. He is cooler, isn't he?"

"*Ja*, he survived the night."

Her head weighing heavily on her neck, Jessie lifted her eyes. "Will he live?"

"God only knows that."

Jessie pressed her fingers to her burning eyes. "Thank you, Doctor."

"I did so little."

"At least you didn't turn me away." She opened her eyes and gazed at him.

He grinned. "My mother taught me never to contradict a lady."

Jessie smiled, but shook her head at his modest humor. Ignoring a dull ache behind her eyes, she wrapped the sleeping child into his blanket. "I'll take him to his parents."

"Tell the mother to give him nothing but the water from boiled rice. If she gives him anything else, he won't survive. Rice is an old remedy for diarrhea. In about two days, she can give him a little of the cooked rice also."

"I'll tell her. Thank—"

"Wait. May I drive you home?"

"I'll manage I . . ." Jessie tried to stand and found she couldn't.

"Let me take the child to his parents, then I'll get my gig."

Jessie felt numb. From that point on, she was aware of voices, fresh air on her face, and that she was being led by the arm, aware of the clip-clop of the horse's hooves on wooden streets.

"Mrs. Wagstaff?" Dr. Gooden's voice penetrated her fog.

She straightened on the gig seat. The sun struggled against the morning mist. "Where am I?" Her mind felt like a roll of cotton batting.

"I hope at your front door."

Jessie looked around her, surprised to find herself at home.

"Ben told me it is the white house with green shutters on Pine Street near the corner of Ontario."

She turned to him. "I can't thank you enough, Doctor."

"My pleasure, Mrs. Wagstaff." He helped her down. "Good day, then." He bowed over her hand.

Jessie walked around the house to the back door. Just as she reached the corner, she glanced back and found the good doctor, still gazing after her.

Chapter 4

"Jessie, I been so worried." Susan hurried down the back steps.

"Little Ben made it through the night." Weariness blunted Jessie's emotions; she shivered in the spring-damp air.

Susan pressed her hands to her breast. "I been praying all night."

Jessie's fatigue dragged her down. Trying to gather her heavy skirts to climb the steps, she half stumbled.

Susan caught her by the arm.

Jessie sagged against Susan. "Will you help me upstairs to bed?"

"I'm helping you right to the kitchen table."

"Too tired to eat."

"You are eating, then sleeping. That's final." Susan tugged her to a hard kitchen chair.

"I'll fall asleep——"

"Don't take long to scramble up eggs." Susan pushed a cup of coffee into Jessie's hand. "Drink that. No arguing, hear?"

The cup warmed Jessie's hands and its aroma lifted her spirits slightly. "I'm not very hungry, really."

"You ain't had a appetite for months now. You're eating."

"Yes." Miss Wright stumped into the kitchen. "You didn't take two bites of your meal last night."

Setting down the cup, Jessie leaned her head into her palm. She couldn't face another tirade.

"The child?" Miss Wright asked with a scowl.

"Ruthie's child made it through the night, ma'am," Susan said over her shoulder.

"Good," Miss Wright muttered. "You can't go on like this, Jessie."

Taking a deep breath, Jessie looked straight into Miss Wright's pointed finger. "You're right." Jessie glanced up as Susan put a plate of eggs and toast fragrant with butter in front of her. "I need to find a doctor to help your people, Susan."

"I'm glad you are finally listening to good sense," Miss Wright grumbled.

Jessie glimpsed Susan's half-grin before she went back to the sink. Jessie began taking small bites. Why did chewing take so much energy?

"The charity hospital took the child in, then?" Miss Wright prompted.

"The matron didn't want to. A doctor came out of the shadows . . ." Jessie's voice faltered. She forced herself to take another bite. Her eyelids drooped. She batted them open again.

"Susan, does she look pale to you?" the old woman asked.

"Ma'am, maybe she just too tired to talk now," Susan suggested gently.

Nodding, Jessie continued chewing laboriously.

"It's about time you eat." Like a watchdog making sure Jessie ate every bite, Miss Wright folded her hands on the top of her cane.

Jessie heard a polite tap at the kitchen door, but she was too tired to care. Susan wiped her hands on her red apron and went to answer it. "Mr. Smith be here, Mrs. Wagstaff."

The man walked in.

Miss Wright sat up straighter. "What are you doing here?"

For once, Jessie was grateful for Miss Wright's outspoken ways. She felt defenseless, unable to deal with his worrying effect on her.

He paused a few steps inside the kitchen. "Just dropped in to pick up my valise and go to Mrs. Crawford's boardinghouse."

"Mrs. Crawford has my sympathy," Miss Wright snapped. "I suppose that means you'll be underfoot day and night."

"Mr. Smith," Susan said, "I found your valise, but I forgot to give it to you last night. Sorry."

Caught up in a floating sensation, Jessie felt as though she had taken a step away from the kitchen. What about a valise?

Smith bowed to Susan and then the spinster. "Thank you for being concerned about a lonely newcomer."

"Humph!" the old woman fumed.

Jessie looked down and watched the fork slide from her fingers as though her hand belonged to someone else.

Lee watched Jessie drop her fork.

"I still don't see why you're here," Miss Wright demanded. "Didn't Mrs. Crawford feed you enough breakfast?"

He opened his mouth to reply, but Jessie caught his eye.

"Catch her!" Susan exclaimed.

Lee rushed to seize her limp body, slipping from the chair. The elusive fragrance of lavender still clung to her and a curious sensation slid through him.

Miss Wright thumped her cane on the floor. "What's wrong?"

He quickly took Jessie's faint pulse. "Did she get any sleep last night?"

Miss Wright leaned forward anxiously. "She returned home only minutes ago. It's just fatigue, isn't it? She didn't catch some contagion at that hospital."

Lee scanned Jessie's pale face. "Her heart beat is slow, but that is to be expected with a case of exhaustion." He swung Jessie up into his arms. The incredible lightness of her body surprised him. With her full skirts and stiff posture, she'd appeared more substantial. But maybe it was only that he was more accustomed to the weight of men on stretchers, not a woman.

"Is she gone be all right?" Susan wrung her hands. "I never see her faint before."

"Why are you asking him?" Miss Wright blustered. "He's no doctor."

Lee smiled at the woman's comment. "Even I can tell whether a woman is feverish or not. Mrs. Wagstaff is not." He turned to Susan. "I'll carry her to bed."

Susan pointed toward the other end of the kitchen. "Please bring her to my bed. Just through here. Then I kin hear her if she need me."

Lee let the young woman lead him through the pantry to her tiny room off the kitchen. Glancing at Jessie's face, so relaxed and soft in repose, Lee waited while Susan turned back the blankets, then he lay Jessie down gently and stepped back. Susan stepped around him and began unhooking Jessie's shoe buttons.

Unexpectedly Lee felt himself moved by the stark contrast of Jessie's slight form, dressed all in black against the white sheets. She looked crumpled and frayed like an autumn leaf after the long winter. He had a sudden urge to gather her into his arms again. With his cheek against hers, he would whisper that he would take care of everything, that she wasn't to worry anymore.

A gnarled finger poked him in the back. "Stop gawking, Mr. Smith. Go out and find a job. Mrs. Crawford doesn't need a charity case on her hands."

He bit back a retort. *This crone could make a preacher swear. And I'm no preacher.* "I'll bid you good day, then." He turned to leave.

Susan's voice followed him. "Thank you, Mr. Smith."

"My pleasure, Susan." Outside, he strode away, valise in hand, letting the cool morning breeze clear his head. *If Jessie Wagstaff wanted to stay up all night nursing sick, probably thankless, people, it was her business, not his.*

After leaving his valise at his new home, he walked briskly toward town. A good night's rest in a pleasant, but reasonably priced, room at Mrs. Crawford's plus a delicious breakfast had given him new hope he would find work today. After years of idleness, he didn't really want a job, but he needed one.

Thoughts of Jessie intruded. *Fool woman. Up all night.* He shook his head. Jessie Wagstaff was obviously an inveterate do-gooder. He blocked these thoughts, turning to his goal. *I'm going to find a job today. I'll stop at the first Help Wanted sign.*

That first sign came quicker than he had expected. A warehouse on Lake Street sported a notice in its dusty window—"Bookkeeper Wanted." Lee stepped inside before he could talk himself out of doing so. He hailed a workman. "Who do I talk to about the book-keeping position?"

A voice came through an open door. "You talk to me."

Lee stepped inside the door. "Sir?"

The man motioned him closer. "How long have you worked as a bookkeeper?"

Lee stepped to the desk and held out his hand. "Lee Smith, at your service, sir."

The man stood up and shook Lee's hand, repeating, "How long have you worked as a bookkeeper?"

This is how they do business in Chicago? So abrupt? "I have no formal experience, but I am very good with figures."

"Sorry, I need an experienced bookkeeper. This is the beginning of our shipping season. " The man sat back down and immediately began leafing through papers.

Out of ingrained courtesy, Lee bowed and left.

Outside the morning was still very young, but Lee felt his confidence slip a notch. *Well, that's strike one, but I'm not out yet.* By the end of the morning, he had been turned down for three more jobs. He had more than struck out.

He headed for some place familiar, soothing. Soon inhaling the scent of ale, he pushed through the swinging doors at Pearl's.

"Hey, the suit's back!" a familiar-looking workman shouted.

Within minutes Pearl had poured Lee his barley water and he was spinning an action-packed account of the previous day's base-ball game for the workmen crowding around. Two men tried to buy him beers, which he waved away with his glass of barley water. All too soon the workmen went back to their jobs and left Lee alone at the bar with Pearl.

"Why the long face?" She swabbed the bar with a large white washcloth.

The edge of genuine concern in her voice loosened his tongue. "I'm new in town and looking for a job."

She looked him over for a long minute. "Ever tend bar?"

Lee shook his head.

"Want to?"

"You mean work here?"

"Yes, here." She stared at him as though daring him to insult her offer.

Caught between competing tides of relief, caution, and shame, Lee's thoughts raced. Wouldn't a saloon be the worst place for him to work? "I don't know . . . what to say. I've never worked as a bartender."

Her tone softened. "It ain't hard."

Lee clenched his jaw. He was surprised at the depth of his embarrassment. *Bartender.* Of all the jobs he had pictured himself taking up, the trade of bartending had never occurred to him.

"It pays only four dollars a week for six days work. Eight a.m. to seven p.m. Not much to raise a family on."

"I'm single."

She nodded. "Too good to tend bar?"

"No, I just—"

"I noticed you stuck to barley water. I can't have a souse working behind the bar, especially during the day. That's when I need to be taking care of things at home. If you've got a problem with drink, tell me now."

He imagined the Widow Wagstaff's reaction to his telling her that he was a bartender. Everyone knew Chicago was prominent in the budding temperance movement. If she found out, it would raise another wall between them. But since he would not be living under her roof, she need never know where he worked.

"Well?"

He recalled the rejections this morning. If he turned down Pearl, he would be forced out onto those lonely streets to begin again. "We could try it and see how it works out for both of us."

"Can't say fairer than that. Remember, I don't allow my barkeeps to drink while working their shift. If someone wants to buy you a drink, just toss the nickel in your mug and tell them you'll drink it later. Can you abide by that?"

A silent sigh of relief vibrated through Lee. "Yes, ma'am."

"All right, then." She held out her hand to him. Her handshake was firm and direct. "Come back and I'll show you the layout."

Jessie slowly came awake. For a moment, she was lost in time. Then she remembered the night before and this morning. She yawned and stretched languidly. Her body still felt leaden. She gazed around the room, noting the little touches that made it Susan's room, a palm from Palm Sunday service, a string of red beads on the beside table.

Years ago waking in the bed in the little room off the kitchen had been an everyday occurrence for her. In her memory, Jessie saw herself at the age of twelve, leaving home with one small valise in hand; her stepfather marching her brusquely up to Margaret's back door, then leaving her there without a backward look. Just the week before, she'd overheard him telling her mother no girl needed more than a sixth-grade education, and it was time to put Jessie out to earn her own living. He'd supported another man's child for nine years. He had done his duty.

So on that cold, dreary November day, he'd abandoned her on Margaret's back step. Feeling a sinking sensation in her stomach, Jessie had sneaked a look up at Margaret's plump and smiling face. With a gentle touch, Margaret had drawn her in and shown her to the little room. The room's new pink gingham curtains had looked so pretty.

Margaret had commented, "I thought you might be partial to pink." Tongue-tied, Jessie only nodded. After her few possessions and clothing were arranged on the small bedside table and the pegs on the wall, Margaret escorted her back to the kitchen where they spent the morning baking ginger cookies. Those sweet, spicy ginger cookies had tasted like manna from heaven, and those few hours of gentle welcome had made all the difference to Jessie. She had loved Margaret, Will's mother, from that day.

Three years later on November 7, 1860, Jessie had married Will, Margaret's only son. Will, ten years older than Jessie, enlisted a year after their marriage and left his wife and his widowed mother and, after a furlough home, his only son.

Now lying on the once-familiar bed, Jessie breathed a sigh that quivered through her. *Margaret and Will made all the difference in my life. Thank you, God, again and again. I never knew laughter. I never knew freedom until I came into this house.* Will's smiling face came to her memory, sweet and teasing as always. His teasing voice said, *"Still in bed, princess?"*

Susan intruded on Jessie's daydream. "You awake, then?"

Jessie looked over at her in the doorway. "I need to freshen up. What time is it?" Looking at Susan brought the frightening incidents of the night before back to mind. She'd been terrified Little Ben would die. She didn't want to face that again.

"You can get up, but you ain't doing much today. I got my eye on you."

Hiding her worry over a problem she had no solution to, Jessie swung her stocking feet down and sat up, the bed ropes creaking under her. She spoke lightly, "How did you get so bossy?"

"Been watching you." Susan grinned.

This unexpected "sass" hit Jessie's funny bone, lifting her heavy spirits. She tried to pout comically, but went into giggles instead. "Oh, Susan, what would I do without you?"

Uneasy, Jessie sat on the back porch, watching. Facing her, with his back to the white-washed shed that housed her goat and chickens, her bad penny, Mr. Smith, rolled up his sleeves and then patted the leather baseball glove on his hand. "Throw it, Linc. Right into my glove," Lee urged.

His back to her, Linc wound up and threw the soft ball. To Jessie, it seemed a feeble imitation of what she'd seen that day of the first White Stockings game.

Still Mr. Smith lunged forward and caught it. He grinned broadly at Linc. "That was a good try. Next." Smith moved forward a few paces. He sent the ball back in an easy toss.

"Got it!" Linc did a bouncy jig.

Jessie celebrated, too, with a smile. With a dark shawl around her to ward off the lingering April chill, she sat sipping her cup of sweet tea while she inwardly experienced a civil war of emotions over the man in her backyard.

Half of her couldn't help rejoicing. This was the very first time a man had offered to play ball with Linc. Linc's face had glowed with enthusiasm when Mr. Smith arrived after supper with a baseball and a leather glove. Jessie had felt the excitement herself.

How many times in the past years had she suffered silently along with Linc, as they glimpsed a father and son playing catch in a park? She never intended to marry again, so having a man willingly spend time with Linc had been an unanswered prayer.

But the other half of her was galled. Why did it have to be this man? Lee Smith used his handsome face and glib charm entirely too much. No matter what she said to him, he always had a smooth reply. And having a handsome, eligible man around would only lubricate the jaws of the neighborhood gossips.

She watched, trying to get the better of her antipathy to this stranger who had forced his way into their lives. Though she'd warn Linc that as Mr. Smith became acquainted with more people he'd probably have less time to play catch, why shouldn't she let her son enjoy tonight? Why shouldn't she enjoy watching him experience it?

Over this joy hung the unresolved, knotty problem of little Ben's illness. What if the next time this type of crisis occurred, a child died? The worry was like a steel band around her head, tightening. Jessie wasn't a doctor. All she knew was what Margaret had taught her.

"Mrs. Wagstaff?" Susan stepped out on the back porch. "You got a caller." Dr. Gooden strode forward.

"Dr. Gooden?" Jessie nearly dropped her teacup.

"Mrs. Wagstaff, I wanted to see if you were well after staying awake all night."

"I'm fine. Please won't you take a seat?" Jessie motioned to another chair.

"Thank you. I can stay only a short time." He sat down and smiled at her.

"Would you care for some tea?" Jessie hoped she didn't appear as flustered as she felt.

The doctor nodded and Susan went in to get it.

Her gaze ran over him. He had an honest face, a firm chin.

"I can't thank you enough for your help last night. You saved little Ben." Impulsively Jessie reached for his free hand.

He gripped her hand briefly. "That was my reason for becoming a doctor. Too many children die and we have no inkling even of what causes the diseases. Sometimes I feel like a man stumbling in the dark."

This man didn't speak in polite nothings, treating her as a mere woman who wouldn't comprehend serious matters. Just as Will had thought her worthy to be included in his work for abolition.

Coming through the back door again, Susan cleared her throat. "Pardon me, Mrs. Wagstaff, you was napping this afternoon when Caleb called to say little Ben is drinking the rice water fine."

"Good." The doctor accepted the heavy white mug.

"Who's Caleb?" Mr. Smith's lazy voice intruded.

Jessie turned an unwelcoming glance to him, then felt a twinge of guilt. *This man had come on his own to pitch to Linc.*

She forced herself to answer in a perfectly polite tone. "Caleb's the minister's son. He often brings us messages."

"Got an eye for Susan, eh?" Smith winked at Susan.

Susan suppressed a grin. "Can I get you a cup a tea, too, sir?"

Lee bit back a groan of dismay. *Barley water at Pearl's. Tea at Jessie's.* He'd never thought he'd drink such pap.

"If you're not partial to tea, there's buttermilk in the icebox," Jessie offered.

Lee swallowed hard. "I'll take tea, thanks."

Linc had followed Lee and stood beside him. "May I have buttermilk? Please?"

Susan turned back to the kitchen.

"I'm Lee Smith." Lee held out his hand to the stranger. He didn't like the man on sight.

Jessie said, "Dr. Henry Gooden, Mr. Lee Smith."

Dr. Gooden shook hands with the man.

"Who is this young fellow?" Gooden asked, nodding to Linc.

"This young fellow is Jessie's son, Linc." Lee ruffled Linc's hair. The boy smiled up at him. Glancing at Jessie, Lee saw his implied intimacy with Linc irritated her. He'd done it to goad the good doctor, but it had come so naturally, so easily that he'd surprised himself. He'd never taken an interest in a child before.

"Lincoln," Jessie said, sounding very formal, "make your bow. This is the doctor who helped little Ben last night."

Linc bowed, but stayed close to Lee.

Jessie went on. "Mr. Smith has just arrived in Chicago."

"Indeed?" The doctor sipped his tea.

Lee leaned back against the porch railing. "Indeed."

Linc leaned against the railing, mimicking Lee.

"Did you find work today, Mr. Smith?" Jessie asked.

"I did. I'm clerking at an office downtown," Lee lied.

Susan came out bearing another cup and a glass of buttermilk. Before Lee's eyes, Linc downed the glass in one long, noisy draught.

Lee found himself laughing out loud. "Slow down, sport. You'll get the colic drinking that fast."

"Yes, sir." Linc looked up at Lee. "Can we play some more?"

"I thirst and I need my tea," Lee said. "Go practice your pitching form."

"What's that?" Linc demanded.

"Practice throwing the ball *without* the ball." Lee sipped his hot tea.

"Linc, it's nearly time for you to wash up for bed," Jessie cautioned.

"Aw, Mother, *please*. I need practice. We're playing ball at recess now and I gotta do better or I won't get picked."

"Just a little longer, then."

Before his mother had finished her sentence, Linc scrambled off the porch. Lee sipped the sweet tea. Tea wouldn't have been his first choice, but it was wet and tasted better than barley water.

"Jessie!" Miss Wright clumped out onto the porch. "That boy needs to get up to bed. And you need to get to bed early yourself."

Out of politeness, Lee stood up straighter, then gritted his teeth. Dr. Gooden also rose. Jessie quietly introduced him to Miss Wright.

Miss Wright's greeting to the doctor was as unwelcoming as any Lee could have hoped for. "Well! It's about time someone helped this woman. She can't go on staying out all hours nursing. She'll ruin her health."

Dr. Gooden bowed. "I must be leaving."

Wise man, Lee said to himself. "I'm afraid I must be going as well."

The evening came to an abrupt halt. Irritated by Miss Wright's high-handedness, Jessie wished both gentlemen good night. Then she and Linc climbed the steps to their attic room. Fatigue and a headache had dogged her all day. Now her arms and legs felt as though they had been weighted down with wet sand. But her mind was busy with Miss Wright's words: "It's about time someone helped this woman."

Susan bustled up the stairs behind them.

"Oh, Susan, I though you agreed to help Miss Wright get to bed. I just don't have the strength tonight."

"She told me to help you first. You set while I watch this boy wash up—"

Linc protested, "I can do it myself."

Grinning, Susan swatted Linc's behind.

Jessie began slipping pins from her hair. Why hadn't she thought of a doctor for Susan's friends before? Surely she could persuade some kind doctor to treat them. At this thought, a load of worry floated off her.

After Linc said his prayers, Jessie preceded Susan behind the dressing curtain where Susan undid the buttons down the back of Jessie's dress, then loosed her corset laces. Jessie sighed at the sudden release. Jessie pulled on the worn cotton gown, and slid between the cool sheets she hadn't slept between for two nights. She wanted to whisper her thoughts to her friend, but was suddenly too tired to speak.

Susan stopped beside Jessie's bed. "Your nights nursing and days working be over. From now on, I'm gone to take better care a you." Susan patted Jessie's arm and left.

Jessie yawned. One last lucid idea flitted through her mind. *She knew just who to ask for help.*

Chapter 5

Jessie, standing opposite her guest, glanced once more around her immaculate parlor with satisfaction. Her parlor gave her confidence. *I can do this.*

With a smile, Dr. Miller, her family's long-time physician, accepted the thin china cup of coffee from her.

"Thank you for stopping before starting your rounds today." Jessie sat down across from him. The tied-back, floor-length bouffant rose curtains she'd made herself fluttered slightly with the warm breeze. "The lilacs will be blooming—"

"Jessie, please," Dr. Miller chided her with obvious affection. "Are you ready to let me know why you sent Linc over with a note asking me to stop by? I've known you since the day you were born and when you get nervous you chatter."

She blushed and smiled. "I don't know why I'm nervous. I know when I explain the situation you will want to help." Despite her brave words, she quivered inside. Five years ago when she had begun to help Susan's friends, she had crossed an invisible line. The War Between the States had brought about emancipation and citizenship for Negroes. But little else. She cleared her throat. "You know Susan?"

"I've seen her around your house. Yes." He took a sip of his coffee.

"When I got to know Susan's people, I found out that they have no one to provide medical care—"

"Your dear mother has told me that you have been helping them. True Christian charity."

She drew herself up. "But I'm inadequate, Doctor. I use everything my late mother-in-law taught me about nursing the sick. But it's not enough. They need a doctor."

Dr. Miller set his cup and saucer without clatter onto the small round table. "Jessie, you don't know what you're asking me."

"I only want you to accept Susan's people as patients. They aren't beggars. They would pay—"

"I cannot help them directly." He moved forward on his seat and reached for the wallet in his back pocket.

Jessie touched his arm, halting him. "Why?" Her pulse sped up.

He frowned. "If it becomes known that I'm treating blacks, I'll lose all my white patients. It could destroy a successful practice it has taken me thirty-five years to build."

Her fingers tightened around his arm. "Doctors volunteer to go to the mission field—"

"That's all right in foreign parts, but not in Chicago." He stood up. "You don't understand the depth of the feeling here that colored people should've stayed where they belonged."

Jessie rose to her feet. Temper flashed red-hot through her. "Do you mean Africa? The slavers didn't allow them that choice."

He took a five-dollar bill from his wallet and laid it beside his discarded cup. "That's to buy medicine. Good day."

He strode out, leaving Jessie standing in her parlor. She heard him close the front door firmly.

"Well, that's that." Susan stalked into the room with her arms crossed over her breast.

"I'm stunned. Dr. Miller is one of the kindest men I know." His refusal had felt like a door slammed in her face.

"To white folks."

Jessie'd known she'd been taking a chance. She'd never asked anyone else to cross the invisible color line and join in her work. What she needed was a man with a larger vision. "Maybe I was meant to meet Dr. Gooden," Jessie said in a thoughtful manner.

"You think he might help my people?" Susan's doubt on this was clear in her tone.

"The Lord doth provide. Let's invite Dr. Gooden to dine with us Friday."

Dr. Henry Gooden stood on the front porch of the Wagstaff House, wondering if he would find here what he had been looking for. A young woman of color answered the door. "It is Susan, isn't it?" Dr. Gooden handed her his hat.

"Yes, sir. Will you step into the parlor, please?" Susan showed him to a chair, then curtseyed. "I'll tell Mrs. Wagstaff you're here."

From the comfortable wing-back chair, Henry examined the parlor. The oak floor and woodwork gleamed in the lamplight. Everything else also spoke of a notable homemaker.

"Dr. Gooden, I'm so happy you could come." Jessie swept in, her hand outstretched to him.

He stood, took her hand, bent to kiss it. The scent of lavender floated from her. He smiled. "For the invitation, I thank you."

"Please have a seat."

As he waited for her to sit first, he gazed at her with admiration. She lowered herself delicately into her chair, then perched on it like a lady with her spine held straight, not touching the back of her chair.

"Have you had a busy day, Doctor?"

He liked her question, the perfect social start to a conversation. Tonight, she was dressed all in black, and though simple, it was cut in the latest mode with the skirt swept toward the rear to a modest bustle. "A day of usual cases. But I never tire of it."

"I understand."

Her two quiet words touched him. This woman did understand. Nodding, he smiled at her. Out of the corner of his eye, he saw the old woman coming toward them.

"Who is this you're sitting with?" the old woman barked.

Deferentially he stood up.

The old woman glared at him. "That doctor? What is he doing here again?"

"Miss Wright, I've invited Dr. Henry Gooden for dinner."

As he bent over the old woman's hand, she grumbled, but the old woman said no more. His hostess was definitely the mistress of her home.

"Mother?" Linc scrambled into the parlor. "Dinner is served."

Jessie rose. "Lincoln, please tell Susan we're coming right in."

Henry wanted to offer his arm to Jessie, but good manners dictated he offer it to the elderly spinster first. When she rebuffed him, he entered the dining room with Jessie's hand featherlight on his arm.

The dining room impressed him as the parlor had. "The carving on your sideboard, it is beautiful."

"My late husband's father was noted for his fine woodworking."

"He was an artist." Dr. Gooden seated Jessie at the head of the table and waited while she introduced him to her other two boarders. The young blonde was a treat to behold, but the redhead was mutton dressed as lamb. While Jessie still wore widow's black, the widowed schoolteacher was arrayed in pink ruffles instead of tastefully in some sober hue.

At the foot of the table at Jessie's request, he gave the blessing. "God, thank you for this home and this meal. Amen."

"So you have family?" Miss Wright asked tartly.

"My mother lives in Cleveland with my older brother and his wife."

"Sir, what made you become a doctor?" Miss Greenleigh, the young blond lady, asked him.

"When I was only eight, my sister nearly died. With the diphtheria. A doctor saved her life. After that, I became his shadow."

"You began your avocation early, then?" Jessie asked.

He liked the way her voice sounded so sure, so confident. The meal went on just as he'd hoped, good food in a genteel setting. He ate his final bite of sweet rhubarb pie with light whipped cream.

Susan came through the curtain. "Mrs. Wagstaff, could Lincoln be 'scused from the table now?"

"Why?"

"Mr. Smith is here. He wanta know can Linc come out and play ball?"

Henry was pleased to see that though Linc eagerly sat up straighter, he did not bolt from the table. Only when Jessie nodded, did the boy disappear in a flash behind Susan.

Mrs. Bolt stood up. "Dr. Gooden, perhaps you'd be interested in attending a temperance meeting with me tonight?"

He shook his head. "So sorry, ma'am. Already I am involved in much charity work."

"Very well." Her mouth primmed up.

"Perhaps Mr. Smith would like to accompany you," Miss Wright said piously.

"Why I hadn't thought . . . I'll ask him." Mrs. Bolt headed for the curtain and disappeared through it.

The old woman snorted.

Miss Greenleigh shook her head as she rose. "Miss Wright, that was very naughty of you, but I have time to read a while tonight. Would you like to hear more of Dickens?"

"Aren't you going to visit that sister of yours this weekend?" Miss Wright asked with a growl.

"No, I'm relaxing this weekend."

"Well, if you haven't got anything else to do. I could stand a chapter or so." Sounding disgruntled, the old woman got up and the two of them turned toward the parlor.

Jessie smiled. Having Miss Greenleigh in her home was a true blessing.

Jessie rose. "Would you mind spending the evening on the back porch? I should support Linc in his efforts to master baseball, his passion these days."

"In this balmy weather, it would be a pleasure."

Jessie inclined her head. Just as she'd hoped, everything about the meal seemed to have mellowed the doctor. When he offered her his arm, she stiffened but accepted it without demur. She had invited this man tonight to ask him for his help, but she had overlooked the fact that he might misinterpret her intentions. Did he think she was pursuing him? Her mouth went dry.

They walked down the steps. Mrs. Bolt hurried past them, her mouth in a grim line.

The doctor murmured, "Mr. Smith preferred a game of catch to a temperance meeting?"

"I suppose so." As Jessie led him around the side of the house, she recalled racing over this same walk with little Ben limp in her arms. This man had saved Ben; she would never forget that debt.

Ahead in the twilight, Mr. Smith stood behind Linc moving Linc's arm forward, obviously demonstrating how to pitch. Linc with a man who cared about him. For a second she wished she could rest her hand on Mr. Smith's arm in silent thanks.

No matter how his cocky attitude grated on her, she owed him so much. His nightly visits had given her son an extra bounce to his step these days. And she'd heard Linc bragging about "his friend Mr. Smith" to the neighborhood boys. Only the presence of Dr. Gooden held her back from the emotional pull that now drew her to Mr. Smith.

Then she saw Dr. Gooden smiling at Linc. This man had a kind heart, too.

Lee called to them, "We meet again, Doctor. Good evening, Mrs. Wagstaff."

Jessie nodded.

The doctor replied, "Mr. Smith."

Lee didn't let the doctor's unwelcoming tone bother him. As Linc babbled to Lee about the ball game that day at school, the doctor was seating Jessie on the porch. *I don't want to miss a word Dr. Gooden says to Jessie.* "Okay, Linc, tonight you go stand with your back to the shed and I'll stay here, close to the porch."

Listening to the doctor trying to charm the Widow Wagstaff would make an entertaining evening.

The doctor cleared his throat. "Mrs. Wagstaff, you recall our discussing the possible causes of milk fever?"

Lee grinned to himself. How many men after dinner would discuss milk fever with a lady?

"Yes, I've often wondered why milk is good for children Linc's age, but harmful to infants."

"And the factor of the time of year is significant also, don't you think? Milk fever comes with the warm weather."

"Yes."

"Have you ever heard of Louis Pasteur, a French scientist?" Dr. Gooden asked.

Lee answered silently, *Yes, I have. What about him?*

"He believes disease is spread by bacteria. A microscope, have you ever seen one?"

"I know what it is."

Now Lee's interest had been caught, too. What was the man's angle?

"Looking in the microscope, Pasteur has identified bacteria, which he says are alive and cause disease. He has experimented with heating milk to boiling. With thirty minutes boiling, all the bacteria in the milk are destroyed."

"Then if mothers boiled the milk before they gave it to their babies, they could destroy the bacteria which causes the diarrhea?" Jessie sounded excited.

Good question, Jessie. Lee caught the ball and tossed it back to Linc.

"But what about the warm weather? How does that make the bacteria worse?" Jessie's interest came across clearly.

Lee strained to hear the answer to this question. He had to admit the widow knew how to delve into a subject without dithering about the constraints of polite conversation.

The doctor's voice showed his excitement at Jessie's interest. "Look around you. When the weather warms, everything grows. Why not bacteria?"

Lee caught another ball. "Good pitch!" He tossed the ball back to the boy.

"A lot of physicians," the doctor said, "don't want to deal with all the new ideas in this century or bother to read the foreign journals."

"That's wrong."

"At least short-sighted. I want to direct a hospital that trains doctors in the latest discoveries, newest medicines. The old doctors won't change, so teaching new doctors must be my goal."

Lee heard the enthusiasm in the man's voice and pitied him. His passion for the innovative would make him an easy target for lesser men.

"I knew when we met you were different from other doctors." Jessie leaned forward, her voice eager. "I believe you were sent to me by God."

"Me, how?"

You walked right into that one, Doc. Lee grinned and tossed a faster ball back to Linc, who yelped happily as he caught it.

"Will you consent to be the doctor to Susan's people?"

Silence fell on the porch.

Lee grimaced to himself. *Go ahead, Doc, talk your way out of this one.*

"This is a deep concern of yours, isn't it?" Dr. Gooden asked.

Tell her you can't do it, Doc.

"I was terrified that night. My skills are inadequate and I haven't found them someone who has the skills they need."

"But, why are you responsible for them?" Dr. Gooden asked.

"My husband, Will, worked for abolition. He enlisted in the U.S.

Sanitary Corps to succor wounded soldiers. What good is freedom to Susan's people if they can't even find a doctor who will treat them?"

Lee felt his face draw down and become stiff, grim.

"What's the matter, Mr. Smith?" Linc gazed at him with the ball poised to throw.

Chagrined, Lee felt exposed. "Nothing. Toss that ball here, sport!"

Dr. Gooden replied, "Some problems are too big for one person to solve. Your late husband didn't end slavery all by himself."

"No," Jessie admitted, "but he did what he could. And so will I."

"I cannot do what you want me to."

At the doctor's simple statement, Lee stood up straighter. *I can't believe he had the guts to tell her the truth.*

"Why not?" Jessie's voices sounded tremulous.

Did you really expect him to just say yes, Jessie?

"If I do what you ask, I put in danger—or worse—destroy all my chances to reach my goal of a teaching hospital."

"Why?" Jessie asked.

The doctor explained, "A good hospital costs a good amount of money."

So Dr. Gooden's a realist after all? Lee tossed the ball. "Catch this, Linc?"

"I need wealthy contributors. I cannot do anything that will endanger my impressing these people with the importance of the work I've been called to do."

You mean impressing them plain and simple, don't you, Doc?

"I would think you'd be taken more seriously," Jessie said.

"This world we live in is not perfect."

Lee waited. The Jessie Wagstaff he knew didn't take no for an answer.

She said, "I don't believe that our goals oppose one another. I can't believe you would turn your back on a person, white or black, who needed you."

A brief silence transpired.

The doctor broke it. "I tell you what. I will give you medicine and information you need to nurse them."

Lee heard the rocker creak. He glanced over his shoulder and saw Jessie take hold of the man's hand.

Jessie said, "Thank you."

Lee's stomach clenched, but why? He didn't care about the widow and the doctor. He walked toward Linc. "It's time we take a rest."

Linc frowned. "I'm not tired."

"I am." He rested his hand on Linc's back. Doing this was starting to feel natural, comfortable. At the back porch, he and Linc leaned back against the railing side by side.

Jessie drew her hand from the doctor's.

"Well, young man," the doctor said, "your catching and pitching, they're improving."

"Did you play ball when you were a boy, sir?"

Lee hung back but let Linc take a step forward.

"Yes, but I was not as good as you or Mr. Smith." The doctor grinned and stood up. "I must go. I am on duty at Rush Medical Hospital early on Saturday mornings."

"Thank you for coming, Doctor." Jessie rose.

The doctor bent over her hand, refused her offer to walk him to the front door, and departed.

Susan walked out onto the porch. "I come for Linc. Time for bed, mister baseball player."

"Mother, please?"

Lee said, "I'm tired myself, sport."

Linc's face fell.

"But if your mother doesn't object, we'll continue our game of catch tomorrow evening."

"Hooray!" Linc jumped straight up.

"Come on, Linc, your bed be callin' you." Susan and Linc started toward the back door. "Oh, I forgot your mama stop and left you a note." Susan pulled it from the pocket in her apron and handed it to Jessie. Then she led Linc away. The boy looked back at Lee until the last moment.

While reading the note, Jessie stood facing him. He could see why the doctor might be intrigued by her. Even dressed in black, and buttoned up tight as can be, Jessie Wagstaff still caught the eye. "So you're trying to find yourself a doctor?"

She surprised him by tearing the note in two and shoving it into her pocket. "So you were eavesdropping? *Yes*, I am. My stepfather has just written me that asking my own doctor to treat them was outrageous. Is that what you think?"

Her vehemence didn't surprise him, but her naiveté about the deep prejudices in this ugly, old world sharpened his voice, "Don't you realize no doctor in this city will take Susan's people as patients?"

"Dr. Gooden has agreed to help me."

"He'll give you medicine and advice, but don't expect him to visit shantytown any time soon." He couldn't keep the sarcasm out of his voice.

"It's easy to sneer at someone who has a higher calling, but what would an office clerk know about the pressures a man like Dr. Gooden faces?" With a swish of her skirts, she swept away like Queen Victoria herself.

He stared after her. *I know all about men like Dr. Gooden. I used to know one like him a long time ago. Watch out, Jessie, a man like that can let people down badly.*

Chapter 6

June 15, 1871

"Beer, *bitte*."

"Not pink champagne, Slim?" Though Lee grinned as he pulled down the spigot of the beer keg, he mentally tried to shrug off a restlessness that had gripped him for several days.

"Funny, Smit'." The large, broad-shouldered German tossed a nickel into Lee's hand.

Lee aimed and expertly flipped it into the cigar box behind the bar, which served as Pearl's cash box. Talking helped keep him from thinking. "How's your day?"

"Six hours more work and tomorrow *ist Sonntag.*"

Lee concurred with the raucous but friendly agreement to this sentiment rippling through the line of men along the length of the bar. With genuine satisfaction, Lee anticipated tomorrow, his day off. Jessie had invited him for the first time to Sunday dinner, to celebrate Linc's eighth birthday. Lee was making progress toward his goal.

Out of the corner of his eye, he saw his pretty boss enter from the rear of the tavern. Several voices around him called out greetings. One man ventured, "Hey, Pearl, you look grand!"

Lee grinned ruefully. He should have expected Pearl to drop in. He forced himself to use a light tone. "Checking to see if I'm pocketing some of the gold from these gentlemen-about-town?"

More laughter approved his sally. One thing Lee had learned about bartending was that the rough men who came into the tavern were starved for amusement.

As Pearl came behind the bar, she exchanged several teasing comments with the customers. He allowed his ironic gaze to rove over Pearl in a charming cranberry red dress with wide bands of ivory lace across her low-cut bosom. He had noticed whenever she visited during his shift, she always made herself a treat to see. That was becoming the problem.

She turned to him. "I came in to pay you."

"So early?" He dried his hands on the towel tucked into the waistband of his white apron. "Are you sure I won't close up and take a nap in the back room as soon as you leave?"

"He's a sly one!" the men warned Pearl. "He's as lazy as a dog with a lame leg!"

"Pooh!" Pearl waved a dismissive hand to them. Lee listened with only half an ear to the banter that continued until the workmen reluctantly went back to their jobs in the nearby factories. Then Pearl took the cigar box into the back room where she had a desk.

While she was gone, Lee served the two drunks who were sprawled at a table in the back. They weren't carrying on a conversation. They were just sipping, slowly and steadily drinking themselves into their daily stupor. He didn't mind serving workmen beer with their lunches. Many of them were German immigrants who had drunk a glass of beer at lunch their whole lives. But these two drunken faces haunted him more every day. Had any bartender ever pitied him?

"Mr. Smith," Pearl called him back to the bar. "Here's your wages." She handed him four one-dollar bills.

Outside, a wagon rattled by and a flume of dust floated over the double swinging doors. Pearl paused, just as he did, to watch the particles dance in the rays of sunlight and finally drift down to the tabletops.

Worry was plain in Pearl's voice. "Yesterday a neighbor boy almost started his father's barn afire."

Lee shook his head. "Everything's as dry as tinder."

Pearl's tone sharpened. "I used it to put the fear of fire into my two."

Two widows had become important in Lee's new life in Chicago. Jessie had been left a house as a means of support. Pearl had been left a saloon.

"I'm off to the bank, then home," Pearl said. "My boy broke another window playing that baseball."

He grinned.

"*This time* he's going to have to work it off. He'll be coming here every afternoon next week and mop the place."

Red flags waved inside Lee, but he said gallantly, "As you wish, ma'am. I will miss doing it myself, but . . ."

She chuckled. "I'd give anything to know who taught you such pretty manners and how you ever let me hire you as a barkeep."

"It was my lucky day." He grinned broadly to hide his uneasiness.

Pearl shook her head at him. As she left, femininely swaying her high and ornately be-ribboned bustle, he knew she was flirting with him. Pearl teased him with a practiced subtlety and great finesse—in contrast to Mrs. Bolt, who launched herself at him like a lovesick adolescent.

He imagined himself telling the "prim" schoolteacher that a bar owner had better manners than she. But why hadn't anyone explained to the redhead that while no man turns from the attraction of a pretty woman, no man ever desires to be the object of such a blatant pursuit? Mrs. Bolt embarrassed herself and him every time they met.

He clenched his jaw as though forcing back these words while he swabbed the bar with a washcloth, tidying up after lunch.

The heat from the blistering, noon-high sun weighed down the stagnant air of the saloon. One of the drunks lifted a hand. Lee grimaced to himself as he picked up the whiskey bottle, then walked toward them.

The odor of whiskey no longer made Lee's mouth water. Instead it made his pulse jump as though he needed to run. This and the fear of greeting Linc with alcohol on his breath kept him dry as their Chicago drought. Nothing must come between Linc and him.

He poured each of the drunks a shot of whiskey, suddenly swelling with a deep repugnance. How had he let himself start work here? The walls around him suddenly felt like a trap. He wished to be anywhere—no, not anywhere. He longed to be in Jessie's backyard.

In his mind's eye, he pictured her image from last evening. For the very first time, Linc had hit a ball over the back fence. Jessie had leaped to her feet. Because of the heat, the top buttons of her high-necked black blouse and the buttons at her wrists had been loosed. Her wavy hair had come a little undone and wisps of hair curled in the faint perspiration all around her temples.

When he glanced to her face, he had been captivated by her animation. Her pinched look of stern widowhood, which he had disliked, vanished. In that moment, he'd glimpsed the sweet, happy woman she'd been before she'd put on widow's black.

* * *

Jessie held herself rigidly, not allowing her spine to touch the back of the pew, the way her stepfather insisted a lady sat. To her right sat her mother, stepfather, and their twin sons. Jessie had tucked in Linc at her left to limit her stepfather's scrutiny of him. If she did anything her stepfather didn't like, he'd snatch her mother and half brothers away home and ruin the day. This worry kept Jessie on poisoned pins and needles.

With the congregation, Jessie stood to sing. Her mind kept slipping back to Susan, who'd stayed home from her own church to prepare Linc's birthday meal. *Thank You, God, for Susan.*

Her mind deserted the church where she was singing and took her back five years to the day she had first met Susan. That Sunday morning she had walked to the Negro church, on the South Side in a warehouse along the lakefront, where the congregation met. Too poor to purchase pews, the congregation stood except for a few older men and women who sat on ladder-backed chairs at the front. Jessie hadn't anticipated that being the only white face in a room filled with dark faces would make her feel so conspicuous.

Unconcerned, Linc, only three then, toddled away from Jessie's side, forward to one of the few older women who was without a child in her lap. In silent request, he held up his arms and the older woman bent, picked him up, and settled him on her navy skirt.

Around her the congregation began singing, "On that great getting up mornin', Hallelu, Hallelu . . ." The people around her swayed to the rhythm. Thunderstruck, she'd never heard such voices, lyrics, melodies, such joy! They stirred her beyond her imagining—awakening her blood, setting it to flow rich and sure through her veins, awakening her spirit from its deep mourning.

The old preacher at the front led the congregation in song, his voice was cellar-deep, grave, powerful. The mood of the music shifted and a song about dying swirled into her heart. They sang this plaintive question: "Were you there when they crucified my Lord?" over and over letting it build, rise, soar. When the low chorus, "Sometimes it causes me to tremble, tremble, tremble," was sung and sung again, the pain of losing Will, of losing Margaret pierced Jessie's heart anew.

Silent tears coursed down her cheeks, unchecked. *Oh, Margaret, Will, how can I go on without you?* This freshly opened grief made her regret coming. She clasped her Bible to her breast as though it were her heart and she had to hold it together or it might shatter.

Then like a wave of cold, clear lake water, a high soprano voice, joyous and true, broke over them, "Sing a ho that I had the wings of a dove. I'd fly away!" Excitement, energy, sensation shot through Jessie. "I'll fly away!"

She imagined Will and Margaret standing on either side of her, lifting them to joy. *All this will pass away in time. I, too, will fly away.* She let its harmonies carry her heavenward. "*Yes, I will fly away!*"

Then with a full heart, Jessie watched the pastor open his well-worn Bible. In his compelling voice, he read the last chapter of John, of Christ appearing to the apostles as they were fishing in the Sea of Galilee and cooking a humble fishermen's breakfast in the chilly, gray dawn on the shore. The picture he made so real took Jessie outside to the shores of Lake Michigan. She smelled the fresh lake air, heard the gulls screech, imagined the brisk morning wind on her face. Jessie tingled with the story of how Peter, when told he would die a martyr's death, turned and asked if that would be John's fate also.

"You see Peter was the Rock," the old preacher said. "Christ had chosen him to be the foundation of his church. But he still was irritated that he wasn't the one Jesus loved best. And the Lord answered Peter, 'What is it to you, Peter, if John live till I come again?'" The pastor repeated the question. His voice dropped, "You see, friends, Peter's spirit was willing, but his flesh was weak. He wasn't happy with just being the top rung of the ladder. He wasn't satisfied. He wanted to be the one—not John—who rested his head upon Jesus' chest." His voice rose, "Did Christ strike Peter dead for this effrontery? Did he?"

The congregation answered, "No!" It made Jessie jump. She'd never heard a pastor actually get a reply.

"That's right! No! And He'll show the same kindness to us! Peter was there with the Holy Christ right beside him, yet he still could think small thoughts. Are we any better?"

Jessie was prepared this time for the "No!" that resounded around her.

"So, brethren, let's be kind to one another. You know we aren't supposed to judge. No, we're not. But we judge anyway. Yes, we do! Are any of us worthy? No, not one. Remember that and be kind." A chorus of "Amen!" followed this and with a simple prayer, the service ended.

The pastor went to the door to shake hands. Jessie and Linc were politely ushered to the front of the line. "Good morning, sister, I'm Reverend Mitchell." Feeling shy, she shook his hand, the first time ever she touched dark skin.

"I'm Mrs. Wagstaff. Reverend, I would like to ask your advice about a matter when you're free."

He replied, "Mrs. Wagstaff, you might as well speak plainly. No one here will go about their business till you state your reason for visiting our service." His words were direct, but spoken kindly.

Jessie blushed. "I'm sorry. I didn't mean to intrude, but I am looking for a woman to help me at home. I'm a widow and I'm going to take in two more boarders to support myself, but I need help. Especially since my son takes up so much of my time."

"I see," said the Reverend. "You want someone reliable."

Jessie nodded, then leaned down to wipe a smudge off Linc's cheek.

A tall, young man at the pastor's elbow said sharply, "Ask her how much she's willing to pay."

The pastor frowned. "I intend to ask that, son."

"I don't know exactly." Jessie bit her lower lip. "I am receiving two dollars a week from my present boarder, so I'd probably be taking in about six dollars a week. But I don't know how much it will cost to feed six people—"

The young man spoke up sharply again, "So you expect her to work for room and board like a slave?" The man's words visibly shocked his father. Many of those standing around cast him upset glances.

Affronted, Jessie looked him in the eye. "No, I was thinking that since the money would be supporting three—the woman, my son, and me—that I would pay her one-third of what is left after expenses each week. Would that be fair?" There had been a moment of silence.

"Yes, ma'am, that sounds fair," the old preacher said. He then cast his eyes over the waiting assembly. "Susan, would you like to work for Mrs. Wagstaff?"

"Yes, thank you, Rev'rund." Susan came forward, clothed in a shabby gray dress with mended lace at the neck.

"How do you do, Susan?" Jessie offered her hand.

"How do, Miss Jessie." She curtseyed to Jessie.

"Please call me Mrs. Wagstaff. I am your employer, not your mistress."

Susan's face registered a flash of happiness and she curtseyed again. "Yes, Mrs. Wagstaff."

The present church pipe organ reverberated with the final chords of the hymn, jolting Jessie's thoughts back to the present. *I must find someone to help Susan's people. Lord, help me.* Jessie sat down amid sounds of skirts rustling and Bible pages turning.

In the discreet well-bred silence that followed, the minister read the New Testament Scriptures for the morning, Galatians 3:28: "There is neither Jew nor Greek, there is neither bond nor free, there is neither male nor female: for ye are all one in Christ Jesus."

Jessie drank in these words of purity and devotion and tried to let love blossom inside her heart for her stepfather. Her mother nodded in Linc's direction. Linc, sitting with his hands folded in his lap, was silently swinging his legs back and forth. Her stepfather demanded all children imitate statues in church. Her stomach burned with her resentment. *Lord, forgive me. I hate him.* Linc looked up innocently. She pointed to his legs and shook her head. A sudden, tiny grin lighting his face, he obeyed. Inwardly she was delighted. It was times like these that she most saw her Will in his undaunted son.

* * *

At long last, the minister concluded his sermon. After two hours of obeying her stepfather's strictures, Jessie felt choked. Any longer and she wouldn't have been able to breathe. Jessie followed her mother down the crowded church aisle, and down the stone steps. She had smiled mechanically to everyone who greeted her, but it was a deceiving mask and she hated it.

Shielded from the noonday sun by their white parasols, Jessie and her mother strolled home, side by side, smiling. Mother rarely smiled when her husband was near. A day in her stepfather's galling company had to be endured as the only way to have her mother with her at Linc's eighth birthday.

In honor of the day, Jessie had put off her "blacks" and worn her more festive dove gray with ivory white lace collar tatted by Margaret. As she and her mother ascended the steps of Wagstaff house, her stepfather hurried forward to open the door for them. Jessie looked away from him as they folded their parasols and stepped inside.

"I smell fried chicken," Mother said.

"Yes, Susan stayed home from church to cook—"

"That's her job, isn't it?" Her stepfather hung his hat on the hall tree.

Jessie swallowed a stinging retort. *I won't give you any opportunity to leave early, stepfather. Mother and I are going to enjoy this day—come what may.*

While her half brothers, Tim and Tom, followed their father's sedate example, Linc ran ahead toward the kitchen. Her stepfather shook his head over Linc's lapse of decorum. Pointedly ignoring the man, Jessie walked with her mother toward the parlor.

"Good morning, Esther," Miss Wright's voice from the parlor greeted Jessie's mother, one of her former pupils.

Mother entered the sunny room and pressed her hand into the old woman's. "It is so good to see you, ma'am, especially on such a happy day."

"Yes, it is hard to believe the little scamp can really be eight today. I was remembering Margaret's delight at receiving God's gifts of a son, then a grandson. I've been enjoying memories all morning. Margaret and I were girls together, you know."

The spinster's mellow mood surprised Jessie, but Will's mother had been the old woman's best, nearly her only friend. "I must check on dinner," Jessie murmured and rustled down the hall through the kitchen curtain.

"I heard y'all come in." Susan lifted the black iron skillet's lid to pierce the sizzling chicken with a large fork, checking its doneness.

"Everything smells delicious. What can I help with?" Jessie reached for her apron.

"You put that apron back," Susan ordered. "Everything's done and this is your day to celebrate. Now get out of this hot kitchen!" Susan matched her words by waving her hands toward Jessie, shooing her.

Jessie chuckled. "Where did Linc disappear to?"

"He went out to water that pup Mr. Smith brought him yesterday. I'll send Linc back to the parlor when his hands is all wash again."

Nodding, Jessie returned to the parlor to sit beside her mother, deep in conversation with Miss Wright. From under her lashes she observed her stepfather's keen gaze looking for dust.

A complacent smile tugged at the corners of her mouth. She'd left no dust anywhere and her floors shone like crystal. Her back and arm muscles still ached from a day spent cleaning and polishing. Nothing her stepfather could say now or later would spoil this day for her mother, Linc, and herself.

A knock sounded on the front door. Jessie rose to open it. She found Mr. Smith standing on the front porch with a bouquet of pink and white carnations.

"For my hostess." He laid them into her arms.

A tingle of exhilaration robbed her of speech. She fingered the slender petals of one carnation. "Thank you. I can't remember when I last received flowers." She felt herself blushing.

Footsteps on the porch. Jessie stepped farther inside and motioned Dr. Gooden in. He held out a bouquet of pink roses to her.

She felt an instant restraint or maybe it was tension, between the two men. She couldn't think why that should be. But the experience of holding two bouquets from two different men struck her speechless for a moment. Then she scolded herself for being silly. Of course, being polite, they would bring hostess gifts to her. Suddenly she recalled her stepfather sat only a few feet away from her. That made her stiffen. "Please come in."

At her request the two gentlemen hung their hats on the hall tree and followed her to the parlor. She introduced them as "Lincoln's friends" to her parents, "Mr. and Mrs. Hiram Huff." Under her stepfather's scrutiny, Jessie held her flowers casually. "I'll have to find a vase for these," she murmured.

Sensing Jessie's insecurity, Lee diverted attention from her. "Where's the birthday lad?"

"He's out back watering Butch," Jessie said.

"Butch?" Huff repeated.

The man's negative tone instantly put Lee on guard. Lee watched the way Jessie took a deep breath and composed her mouth into a forced smile. He couldn't recall Jessie ever behaving so unnaturally before.

"Butch is the puppy Mr. Smith gave Linc for his birthday," Dr. Gooden said approvingly. "A fine pup."

Lee glanced at the doctor, surprised at his support.

"A dog," Huff blustered.

One of the twins asked in obvious awe, "Linc got a dog?"

"Children," Huff barked at his son who flushed a deep red, "are to be seen and not heard." He glared at Jessie. "You have heard me say time after time, town dogs are just a nuisance. He'll dig up your yard, draw flies, and infest your house with fleas. What will your boarders say to that?"

"Butch *isn't* a house dog," Miss Wright spoke up.

Lee could hardly believe his ears. *I didn't know the old woman had it in her.* Lee eyed Huff with distaste. "That's correct. Linc and I built a doghouse together for him, sir."

Dr. Gooden nodded and added, "Linc promised to walk him each morning and each evening. I told him he must keep Butch tied up and wet him down in the hot afternoons."

Reluctantly Lee gave the doctor an imperceptible nod of thanks. The stepfather choked back his ire with evident displeasure. He might bully the women, but how could he argue with two men who approved of the pet? *Linc is going to have his dog whether you like it or not.*

"Mr. Smith, it's very good of you to take time for Lincoln," Jessie's mother said quietly.

"My pleasure, ma'am."

"Mother!" Linc burst into the sunny room, hugging a small brown-and-white pup. "Everyone's in the backyard! Come on!"

As Huff lunged toward the boy, Lee moved forward protectively. When his mother didn't move, Linc grabbed her hand and pulled her through the hall and kitchen.

Lee, followed by Dr. Gooden, had to nearly run to keep up with them. The four of them came to a halt on the back porch, next to Susan who stood stock still on the top step, transfixed.

A dozen of the black community had gathered in Jessie's backyard. Lee recognized these friends of Susan's whom he had seen come and go through Jessie's back door. In their midst, Lee picked out the face of the bent old but untroubled preacher who had called on Susan just the week before. Beside him stood a very round, short woman with gray hair, peeking out from under a calico turban. The old woman's clothes were faded, tattered and her wide feet were bare.

Suddenly Susan came out of her shock and shrieked, "Ruby! Grandma Ruby!" As the girl raced down the steps, the old woman tottered forward. Susan threw herself into those open arms. "Grandma Ruby, I never thought I'd see you again! You're alive!"

"I been lookin' these last five years for you, my honey." Ruby rocked Susan back and forth in her arms as though the young woman was just a child once more. "I walk miles and miles and ask a thousand people 'n' more—where be my girl, my onliest girl? Praise God!" Ruby burst into tears.

Lee felt his throat thicken. A homecoming. A reunion.

Jessie stood like a statue pressing both bouquets to her breast. She must have felt Lee's attention on her because she looked up at him. She murmured, "Susan was sold away from her only relative, her grandmother, when she was only thirteen."

He acknowledged her explanation with a subdued nod.

Dr. Gooden cleared his throat. "It is hard to believe that the Emancipation Proclamation is only signed eight years ago."

Lee nodded soberly, watching the two women cling to each other, kissing, weeping, and laughing.

Jessie hurried down the steps straight to the two women. Susan, her face ashine with laughter and tears, turned her grandmother toward Jessie. Without waiting for a word of introduction, Jessie gave the bouquets to the old woman and threw her arms around her. "Welcome."

From behind Lee, Huff's outraged voice snapped, "What is all this commotion?"

Lee glanced coolly over at him.

But Dr. Gooden answered, "Susan is reunited with her long-lost grandmother."

"That is all good and well, but the girl could go to her in their neighborhood. These people have no business here." He clattered down the steps, headed straight for Jessie.

Lee couldn't help but smile. He often didn't like Jessie's determined ways, but she wouldn't tolerate this man ruining Susan's reunion. He followed Huff at a discreet distance. *I wouldn't miss this for the world.*

Keeping pace with Lee, Dr. Gooden leaned to speak close to Lee's ear, "That man doesn't know his stepdaughter very well, does he?"

"So it seems," Lee replied with a wicked grin.

Huff's voice boomed over the backyard, "Jessie, these people don't belong here!"

Jessie replied, "Stepfather, this doesn't concern you. Won't you return to the parlor?"

Huff stopped directly in front of her. "These people must leave. What will the neighbors think?"

Lee watched Jessie lift her chin. *Now the sparks will fly.*

"This is no concern of my neighbors or of yours."

Lee suppressed a grin at the honed steel in Jessie's tone.

Hat in hand, the Reverend began edging away, "We'll be leaving then, Mrs. Wagstaff. We didn't come to cause friction. When we learned it was Susan our sister Ruby was searching for, we just couldn't wait; we had to bring them together."

Jessie put out her hand to forestall him. "There is no reason for you to leave on this happy occasion. Susan has made enough fried chicken and cake to feed an army. You can celebrate Susan and her grandmother's reunion in my backyard while we celebrate Linc's birthday in the dining room." Jessie touched Susan's arm.

Lee said to himself, *That makes sense, Jessie, but Huff won't buy it.*

"But, Mrs. Wagstaff—" Susan began.

"Jessie." Her stepfather grasped Jessie's arm. "This will not do. Your neighbors will be appalled. Susan can visit her grandmother when she has her day off."

Lee couldn't wait to hear Jessie's reply.

Jessie pulled away from Huff's grip. In a deceptively soft tone, she said, "You are not the master here."

Chapter 7

Lee read the despair on Mrs. Huff's face as she stood beside her young sons and Miss Wright. She hurried down the back steps. White-faced, she opened her mouth.

Her husband silenced her, "We are leaving, Esther. Your stubborn daughter is making a spectacle of herself and I won't subject you and our sons to such goings-on."

"Goings-on?" Lee heard himself say. "She just wants Susan's friends to eat cake in her backyard."

Huff reached for his wife's arm. She pulled back, eluding his grasp. "Please, Hiram," she pleaded.

The anguish in the woman's voice sliced through Lee like a scalpel.

"Esther, we're leaving."

The woman hesitated, visibly torn. Giving in to tears, she covered her mouth with the back of her hand. She stepped in front of Linc, who still clutched his pup, and dropped to her knees on the dried-up grass. She pulled him to her, hugging him.

"Esther," her husband insisted.

Lee fought the urge to confront Huff, the hard-hearted jerk. Lee's hands curled into fists.

With a smothered sob, Jessie's mother tore herself away from Linc. She rushed past her husband. When she reached her sons, she took each by the hand and hurried them into the house. Without a backward glance, Huff marched after her. From her place on the porch, Miss Wright huffed her displeasure and turned away, too.

Lee burned with outrage for Jessie. Lee imagined the satisfaction of his right fist connecting with the holier-than-thou's jaw.

"Mrs. Wagstaff," Reverend Mitchell said, "we didn't mean to cause a break between you and your mother—"

"You didn't." She lifted her chin. "She made her choice years ago when she married Hiram Huff." Then she smiled, a tight, a pitiful smile. "Frankly, Reverend, I prefer your company. Come, Susan, bring your grandmother up into the shade of the porch."

Touched by Jessie's brave front, Lee stood with his hand on Linc's shoulder. As Jessie passed him, she asked, "Are you staying, then, Mr. Smith?"

He made his voice match hers in bravado, "Ma'am, the mere thought of Susan's fried chicken makes my mouth water."

"Dr. Gooden?" She paused in front of him.

He bowed. "I can only echo Mr. Smith."

She smiled at both of them. "Come. I'll need your help."

"Mother, why doesn't step-grandfather like us?" Linc struggled, but his puppy finally wiggled out of his grasp.

Jessie bent and kissed her son's forehead. "It isn't our fault, son. He doesn't like very many people."

And I imagine very few really like him, Lee commented inwardly.

"Mother can I . . . may I," Linc amended, "get out of my Sunday clothes?"

"Lincoln, just because we won't be eating in the dining . . ." she stopped. "I'm sorry, Linc. Of course, you can . . . *may*."

Linc ran to the house with a "Whoop!"

Jessie murmured, "I hate it when I start to sound like *that man*."

"Your stepfather is of a strong temperament. It is hard to overlook." Dr. Gooden smiled wryly.

Jessie grinned. "How perceptive. And you just met him today."

"I'd say, he's a man who's easy to know, and hard to avoid," Lee added.

This forced a chuckle from her.

Pleased, Lee followed her up to the porch.

She called out, "Caleb, Ben, will you come in and carry out the kitchen table. Dinner is ready."

Lee along with the other men brought out the kitchen table, chairs, napkins, plates, and silver. His appetite awoke as women arranged bowls of creamy mashed potatoes, yellow corn bread, and platters of golden fried chicken on the long table with its white oilcloth. The fragrance of butter and the chicken did indeed make his mouth water. Throughout the bustle, the pup he'd given Linc yapped excitedly, nipping at the men's pant legs and racing back and forth under the women's wide skirts.

When all was in place, Reverend Mitchell took off his hat and bowed his head. Lee noticed Susan reach for her grandmother's hand and something deep inside him ached for a similar touch. His eyes automatically sought out Jessie. Their gazes met over Linc's blond head. When Dr. Gooden edged closer to Jessie, Lee felt a grinding inside.

The pastor cleared his throat. "Father, we know it was Thee who brought Susan and Ruby together once more. Give Mrs. Wagstaff and her son back the kindness that they show us each day, pressed down and overflowing in abundance. Thank Thee for Lincoln on this day of his birth and for this dinner and the hands that lovingly prepared it. In Christ's name, Amen."

Immediately excited chatter and laughter broke out as the buffet line formed, but everyone stood back waiting for someone to go first.

Then Linc, pulling Lee along with him, headed to the table. This brought chuckles. When Jessie shook her head at the boy, Lee held his hands out in a gesture of helplessness.

"It is the boy's birthday, Mrs. Wagstaff," Dr. Gooden said.

Then Lee offered Jessie a plate and urged her to follow her son. For once, she did not balk at a suggestion of his. But when she drew Dr. Gooden with her in line, Lee averted his gaze. When Lee served himself, he complimented Susan who stood behind him, "You've outdone yourself."

Susan smiled. "I didn't know when I was cookin', I was cooking for my grandma." She wiped away fresh tears.

Soon the picnickers, except for the elderly who had accepted kitchen chairs, were sitting on the grass in the slender shade cast by the shed and porch. Though Jessie had invited Susan and Ruby to sit on the porch, they observed a decorous separation of races by positioning their chairs on the lawn, just inside the shadow of the porch. Jessie, Linc, Lee and the doctor were the only ones who sat on chairs on the porch.

Lee wondered if Jessie realized that her black friends did this to protect her. Did she realize the backlash she might reap if she continued to flout the standard separation between the races?

After dinner, Linc blew out the candles on his cake. Lee, like everyone else, settled back comfortably, Lee tilting his head back, as he looked up into the clear, blue sky. Life is good again, his heart whispered. He savored Jessie's words to Huff: "You are not the master here." How delightful to witness Jessie's routing of the hypocrite! Smiling, he turned to her.

The doctor was speaking close to Jessie's ear and she was smiling. The sight triggered the grinding feeling again. This time he identified it—jealousy. *What's happening to me? I can't be jealous of Jessie and the good doctor. He's just the kind who'd make her a good husband.* But Lee squirmed at the thought.

Ruby spoke up, "This surely be the best day of my life. Till I find my girl, my onliest girl, I never enjoy my freedom." Ruby leaned over and kissed Susan's cheek. Susan gave way to tears again, hugging Ruby. Lee noticed Jessie dab her eyes. He edged his chair closer to her and whispered, "I wish your mother could be here."

"My stepfather has always forced her to choose him over me," she whispered back.

"A shame."

She turned away from him, raising her voice, "He's a shame to all Christians."

Lee admitted to himself he admired Jessie Wagstaff. She might be bossy, but when an issue of right and wrong was concerned, she was unmoved by criticism. Since the war, she had become more determined to fight for her ideals while he had deserted his altogether. Unfortunately, this might put her in harm's way.

His good humor ebbed.

Susan and her friends began to hum and sing, "O, happy day when Jesus washed my sins away. O, happy day . . ."

After his years in the South, Lee was familiar with this spiritual—"O, happy day . . ." He hummed along, feeling the joy in the words, their balm pouring through him like the bright, hot sunshine around them all. Glancing toward Jessie, he saw her lean closer to Dr. Gooden again. Lee strained to hear her words.

"Doctor, if it were a matter of life or death, would you come—if I needed your help?"

Dr. Gooden looked around him solemnly. "If it is life or death, I will come."

Lee sat back in surprise. Dr. Gooden had unexpected depths.

As the song ended, Ruby sighed. "Rev'rund, today I want to hear the song we couldn't sing."

Without hesitation, Caleb stood up, tall and straight, his dark, handsome face fiercely proud. "I was born free, but I sing this song for the day when we'll all be really free."

The way Caleb Mitchell said the words "really free" made Lee certain the man wasn't alluding to heaven. And Lee knew only one spiritual had been forbidden in the South before the war.

Caleb sang: "When Israel was in Egypt's land, Let my people go! Oppressed so hard they could not stand. Let my people go!

"No more in bondage shall they toil, Let my people go! Let them come out with Egypt's spoil, Let my people go!" The low tones of Caleb's voice vibrated through Lee's bones and sinew and the stark longing in them sobered him.

Then Susan's rich soprano lifted above Caleb's voice in exaltation: "Thus saith the Lord, bold Moses said, Let my people go! If not, I'll smite your first-born dead, Let my people go!" A shiver sliced through Lee.

As the people around joined in the final chorus, a long repressed sadness, longing, and defeat surged through Lee. "When Israel was in Egypt's land, Let my people go! Oppressed so hard they could not stand. Let my people go!" The final notes, Caleb's and Susan's, reverberated in total silence. Lee felt himself near tears and couldn't think why. Slavery had ended. The war was in the past.

Linc leaned back against Lee's leg as though seeking comfort. Lee reached down and ruffled Linc's hair.

"Uh-oh," Linc murmured a warning.

Lee followed the direction of the lad's gaze. A tall, angular woman came from the house on the other side of Jessie's home.

Jessie rose and went to meet her neighbor. "Mrs. O'Toole, how nice. You're just in time for a piece of birthday cake."

"It's not for the cake I'm here," the woman snapped. "You send these people home. They don't belong here." She crossed her arms over her meager bosom.

Lee knew Jessie would never back down.

Jessie stood straight. "These people are *my* guests on *my* property—"

"This is outrageous. 'Tis bad enough you've hired a black girl instead of my niece an honest Irish girl—"

"Mrs. O'Toole, I think it's time you went home."

Lee shivered at Jessie's tone. He had heard captured Rebel soldiers reply to Union officers in warmer tones. The tall woman stalked away.

Linc let the pup go. Butch charged after the woman yapping and growling at the intruder. Linc paused a moment; then chasing after the dog, he snatched up Butch just as he was about to follow Mrs. O'Toole through her gate. Linc ran back to his mother.

When the dog quieted, Dr. Gooden patted Linc on the shoulder. "Happy birthday again." He pressed a silver dollar into the boy's hand.

Linc shouted, "Thank you, sir!"

The doctor grinned. "I will show myself out, Mrs. Wagstaff."

"Thank you for coming," Jessie said as the doctor bowed over her hand in farewell. He nodded to Lee and walked toward the front of the house.

The doctor's departure seemed to signal an end of the celebration. The men pulled on their black hats. The women shook out their full skirts and straightened their hat pins.

"Please don't go," Jessie implored. Her words were cut off by the arrival of three mounted police. She gasped.

Lee stepped forward to intercept them, protect her. "Good afternoon, gentlemen. What can we do for you?"

The oldest of the three officers swung down from his saddle. "We received a report of a black mob—"

"Mob?" Jessie repeated the word incredulously. "Does this look like a mob?"

Shaking his head at her to be still, Lee stepped closer to the officer. "It seems you received a false alarm."

"Appears so, but—"

The preacher approached them. "Begging your pardon, officer, but did you mention a rumor of about a black mob?"

Lee felt as uneasy as the black pastor sounded.

"I'm afraid so," the policeman replied. He gave the preacher a meaningful look. "You know how rumors—"

"Spread," Lee finished.

"Would you escort us home, officer?" the pastor asked.

"What?" Jessie objected.

"Jessie," Lee restrained her with a hand on her arm. "You don't understand."

His face stormy, Caleb spoke up, "Mrs. Wagstaff, what he means is if a rumor about a Negro mob spreads, our people could be in danger not just here but all over the city."

Reverend Mitchell intervened, "But if these policemen will give us escort home, the rumor will be blunted."

"He's right, Jessie. Matters could get out of hand in no time. You don't want people hurt." Memories from the past flared inside Lee. He'd seen what evil men were capable of.

"Susan." Jessie turned and took both Ruby's hands in hers. "Ruby will stay here with us."

Susan protested, "But what about the neighbors?"

"She stays, Susan." Jessie looked to Lee. "Are you deserting us, too, Mr. Smith?"

Challenged, Lee found he couldn't disappoint the appeal in Jessie's imploring gaze, especially when Linc also looked up at him hopefully. "I'll walk the Reverend's congregation home." The phrase came out before he could hold it back.

Jessie reached for his hand. "Thank you, Lee."

She'd touched him and called him by his given name for the first time since he arrived on her back porch. A fierce protectiveness stirred in him for this woman and her son. Words from deep inside him bubbled up, "Don't worry, Jess. Everything will be all right."

Chapter 8

Inhaling the clean fragrance of fresh starch, Jessie shrank from taking a long-dreaded step today. *But it must be today.* "Your grandmother stays." Jessie punctuated her sentence by snapping off the stems from a handful of garden string beans, dropped them into a large pot in her lap. Snap. Snap.

Standing at the ironing board, Susan began pressing Linc's white Sunday shirt, the iron hissing on the damp fabric. "But the neighbors—"

"My hiring a cook is none of their business." The cloying heat and quiet of the afternoon wrapped around Jessie. "Susan, are you sure you should be ironing in this heat?"

"I used to pick cotton on hotter days. Don't be trying to turn me. We just ain't got enough room," Susan protested.

Jessie's stomach tightened at this reminder. "Leave that to me."

Susan slid a black blouse of Jessie's onto the board. "When are you gone get out of mourning?"

"Don't *you* try to turn me." Jessie pointed a string bean at Susan. "Ruby's staying."

Susan paused, holding the iron in the air. "You're too good for your own good."

"You mean stubborn, don't you?" Jessie grinned.

Susan snorted. "I wish everybody stubborn like you."

Jessie snorted in turn.

In the overpowering heat, the two of them fell silent.

To the homey beat of the iron as Susan worked, Jessie's mind drifted. Her mother's siding with her husband against Jessie on Linc's birthday still stung. Not even Susan's nearness prevented a stunning loneliness from sweeping through her. *He always made certain I came last with my mother and I always will.* Setting the pot of beans on the table, she stood up before she could give way to tears. Besides she shouldn't put what she must do off any longer. "I'll go tell Miss Wright—"

"Tell me what?" the old woman, drooping over her cane, asked from the doorway.

Jessie, wiping her hands on her apron, walked to Miss Wright. "Let's go into the parlor. It should be cooler on the east side of the house by now."

Though the spinster scowled, Jessie drew her into the parlor and helped the older woman to sit down on the rose-sprigged sofa by the front window. "We have to make a change. I am going to move you downstairs into the parlor—"

"Where anyone can walk in or look in from the entryway."

"I'll keep the pocket door to the foyer closed from now on." Jessie pressed her hankie to her perspiring face.

"You're doing this because you're taking in that girl's grandmother. How can I make you understand? Susan's people belong in Africa where God put them. Some are smart enough to go where they belong."

Jessie had anticipated Miss Wright's objections. But just as the day's heat and humidity, these successive waves of opposition were wearing her down. She tried to sound patient. "How can I send Ruby to live apart from Susan? I know I would give anything to have Margaret here again."

"I'm not saying you should send the woman far—"

Jessie's forbearance snapped. "Ruby isn't the only reason I'm making this change. Soon you won't be able to get up and down the steps and you know it."

Miss Wright flushed red at Jessie's blunt words. "If Margaret were here—"

"You know Margaret would never turn Ruby or anyone else away if they needed help." *Margaret didn't turn you away.*

The elderly spinster blinked back tears.

Jessie regretted upsetting her. *But what must be said must be said.*

Miss Wright looked away while dabbing a handkerchief at her eyes. "You didn't know Margaret as long or as well as I did."

"Every time I do something *you* don't want me to do, you use Margaret against me."

"I'm trying to make you see reason." The spinster's voice was thick with unshed tears.

Jessie couldn't keep the anger from her voice. "Why am I the one who must see reason? Is it reasonable for my neighbors to call out the police merely because my guests have dark skin?"

"You don't seem to understand the boundaries of accepted conduct—"

But in her anger, Jessie continued, "Is it reasonable for doctors to refuse patients merely because of the color of their skin? If these things are reasonable, then I'm glad to be thought unreasonable."

Miss Wright crimped her lips and said in a tight, voice, "What will you use for a parlor, then?"

"The dining room. It's warmer in the winter and I think I can fit a few of these chairs at one end."

Suddenly aware of the tension in her neck, Jessie rotated her head to loosen the taut muscles. "I will help you move your things down as soon as I have the curtain sewed and Ben to help me move the furniture."

"What curtain? You already have curtains on the windows."

"It will be a privacy curtain, dividing the parlor into two rooms."

"*Who* is going to share this room with me?" Miss Wright's chin lifted.

"Linc and I."

"Why?"

Jessie took a deep breath. "Ruby can't climb two flights of steps to the attic, so Susan will give her grandmother her own little room off the pantry and Susan will take my attic room. Linc and I will move into the other half of the parlor with you. I need to rent out your room. Linc is getting older and I don't want him to have to leave school early to go out to work."

"And if I don't want to share the parlor with you and Linc?"

Jessie would not say the words they both dreaded: *It will make it easier to care for you when you can no longer walk at all.* "Moving you downstairs will be better for you." Their eyes met and held with tacit understanding.

Miss Wright stood up, grunted with pain. "I'll go and sit on the porch."

Impulsively Jessie stood up and reached out to touch the old woman, but stopped just shy of her sleeve. Hands at her sides, Jessie watched the old woman shuffle out of the room.

Jessie folded her arms over her breast. *I'll keep my promise to Margaret and care for Miss Wright for the rest of her life. Miss Wright has forgotten how kind Margaret was.*

The bright Saturday sunshine made Lee pull the brim of his hat farther forward as he walked along the side of Jessie's house.

"You're a liar!" A childish voice shouted from the backyard.

"Am not!" Linc insisted.

"Are too!"

"Am not!"

Linc's pup began barking and the unmistakable grunts of boyish fisticuffs made Lee hurry into the backyard. "Lincoln!"

Startled, the boys parted, but the acrimony between them blazed on their sweat and dirt-smudged faces.

"Explain yourselves," Lee said in a stern tone.

"He said I lied," Linc declared, his expression stormy.

Lee spoke to the other boy. "Who are you, young man?"

The boy said, "I'm Tom. Live next door."

"Well, Tom, what do you think Linc was lying about?"

"He said you played ball with the Knickerbockers."

"Yes, while visiting friends in New York, I did get to play an inning of a practice game with that famous team." Lee had to keep from grinning. The way Tom eyed him left no doubt that he didn't believe Lee either. "Tom, I wouldn't lie to you or Linc."

Yes, I would. I did. Lee had to close his lips firmly to hold back these words from pouring forth. The more time he spent with Linc, the harder it became to conceal the truth from the boy. "Now, you two shake hands like gentlemen."

Reluctantly the boys shook once. Tom dug his hands into his pockets and turned to leave.

"Hold on, Tom," Lee suggested nonchalantly, "Why don't you stay and we'll toss the ball a while?"

"You mean it?" Tom's face glowed.

"Sure." *Perhaps I can't tell the truth, but I can do some things right.* The events of the Sunday before still lingered vividly in his mind. He hadn't wanted to end up helping Jessie's "cause" by escorting the black congregation home. He wouldn't let anything like it happen again. Jessie's crusade would stay hers alone, he told himself firmly. *That wasn't my promise to Will.*

Jessie overheard the voices. She walked out and sat on the back porch railing to watch. Lee and the boys tossed the ball in a game of catch while Butch scampered, yipping cheerfully.

Outwardly calm, Jessie fanned herself. Her confusion over Lee's place in their lives made her bubble inside. Mr. Smith hadn't yet tired of spending time with Linc as she had expected. And with his gift of a pup, he'd taken Linc's heart completely. Some intuition told her there was something about Lee that didn't ring true. Was it just his cynical streak or something more?

"It's time to go, Mother!" Linc tied yapping Butch to the porch railing near the doghouse. The look of joy on her son's face meant more to her than pure gold dust.

Jessie stood and brushed back her son's hair. "Have a good time at your ball game."

Mr. Smith strolled up behind Linc. "I'll have him home before supper."

Jessie nodded. "Thank you, Mr. Smith."

"I thought you dropped the 'mister' last Sunday, Jess." He smiled a wicked, teasing smile at her.

She folded her hands together. The man never stopped pushing.

Lee brought Linc home from the ballpark, then stayed for supper. While Susan left to help Linc, Miss Wright, then her own grandmother to bed, Lee followed Jessie out to the back porch. Lee knew he should go. But the temptation to spend time with Jess alone drew him against his will. "Mrs. Wagstaff!" Caleb hailed Jessie from the walk.

Jessie sat up straighter. "What's wrong?"

"My father can hardly breathe. Will you come?"

Jessie stood. "It's his heart." She hurried inside and started gathering various herbs into a basket.

Lee pursued her. "What can you do if it's his heart?"

"I'll do what I can." Fastening her bonnet, she started out the door.

The sudden destruction of their private moment irritated him; he hurried after her. "Caleb, why did you come here? This woman is not a doctor."

Caleb clenched and unclenched his fists as if he'd like to punch Lee. "Don't you think I know that? He's my father. I have to do something."

Lee was going to turn away. This wasn't his business.

"Caleb," Jessie said, "why don't you try to find Dr. Gooden?"

"He won't come," Caleb put voice to Lee's opinion.

"He said he would come if it were life-and-death," Jessie said.

Caleb turned and stalked off without a word. Lee couldn't decide whether it was pique or he was going to do Jessie's bidding. Jessie started off and Lee hurried to keep up with her. He knew he could not persuade her to stay home, but he couldn't persuade himself to not escort her.

In due time, Jessie led him into a small house. The sky had been darkening steadily and his eyes adjusted to the low light of one feeble lamp on the table. He heard Reverend Mitchell's labored breathing before he saw him.

"Good evening." Jess set her basket on the table and began removing her hat and gloves. "Are you experiencing pain in your chest again?"

"And in his arm," Ruth, who sat by the bed, answered.

When Lee accompanied Jess to the narrow bed, he recognized the clear signs of dropsy. The thin man's feet, legs, and abdomen were swollen. "I'll try a stronger dose of Margaret's heart tea," she said.

Lee fell back. As Jessie brewed tea, he felt like a pale wraith in a murky netherworld. Lee did not want to look death in the face again.

He turned to leave. "Will you help me?" Jessie asked. Her simple question in the dark held him in place. Oh, how he wanted to leave. But he could not let Jessie face death alone.

Soon with Lee supporting the pastor from behind, Jessie lifted the cup to the old man's grayish white lips. His whole body strained with each breath.

He stopped breathing.

Jessie cried out. The tea cup fell from her hands and shattered at her feet.

Lee's heart pounded so violently that he felt nauseated. He bent his head to draw up his strength. *Breathe, breathe.*

Then the old man gasped, choked. He took a shallow breath. Lee realized he'd stopped breathing too. *I can't do this.* He moved to lay the pastor back down, but was stopped by Jessie's hand. "Support him while I make more tea."

He wanted to shout at her that no tea in the world would help repair this worn-out heart.

"Please," she whispered.

Lee found himself nodding. There was that same buzzing in his ears . . . the buzzing that had driven him to drink. *The war is over. This is an old man, dying of an old man's disease. It isn't the same.*

Jessie brewed tea; Lee helped her administer it. Then he paced back and forth and listened to each breath the old pastor drew. As each ended, he waited for, urged the next to come. Time passed, measured breath by breath.

In the humid night breeze, mosquitoes buzzed around Lee's ears till he tied a handkerchief around his head. He remembered how death drew flies. Adrenaline pumped through him. He wanted to run away. But Jessie hovered nearby and he couldn't leave her to face death alone.

She kept going to the door, looking out. He heard her praying and the words, "Dr. Gooden," were loud enough for him to hear. "He's not coming," Lee said, bitterness gnawing him. Lee's nerves had become taut, an overtightened wire. Would it snap again?

"Caleb hasn't yet returned," was her reply.

He muffled the sound of disgust he could not hold back. In spite of nightfall, the stifling heat refused to relent. Jessie discreetly unbuttoned her collar and her cuffs and Lee shed his coat on the back of the chair as he finally sat down. Head bent, elbows propped on knees, hands folded, he forced himself to sit still and hold on.

"Are you all right?" her voice came softly.

"Jessie?"

Dr. Gooden's voice came from the doorway before he could reply. Lee bolted upright nearly upsetting the chair.

"You came!" Jessie sounded tearful, almost hysterical.

"Caleb had many places to go before he found me," the doctor replied. "I have worked a busy day." He immediately crossed to the table and opened his black bag. "Reverend Mitchell, your son told me of your symptoms and I have brought a powder for you."

At the doctor's request, Jessie poured water from the kettle into a cup. And the doctor opened a small white packet, measured out a few grains of powder and swirled the cup. Caleb propped up his frail father and the doctor helped his patient painstakingly sip the mixture.

Lee watched from the shadows. The doctor had come. Shock and something else shimmered through Lee's fatigue. Was it resentment? But Lee hadn't wanted the old man to die. He should have been relieved, but he wasn't.

"This is a new mixture of digitalis." Dr. Gooden motioned Jessie to sit in her chair by the door. "It should bring relief almost immediately."

"Hello, Doctor," Lee finally forced himself to say.

"You, here, Smith?" The doctor offered Lee his hand. "I'm so glad you stayed with Mrs. Wagstaff until I could arrive."

Lee wanted to spit in the man's eye. He didn't want to delve into the why of this. On the other hand, he was grateful the man had brought medicine to the Reverend. He didn't know what to think.

The doctor snapped open his pocket watch, leaning toward the lamp. "It's near midnight, Mrs. Wagstaff. We stay up together another night."

She reached for his arm. "I'm sorry to call you out, but—"

Reaching out, he grasped her hand. "I gave my promise."

Under the cover of night, she lifted his hand and pressed its back to her cheek. She whispered brokenly, "I've fought alone for so long."

"Jessie," he murmured. "I'm here now."

A silent witness, Lee burned at his own helplessness. He should have been the one to help her. But he couldn't do this. Lee didn't trust himself to speak.

"My father is sleeping easily." Caleb walked to them in the doorway. Faint moonlight silvered the strong features of his face. "I owe you, Doctor."

"I charge only fifty cents for a call. I'll leave you another packet of medicine."

"I owe you more than money."

Dr. Gooden offered Caleb his hand. They shook.

Caleb turned to Jessie. "And Mrs. Wagstaff, you always come whenever you're needed."

She touched Caleb's arm. "You should sleep now. Will someone stay with your father tomorrow while you're at work?"

"Ruth stays with him during the day."

Jessie nodded. As she gathered her bonnet, gloves, and basket, the doctor and Lee waited outside.

The three of them crowded into the doctor's gig. Soon they were making their way home through the nearly empty streets. The doctor didn't hurry his tired horse. Its hooves made a sad clip-clop on the wooden streets.

The doctor stopped at a corner near Jessie's house. "I'll let you down here, Mr. Smith. You do not live far, do you?"

Lee wanted to refuse. "Thanks," he said as he climbed down to the street. Irked, he watched the gig drive away.

Almost without realizing it, Jessie leaned against the doctor's side. She knew she should draw away, but when he took her hand in his free one, she didn't pull away. Having someone to lean on, after standing alone for so long, just felt too good to deny.

Finally, the gig stopped in front of Jessie's house. She sat up, but when she tried to pull her hand from his, he prevented her.

"A moment. I ask a favor."

Jessie cleared the sleep from her voice. "What is it?"

"In a little over a week, I will attend a party at the Potter Palmer home."

"The Palmers?" Jessie was surprised. The Palmers were high society.

"Yes, I am invited by Mrs. Palmer. She toured Rush Hospital this week and was very interested in my ideas for better public health through cleaning up Chicago."

Jessie felt a lift. "Oh, that's wonderful."

"Yes, I think I'm beginning to make the contacts I need for my future work. But for success I need one thing more."

"What?"

"You to go with me."

His words shocked her into silence.

"I need a woman like you on my arm. I need you to charm the men and speak with intelligence to the women. As Linc would say, I need to cover all of my bases. Will you help me, Jessie?"

So many thoughts rushed through her mind she couldn't speak at first. "I'm not the kind of woman you need. I'm just a poor widow."

"You are poor only in money. I will buy you a dress for the occasion."

"Oh, no! You can't!"

"Please. I need you. I'm counting on you, Jessie."

If he'd said any other words, she could have refused. But how could she deny this good man her help?

She bowed her head. "If you think I'd be of help to you, I'll go." Bending toward her, he kissed her hand.

Jessie felt a chill go through her when she realized he had kissed the palm of her hand, not the back.

Chapter 9

June 27, 1871

The sharp rat-a-tat on the front door caught Jessie on her knees polishing the railing of the front staircase. "A delivery from Field & Leiter's for Mrs. Jessie Wagstaff," a voice called from outside.

Oh, no! Jessie pushed herself up, yanked off the apron, and hurried to the door. She summoned up a smile for the boy in the blue uniform with brass buttons who gave her a large box, saluted, and left.

Closing the door, Susan took the box from Jessie. "Now what's this?"

Shock seizing her, Jessie felt unable to explain. How had Dr. Gooden protected her reputation when purchasing an appropriate dress for her?

Plus the unusual occurrence of a department store delivery had garnered an instant audience. Miss Greenleigh on the landing above, flanked below by Miss Wright in the doorway to the parlor, and Ruby in the one to the dining room. Why couldn't the delivery have come when everyone was out?

For just a second, Jessie longed to run up into the attic and hide. She'd hoped Dr. Gooden would reconsider his invitation. Should she tell them he'd bought her the dress? *Never.*

Ignoring the fluttering of her heart, she announced, "Dr. Gooden has invited me to accompany him to a dinner party this Saturday evening. This is my new dress." Suddenly she envisioned Mr. Smith's reaction, a negative one, to this dress and the doctor's invitation. Confused, she pushed the thought from her mind.

Around her, the women hummed with excitement as they all hurried to Jessie. "Susan, would you please get my sewing box from my room?" Miss Greenleigh said. "We'll have this fitted to Jessie in two shakes."

After a flurry of activity around her, Jessie stood behind closed doors in the dining room. Susan slipped the black dress off over Jessie's head, revealing Jessie's embroidered white corset cover and starched petticoats. Then Susan slid the silk dress over Jessie.

A spontaneous "Ahh" breathed through the ladies surrounding Jessie who was still having trouble remembering to breathe.

"Oh, it look just like the dress Miss Charlotte wore to that fall cotillion her daddy give in fifty-nine." Ruby rubbed her hands together.

From the elegantly carved wooden sewing box, Susan lifted out a round pink pincushion. "But, Grandma Ruby, see how the overskirt sweep up into this bustle. Miss Charlotte's dress had a hoop."

"It does outline your tiny waistline perfectly." Miss Greenleigh grinned.

"Very nice." Miss Wright lowered herself onto a chair.

Being the center of attention was a new experience—both thrilling and horrible. Jessie had a hard time lifting her chin to face them. But she had to or the hemline would suffer. And the thought of revealing that Dr. Gooden had bought the dress for her still made her heart throb. She'd have to find some way to pay him the money back, bit by bit. And Mr. Smith must never find out about this. His sarcasm would be hard to bear.

While Ruby hovered nearby in the doorway, Miss Greenleigh and Susan deftly lifted and adjusted the fit at the cap of the sleeve. "Ruby!" Miss Wright's sharp voice made Jessie and the other three women jump. "You're too old to be standing. Sit." She pointed her cane to a dining room chair.

Ruby hesitated.

"Sit!" Miss Wright ordered her.

Ruby sat.

Jessie, Susan, and Miss Greenleigh exchanged covert glances that told Jessie they were just as surprised as she about Miss Wright's concern for Ruby's comfort.

"Mrs. Wagstaff," Miss Greenleigh said, interrupting the alterations. "There's something special about this dinner party. This is really an evening gown, isn't it?"

All of the women, even Miss Wright, gazed at Jessie, who felt as though a brick had become wedged sideways in her throat. "Mrs. Potter Palmer toured Rush Hospital last week. Dr. Gooden had the opportunity to explain some of the new concepts of better health through public sanitation—"

Miss Greenleigh squealed, "You've been invited to dinner at the Palmer mansion?" The young woman danced a little jig. "I can't wait to tell Mrs. Bolt. She'll turn absolutely pea green!"

"Potter Palmer?" Ruby quizzed Susan. "Who that?"

Susan exclaimed, "One of the richest men in the city—that's who!"

"Lord, have mercy!" Ruby clapped her hands.

"But how can I go to Potter Palmer's?" Jessie voiced her worry. "No matter what I wear I'm nobody—"

"You're the equal of any of those society women." Miss Wright's adamant words halted everyone. She drew her bent body up to lecture them. "I, for one, see clearly why Dr. Gooden wants you by his side."

"Then explain it to me." Jessie folded her arms over each other.

"Dr. Gooden knows that the men he'll meet are all busy making and tending their fortunes. In the matters of charity, it's their wives who must be influenced. That's why he needs a woman like you Jessie."

Looking thoughtful, Miss Greenleigh went on: "I see. A single man like the doctor must tread warily around these married women. He mustn't give the wrong impression. But if he comes with a lovely, intelligent woman on his arm, he'll give just the right kind of impression."

Jessie's feelings of inadequacy nearly choked her. "But I'm not lovely or intelligent."

"Stop that nonsense right now." Miss Wright thumped her cane.

"Look at your beautiful brown eyes. This dress looks gorgeous on you," Miss Greenleigh insisted. "And how many times in your life will you be invited to the Potter Palmer mansion?"

I didn't even want this one time. And Jessie for some unknown reason felt traitorous to Mr. Smith. Was it because he'd come with her to nurse the Reverend?

"Besides," Ruby urged, "if the doctor need you, you got to help him."

Miss Wright spoke up, "Now, you two young women, step back so I can see the effect. Jessie, turn slowly, so I can see the dress on you."

Jessie did as she was told.

Miss Wright nodded. "Elegant. And remember, Jessie, you're the equal of any woman there. They're just women who married men who made money. The Wagstaff name has been respected in Chicago for over thirty years and don't you forget it!"

What could Jessie say? But she still felt her head shaking no.

"Mrs. Wagstaff," Miss Greenleigh suggested, "why don't you come up to my room and look at yourself in my full-length mirror. If you only saw yourself, I'm sure—"

At the idea of seeing herself in anything but black, Jessie panicked. "Oh, no!" The women all stared at her as she flushed, surprised at her own vehemence.

Then Susan muttered, "One of these days I'm gone burn every black dress in this house."

"Amen to that," Ruby said.

"Dr. Jones, can't I say anything to change your mind?" Jessie, clutching her purse with both hands, tried to keep the quaver from her voice as she tried to persuade the fifth doctor.

The young man with a fair beard shook his head. "I'm sorry. What you suggest is impossible."

"But you've just opened your practice—"

"If I take in black patients, my practice will close even more quickly than it opened."

"But . . ." Jessie's mouth was so dry she couldn't finish her sentence.

A bell jingled.

"My next patient." He smiled with tight lips and showed her to the door.

Crushed, Jessie departed without another word. A horse trolley passed her, raising dust from the unpaved street. She pressed a handkerchief to her nose and mouth to filter out the dust as she breathed.

She walked blindly for several blocks, trying to understand why everyone couldn't see the obvious. Susan's people needed medical help regardless of their dark skin. How could people just ignore such a glaring need? She hunched forward as though carrying a heavy burden.

Coming back to herself, she realized she was only about a half mile from her mother's home and her stepfather would be at work. She hadn't seen her mother since Linc's birthday. The chance of a quiet visit alone with her mother was too inviting to be ignored. She strode down the familiar street and turned up the alley.

Smiling, she ran lightly up the back steps to her mother's home. "Mother!"

"Jessie!" Esther threw open the back door and wrapped her arms around her daughter. "I saw you coming!"

Tears sprang to Jessie's eyes. Her mother's embrace was more than she had hoped for. How many times in the lonely years after losing Will and Margaret had she yearned to feel her mother's touch?

"I'm so glad you came," Esther murmured. "I was afraid after . . ." Her voice ebbed, then died.

"Let's not discuss him," Jessie replied, dabbing her eyes with a handkerchief.

Esther put her arm around her daughter's shoulders and drew her into the kitchen. Jessie sat down at the dark oak kitchen table. Glancing at the stark white walls, she felt a painful tug at her emotions. As long as she could remember, her mother had longed for a blue kitchen, but Hiram Huff decreed the extra charge for tinted paint was an unnecessary extravagance. After all, his mother's kitchen had been plain white—like a kitchen should be.

But Jessie wouldn't let Hiram Huff spoil this rare, private visit with her mother. "How are the twins?"

Esther set two cups of coffee onto the table. "They're working hard, preparing for the sixth-grade spelling bee."

"That's nice." An uncomfortable pause began. Jessie craved sympathy and encouragement in her effort to find a doctor for Susan's people, but knew—out of a sense of duty—her mother would not voice any opinion that countered her husband's. The memory of Mr. Smith's face as he'd agreed to escort Susan's friends home popped into her mind.

"Mr. Smith seemed like a very nice man," Esther said softly, then looked into her daughter's face.

How had her mother known she was thinking about Lee Smith? Avoiding her mother's glance, Jessie sipped her coffee. "He's been very good to Linc. He comes every evening to play ball and takes him to Saturday games as often as he can." Again an uneasy, unnatural silence cropped up between them.

"I was happy Susan's grandmother found her granddaughter again." Esther traced the rim of her cup.

"Yes." *As happy as I would be if I could be close to you, Mother, as I've always wanted to be.*

"It must have been a terrible thing to be separated from your only living relative like that."

"Yes." *I know how that feels.* Tears threatened Jessie again. She regretted coming. Sitting near her mother, trying to chat politely made Jessie's emotional separation from her mother feel more stark, more cruel than ever.

Esther took a deep breath. "I wish—" She broke off at the sound of heavy footsteps coming up the wooden back porch steps.

"Esther—" Hiram stepped into the kitchen and halted. "*You're* here?" Her stepfather wore his fire captain's uniform, blackened with smoke.

"Yes." Jessie rose to face him. "I happened to be in the neighborhood."

"I didn't expect you home, Hiram," Esther said, also rising.

Jessie silently fumed. How did he manage to make them feel as though they had been caught doing something wrong?

"Didn't you hear the alarm bells all night?" he snapped. "My men are exhausted. I had to call the next shift in early." He pulled off his fire hat and raked soot-blackened hands through his hair.

Esther murmured, "I'm so sorry—"

"One small fire after another and then an abandoned warehouse down by the river. Someone's careless match destroyed it. We barely contained it. Water pressure was dangerously low."

He glared at his stepdaughter. "Evidently having a new cook gives you time to gad about, missy."

Hot words frothed up inside her throat. She choked them back for her mother's sake. "Missy" was the childhood name he had used when he'd scolded her. He must know his using it would goad her. He nearly succeeded in making her say something indiscreet, but she wouldn't give him the pleasure of knowing he'd vexed her. "I do need to go," she said in a carefully colorless voice.

"Even a few of my men had heard about your colored party. Everyone in your neighborhood is outraged by your ridiculous display, missy. You don't seem to have any sense about what is proper or how gossip might affect us."

Jessie stood stock-still, her face warm with a deep flush. "Stepfather, I don't dignify gossip by regarding it—or do I regard those who spread it." Out of the corner of her eye, she caught her mother's pained expression.

If she continued, her mother would suffer for it, not with blows, but with endless hectoring. Her eyes averted, Jessie walked past her stepfather. Without a wave or backward glance, she said, "Good day, Mother."

Tense and afraid to sit down and possibly wrinkle her dress, Jessie stood in the middle of her parlor. Earlier Miss Greenleigh had done Jessie's hair and buffed her nails. She'd loaned Jessie long gloves and a gossamer shawl. Before that, Miss Wright had surprised Jessie by giving Susan the money to buy a pair of shoes of silk dyed the same color as Jessie's deep amber dress. This occasion had drawn them together in some way.

"You will do fine," Miss Wright said gruffly.

Jessie looked askance at the old woman who kept watch with her. "I'm worried I'll do something that may reflect poorly on Dr. Gooden."

"Be brief. Tell the truth, but don't explain."

"You mean that we're as poor as church mice?" Jessie managed to smile.

"We're not poor, just thrifty. This is America. Remember you're the equal of any of the ladies you'll meet tonight."

"And I married Will." Her eyes strayed to his daguerreotype on the mantel. What would Will say to her in this silk dress? She knew. He'd say, *"You look beautiful, princess."*

The sound of the carriage brought both their eyes forward. "He's here," Jessie croaked. Her skirts whispering around her, she moved slowly toward the table where she laid her long gloves. Then carefully drew them on. The knock at the door came. Susan walked sedately through the hallway to answer it. Jessie heard Susan greet the doctor, then held her breath as he walked toward her.

"Jessie, how lovely you look tonight." He took both her hands.

"Good evening, Doctor." Miss Wright called his attention to herself.

The doctor continued to hold Jessie's hands, but he turned and bowed to the old woman. "Miss Wright."

The doctor deftly arranged Jessie's shawl around the top of her shoulders. As his finger tips brushed the nape of her bare neck, she shivered involuntarily, not appreciating his touch. "Shall we go?" The doctor offered her his arm.

Jessie nodded and tucked her hand into the crook of his elbow. As they stepped into the hall, Mrs. Bolt called down to them from the landing, "Don't you two look charming!"

Jessie cringed. She'd noticed that Miss Greenleigh had stayed discreetly upstairs in her room. Ruby and Susan had lingered in the dining room while Miss Wright had stayed in the parlor to bolster Jessie's resolve. Her confederates had tactfully given her the privacy and support she needed to nerve herself to the task at hand. But, of course, Mrs. Bolt had no tact.

"I hear you two are off to a special evening," the redhead said archly. "Though how a poor widow can afford a silk dress, I'm sure I don't know." She finished with a trill of laughter.

Jessie squeezed the doctor's arm.

"I am sorry, ma'am. We do not have time to chat. Good evening." The doctor swept Jessie outside.

With a jolt, Jessie saw Linc and Lee at the bottom of the front steps. Earlier Linc had left to go for a walk with Mr. Smith. She'd told her son she was going to a party, but she'd hoped to avoid seeing Mr. Smith. As he looked up the steps at her, she felt exposed, vulnerable.

"Mother! Where did you get that dress? It isn't black." Her son spoke loud enough to alert everyone in the neighborhood.

More gossip. What trumped-up story would be spread to her stepfather now? "Hello, Linc," she said as calmly as she could. Dr. Gooden led her down the steps.

"Good evening, Mrs. Wagstaff." Mr. Smith swept off his hat and bowed low, somehow making this polite gesture a taunting one. He lowered his voice, "Or should I address you as 'my lady' this evening?"

At the subtle mocking in his tone and words, Jessie's face flamed. As if completely unaware of the other man's ill temper, Dr. Gooden drew out his watch. "We cannot stay to chat or we will be late."

"I wouldn't want to make you late," Mr. Smith sneered.

How did Mr. Smith make her feel the hypocrite? She wanted to shout at him, Yes, I know I don't belong in this dress or going to this party, but I must. Dr. Gooden has proved he's a fine man and he needs my help. Avoiding Mr. Smith's derisive gaze, she looked down at her son. "Be good, Linc. I'll be home very late. Good night."

She hurried past them, but at the last moment, she couldn't stop herself from looking back at Mr. Smith. The naked chagrin on his face surprised her far more than his scorn. As little as she wanted to encourage either man, she'd have to be a ninny, in Miss Wright's parlance, not to realize that Mr. Smith resented her going out with Dr. Gooden.

The doctor helped her into the hired carriage and shut the door. In the dimness and privacy of the carriage, she tried not to dwell on the Dr. Gooden–Mr. Smith complication. The driver "chucked" to the team and they started off, rolling down the street.

"You look well, Dr. Gooden."

He smiled. "Now, Mrs. Wagstaff, I ask you a favor. We have not known each other long. But tonight I wish that you will call me Henry."

"Henry?" She edged forward. She remembered him calling her Jessie the night he'd invited her. How had she let their acquaintance move so quickly? *Why did I let myself get drawn in like this?*

"Yes, it is better that we seem to have had a longer acquaintance."

Her mind went back to Miss Wright's explanation of why Henry wanted her to accompany him and she relented. "Just for tonight," she said with determination. *This won't happen again.*

"Good. Mrs. Palmer, our hostess, and Mrs. Field, the wife of Mr. Marshall Field, are the two women most likely to help in my work. Both of them have begun to follow the example set by English ladies in sponsoring charity work."

Jessie nodded. She'd come to help the doctor and now she must see it through. No matter what Lee Smith thought. Still, by the time their carriage pulled up in front of the Palmer residence, Jessie felt queasy and shaky. Only a quick prayer gave her legs the strength to carry her toward the house. *House?* The Palmer mansion loomed above her like a castle of old. A castle alight with gas lamps, but to Jessie it appeared more like a formidable fortress whose battlements she was about to breach.

Gripping the doctor's arm like a lifeline, Jessie moved up the red carpeted steps and entered the massive double doors. Her pulse thrummed in her ears. Only a childhood spent concealing all emotion from her stepfather came to her rescue. Henry handed an engraved invitation to the butler.

"Ah, yes, Dr. Gooden," the man said dourly. "And the lady?"

"Mrs. Jessie Wagstaff." Henry patted her hand.

The butler inclined his head in greeting as they walked down the thickly carpeted hall. Gaslight flames danced in their protective glass globes along the richly papered wall. Jessie, too keyed up, merely absorbed the surroundings in terms of rich color, spaciousness, and elegance. They arrived at last at the drawing room door and were announced.

A tall woman, wearing a dress of gray silk and a rope of silvery pearls, stood up and swept toward them. "Dr. Gooden, welcome to our home."

Henry stepped forward and kissed the woman's gloved hand. "Mrs. Palmer, thank you again for the kind invitation. May I introduce you to my friend, Mrs. Jessie Wagstaff?"

Mrs. Palmer and Jessie curtseyed to one another. Then the lady took both of them around the ornate gold and maroon room, which could have held the whole first floor of Jessie's house twice, to introduce them to her husband and eight other couples.

Mrs. Palmer ended by saying, "So you see it's an intimate group really. I didn't want either you or the good doctor to feel overwhelmed."

Jessie felt overwhelmed. But she smiled and nodded. The only names and faces which had stuck in her mind were Mr. and Mrs. Palmer and Mr. and Mrs. Marshall Field because Henry had mentioned them.

The women's gowns glittered, shimmered, frilled. *I must seem a sober red hen.* If only the ladies back at home could see how her own amber silk dress and simple pearls were overshadowed in this lavish setting.

The butler approached Mrs. Palmer. "Dinner is served, Madame."

Mr. and Mrs. Palmer led the way into the dining room. Glittering crystal, gleaming silver, flickering candles, glinting golden candlesticks, sparkling chandeliers. Jessie blinked her eyes, trying to accustom them to the golden light—reflected and multiplied.

She saw name cards at each place. Dr. Gooden was already drawing Jessie to two seats side by side near the middle of the table. He pulled out her chair and seated her.

Glancing down, Jessie glimpsed a heart-stopping row of forks and spoons flanking the gilt china setting. She closed her eyes, then opened them. The array of silverware stared back at her with a contemptuous gleam.

A footman stepped over and with a flourish placed a large white napkin in her lap. She swallowed a small gasp. "I've kept the menu very light this evening," Mrs. Palmer's voice fluted over the genteel conversation. "I don't believe in heavy meals in this dreadful heat."

Jessie nodded politely. But eyeing sideboards covered in white linen, laden with serving dishes, Jessie doubted Mrs. Palmer's concept of a light meal would agree with her own. Unfortunately, Susan's extra tug on Jessie's corset strings would prevent Jessie from doing any real eating tonight.

Listening carefully to the discussion about the mechanics of changing the course of the Chicago River, Jessie ate tiny bites of only a few foods. It was all too much.

Without warning, Mr. Palmer addressed her, "Mrs. Wagstaff, yours is a name I know. You're related to old Will Wagstaff?"

Jessie steadied herself. "He was my husband's father."

"The man was an artist. He designed the sideboard behind you."

Jessie glanced at it. "Yes, that looks like his work."

"He was a master. Do you know a duke tried to buy that sideboard from me?" At this sentence, every head at the table turned toward the sideboard. "The duke told me to name my price. The one in his castle had been damaged in a fire. He said he hadn't seen such workmanship in years. You were married to his son?"

"Yes."

"I heard he fell in the war. He had shown great promise as a wood craftsman, too, I believe. A sad loss."

Jessie nodded. The mention of Will and his father made sitting at this table even more unbelievable.

"Indeed the war left a sad harvest." Mrs. Palmer motioned the butler to begin the dessert course.

A woman whose name Jessie couldn't recall said, "Yes, how wonderful that he left you well provided for." From a footman the woman accepted a dessert plate, trimmed with a doily. "Some poor widows have even been reduced to taking in boarders."

Jessie stiffened. She sensed that Dr. Gooden had become completely still beside her. Jessie struggled with feelings of outrage over this woman's easy condescension. Miss Wright, for once, had been correct. She was their equal, and if she were here not for Dr. Gooden's benefit, she would have told them what she thought. But she would tell them nothing of her true feelings. Perhaps this was why Mr. Smith had sneered at her foray into society.

Chapter 10

With the back of her hand, Jessie wiped away perspiration trickling down her forehead, even though it was barely an hour since sunrise. She then returned to scrubbing at the washboard. In the shade of the back porch, Susan stirred the simmering pot of white laundry with a broom handle.

All Jessie's uncertainties over the dinner and the subtle competition between Mr. Smith and Dr. Gooden roiled around inside her like the soapy water bubbling in Susan's laundry tub. She'd kept her peace about the Palmer dinner, but what were the chances the ladies of her house would let this continue?

With a mug in each hand, Ruby waddled out. "I got coffee."

"Thank goodness." Jessie straightened up, tossed Linc's shirt into Susan's pot, then accepted one of the mugs.

Miss Wright stumped out. With a coffee cup in her hand, she sat in one of the rocking chairs. "It's time you told us, Jessie, about that dinner party."

"Yes, that's what I came out for." Also with cup of coffee, Miss Greenleigh in a rose-pink cotton wrapper pulled up a chair beside Miss Wright. "Mrs. Bolt is still sound asleep, so this is the perfect time for you to tell us *everything*."

Lowering herself to the top step, Ruby nodded in agreement. "We waited all day yesterday for that woman to get gone. But she stuck like a burr."

Still churning inside, Jessie sank onto a lower porch step and looked up at her audience. The dinner party was still too personal, too troubling, yet these women had earned a stake in it, too.

Susan joined Ruby on the top step. "Did you have a bad time?"

"What was it like inside the Palmer mansion?" Miss Greenleigh leaned forward.

Buying time, Jessie sipped coffee. "Luxurious. Lovely paintings. Flocked wallpaper. Rich Persian carpets." Jessie tried to put enthusiasm into her voice.

"What were the ladies wearing?" Miss Greenleigh prompted.

"Mrs. Palmer wore a gray silk dress with a rope of pearls. The other ladies wore sateen or silk dresses in brilliant colors—royal blue, green, purple, all shimmering in the gaslight."

Jessie didn't mention how overshadowed her simple gown of

amber silk had been. Perhaps working might mask her reluctance, agitation. Putting down her empty coffee cup, she went back to the washboard.

"What they serve?" Ruby asked.

Jessie picked up another shirt, soaped the inside of its collar, then rubbed it against the washboard. The harsh soap stung her fingers like a just punishment for her foray into pretension. Pretension—that's what Mr. Smith's expression had pronounced on her. "We had consommé, turkey and fish, so many side dishes. For dessert we had fresh fruit and Italian ices."

"Just right for a summer dinner," Ruby approved.

Jessie didn't mind reciting the simple facts. *Just don't ask me how I felt about it. Please.*

Ruby began, "I 'member—"

Miss Wright interrupted, "Jessie, did you notice the sideboard in their dining room?"

Jessie tossed the shirt into the pot. So Miss Wright knew about that. "Yes, Mr. Palmer made the family connection between me and Will's father. He said a British lord had tried to buy the sideboard from him."

"Really?" Miss Wright sounded pleased. "I'm glad to hear they hadn't bought something newer."

"No, Mr. Palmer was quite complimentary about Will's father's skill." Jessie couldn't voice Mr. Palmer's kind words about her Will.

"Margaret was always so proud of her husband's work." Miss Wright's voice shook. "Will had the gift, the love of wood and fine detail, too."

Susan walked back to the bubbling pot to begin stirring again. "Jessie, you don't sound like you had a good time."

Jessie couldn't hold back her misgivings any longer. "It was a difficult evening. I felt . . . out of place."

"I cook my whole life in the big house," Ruby grumbled. "Don't you never think fine clothes and gilt on they china mean no sorrow or sin."

"Well said," Miss Wright glanced at Ruby approvingly.

These words freed Jessie from the last of her constraint. Her revulsion at being less than honest bubbled up from inside her. "I felt like an actress playing a part. I would never have gone if it hadn't been to help Dr. Gooden."

"What about Dr. Gooden, Jessie?" Miss Wright demanded. "Is it your intention to remarry?"

The unforeseen words knocked the wind out of Jessie. She gasped for breath. "Marry the doctor?"

"Yes, do you plan to marry the doctor or do you intend to marry Mr. Smith?" The spinster stared at her with narrowed eyes.

The urge to run away surged through Jessie. "I haven't encouraged either gentleman to think I favor him."

"Is that what you think?" Miss Wright "humphed," then went on: "That's not what the neighbors think. What with the both men hanging around this back porch practically every evening."

Jessie tasted bile on her tongue. *Marry? Me?*

"She right." Ruby nodded. "They be your gentlemen callers. Everybody see that."

"I will never marry again." Jessie slapped a petticoat onto the board and began rubbing furiously. "Mr. Smith is Linc's friend not mine. We can't be together for more than a few minutes without his trying my temper."

Miss Greenleigh said slyly, "Yes, I've noticed that."

Before Jessie could think how to answer this, Miss Wright said in a starched-up tone, "This avoiding the truth will not wash, Jessie. Dr. Gooden and Mr. Smith may not have said anything plainly, but no man comes every evening just to play ball or talk about medicine."

"You got that right," Susan said under her breath, so only Jessie could hear her.

"Must I be held accountable for how two men choose to spend their evenings?" Jessie scrubbed faster, harder.

"That's enough scrubbing on my petticoat," Susan objected. "I hanker to wear one without holes."

Jessie flushed and threw the wet petticoat into the tub.

Miss Wright continued lecturing her: "If you don't wish to encourage these gentlemen, you must let them know that their suit would not please you."

"But why shouldn't their suit please you?" Miss Greenleigh countered, wide-eyed. "Both of them are eligible. There's nothing wrong with a widow remarrying. You've been alone for over six years now."

Jessie grumbled, "I am still not convinced that either of them is looking for a wife or looking at me as a prospective wife." Certainly Mr. Smith had never voiced such an intention.

Miss Wright shook her head. "I see how that doctor looks at you. That man has marriage on his mind."

"He a busy man," Ruby seconded. "If he ain't interested in you, he don't spend that much time here."

Miss Greenleigh said, "I think Mr. Smith would make an excellent stepfather for Linc."

As though pricked with a sharp needle, Jessie snapped, "Never! Linc will never live under a stepfather." Hands on her hips, she faced the women ranged on the porch. "I made Linc that promise the day we held his father's memorial service."

The women looked back at her, obviously shocked at her outburst.

"I will never marry again," Jessie declared, vibrating inside with a mixture of fear and worry. *Then why can't I just send them away?*

Miss Greenleigh crossed her arms over her breast and observed, "Then you'd better tell that to these men. Just dressing in black has not dampened their interest."

Susan spoke up, "Why you think it would be so bad for Linc to have a stepfather? Not every man be hard like your stepfather. Maybe Linc want a stepfather—especially if he be someone like Mr. Smith. Did you ask your boy?"

Jessie tightened her mouth and bent over the washboard. "I know what's best for my son."

* * *

July 4, 1871

In the deep twilight, another wave broke around Linc making him squeal. "Mother!" Linc in a one-piece swimsuit splashed through the shallows at the Oak Street Beach to her at water's edge. "I found some more shells." He slid the tiny wet shells into her hand.

Before she could add them to the sandy collection wrapped in a handkerchief in her pocket, Linc charged out to meet another white-capped wave.

With his pant legs rolled up, Lee waded over to her. "I have never seen such waves on this lake before."

"An east wind brings the waves in high and warm. When I was little, my mother brought me here whenever the wind was right," Jessie murmured. She fell silent, recalling the severe scolding her stepfather had given her mother for going into the water with her.

Suddenly a blast of loud brass band music fluttered to them on the wind. "It must be nearly time for the fireworks," Jessie said.

"Will we really see them from here?" Lee asked.

"Yes, they do them at the lakefront." Jessie sank down onto the rented beach chair and modestly arranged herself. A smile she couldn't quell shaped her face.

The cooling lake breeze made her feel wonderfully comfortable and relaxed. Linc splashed out of the waves and collapsed onto the sand beside his mother's chair.

"Thanks for persuading us to come, sport," Mr. Smith said.

"It's Independence Day. We had to do something special." Linc leaned against Jessie. The sky turned from brass to deep violet to slate. For once, Mr. Smith wasn't ironic or sardonic with her.

While Mr. Smith still irritated her with his care-for-nothing attitude, how could she feel anything but gratitude to him? His kindness to her fatherless son had put her deeply in his debt. But she refused to believe Mr. Smith was interested in her. Miss Wright was completely "off base" in regards to Mr. Smith. She smiled over her own use of the baseball term. Linc's passion for the game had infiltrated their life.

Night came. Without speaking, Jessie and the others turned south toward the carnival and waterfront. The warmth of the day lessened.

Boom! The first fireworks exploded overhead with golden streamers. The pyrotechnic show proceeded quickly. Jessie lost herself in the dazzling colors, pounding explosions, and the cascade of oohs and ahhs from the shore and water. She glanced at her son and took pleasure from the joy in his expression. Her eyes strayed and caught sight of Mr. Smith, too. Everyone else's eyes were skyward, but Mr. Smith had buried his face in his hands.

Why?

The answer came quickly. The war. She'd heard stories of veterans who jumped at any loud noise. Was Mr. Smith remembering the dreadful thunder of cannons and red flares of the bombs overhead? Her lips pressed together. Mr. Smith shivered suddenly as if it were cold. She thought she heard him moan. The man often irritated her with his care-for-nobody air. But was that to conceal the pain from his past? *I never thought of that.*

The fireworks ended with a fantastic series of explosions in gold, brilliant blue, crimson, and startling green. The city's gaslights twinkled against the charcoal sky. All around her, mothers and fathers gathered sleepy children for the walk or trolley ride home. The voices were soothing, homey. An overtired child began crying and his mother sang him a weary-sounding lullaby. This sound fit her mood. Why hadn't she ever thought of this man's suffering?

Soon few people were left. Jessie became aware that Linc had fallen asleep heavily against her. Still she didn't speak or move. Mr. Smith appeared to remain wrapped up in his inner turmoil. Jessie did not want to disturb him. What tormented him tonight? Finally he looked up. She expected him to look to Linc's face first. When he looked to her first, her heart tightened. But his expression remained distant, veiled.

In the lamplight, the white-capped waves still rushed the sandy beach, racing up the shore. If this man had been to war just like Will, what had he brought with him from that experience? She couldn't ask. At last, she murmured, "Linc has fallen asleep. We need to get home."

Mr. Smith stood, then bent down. "I'll carry him." He swung Linc up into his arms. The boy didn't waken. Jessie and Lee walked silently through the quiet streets and down her alley. As they approached her house, she stumbled and Lee caught her arm. She noticed Mrs. O'Toole's curtain twitch. Well, the gossips would talk no matter what she did. She tried to take a step and cringed. "My ankle."

"Twisted it?" Mr. Smith asked.

She clung to his arm. "Yes."

"Lean on me. It's only a few steps to your back porch."

She had no choice. Yet she'd not been this close or touched a man like this for a long time. Mr. Smith had left his coat at her house, so only his shirt separated her skin from his. In the cocoon of night, she was very aware of his breathing, of his masculine scent, of the sinew of his arm. Women and children were so soft, cushiony, and men so solid to the touch.

At her back steps, she let herself down onto the second one. "Take Linc to bed," she murmured. "Send Susan out to help me."

He left with only a nod. She rested her head against the railing, letting the images from this happy day play through her mind. Mr. Smith and Linc running down the beach toward the water, racing to see who could shuck his shoes and socks and make it into the water first. The two of them devouring her fried chicken and competing over who could spit watermelon seeds the farthest. The day's joy zipped through her.

"Jess?" Mr. Smith's voice came to her and then he was raising her and helping her up the steps. "Susan isn't back yet."

Jessie nodded against him. They were all alone, a rare occurrence, and she wanted to say something to this man who loved her son. This man who'd likely suffered loss, pain, and deprivation in the cruel war. But what could one say? "Lee?" she said his name for the first time.

He stopped. "Jess?"

A shaft of moonlight illuminated his eyes. She reached up and stroked his hair. It was springy and thick. Her hands liked the feel of it. "You've given us so much." She didn't know where the words came from.

"Nothing. Not nearly enough." His voice came out raspy.

Her fingers went through his hair again. "You hurt tonight. I'm sorry."

"I don't want you to be sorry." He pulled her closer. "Don't pity me."

"I don't. I'm grateful." She looked up, her emotions and thoughts hopelessly tangled with her sudden attraction to this bedeviling man. "I . . . I . . ."

And he kissed her.

Sensation crashed through her. His lips moved over hers igniting sparks throughout her veins. She leaned into him and then breathed in his breath.

Suddenly he pulled away. "What am I thinking?" He swung her up into his arms, carried her through to the parlor and left her on her bed, stunned and horrified at what had happened. *I let Mr. Smith kiss me.*

Chapter 11

August 30, 1871

Jessie stood in Miss Greenleigh's room, normally so neat. Today it was a riot of clothing and new tissue paper. Like the face of a daisy attracted to the sun, Jessie had been drawn here. Kneeling in front of her trunk, the bride-to-be was carefully folding the multitude of her underthings: corset-covers in white and pale pink, fine-woven chemises frilled with ruffles and flowered embroidery at their yokes. Jessie suppressed a tiny nip of envy.

"Yes," Miss Greenleigh replied to Mrs. Bolt, sitting in the only chair, "my fiancé is fifteen years older, but we're in love—"

"You ought to be marrying a man nearer your own age," Mrs. Bolt interrupted. "You'll end up a young widow."

"I could die before Matthew." The young woman continued her careful folding.

Mrs. Bolt shrilled, "Just because you're afraid of being left an old maid—"

Miss Greenleigh didn't look up. "This year I received two proposals."

The redheaded widow's mouth crimped into a sour pucker. "*Well*, I see that my words of wisdom are wasted here." Mrs. Bolt rose, brushed past Jessie, and clattered away.

Ill at ease, Jessie turned to leave.

"Please come in and close the door." Miss Greenleigh beckoned Jessie who complied and sat down, wondering what the pretty blonde had to say.

"Since I will no longer be living here, could we use our given names?"

Jessie smiled. Their relationship as landlady and boarder had made them keep their distance. "I'd like that, Eileene."

"I wasn't completely truthful with Mrs. Bolt, Jessie."

Jessie raised her eyebrows.

"This is my *third* proposal in the past twelve months." A puckish grin enhanced Eileene's radiant face.

"But—"

"I met many gentlemen when I spent weekends with my sister—my matchmaking sister."

"Perhaps we could hire her for Mrs. Bolt." Shocked at herself, Jessie clapped her hands over her mouth.

Miss Greenleigh whooped with laughter. "No." She sat back on her heels. "I wish I could give Mrs. Bolt some 'wise words' about her coy and graceless behavior around Mr. Smith. If she continues the way she is going, she will never marry again."

Jessie lowered her voice. "I wonder if she was happy in her first marriage. If she had been, perhaps she wouldn't be so overly eager." Jessie confided, "I can't imagine being married to anyone, but my Will. I hope you and Matthew will be as happy as we were." The memory of kissing Mr. Smith caused Jessie a twinge.

"I think we will be." Eileene paused.

With the toe of her shoe, Jessie pensively traced the rose pattern on the small bedside rug. All this talk about marrying highlighted her strained relationship with Mr. Smith. She still couldn't believe she'd let him kiss her on the Fourth of July. "You were right—all of you," Jessie muttered without planning to.

"About Mr. Smith and the doctor?"

Jessie hung her head.

"May I be honest?"

Jessie tilted her head to the side, assenting.

"It isn't good to raise a lone boy in a household full of females."

Eileene's softly spoken, but undeniable words dropped like boulders onto Jessie's heart. Gathering her composure, Jessie rose. "I should be in the kitchen, helping Susan. And Eileene, my best to you and Matthew."

"I'll send you a wedding invitation."

"Please do." Jessie clasped hands with Eileene. Deep in thought, Jessie walked down to the kitchen.

"She done packing?" Susan had her hands deep into a batch of bread dough.

"No."

"She the nicest boarder we had."

Jessie stepped to Susan's side. "She said Linc shouldn't be raised in a household of women."

"She right. Why don't you rent her room to Mr. Smith? That's what he come for in the first place."

"Linc need a man around here." Wheezing softly as always, Ruby walked in, her large body shifting from one unsteady foot to the other. "What you mauling, child?"

"Six loaves a bread."

Jessie's worry dragged her mind away from the kitchen. *Yes, Linc needs a man in his life.* But would Mr. Smith be content to be there for Linc, yet expect nothing from her? In the weeks since they'd kissed, he'd been a pattern card of a gentleman. But there was still something about him that warned her away. *And my heart will always be Will's. Then why did I let him kiss me?*

After lunch Jessie carried a lapful of mending out onto the shady back porch. In the heat of the afternoon, everyone else napped. Jessie sighed and threaded a needle.

"Jessie?" Her mother whom Jessie hadn't seen in weeks came up the backyard path.

"Mother, how did you ever get away?"

"I had to come and see you. I don't care what Hiram says."

Heedless of the mending, Jessie stood, welcoming her mother with open arms. For a few moments they clung to each other. Jessie urged her mother into a nearby chair. "I'll get you some tea."

"No, I can only stay a few moments, but I had to come. I've felt so terrible ever since your last visit."

Anger drove its claws into Jessie's heart. "Hiram should feel terrible, not you. He's forbidden you to speak to me, hasn't he?"

"Jessie, please. Hiram's a good man. No fire captain in Chicago is as conscientious."

"No doubt, but he always puts himself up as the judge of the world. I can't forgive the things he said about Will. How your husband had the gall to tell me—in front of Margaret—that a son's duty was to stay home and provide for his widowed mother."

"It would have been better, for you and Linc, if Will hadn't volunteered—"

"I would *never* have asked Will to avoid the draft the way your husband did." Jessie's hands fisted.

Esther hung her head.

"I'll never forget that your husband paid a man three hundred dollars to be drafted in his place. I have always wanted to ask Mr. Hiram Huff what it feels like to hire a man to *die* in your place?"

"It does no good to stir up the past—"

Words rushed to Jessie's lips. "I can't hold everything back anymore."

Jessie stood and began pacing. "I'll never forget the day when he left me—only twelve years old—on this porch. I'd never been so frightened. Mother, why didn't you, at least, come with me?"

"Hiram said I would cry and upset you—"

"*Hiram said,*" Jessie parroted. "Mother, why did you ever marry him?"

Twisting her handkerchief, Esther flushed scarlet. "Please."

"He has continually separated us."

"No—"

"It's true and you know it."

Esther stared down at white cotton-gloved hands folded in her lap. "No, he's a hard man, but I never let him use a switch—"

"Words and looks can sting harsher than any switch."

"Please. If he hadn't been so exhausted and worried about the drought and all the fires, he wouldn't have argued with you—"

"You still choose to defend him." Jessie clenched her hands. "I will never remarry." *I'll never kiss Mr. Smith again.* "I will never put Linc through this."

"Please don't say that. Mr. Smith . . . Linc loves him so much . . . I was hoping . . ."

While her mother rambled tearfully through these phrases, Jessie shook her head. "Since I was three years old, Hiram Huff has cheated me of my mother's love—"

"No."

"I grew up thinking you didn't love me. Margaret had to explain that you did love me, you just couldn't show it because of my stepfather. Every time I would reach for you, he would step between us, scolding me."

"But Hiram speaks highly of you now. He was especially pleased that you didn't rent to men. He says most widows are 'shameless'—"

"Mother, on his birthday Linc asked me why his step-grandfather didn't like him."

Esther moaned.

Jessie drew herself up. "You are always welcome here. But if I never see Hiram Huff again, it will be too soon."

"Jessie," her mother pleaded, "I know he has wronged you, but you are a Christian. You must forgive."

Jessie looked away, hardening her heart against the crushed expression on her mother's face. "I can't help how I feel. I won't lie any more."

Esther rose slowly and left. Feeling close to tears herself, Jessie turned her back and went into the kitchen. She was done with Hiram Huff and with kissing Mr. Smith. Linc came first.

In the waning light of sundown, Jessie approached her home, crumpled, downcast. When would the cool, rainy fall days begin? Dry leaves dropped and shattered on the parched brown lawns and dusty wooden streets. The lingering drought and her own futility oppressed her.

As she hastened up her back steps, she tried to put aside the pain of her seventh rejection by a physician. She had been certain this doctor who'd studied for the mission field would say yes. The man's hypocrisy had staggered her. As long as he was miles away, on their soil, he did not mind treating dark "natives." But not in Chicago.

Voices coming from the kitchen drew her attention. Caleb opened the door for her. "Mrs. Wagstaff, I'm so glad you've finally come home."

"What is it? You looked worried."

"My father . . . his heart. . . ."

Jessie grasped his hands. She didn't want to face this alone. Though she'd kept Dr. Gooden at arm's length since the night of the Palmer dinner, he'd come now. *Wouldn't he?*

"The Rev'rend wants you to come," Susan said, her voice breaking. "We bin waiting for you."

Lee entered through the kitchen curtain. "Linc's in bed." When he spotted Jessie, he halted. "Linc and I missed you tonight, Mrs. Wagstaff. Was your mission successful?"

His behaving as if he belonged in her house irritated her. "I don't have time to talk now."

Lee surveyed the company gathered around Jessie. "Something's wrong."

"Caleb's father is mortal bad again," Susan said.

"What are his symptoms?" Lee asked automatically.

"He's experiencing chest pain and can barely breathe." Caleb's face twisted. "It's worse than last time."

"Heart failure." This medical pronouncement slipped out of Lee's mouth before he could prevent it.

"Caleb, go to the doctor's hotel. The Reverend needs him. Susan, let us go quickly," Jessie urged.

"I'm coming, too," Lee said in spite of himself.

"You're not . . . needed." Caleb glared at him now.

This goaded Lee. "I'm coming anyway." Jessie objected but he went on: "Mrs. Wagstaff will need an escort home."

Jessie glared at him, but Lee doubted the good doctor would come and he couldn't let her face the disappointment alone.

Jessie, Susan, and Lee covered the few miles to a one-room house. Somber people hovered around the dwelling. With a sinking feeling, Lee recognized that the Reverend's flock wouldn't come unless they thought this the end.

Susan led them inside. Homemade candles, clustered on the bedside table, cast flickering shadows on the unfinished walls. Lee looked at the spent, old man who lay just as he had that other night.

"Mrs. Wagstaff?" the old preacher's low voice sounded like sandpaper on rough wood.

She went to sit on the only bedside chair. Lee, feeling out of place, slipped to the rear of the crowd, surrounding the bed.

"Reverend." Jessie took the gaunt hand. "Shall I make you a cup of Margaret's herb tea?"

"I don't think . . . it will be of any . . . further help to me." The old man wheezed as though he had been running for miles.

Lee vicariously felt the effort it cost the preacher.

Jessie clung to his frail hand. "I've sent Caleb—"

Unexpectedly, Caleb's voice came from the doorway, "I left word for the doctor at his hotel."

"Mrs. Wagstaff, God bless you. . . ." The old man gasped between phrases. "Let your light so shine. . . . Whatever you have done for the least . . ."

"I haven't done anything anyone else couldn't do better," Jessie objected.

The tears in her voice wounded Lee.

"But who else does anything?" Caleb's voice sounded harsh in the velvet cocoon of the dark room.

"Son, forgive. Bitterness . . . will destroy you." The Reverend's breathing rustled like a tide of dry leaves swept over pavement. He choked.

Jessie looked helpless, frantic.

Unable to resist her silent appeal, Lee arranged the pillows under the old man's featherlight upper body. The man was literally drowning from within; fluid pooling and compressing his lungs. As Lee pictured the laboring worn-out heart, he felt pressure on his own chest.

"Music," Reverend Mitchell whispered. "Sing."

A momentary silence greeted this. Then a woman started humming; another sang softly, "My Lord, what a mourning. My Lord, what a mourning. My Lord, what a mourning when the stars began to fall." More women joined in, reverently humming and singing the chant. The melody took Lee back to war days in Mississippi and later Virginia. In this humble setting, the genuine feeling in the words opened emotions long buried.

As though expecting the doctor, Jessie walked to the door and looked out.

Don't get your hopes up, Jess. The good doctor will disappoint you. Maybe tonight.

Without pause, the next spiritual began. "Soon I will be done with the trouble of this world." An almost physical longing crystallized within Lee. If only one could be done with the trouble of this world. "Soon I will be done with the trouble of this world. Goin' to live with God." He drew a painful breath. Penetrating, unanticipated grief weighed him down. He leaned back against the rough wall.

Song followed song. In the funereal glow of the candles, Lee could not take his eyes from the old man. Jessie paced in front of the door, looking outside at the sound of each passing wagon.

Lee felt hard-earned barriers against memories of the war begin to crumble. He wanted to escape this room, from remembering, but he couldn't leave Jess. The doctor wasn't coming tonight, yet Lee took no satisfaction in being proved right.

"Son," the old man's raspy whisper sounded loud in the silent room.

Caleb knelt on one knee and gripped his father's thin hand. "Father."

"Forgive, son. Let go . . . of hate. . . ."

Caleb pressed two fingers to the bridge of his nose as though forcing back tears.

"You will . . . never know peace." The old man wheezed again under the killing burden of fluid and blood.

Breaking the silence, one of the mourners intoned in a rich bass voice, "Swing low sweet chariot comin' for to carry me home." A crescendo of harmonies and emotions coursed through the grief-saturated room.

The old preacher raised one hand. "Caleb, it's beautiful," the Reverend mumbled. "I see it."

Jessie came to Lee. He held out his hand. She accepted it, staying beside him. The touch of her hand in his strengthened him against the sorrow around him.

The old man tried to lift his head. "Praise God." The dying man collapsed against the pillow. Silence descended. No one moved.

Lee waited until he realized that foreboding had immobilized everyone. He stepped close to the bed and pressed his hand to the man's throat, feeling for a pulse. "He's gone." Lee tenderly closed the old man's eyes.

A moan. A cry. A heartrending sob.

Lee felt his low spirits sink farther. In a heartbeat, he was transported to the past. He stood at the edge of a battlefield at daybreak. The moans and shrieks of wounded men ripped and shredded the peaceful dawn. Lee began trembling. Before it could overtake him completely, he fled the house.

Heedless of her own tears, Jessie accepted and returned the embraces of the other mourners. Inside, she felt scoured out by grief and disappointment. *Dr. Gooden, why didn't you come?*

After Susan released her from a fierce hug, Jessie searched the room for Lee. *Gone.* She threaded her way through the mourners until she was able to escape outside. By the glow of the streetlamp, she spotted him and hurried to him.

Before she could speak, he took her arm and began to rush her along the alley. She couldn't keep up with him; she pulled against him.

Abruptly he pulled her close. Only then did she become aware of the trembling of his hands. "What is it?"

He groaned. The sound unnerved her, standing alone in the dark. Drawn against her will, she moved closer to him, closer. She rested her forehead on his chin. A drop of moisture, then another fell onto her cheek. Looking up, she realized the tears were not hers, but his. "What is it?"

He gripped her arms. "Oh, Will . . ." He swallowed convulsively and his grip tightened on her. "Hurry, Will! They're dying. Why don't they send us more wagons, more men?"

At the stark despair in his voice, she wrapped her arms around him. He was shaking. Like a mother soothing a child, she stroked Lee's back, murmuring comfort. His arms closed around her. One last harsh groan escaped him. He was still.

Then she felt him lower his cheek to hers. This slight adjustment completely altered the mood of their closeness. No longer were they mother, son. Now they were man and woman. His embrace made her feel light, small, feminine. His breath feathered the small curls at her temples. Breathless, she turned her face into the crook of his neck.

"Jessie," he sighed her name. He lowered his lips to hers. She did not resist. He kissed her, a demanding kiss, not a kiss to be ignored.

She gasped and he deepened his kiss. A yielding sigh drifted from her mouth. She knew she should pull away, but the same inexplicable pull she had experienced on the Fourth compelled her to remain against him

When his eyelashes flickered against her face, she trembled with her need for him. Shocked at her own response, she forced herself to step back. Grudgingly he let her go.

"You were remembering the war?"

"Yes," he admitted curtly. He took her arm and started down the dark street.

She tried to keep up with him. "Why now?"

"I don't want to talk about it. The war should never have happened." His pace became brisker.

"Then Susan wouldn't be free." Jessie tugged against him, forcing him to slow.

"If the South could have foreseen all that the war would rob them of, and all that it would force them to endure, they would have let Susan's people go, and gladly."

"I doubt that."

"What do you know about it? We all joined to 'Save the Union' and later 'Free the slaves.'" His voice became fierce. "On enlistment posters they don't say: 'Give us your youth,' 'Leave your wives widows and your sons orphans,' 'Die like dogs—worse than dogs.'"

He halted, gripping her wrists. "I have seen amputated legs stacked like cordwood. After winter battles, we had to chip men out of pools of their own frozen blood." He jerked her closer. "The war was a travesty. No cause justifies war."

The visions his words evoked terrified her, but suddenly she recalled all his words. She said in a dazed voice, "You said Will. You knew my husband. You're Smith. You drove an ambulance for the Sanitary Corps, didn't you?"

His mouth opened and closed, but no words came out.

She touched his arm. "I won't make you talk about it. But I need to know."

He closed his eyes as though drawing inner strength, then he nodded.

"I'm glad." She searched for words to strengthen him. "You and Will did what you had to do. Some things are worth dying for, but we, you have to go on."

He said at last, "Always the crusader."

Exhausted, Jessie did not speak, but she took his arm, leading him home. She ached for Caleb in his loss and for Lee, but she could not heal their pain. Only God could. And she doubted either man would seek God's healing. Lee had suffered with her Will. He deserved peace, comfort now. Then her mind pulled up another painful thought. Dr. Gooden hadn't come.

As they were parting on her back steps, she couldn't hold back the words. "Would you be interested in renting Miss Greenleigh's room?"

"I thought you never rented to men."

"I've—I've changed my mind," she stammered.

"Then I would like the room." He looked her full in the face.

She avoided his eyes. "At the end of the week?"

"The end of the week."

Her gaze followed him as he ambled away. It was done. She should have sent him away; instead, she had brought him closer to her, to Linc.

I let him kiss me again. Her lips tingled with the memory. She resisted the warm tide, engulfing her. How did this man make her go against her common sense and convictions? What power drew her to him? Walking through her back door, she hummed, "My Lord, what a mourning when the stars begin to fall."

After Reverend Mitchell's evening funeral, the lake breeze was blowing through Jessie's parlor windows, swelling the sheers. Jessie pulled the crisp, white sheet up to her son's chin and patted his cheek. "Good night, son. God bless you."

Yesterday it had been laundry day and in spite of Susan and Ruth's help, her back ached from bending over the washboard. She knew she should kneel beside her son's bed and pray with him at bedtime, but most nights she felt that if she got down on her knees, she would merely lie down on the wooden floor and go to sleep.

If only Will had come back from the war, there would be someone with strong hands to rub her back. She could easily picture Will humming softly as he worked the tenseness out of her tired muscles. Sitting down on the chair at the foot of Linc's narrow bed, she sighed.

She forced herself to stop this downward spiral into self-pity. Will had loved her, had given her a son, and left her a house with which she could support herself and their son. Many women were in much worse circumstances. Slowly she unhooked the buttons of her shoes, one by one, then she slid down her garters and black cotton hose. The first breath of air on her legs was refreshing and the bare floor felt cool to the bottoms of her feet.

The full moon flooded the room with silvery light. Linc's breathing became regular, telling her he was deeply asleep. Miss Wright snored on the other side of the curtain. She pressed down the images from the funeral tonight. Caleb's stolid grief.

Beside her chair sat her old trunk. She opened the lid, careful not to make a sound. Under her winter woolens lay the packet of letters from Will tied up with a faded blue ribbon. Keeping the ribbon in place, she let her fingers walk on top of the letters' edges.

Lee's knowing Will explained why he'd sought her out in April and had befriended her son. In this private moment, she admitted she looked forward to Mr. Smith's nightly visits as much as her son did. She closed her eyes willing images of Lee and Linc playing together away. Now that she'd invited Lee to move into her house, she needed to reinforce her memories of Will. Biting her lower lip, she opened a letter from the middle of the packet.

"Dearest Jessie." Will's greeting still had the power to move her six years after his death. Her eyes scanned the page and then more pages—accounts of battles, bravery, deaths. Then a notation jumped out at her. "March 3, 1864. Jess, bad news today. Smith, the driver, died last night. I am sorely grieved."

She pressed the letter to her throbbing heart. If Smith died March 3, 1864, who was the man who had mourned with her tonight at Reverend Mitchell's funeral?

Chapter 12

September 28, 1871

"Oh, Mr. Smith, are you leaving now, too?"

Just as he was about to leave Jessie's house, Mrs. Bolt's insinuating voice froze Lee's insides. "I didn't expect you to be up and out so early on a Saturday morning."

"I have a little shopping to do downtown. How nice we are going the same way." As slick as an escaping cat, the redhead slipped her arm into his.

The urge to box the woman's ears nearly overwhelmed him, but taking a deep breath, he nodded. The stroll to town began. The widow kept up an uninterrupted gush of meaningless chatter.

Lee held his temper precariously. Her proprietary manner—as though she had some claim on him—aggravated him. *I don't know how much longer I can be polite to this woman.*

At the sight of the first office building they came to, he halted. "I must leave you here, ma'am." He disconnected himself from her clinging gloved hand.

"Oh, could I see your office?" she cooed as she stared up at the sandstone edifice.

"So sorry. I'm due in a meeting immediately. Good day." He charged into the building and up its flight of marble stairs. By the second floor window, he watched as the redhead disappeared up the street. Within minutes, he headed south for the Workman's Rest. When he entered its alley door, he found Pearl waiting for him.

Wearing a dress of royal blue cotton, she gave him a sidelong glance. "You dress like a banker, but you don't work banker's hours, Mr. Smith."

"I was delayed by . . . ah . . . business."

Pearl gave him a provocative smile. "You could move up your position here, you know. How would you like to be proprietor?"

Lee's mouth went dry. *Why did I ever let a flirtation with my boss start?*

"Think it over." Letting her lacy, royal blue bustle sway, Pearl walked away into the main room.

Think it over? Lee groaned inwardly. He should never have—even subtly—encouraged his employer's initial forays into flirtation. Instead, amused by it, he had let it go on. He had misled her and for that he felt guilty.

Lee hung up his coat and hat, tied on his white apron, and tucked a clean towel in its band.

I'm surrounded. Pearl at work. The redhead at the Wagstaff's house.

Jess's face appeared in his mind. *Jess.* He felt her lips against his, her soft body pressed to him. *Jess.* Holding her had been bliss. But the comfort in her caring touch had meant more to him than any passion he had felt.

Jessie continued to clothe herself in black and gray, trying to conceal her beauty. To the world, she presented a stern-widow mask. It no longer fooled Lee. Jess was a tenderhearted, loving woman.

He felt unprepared for this turn of events. His years in the army and his life after the war had kept him immune to affairs of the heart. He had only the remembrance of a few infatuations in his salad days.

Had he fallen in love with Jess? He rubbed his forehead, wishing he could reach inside, smooth out his thoughts, and make sense of this. He took the broom to the sidewalk in front of the saloon.

He swished the broom back and forth, his pointless action mimicking his mental confusion. With an exasperating combination of softness and fortitude, Jess insisted on taking care of Miss Wright, an old witch anyone else would show to the door. She brushed aside his attempts to give her money to help with expenses, even for Linc. When the good doctor, who was still courting her, had explained his not coming to the Reverend's aid because he was caring for a critically ill child, she'd forgiven him, much to Lee's dismay. Jess was absolutely genuine. She would never play him false.

And I lied to her.

Her crusade to find a physician for Susan's people made it impossible for him to reveal his true identity now. With shame, he recalled how after each rejection, she'd returned home, looking crushed. What if she ever found out the truth about him?

If she finds out, she'll never forgive me.

"Missy, we need to have a talk."

Recognizing her stepfather's harsh voice, Jessie paused in midswing with the rug beater, held in both hands like a bat. The rag and woven rugs from the bedrooms hung over the clothesline on the side of the house. "Why are you here?"

"I see you no longer make any attempt at common politeness—"

"Why should I?" She continued swatting a rug with an even rhythm. "You've never shown any politeness to me—that was more than a paper-thin mask." Out of the corner of her eye, she saw his lips crimp in disapproval.

"I am here—for your own good. The way you have been behaving has reached my ears once more, missy."

She tried to avoid the coming argument. Looking at the rug, Jessie did not miss a stroke as she moved ahead to beat the next rug.

The stale scent of dust hovered around them. "I'm not interested in anything you have to say. For my mother's sake, please leave."

He drew himself up. "I'm not leaving till I've said what I've come to say."

"Suit yourself." She went on swinging the beater, feeling each impact through her arms and back.

"Put that rug beater down. I think we should go in so we won't be overheard."

"I've told you I don't want to hear what you have to say and I've asked you to leave."

"As your father, I have a responsibility—"

"You are not my father. You have never treated me as though you were my father—"

"I provided for you for nine years—"

Jessie moved to the next rug and swung at it, matching each swing to the beat of her words. "*And* I'm *sure* you have *written* down in your household ledger *every* penny you were *ever* forced to *spend* on me. *But* since you made me *work* off each *penny*, I feel *no* obligation to *you*."

"Your attitude is totally unacceptable—"

"Thank you." She moved on to a rose-patterned rug and attacked it.

"Enough of this." Huff hurried forward. "This morning one of the other fire captains, who has a brother who is a doctor, asked me if my stepdaughter's married name was Wagstaff."

Jessie kept the clothesline dancing rhythmically. With each moment, her irritation expanded, growing into anger.

"He proceeded to tell me about an embarrassing visit you made to his brother."

"His brother should be embarrassed." Jessie spoke through gritted teeth. "Indeed, he should be ashamed for not helping people who need him."

"No one elected you his judge. 'Judge ye not, lest ye be judged.'"

Her anger blazing white hot, Jessie stopped in midswing. "How dare you quote scripture to me—you hard-hearted, mean-fisted hypocrite! Have you ever heard—'Love one another even as I have loved you'? When have you ever loved anyone, but yourself?"

He spluttered with outrage.

Jessie felt herself lose control. Scalding words long held back poured forth, "I have never forgotten how you criticized Will when he enlisted to help free the slaves. But how could you understand his love for people he didn't know—when you don't even love the people *you do know.*"

With a hand upraised, Hiram crowded close to her. Automatically Jessie took a batter's stance, gripping the rug beater like a baseball bat.

Hiram stopped. "You'll never see your mother again," he hissed. He turned and marched away.

Jessie felt light-headed, her head throbbed. *He was going to strike me.*

Esther was polishing silver when her husband walked in, slamming the door behind him. She dropped the spoon she held. It clattered to the floor. "Hiram, what has happened?"

"That daughter of yours!" he thundered and started pacing. "I went to her house to confront her about the way she's been disgracing us all over town. Captain Phelps described your daughter's outrageous attempt to persuade his brother to take on her black friends as patients—"

"But those people do need a doctor," Esther said softly. Her heart sped up as she added, "Perhaps God wants Jessie to do this."

"Nonsense! God wants no such thing!"

"Do you speak for God, Hiram?"

Silence. Hiram stopped pacing. "Esther, you have never spoken to me like this before."

She clutched the edge of the table, her knuckles white. "You have never spoken for God before. I know it's your nature to feel things strongly and to express yourself strongly—"

"A Christian wife does not contradict her husband."

Her voice remained soft, but she stood up, facing him. "Even when he is wrong?"

"I'm not wrong! Your daughter—"

"Again. Do you speak for God?"

He stared at her as though he doubted his ears.

She looked at him, frowning a crease between her brows. "I have been doing a lot of thinking over the past few weeks. We have been married for over twenty years. In that whole time, Hiram, I have never once said what I was truly thinking. That's a long time to keep silent."

"Thinking?" he sputtered.

"I know it has probably never occurred to you, but I have my own thoughts and feelings. Last week Jessie told me that when she was a child, she thought I didn't love her." Her voice cracked. "Can you imagine how that wounded my heart?"

"That has nothing to do with this—"

"It has *everything* to do with this. Do you remember what you promised me about Jessie before we married?"

"I told you I would treat her as my own child."

"Yes." A sob formed deep inside her, but she held it in. "But how was I to know what a rigorous and unloving father you meant to be?"

"What?" His face registered disbelief.

"You browbeat our sons with your rigid rules and cold discipline. You never show them love or even common kindness." Esther looked down at the floor, ashamed of her words.

"You're losing your mind." He sounded incredulous.

She faced him. "No, I am *speaking* my mind for the first time."

He stepped up to her. "It's your daughter's rebellion I've to thank for this attitude. I will tolerate no more of this defiance from either of you." He gripped her arms painfully. "You will not speak to her again till she apologizes to me."

"No."

He squeezed her arms tighter.

She wrenched away from him. Feeling as brittle as the first, thin sheet of winter ice over a pond, she turned to leave the room. "You have always wanted to separate me from my daughter."

"Esther, I forbid you to speak to your daughter until she apologizes to me. You will obey me."

"No, Hiram, I will not obey you in this."

He lunged forward, grasped her arms once more and jerked her toward him, hurting her, his livid face just inches from hers. "You promised to love, honor, and obey me. If you defy me, you will be breaking your wedding vows."

Esther ignored his agitation and the pain in her arms. "Hiram, you promised to love, honor, and cherish me. You have never kept even one of your vows to me. Let God judge between us."

Hiram raised his hand so quickly Esther didn't have time to dodge his blow. Her head swam and she couldn't get her breath. Trying to speak, she felt herself losing consciousness.

Mrs. Bolt held herself upright, making the most of her five foot four inches, as she marched at the front of a dozen or more of her compatriots in the Temperance Union. Everyone around her chattered with excitement. Their common zeal had finally prompted them to take action against liquor. A thrilling combination of trepidation and ardor carried Mrs. Bolt up to the swinging doors of the first gin mill where she would crusade this evening.

Ever since childhood when passing any saloon, she'd crossed to the other side of the street. This was her first chance to peer over swinging doors. A striking blond woman, standing at the bar in the long, narrow room caught Mrs. Bolt's eye. *A fallen woman!* Mrs. Bolt avidly absorbed every detail of the woman's costume. Though somewhat disappointed by the modesty of the apparel, she gloated that no decent woman would wear all that showy lace atop the flaring blue bustle.

Mrs. Bolt chanted along with the others while she observed the woman flirting in a common and obvious fashion. The fallen woman tapped the arm of the man standing beside her. Mrs. Bolt caught the end of the hussy's sally, "I should pay the most charming bartender in Chicago more." The blonde counted four dollars into the open palm of . . .

When Mrs. Bolt recognized the face of the man, she smothered a faint shriek.

Aching with fatigue, Jessie sat at the head of the dining room table. As she slipped a handkerchief from her pocket and wiped away the perspiration at her temples, she wished summer would finally end and the cool, damp days of fall would begin. Her confrontation with her stepfather in the backyard that afternoon had shaken her.

"That was a delicious meal, Mrs. Wagstaff."

"Thank you, Mr. Chaney."

Mr. Chaney, a young carpenter journeyman, had rented Miss Greenleigh's former room yesterday.

"My condolences on the loss of your husband," the young man said.

"What?" Jessie asked, startled.

"You're still in mourning. I realized I didn't mention it yesterday. Please excuse me."

Miss Wright directed her attention across the table to the young man. "Her husband has been gone for over six years now. It's time you put mourning clothes behind you, Jessie."

Before Jessie could think of what to say to this, Lee ruffled her son's hair. "Go get the checkers and board, Linc."

Over the intervening days, Jessie kept trying to come up with a logical reason why Mr. Smith had lied to her. Had he just wanted to be connected to her and Linc? Had he just been upset that night and not understood her?

"I'll play too if you don't mind," Mr. Chaney said. Jessie hoped Mrs. Bolt wouldn't make his life miserable with her flirting. The fact the young man was over ten years younger than the redhead probably wouldn't deter the woman.

Linc brought out the game in a tattered cardboard box. The boy and Lee set up the checkers on their board.

Jessie heard a new voice in the kitchen. She stood up as Susan came through the kitchen curtain.

"Mrs. Wagstaff, your mother here."

Jessie followed Susan back into the kitchen. Ruby was hovering over Esther where she sat at the kitchen table.

At the sight of her mother's bruised and swollen face, Jessie rushed to her. "Mother!"

"That man hit her!" Ruby declared fiercely.

Jessie knelt in front of her mother, taking her hands. "It's because of me—"

"No, Jessie," Esther whispered. "This is his fault. After he went back to work, I . . . I left the twins with our neighbor. I can't go back—"

The slamming of the front door and a strident female voice shouting made the four women turn their attention from Esther.

"Mother, come quick!" Linc stood in the middle of the parted curtain. "Now!"

"Go!" Esther pushed her daughter by the shoulders.

"Now what?" Jessie got up and hurried into the dining room with Linc. Everyone except Miss Wright had risen to face Mrs. Bolt, who stood in the doorway of the dining room. Jessie halted.

"Don't try to deny it." Mrs. Bolt pointed her finger at Lee. "I saw you with that painted woman."

"What are you talking about?" Jessie demanded.

"Vile deceiver." The redhead's voice became thick with outrage.

"What are you talking about?" Jessie repeated.

"Mr. Smith is a bartender!" the redhead shouted.

Two shocks within as many minutes—her mother bruised, Lee, a bartender?

"I am a bartender." Chagrin and shame combined in Lee's voice. Linc dropped his mother's hand and went to stand beside Lee.

Mrs. Bolt's face turned scarlet. "He isn't fit to sit at the table with decent people. Out of loyalty to you, Mrs. Wagstaff, I have endured painful criticism for living here despite your outrageous behavior. My forbearance is repaid like this."

Esther came through the curtain with Ruby and Susan hovering behind her. The sight of Esther's bruised face made Miss Wright gasp. "Esther, what has happened to you?"

"Oh, Miss Wright," Esther sobbed, covering her face with her hands.

"Why isn't anyone paying attention to me?" Mrs. Bolt, hands on her hips, demanded.

"Because you wore out your welcome here months ago, you tedious ninny," snapped Miss Wright. "Pack your things. Mr. Smith isn't going to propose to you. A blind nitwit could see he's sweet on Jessie. You've stayed here for nothing."

The redhead colored to a hideous red. Her voice shook. "Is this true, Mrs. Wagstaff?"

Jessie spoke quietly without taking her eyes from Lee's face. *He's sweet on Jessie* echoed in her mind. "Mrs. Bolt, I need your room for my mother and I do think you will be happier elsewhere."

Mrs. Bolt burst into tears and rushed from the room.

Chapter 13

At midnight, Jessie finally gave up trying to sleep. Slipping on her thin cotton wrapper, she crept from her half of the parlor bedroom out to the refuge of the clematis vine–sheltered back porch. Butch, sleeping in his doghouse on the corner of the porch, opened his eyes, but closed them when she murmured his name.

The wood floor felt cool under her bare feet. Too distracted to braid her hair for the night, now she lifted her unbound hair off the back of her neck, laying it on her shoulder. The breeze brushed her neck.

Massaging her temples, she paced up and down on the rough floorboards. In her mind, Mrs. Bolt's spiteful voice repeated over and over, "Vile deceiver." Unbidden, Linc's small voice at bedtime came to mind, entreating her, "Mama, say you won't make Mr. Smith go away. Please, Mama."

What a dreadful scene. What a dreadful evening.

After a continuous tirade of venomous recriminations, Mrs. Bolt had departed. Then Jessie had done her best to soothe Linc and help her silent mother get settled in Mrs. Bolt's former room. Her mother had gone through the motions of dressing for bed like a woman walking in her sleep.

What am I going to do? Twice now Lee has deceived me. Twice that I am aware. What else might he have lied about?

When did I start thinking of him as Lee, not Mr. Smith? And what does it matter? Are either of the names are really his? And why haven't I asked, no, demanded he tell me the truth? She arched her neck backward as a wave of tension rippled through her.

She moaned in exasperation. "I'm doing it on my own again, Margaret." She took in a deep breath and let it out gradually. She heard Margaret's voice: "When a mist clouds your spiritual vision, only God's light will help you see clearly." Jessie knelt beside the porch railing. Through the cotton, the old floorboards bit into her knees. "Dear Lord, I don't understand. Help me."

Bending her head against the railing, Jessie waited for God's light. She let the muted sounds of crickets and cicadas wash over her. Her thoughts roamed. She repeated, "Father, send your light." Soon the painful pressure on her knees prompted her to lift herself to sit on the railing.

Her heart slowed to its normal pace. The throbbing in her head ebbed and disappeared. Sighing, she eased herself back against the corner beam of the railing, enjoying the cooling lake breeze swirling around her bare ankles.

She whispered, "Spirit of God, open my eyes. Help me understand why I haven't been able to confront this man?"

A wave of physical attraction rocked her. She felt warm, alive, feminine. In her imagination, she felt strong arms surrounding her, Lee's arms. She leaped to her feet, her heart pounding. "No," she whispered.

"Jessie?"

She whirled around. "Lee?"

"I'm sorry . . . I couldn't sleep. I didn't . . . I had no idea anyone would be out here."

Barefoot and clad only in her thin gown and robe, she felt stripped of the everyday barriers between men and women. She stepped back into the deeper shadows close to the house while her awareness of him burned its ways through her senses. His chestnut hair was tousled. Though he still wore his dark slacks, he was shirtless. His bare skin in the scant moonlight made her hands tremble. She imagined it as satin under her fingertips.

Her prayer for understanding had been answered. She had not confronted him because she was attracted to him. Why hadn't she gauged her spiraling desire? Was she so blind to her own weakness?

"I'll go back in," he mumbled.

"No." She held up her hand as though reaching for him.

He turned toward her, but stopped when she folded her arms.

"I think we need to talk." She swallowed, trying to relieve the dryness of her mouth. Her mind whirled. She could keep silent no longer, but she first had to protect herself from her forbidden attraction to him. "Sit on the steps with your back to me."

Hesitating, Lee tried to think of something to say, but then gingerly obeyed. His face toward the alley, he rubbed his moist palms on the tops of his thighs. "I'm sorry about all this—about my job. That blasted redhead . . ." In agonized uncertainty, he waited for her response. "Would you like me to change my line of work?"

"That isn't important now." Jessie's voice shook. "I want you to tell me what your real name is."

The words shimmered in the air around Lee's head. Pinpricks tingled up and down his spine.

"I know Lee Smith died in sixty-five."

Earlier, when Mrs. Bolt had called him "Vile deceiver," he'd thought she'd discovered he was living under an alias. *But how could Jessie already have known? Why hadn't she confronted him before?* He almost choked on words, explanations, lies.

"I've known since just a few days after Reverend Mitchell's death that you'd given me a false name."

He stood up and spun toward her.

She retreated from him farther into the shadows of the trellis.

"I can't believe you've known, but said nothing," he said.

"Is there a warrant out for you? Do you owe money?" Her voice was cool, demanding. The warm, responsive woman he had held only days before had vanished.

"Nothing like that."

"You've taken a dead man's name and I have to know why—"

He started pacing. "I spent five years trying to forget the war—running from the past. Finally I couldn't run anymore. I came here to start over." He halted, only a few steps from her.

"Who are you?" Her tone was implacable.

She was Jessie. He couldn't tell her the truth. He had to stall her. It was his only defense. "I need time."

"Time? How will time change the truth?"

He laughed without humor. "Oh, Jessie, you're so . . . Jessie."

"What does that mean?" she asked indignantly.

"I thought once you decided something was right and must be achieved, you'd pursue it to the ends of the earth."

"*I* am not the issue here. Who are you?"

He groaned and raked his fingers through his hair. He couldn't let her know who he was. She hadn't yet connected him with Dr. Smith. The price of practicing medicine again could be the loss of the blessed sanity of his first sober year in decades. He couldn't chance a final descent into drink and delirium tremens.

"Who are you?" Relentless, Jessie prompted him.

The whole truth could destroy him, destroy their chance together. How much of the truth could he tell her without revealing that he was a doctor? "I still haven't been able to let . . . the war go," he stammered. "I hate the cliché, but I couldn't run away from my past."

"But you must still be running away if it keeps you from telling me the truth."

He flinched. She had jabbed a needle right in the center of his wounded soul. He knew she would never be able to understand why he could never again risk making the life and death decisions a doctor must always be prepared to make. "Do you think it's easy to face the ugly truth?"

"The truth will set you free."

"Don't quote scripture to me."

"I cannot have a man who is living a lie around my son. I cannot allow Linc to be in danger of heartbreak. If you are hiding something that—in the end—will force you to abandon him . . . or shatter his trust in you. . . ."

He groped madly for an explanation or distraction. More and more he had become aware of her nearness, of the fragrance of lavender that clung to her, of the impression of her dark hair swept to one side of her head, its waves, a cascade down one of her slim shoulders.

He took a step closer. "Nothing I've ever been or have ever done can harm Linc. That's the truth."

"You've lied to me. How can I believe you?"

"I can show you why you should believe me," he said persuasively.

"How?"

He slid forward, tucking her into his arms. She gasped, but resisted only a moment. He sensed her acquiescence and breathed in the scent of her, exulting in this intimacy. "Oh, Jessie, you are the most irritating woman, the most determined, the most giving. And you don't know how irresistible you are."

Jessie struggled with herself. His touch was fire and it was all she craved and more. But moments ago she had stepped away from him, torn by unanswered questions. Her body and mind wrestled for control. As he began to stroke her back through the thin cotton, she gave up trying to think and shivered with his touch.

"Jessie," he whispered, "can't we let the dead past bury itself? Jessie, the truth is I want to kiss you." Not waiting for permission, his lips sought hers.

She turned her face as though to avoid them, but her lips wouldn't obey her. They wanted Lee's kiss. And his kiss was full and sweet.

She trembled with the same passion as she had just moments before he'd joined her. Her conscience fought to the surface of this sensual undertow. She pushed herself out of his embrace. "No."

With arms suddenly empty, he stumbled a step forward and then halted.

"I wanted you to kiss me, but I can't let that sway me. I must know the truth." She stepped another step backward and folded her arms in front of her, warning him away.

"I'll tell you everything," he pleaded, "when the time is right."

"When will that be?"

"I can't say." He reached out to her.

She turned her back to him.

"Don't go. Jessie, I can't lose you."

She bent her chin to her breast, pondering. Then she lifted her head, though she faced away from him. "I'll give you one more month. April to November is six months. If you can't be honest with me after we've known each other half a year, then it's better we part." She turned to confront him, her voice emotionless. "If you can't tell the truth by then, you'll have to make some excuse to Linc for leaving town and go."

He felt icy fingers of despair clutch his heart. *One month and then I lose her and Linc.*

October 2, 1871

Lee stood outside staring up at the three-story brick building's sign, "Field & Leiter's Department Store." Glancing at his reflection in the gleaming shop window, he straightened his tie. His leave-taking from the Workman's Rest had been a delicate operation. He honestly liked Pearl Flesher and felt he had led her on with his teasing encouragement of her flirtation. Therefore, he had employed all his tact and finesse with aplomb to leave her employment without wounding her with the truth. All for naught. When he'd turned to leave her, Pearl had asked, "So what's her name, handsome?"

He shouldn't have been surprised. Pearl was nobody's fool. "Jessie."

She had nodded. "Good for you. Let us know how you get on, okay?"

Thus Pearl had shone herself a lady. Mrs. Bolt would not agree, but the redhead had shown her true colors to all.

Lee walked into Field's and headed to the desk at the rear of the first floor, impressed by the fine wood paneling, the polished marble columns and floors.

After two preliminary interviews with floor managers, Lee, ushered into a small, but commodious office, introduced himself to Mr. Field. The interview ended with a handshake and an offer to begin the next day to train as a salesman in the Gentlemen's Finer Attire Department. Working at Mr. Field's department store would certainly be a contrast to bartending. Since he couldn't tell Jess the truth about his past, he had to convince her the past was dead and gone, his future was all she need be concerned about.

Outside, Lee paused to tip his hat to a fashionable lady. He felt like tipping his hat to the world. Lee whistled as he planned the best way to tell Jessie about his change in employment.

On his way home, he passed Drexel Park. A young woman walked by him pushing a honey-colored wicker buggy. He glimpsed the rosy bundle inside. Suddenly he pictured Jess strolling with their child. The image was electrifying. A family of their own. *Jessie and he. Wife and husband. Mother and father.*

In white aprons, Jessie and her mother sat at the kitchen table. Jessie peeled one potato after the other with deft, swift strokes.

Esther still held her first potato, untouched. "I never meant to neglect you. When Hiram courted me, he was so polite to you. He said he'd treat you as his own."

"He's not much kinder to the twins."

"I know, but when we were courting, he showed me such courtesy, such respect . . ."

"Is that why you married him? It wasn't love, was it?"

Closing her eyes, Esther sighed sorrowfully. "No, I've never loved Hiram, not the way I loved your father. Maybe a woman only loves that way once. Your father died so young and neither of us had much family to fall back on. Times were hard. By the time Hiram proposed to me, I was nearly desperate."

"So you married him?"

"Yes, he was a decent Christian man and he was the only one who wanted me." Her voice cracked on the last word.

"Mother." Jessie wiped her hand on her apron, then touched her mother's hand briefly.

"I've prayed and prayed, but he never changes. I don't blame God. How can He change a man who thinks there's no need to change since he's about as perfect as a mortal can be? He gives no room for God at all. He attends church. He reads his Bible, but nothing touches him. Sometimes I have felt that I married a man of brick and iron."

Jessie kept her eyes on the potato she was peeling, embarrassed to hear the pain in her mother's voice.

"Every harsh word he ever said to you broke a bit of my heart. A change in Hiram's heart—I have prayed for that—for over twenty years. I would give anything, to change his heart, fill it with God's healing love."

"He'd have to grow a heart first."

"Please, daughter. Don't let what happened to me make you bitter. You and Will were so happy with each other and Mr. Smith is so good with Linc—"

The scene from the night before—Lee holding her in his arms— swooped into Jessie's mind. The passion she'd felt in his arms sluiced through her senses, undiluted by the passing of the night. How glad she was that she'd stepped away. She'd been playing with fire last night. Never again.

Jessie spoke, her voice shaking: "I will never take the chance you did. I knew when I lost Will, I would raise Linc alone. My son can't have his father, but he will have me—all of me. I will never re-marry." *Lee, there will be no more kisses in the dark.*

"Jessie, please don't say that. If not Mr. Smith, what about that doctor?"

"He has never said anything about courting me. I think he's come to realize it's not possible." Jessie hoped she was speaking the truth. She didn't want an embarrassing scene with Dr. Gooden.

"Daughter, I've made my mistakes. Don't make decisions for your life based on mine. God has given you a life different from mine. You are very different than I. You have more fire and spirit."

Jessie looked at her mother. She didn't quite understand what her mother meant. She knew she'd only wanted to be the wife of Will Wagstaff and nothing had changed that.

Linc held up his small slate board. "Mother, look Mr. Smith helped me with my arithmetic."

Jessie sat at the end of the dining table, knitting another pair of socks for Linc. In the heat of the room, she wondered if the cooling autumn winds would ever come. "That's good, Linc." She smiled mechanically. "Now why don't you go do your problems sitting by Butch?"

Miss Wright dozed in a rocking chair. By the window Mr. Chaney was reading an evening paper while Esther read her Bible. She had not realized how irritating Mrs. Bolt had been until they were free of her. Eileene Greenleigh had been correct in her advice. The circle of people around the table provided more of what a growing boy needed.

Jessie hoped the steady clicking of her needles would calm her. Linc shouldn't be allowed to become any closer to Mr. Smith. And she needed to distance herself, too. How?

The front door opened with a bang. "I'm here to get my wife." Hiram's voice shattered their tranquillity. Jessie dropped her knitting. Esther hopped up and started for the kitchen.

"Don't run away, Mrs. Huff," Lee said. He rose. Mr. Chaney, folding his paper, also moved to stand beside Lee in front of the women. Hiram stalked in.

"Good evening, Mr. Huff," Lee said.

Ignoring Lee, Hiram tried to push past him. Jessie felt her pulse race.

Lee's arm shot out, checking the other man. "I said good evening."

Hiram shifted his attention to Lee. "I'm here to take my wife home where she belongs."

Jessie opened her mouth, but was cut off.

"At the moment Mrs. Huff's home is here." Lee stood firm, blocking the other man's path.

"This has—" Hiram jabbed his finger into Lee's shirtfront with each syllable— "no-thing-to-do-with-you."

Jessie stood up and Esther took a few steps back.

"Hiram Huff, you are just like your mother." Miss Wright's strident voice startled them all. "Your mother moved here and into my fourth grade and she was an officious little brat even then."

Jessie couldn't believe her ears.

At first, even Hiram's shocked response stuck and garbled in his throat, then he declared, "This has nothing to do with my mother."

"It has everything to do with why you have lost one of the sweetest wives in Chicago. Esther is a saint because only a saint could have stayed married to you for over twenty years."

Hiram's face turned a beefy red. "Esther, I'm taking you home tonight."

Esther drew herself up, "Hiram, when you decide to keep your vows to me, I will come home."

"You are making no sense." Pushing Lee aside, Hiram started forward again, but halted when Mr. Chaney moved between Hiram and his wife.

"It's simple," Esther continued, "I want your love, Hiram, and not only for me, but for my three children, too."

"Your children. Hah! A lot you cared for your children. Leaving them alone while I went to work. I can't believe you abandoned them like that."

Jessie shook, holding back hot words.

Esther said, "I would have brought them with me if I had the wherewithal to provide for them. But I couldn't expect my widowed daughter to take in two more mouths to feed."

"The twins are always welcome," Jessie said with all the dignity she could muster.

"Keep out of this, missy," Hiram growled. "This is all your fault. You're the one who drove a wedge between me and my wife."

"No, she isn't," Esther said.

"Esther, if you persist in this folly, I will make certain you never see your sons again."

Esther blanched and covered her mouth with her hand.

"I think we've had enough of you tonight," Lee said, then took Hiram by the back of his collar and seat of his pants and propelled him past Susan and out the front door.

Jessie couldn't stop shaking.

Lee returned, dusting his hands. "I've wanted to do that ever since I met that man."

Ruby stepped into the room. "Miss Esther, you come in the kitchen. I make you a cup a tea." Esther, wiping away tears, agreed and followed Ruby. Mr. Chaney bid them all a tactful good night and went upstairs.

Jessie heaved herself back into her chair. "I feel as though I have just run a mile."

"Strong emotion always takes its toll," Miss Wright said.

Lee rounded on her. "You, our dear Miss Wright, deserve an award. No one else could have said what you did and have gotten away with it."

Miss Wright let a momentary hint of a smile flutter over her features. "The man's a fool, but that doesn't help our dear Esther.

He will keep her from her boys and he will make her as miserable as he is able."

"I'm afraid he is a top hand at making people miserable," Jessie said bleakly.

Miss Wright struggled to her feet. "Only God can melt a heart of stone like Hiram Huff's."

"But so far God hasn't seen fit to act." Jessie massaged her neck muscles with one hand.

Miss Wright turned to her. "If you start telling God what to do or if you let yourself hate Hiram Huff, you'll be no better than he is. And I don't care what you think, that *is* what Margaret would say."

Jessie stared at the old woman in surprise.

Miss Wright grunted with pain and hobbled from the room, but tonight even her cane thumping was subdued.

"Are you all right, Jess?" Lee sat down in the chair beside her.

His closeness made her feel like a canary with a tomcat at its cage door. "I'm fine. I thought my stepfather would come sometime, and he'll come again." She stood.

"Most likely. But you aren't alone." He stretched out his hand to take hers.

Jessie ignored this gesture. She didn't want to be alone with Mr. Smith. "I'm going to the kitchen to help Ruby and Susan comfort my mother."

Looking disconcerted, Lee shoved his hands into his pockets. "I'll go out and keep Linc and Butch company."

They both passed through to the kitchen. He went on out the back door while Jessie sat down in the chair next to her mother.

"Miss Jessie, you want some tea, too?" Ruby asked from the stove where she stood by the kettle making the thrumming sound of water near boiling.

"No, thank you, Ruby."

"Grandma, you come sit down," Susan said. "I'll make the tea."

"You ironed all day long," Ruby objected. "Sit. I'm too old to do much but I kin still boil water."

Esther wiped her eyes with a lacy handkerchief. "I'm so sorry, Jessie. I don't know what poor Mr. Chaney thought of such a scene."

"Don't worry, Mother. He seemed to take it in stride."

"He a nice boy, that's for sure." Ruby shuffled ponderously, carrying the steaming tea kettle to the table and set it on a cast iron trivet.

"I surely was glad he and Mr. Smith was here." Susan folded her arms over her breast. "But don't you fret. We'll make sure that husband of yours don't fine you alone."

"Best he not fine her here a-tall," Ruby spoke up, surprising Jessie.

"Grandma," Susan scolded.

"I don't mean what you thinking. I mean this lady should shake that man up good. Let him know she ain't gone put up with his orneriness no more."

"What do you mean, Ruby?" Esther dried the last of her tears.

"I mean he think you depending on him alone. He think he just need to talk and talk and get mad and finally you come home."

"Yes," Jessie encouraged.

Ruby pointed to Esther with her free hand. "You need to get you some new clothes and wear them where he kin see you. You need a new bonnet, new gloves. You need to make him see that you ain't gone just sit around crying over him."

"But how?" Esther asked.

"You go get you a job." Ruby nodded with each of her words. "Not cooking or cleaning—get something at one of them big stores I seen downtown. That'll make him worry." Ruby poured out the steaming water into the teacups.

Could Ruby be right? Jessie wondered.

Ruby sat down and picked up her teacup.

"I'll do it," Esther said quietly.

"A job? Mother, I don't want—"

Esther sat up straighter. "Don't tell me what I can and can't do, Jessie. Hiram's done that for twenty-three years. Besides I don't want to be dependent on you and you don't need me with Susan and Ruby to help you around here—"

"Mother—"

"No, Hiram Huff thinks I'll come crawling back to him. If I take a job and begin making my own way in the world, maybe he'll take me seriously. In any event it'll give me something more to do than cry all the time." She smiled at Ruby. "Thank you."

Lee and Linc came in. "Linc's homework is done. I'm going to walk him to his room."

"I'll come, too." Jessie stood up. Maybe now would be a good time to tell Mr. Smith that she wanted him to begin distancing himself from her son. Unless he'd decided to reveal the truth. The three of them walked through the dining room to the foyer. Linc submitted to having his hair ruffled by Lee and to being kissed by his mother. Then he went into their half of the curtained-divided parlor. Jessie slid the pocket door nearly shut. Then she found herself face-to-face with Lee.

"I'd like to talk to you privately," Lee murmured.

"I need to stable the goat. Would you like to come with me?" Jessie led him outside.

Lee felt awkward. Maybe it was due to Hiram Huff's visit. Jess untied the goat from her stake. In the alley, Lee propped open the shed door and Jessie led the goat in. The musky smell of goat surrounded them and the chickens were already tutting in their roost for the night. Jessie murmured soothing sounds to the nanny as she tied her rope to the ring in the wall.

"Jess, tomorrow I begin training for a position in Gentlemen's Finer Attire at Field & Leiter's."

"I don't care what you are now. What were you?"

"Jess." His right arm hooked the inside of her elbow and swept her into his arms.

She tried to push herself out of his arms.

"Please listen, Jess. Today I turned over a new leaf. I'm going to prove to you I'm worthy—"

"You don't have to prove anything to me. Just tell me the truth." Her eyes avoided his.

"The truth is I'm not the same man I was when I came to Chicago. The past doesn't matter to us—only the future, our future together," he said persuasively.

Pulling away, Jessie scattered fresh straw over the floor.

"It's hard to put my feelings into words because I never thought I would ever say them to anyone. Jess, will you be my wife?"

Jessie took a step back from him. "I won't remarry."

He couldn't believe her words. "But we . . . I have fallen in love with you, Jessie. Doesn't that mean anything to you?"

"I thought you realized. I've always been careful never to—"

He felt himself stir, feel frantic. "Jess, you don't understand. I feel . . . everything's changed." He rushed to explain what he'd experienced earlier. Certainly she'd understand. "Today in the park, a young woman was out walking her baby. Suddenly I wanted it to be *our baby*." He searched her expression for a softening from understanding of what he was trying to express.

Jessie avoided his eyes. "I will never remarry."

"You can't tell me you don't have feelings for me. I am the man you were kissing last night—"

"I'm sorry if I mislead you."

"Why are you doing this? We could have a good life together." Panic twisted his stomach.

"I do not want Linc to grow up under a stepfather—"

"Under a stepfather? You can't mean you think I'm like Hiram Huff." His heart began to pound.

"No, of course, not." She frowned. The nanny goat settled down into its bed of straw, her bell clanging dully.

"Then you're not being logical. I would never treat Linc like your stepfather treated you."

"You wouldn't mean to——"

"You're wrong." He tried to sound logical though his fear was rampant now. He reached out to take her hands.

She took a step back from him and came up against the back wall of the shed. "You're wrong. Don't you see?"

"No, I don't." He now understood the saying "hot under the collar," and couldn't keep the sarcasm out of his tone. "Explain to me how I'd treat Linc like *your* stepfather."

Jessie's face flushed. "You said it yourself. You said 'our baby.' Lincoln will never be 'our baby.'"

"What has that to do with anything?" he demanded.

"If we married, we'd always have a divided home. There would always be *my* son and *your* children."

Lee flung up his hands. "You're not making sense. I love Linc."

She drew herself up. "You're not making sense. How could I marry a man who won't even tell me his name."

Her last words left him silent and staring angrily into her stormy eyes.

Finally Jessie said in a taut voice, "I'll bid you good night." She pushed past Lee and left him standing alone in the deep twilight.

Chapter 14

October 6, 1871

At first, Lee couldn't think, then he hurried inside Jessie's front door. He yanked his hat and jacket from hooks and scuttled down the front steps. Raging against women's illogical thinking and Hiram Huff's hypocrisy, Lee broke into headlong retreat.

Heedless of direction, he hurried down block after block. Finally a church clock tolling ten stopped him. Looking around the night-shrouded street, he found he was on the South Side near railroad tracks where shabby dwellings huddled among warehouses.

He rubbed his face with one hand as though trying to clear away the turmoil in his mind. *I should go home to bed. I have a new job in the morning.* But going home and meekly to bed—in the room above Jessie's—struck him as impossible. As impossible as convincing Jessie that his past was not important to them.

He began trudging the darkened streets again. *I can't expect her to understand what it meant to live through the war as a surgeon. No one who didn't go through it could understand.*

Suddenly he needed to hear someone agree with him. Mentally he went through the short list of men he had become acquainted with in the past months. He recalled Jessie mentioned Caleb had served in the Union Army, too. Caleb didn't like him.

Still, the idea appealed to Lee. He didn't want platitudes about duty or any other soothing pap. He needed a man who would be completely frank, a man who would understand the way the war had really been, not the way people were already beginning to romanticize it. Caleb would understand. Lee looked around and figured out how to reach the late Reverend's house.

In the warm summerlike night, he heard the faint clanging of a fire bell. Small brush fires on vacant lots had become commonplace after a summer-long drought. His heartbeat matched the pealing of the discordant bells. When Lee found the one-room house, no light shone in the window. Lee hesitated in the yard, thinking what to do.

"What are you doing here?"

Startled out of his thoughts, Lee whipped around. "Caleb."

Caleb stopped in front of him, leaning forward belligerently. "I asked what are you doing here."

"I . . . I just came to talk." Lee knew it sounded lame as an explanation, but it was, after all, the truth.

"Why?"

The man's unconcealed hostility turned Lee's stomach sour. Still he went on, "I . . . you . . . I need to talk to another veteran."

Caleb pushed past him. "All right. Come in." Lee followed, sorry he had come. While Caleb struck a match and lit a lamp on the table in the center of the room, Lee stood by the door. He remembered too clearly the Reverend's death in this house.

The circumstances of tonight's visit already rendered him uncomfortable. And he couldn't look around the room without seeing it filled with phantom mourners and hear again the melodies they'd sung.

"Sit."

Lee could recall hearing warmer welcomes from Southern women pointing loaded rifles at him. He eased down on a ladder-backed chair near the sputtering lamp.

Caleb swung his chair around backward and sat down astride it; his long arms draped over the chair back.

"It's difficult not to think of your father—"

"You hardly knew him—"

"I didn't have to know him long to respect him, just seeing him die . . . He was an exceptional man."

"Thank you." Caleb's tone was grudging. His face twisted. "What did you come to talk about?"

Lee shifted in his seat. *How to start?* "What was your outfit?"

"I was with the Fifty-fourth Massachusetts Regiment. And you? . . . Susan told me you were with Mrs. Wagstaff's husband?"

"Yes." *But I wasn't Smith, the ambulance driver.* Lee didn't know how to go on. Silent seconds ticked by.

Caleb slapped a hand down on the tabletop. "Are you going to tell me why you're here or am I supposed to guess?"

The man's sarcastic tone goaded Lee. "I need someone, someone who went through the war, who will understand—"

"Understand what?" Caleb barked.

Lee grimaced. "I was with Will Wagstaff, but I'm not Lee Smith."

"You lied to Mrs. Wagstaff?"

"I had to—"

"Who are you?"

Caleb had Lee cornered and it was all Lee's own fault. He'd wanted to rid himself of the guilt he carried by telling someone his awful secret, to be absolved, not challenged. But in a haze of half-baked emotion, he'd gone to the wrong person. The Reverend's son would, of course, side with Jessie. But Lee had come too far to turn back. He propped his elbows on his knees and buried his forehead into his hands. "Did you ever spend time in an army field hospital?"

"I carried a few comrades to them." Caleb's voice sounded wary.

"Did any of them live?"

"One did."

"What did he lose?" Lee asked grimly.

"An eye."

"A fortunate man." Lee exhaled and sat up. "I have nightmares of those awful days and nights. The screams and moans still have the power to wake me. The stench of the blood and sweat . . . You've been there. You know what I'm talking about."

In the low lamplight, Caleb nodded reluctantly. "I know Mrs. Wagstaff's husband served in the Union army with the Sanitary Corp. It sounds like you were, too. What did you lie about?"

Lee took a deep breath. "I'm not *Lee* Smith. He was an ambulance driver who served with us till he died in sixty-four. My name is Leland Granger Smith."

"So?"

"Will was my best friend. I'm *Dr.* Smith."

"Doctor? You're a doctor. You mean you stood by when my father died and you did nothing!" His fists clenched, Caleb reared up like a fighter coming into the ring.

Lee flung his hands up. "No medicine can give an old man a new heart. I did what I could for your father!"

Caleb halted, breathing hard. For long moments his eyes fixed on Lee's face. Then he settled down again on his chair and ran his big hands over his forehead. "I guess you're right about that."

Lee lowered his own arms. "All I could do was make him more comfortable . . ."

"And pronounce him dead."

Lee gave a dry, bitter laugh. "I had plenty of practice at that. I could do it in my sleep. I often did."

"I still don't get what your problem is. Just tell Mrs. Wagstaff. She'll understand. You've been good to her son."

"I want to marry her."

"So?"

Lee resented the question, but he had started this and he must finish it. "How can I tell her I'm a doctor when she has been looking for one all summer?"

"Just tell her the truth and offer your services."

"Well, now that's the rub," Lee said, his pulse speeding. "I can't ever practice medicine again."

"Why not?"

Lee's face twisted into a mockery of a smile. "Practice peacetime medicine? I wouldn't know how. I came straight out of medical school into the army. For four years, all I did was dig out bullets, cut off shattered or gangrenous limbs, and stitch up sword and bayonet slashes. I'm no physician. I'm a butcher. Give me a slab of meat—not a human."

Caleb didn't speak at first. "You could start over, learn."

"I can't. Can't you see? Just the thought of doctoring again makes me literally sick to my stomach. My hands shake just thinking of holding a scalpel. You were there. I can't explain it to Jess. She couldn't know what it was like."

"She's a good woman. You'd just have to take time—"

"No. I can't face it. I can't even talk to her about it. In the last two years of the war, Will, my best friend, and alcohol were the only things that kept me going. And after Will died, that left only whiskey."

"Susan told me you quit being a bartender, but she didn't tell me you drank."

"I don't drink anymore. But I wasn't sober from the night Will died until early this year." In spite of the stuffiness of the room, Lee shivered sharply. He couldn't stop now. "It's more than that. My family hushed it up, but the army sent me home under restraint. I was out of my mind with drink, with . . ." He fought the images of that last hellish night of surgery when he'd begun screaming and couldn't stop. Even when he was too hoarse to make a sound, he'd gone on. A cold sweat broke over Lee, shaking.

"What brought you to Chicago, then? If you didn't want to face this, why come to Will's family?"

Lee clamped his legs together and clutched the sides of the chair. The trembling lessened. He cleared his thickened throat. "I promised Will I'd take care of Jessie and his son."

"I see." Caleb bent his elbow to the chairback and rested his chin on his fist. "You lied to Mrs. Wagstaff, so she wouldn't have to know you were a doctor. Now you need to tell her the truth because you want to marry her." He looked up. "Why not just keep on lying?"

Distant fire bells started up again, sending their message of danger. They suited Lee's mood. Alarms within. Alarms without. "She read some of Will's letters and found out Lee Smith was dead. She's known since a few days after your father's death."

"That long? That's not like Mrs. Wagstaff. She doesn't stand for things for a minute. There's your answer. Susan was right."

"What's my answer?"

"Mrs. Wagstaff cares about you. She's not a woman to hide from the truth. She must have feelings for you or she would have had it out with you right then and there." Caleb sounded sincere.

"You think so?" Lee wanted to believe him.

"She'll be upset when you tell her, but she can't make you practice medicine—on whites or blacks—if you don't want to."

"I'm afraid I'll lose her and Linc." Saying the words made Lee sick with dread.

"She'll be angry. She has a right to be. I don't like people lying to me—"

Lee's pulse raced. "Jessie and Linc mean everything to me!" *Without them, I don't have a life.* He couldn't say this out loud.

"She'll forgive you," Caleb said it almost kindly. "You have to trust her."

"I'm afraid I'll lose her."

"If you don't tell her, you *will* lose her." Caleb's words, though spoken quietly, hit and echoed through Lee like a hammerblow.

Jessie and her mother stood looking at Field & Leiter's Department Store. Esther gave her a nervous smile. "It's a very imposing, isn't it?"

"You don't have to do this, Mother."

"No, Ruby is right. I must help myself."

"Very well." Entering, Jessie escorted her mother to the store office, where a gentleman asked Esther to his desk for an interview. Jessie squeezed her mother's hand. "I'll go browse, but I'll be back. I'll meet you here."

Esther nodded timorously, then went with the gentleman.

Jessie wandered through the aisles. With money so dear, she rarely let herself enter a store. Today would be a rare treat. In the millinery department, a hat on a mannequin head brought her to a complete stop. It was fashioned like a wing, reddish brown like oak leaves. It sported a pheasant tail feather over the crown and in front a delicate veil to draw across the face. Her fingers itched to lift it from the form and set it on own her head.

"May I help?" A young, modish saleswoman approached.

"No, I—I was merely browsing." Jessie felt like she'd been caught stealing and had the urge to run out of the store.

"Certainly, but wouldn't you like to try that on?" The woman nodded toward the striking hat.

"N-No, I really shouldn't," Jessie stammered.

The woman scanned the nearly empty department. She smiled and said conspiratorially, "Why not try it on—just for fun? I'm not busy. Come sit down."

Jessie objected feebly but soon found herself sitting in front of an ornate vanity with trifold mirrors. The young woman removed Jessie's worn bonnet and arranged the new hat on her crown, securing it with hat pins.

The transformation in Jessie's appearance was so startling for a few seconds, she couldn't speak.

"An excellent choice," the saleslady murmured. "It brings out the warmth in your hair and eyes."

Jessie, unaccustomed to compliments, blushed. She half rose. The woman gently urged her back into her chair. "The effect isn't complete yet. Allow me." The woman reached into a drawer of the vanity and lifted out a large silk scarf of the same rich autumn hue, which she draped over Jessie's shoulders.

Her reflection as a staid widow vanished from the mirror. Looking back at her was the image of a comely, young woman with russet-tinged brown hair. She gasped, "It doesn't look like me."

"I've seen this happen before. When a woman has been in mourning for a year or more, she forgets how she looked in colors. Have you been in mourning for more than a year?"

Jessie nodded. *Six years*.

"Out of respect for the loved one, it's difficult to leave off mourning clothes, but your loved one would want you to go on living. You are young and attractive. It's time you let it show again."

The words sank into Jessie's mind and heart like misty rain on a dry garden. Inside, a tight clasp—which had trapped her spirit—swung open. A thrill of pleasure shimmered through her. "How much is this?"

"Only one dollar and seventy-five cents. A bargain."

"Oh." Jessie's voice fell. "I don't have that much with me."

"We have an easy time-payment plan. Merely put down fifty percent and then you can make a few weekly payments and it's yours."

Jessie's conscience balked, but one glance at the reflection in the mirror silenced it. "I'll take it."

As she watched the saleslady wrap the hat delicately in tissue paper and tie it up in a charming mauve hatbox striped with gold, she felt free, airy. In her whole adult life, this was her first extravagance. And Lee came to mind. "Where is Gentlemen's Finer Attire?" she asked.

The saleslady handed her the ribbon-handle of the box. "Upstairs."

"Thank you."

"I'm happy you found such a flattering hat. I hope you'll let me serve you again."

With quick, light steps she ascended the marble and mahogany staircase. When she topped the steps and scanned the second floor, she located the gentlemen's department easily, but she did not see Lee. She walked among the mannequins, displaying men's suits that fit the description of Gentlemen's Finer Attire. Then she saw Lee just beyond her in the aisle.

Jessie felt herself beaming. She paused behind two mannequins, trying to decide why she'd sought him. She hadn't seen him since she left him the night before in the goat shed. When he hadn't come home by morning, she had worried in spite of herself.

Before Jessie could come out from behind the mannequins, a tall, elegantly dressed woman glided up to him. "Leland, is it really you?"

"Eugenia! Sister!" Lee exclaimed. "What are you doing here?"

"Well, I surmised that Chicago might be where you'd gone to start over. So when Mrs. Field invited me here to consult with her about charity work, I thought it would be the perfect opportunity to try to discover if I were right and how you were."

"Charity work?"

Jessie echoed his question. Her mind frantically tried to make sense of this.

Eugenia continued, "If you had been paying any attention to your family in the last six years, you would have known I've made myself one of the foremost women in the nation—"

"Yes, yes, Eugenia, I'm sure you have. Did you really come looking for me?"

"Yes, but I never expected to find you without even trying. I had asked Mrs. Field about doctors here, trying . . . Good heavens, Leland, you don't *work* here, do you?"

Doctor. Jessie's temples throbbed. *He couldn't be.*

"Yes, sister dear, I am employed here in Gentlemen's Finer Attire."

"Leland, with all your education. Couldn't you find something more appropriate?"

"I told you in Boston, I will never practice medicine again."

He is a doctor. Jessie clutched the hatbox ribbon with both hands. *Dr. Smith?*

"Very well. Father and I never understood why you wanted to be a doctor."

"That is old news, sister."

Not to me, Jessie wanted to shout.

"How's our esteemed father?"

"I don't know why you never could get along with father—"

"Eugenia, do we have to go over ancient history? How long are you going to be in Chicago?"

"Just another few days. Tonight the Fields are hosting a soiree in my honor at the Hotel Tremont." A self-satisfied smile lifted Eugenia's long, plain face.

"Indeed?"

"Yes," Eugenia lowered her voice, "and though I realized Mrs. Field invited me to advance socially, I've found her to be not quite as gauche as I had thought she'd be. And Mr. Field is quite droll."

"I thought so myself."

"Do you know him?" Eugenia's eyes widened.

"He interviewed me for this job."

Eugenia put her hand to her forehead.

Jessie felt like screaming at the patronizing woman.

"Don't worry, sis. I'm using the name, Mr. Lee Smith, not Dr. Leland Granger Smith."

"Thank goodness!"

Lee chuckled. "And I'm afraid I will be unable to attend tonight's soiree. My evening clothes are still in Boston."

"Your regrettable sense of humor, Leland." She shook her head at him.

Alternate flashes of heat and cold coursed through Jessie. How could Lee be Dr. Leland Granger Smith, her Will's best friend? She'd read Dr. Smith's name on the death lists, but there'd been so many mistakes on those lists. Dr. Smith hadn't died. Giddy, she was afraid to move for fear she'd faint.

"You should give me your address in case I ever need to get in touch with you."

"Send any letters here to Lee Smith. If I quit, I will leave a forwarding address with the office."

"Very well. Oh, did you locate your friend Will's widow?"

A silent gasp caught in Jessie's throat. *It was all true.*

"Yes, I did. I'm staying at her boardinghouse."

Looking over her brother's shoulder at a large, free-standing mirror, Eugenia adjusted her hat. "And how about her poor little son?"

Jessie's face flamed.

"He's not a poor little boy. He's great lad."

"Of course." Eugenia glanced at the gold pendant watch that was pinned to her gray bodice. "I'm sure they are grateful for your help."

Lee spoke stiffly, "So far Mrs. Wagstaff won't accept any money from me."

"A charity case with foolish pride. Ah, there is Mrs. Field." Eugenia wagged one finger to another well-dressed lady and turned away from Lee. "Goodbye, brother."

"Miss Smith," Jessie overheard the other lady say. The rest of her sentence was lost to Jessie in her welter of emotions.

Now she knew this man was Will's unlikely best friend, Dr. Smith, son of a wealthy Boston banking family. Dr. Granger had defied his family by taking up medicine, then by enlisting as an army surgeon. And this man's sister thought of her and Linc as just another "charity case." *Foolish pride?* Her face flaming with outrage and shame, Jessie whirled away down the steps.

The nearby church bell tolled six times. Though the sunlight was deepening into dusk, the heat of the long day was undiminished. Jessie, alone on her front porch, paced.

"Jessie, what is it?" Her mother finally returned from Field & Leiter's.

Jessie halted, wringing her hands. "How did your interview go?"

"I'm glad you didn't wait for me. I started in Infant's Wear immediately. I love it." Then Esther came up the porch steps. "What is the matter, Jessie?"

"Nothing—"

"Look at your hands!"

Jessie glanced downward and immediately let her hands drop to her sides. "Please go in. Tell Susan to go ahead and serve dinner without me."

"Jessie?"

"Please, Mother."

Esther paused at the front door to cast a worried glance at her daughter. With a shake of her head, she left her.

Back and forth, Jessie paced, her hands knotted together and pressed to her mouth. She waited for Lee.

"Mama, why won't you come to supper?" Linc appeared beside her.

"Lincoln, it's nothing you need to be concerned about—"

Lee sauntered around the corner of the block, headed right for them. Jessie panicked. "Lincoln, you must go in *now*." She pushed him toward the door, but, seeing Lee approaching, Linc struggled against her.

Lee walked up the steps. "Lincoln, if your mother wants you to go in, do so immediately."

The boy ceased struggling and the door closed behind him. "What is it, Jess? You're upset with me, but—"

"Upset?" She forced her voice to stay low. "I'm incensed. Why didn't you tell me you were Will's friend, Dr. Smith?"

Lee's mouth opened in shock.

"You're a doctor and you knew how I needed one! How could you keep still?"

"How . . . how—"

"Today at Field & Leiter's I saw your sister—and heard her. Foolish pride." Her face burned again. "Yes, I suppose I am only a charity case to you, but, at least, I know how to tell the truth."

"Jessie, listen—"

"Your valise is here and inside is the money you paid for next week. Don't come back." She spun away from him through the front door, shutting it firmly behind her.

"Mama, no!" Linc's voice called through the door.

Hearing Linc's frantic pleas, Lee stood, petrified, his mind blank. Slowly, slowly, he became aware again of Jess's door shut to him. From his memory, a deep voice spoke weakly, "Take care of them, Lee. They'll need you."

Lee whispered, "I've failed you again, Will."

Chapter 15

Returning from Sunday evening service, Jessie and Esther mounted the front steps. Strong currents of hot wind swirled around them, catching and flaring the hems of their skirts. "Where did this hot wind come from?"

A sudden gust kicked Esther's bonnet forward, so that it fell over her eyes. "Oh, Mother!" Jessie pressed her hand over her mouth, suppressing a chuckle.

"Go ahead laugh at your poor mother." Esther giggled as she righted her bonnet. "I'd forgotten how wonderful it felt to really laugh."

"Mother, I . . ." Jessie paused and stared as though looking far away. When she spoke, her voice held a quality of wonder. "Cherries all around me on the floor. Cherries in my mouth and we're all laughing. What does it mean?" She looked to her mother.

Esther said with hushed awe in her voice, "I can't believe you remembered that. You were only a toddler. I'd picked a pan of sour cherries for pie." She took Jessie's hand. "Your father called me outside. When we came back, there you sat, the pan upside down and cherries all over you. Your cheeks bulged like a greedy chipmunk's. Your father and I laughed until we couldn't laugh any more." Esther wiped tears from her eyes. "Fancy you remembering that tonight."

"Mother, I love you."

Esther hugged Jessie to her. "Daughter, I love you, too. These past few days have been difficult, but they've given me the chance to be close to you again and to Linc for the first time."

"Oh, Miss Jessie, Miss Esther, what we gone do?" At the door, Ruby was twisting her apron with nervous hands.

"What is it?" Jessie asked.

"Your boy finally come back after you been gone. I give him a good scold for missing church and sent him to his bed like you told me."

"What has happened?" Esther asked.

Ruby twisted her apron more. "A while and I goes to check on him. He gone, left this paper on his pillow. What it say?" Ruby pulled a scrap of paper from her apron pocket.

Jessie read the scribbled message aloud, "Mother, I'm going to find Mr. Smith. Linc."

Though Jessie stood, she felt as though she were falling down, down.

"Now, Jessie, boys do this," Esther spoke up. "We'll find him. Ruby, is Susan home yet?"

"No, ma'am."

"Then you stay here to tell her what has happened. Jessie, you go through the neighborhood. What was the name of that saloon where Mr. Smith worked?"

"Linc wouldn't go there," Jessie objected.

"He might," Esther said. "Maybe Linc thinks someone there would know where Mr. Smith is."

"The Workman's Rest," Ruby supplied. "I heard that redhead yell it all the way in the kitchen."

"I'll be back as soon as I can!" Esther hurried down the front steps.

"Mother!" Jessie called after her. "Be careful!"

The increasing wind carried her mother's response back to her. "Of course, dear!"

Jessie dashed down the steps. Calling Linc's name, Jessie ran through the neighborhood, stopping at every house. Near desperate tears, she ran down every alley and every street within a square mile around Wagstaff House. The wind blowing harder, harder, Jessie finally returned, bursting into the kitchen. "Is Linc here?"

"No, he isn't." Miss Wright stood, her hands resting together on the head of her cane.

Jessie panted, tried to come up with a plan. *Linc, where are you?* Susan stood beside the cold stove. Ruby shuffled forward. "Boys run away. Then they come home hungry."

"I know I shouldn't be so upset." Jessie ran her hands over her disheveled hair. "But this wind."

Gusts of wind brought the jangling distant fire bells in a ominous ebb and flow. "Another fire," Miss Wright grumbled. "Those bells kept me up last night."

Jessie approached Miss Wright. "I'll help you get settled for the night."

Outside the wind tore a shutter loose on the side of the house and it banged wildly. "I'll go pound that back into place." Susan hurried out the back door.

Letting the older woman lean against her, Jessie helped Miss Wright prepare for bed. "I don't know why we're bothering. With Lincoln running off and the fire bells, I won't sleep a wink."

With Susan pounding the shutter, Jessie tried to think of something soothing to say to this, but couldn't. "Good night." She returned to the kitchen and sat down at the table with Ruby. Susan rejoined them. A look of helplessness passed between the three women as they glanced at each other.

"I think it be time to pray," Ruby announced. She raised her hands. "Oh, Lord, the wind is blowing. Fires is burning and Jessie's child done run away. Nobody know more'n I do how bad it hurt to have your child took from you. Oh, Lord, the heartbreak. You 'member how it was. More'n ten years I mourned and searched. Finally you bring me here, to my onliest child. Now bring Jessie's boy home safe like you bring me to Susan. I thank You, Lord. Amen. Miss Jessie, God won' let you down."

Jessie swallowed tears. "Thank you, Ruby."

Ruby hugged her, then lowered herself ponderously to the kitchen chair. While Ruby sat stolidly keeping vigil, Jessie and Susan paced, looking out the front and then back door.

Hours passed. Jessie and Susan sat at the table with Ruby. The alarms and rushing wind combination was wearing them down.

"I'll make us more coffee." Ruby struggled to her feet. "Look out the window! It look red like Judgment Day."

Jessie and Susan crowded around Ruby, puffing with her customary shortness of breath. "It must be the fire," Jessie said, heading out the back door with Susan at her heels. When Jessie, followed by Susan, ventured away from the shelter of the porch, the wind slapped her in the face like an angry hand. And then it tossed Susan's skirts high and plucked out Jessie's hairpins. Fire bells to the south pealed incessantly.

Jessie joined hands with Susan and ran to the fence.

With the southern skyline lit by an eerie red light, they moved closer together. A sudden explosion, frightening even muffled by distance, halted them.

Holding her hand by her mouth to funnel her words into Susan's ear, Jessie asked, "What was it?"

"It sound like the war all over again," Susan called to her over the wind even though they were inches apart. "The cannons start fires and they burn all night."

"Susan, Mother should have been back hours ago. I'm frightened for her."

Susan put her arm around Jessie's shoulder. "She be all right. We put her and Linc in God's hands—"

A burst of wind flew around the side of the small shed on the alley. It picked up Jessie and Susan like cotton fluff and threw them against the fence. "It can't be a tornado!" Jessie struggled to pull herself upright. "There isn't any rain!"

"I never feel a wind like that." Against the wind, Susan fought her way back to Ruby. "Grandma, you get inside."

"There's more-a me to knock down than you two. Get up here on the porch."

Jessie, Susan, and Ruby huddled near the back door, each holding on to the railing. But they didn't go back inside. The scarlet southern sky was too dangerous, too compelling to ignore. Other neighbors, some clutching shawls around flapping nightgowns endured the violent currents of air to stand and stare at hellish red sky. Soon the ringing of the fire alarms echoed louder—closer.

A man, running up the alley, startled them all. Jessie followed by Susan raced to catch up with him. "What's happening?" she called, cupping her hands. "Where are you coming from?"

Gasping, the man stopped and bent over, pressing his hands to his knees. "The whole downtown is on fire," he said hoarsely. "The fires are out of control. The wind fans the flames and they jump from roof to roof."

As the man took off once more, Susan shouted, "Where you running?"

"The fire's headed this way! I'm packing my stuff and heading west! You should, too!"

Everyone in the alley offered an opinion, but the wind snatched them away. A savage gust slammed against Susan and Jessie. With heads bent into the gale, Jessie holding Susan's hand trudged back up the path. When they reached Ruby on the porch, Susan said, "It don't sound very good."

"You think the fire gone get this far?" Susan asked Jessie.

"It never has before." Jessie bit her lip and looked to the fiery sky.

"Has the sky ever looked like that before?" Ruby worried aloud.

"Never."

"Then it could happen." Ruby folded her hands over her large abdomen.

Jessie began pacing again. "I should have gone after my mother hours ago."

"If you gone out, you would just miss her coming home. It's always that way," Ruby added. "Your mama is a clever woman an' she know this town better-n you. 'Sides, we already prayed her into God's hand along with your boy."

Jessie's fear threatened to fly out of her control. But she couldn't let it. Both Ruby and Susan were looking to her to take the lead. She took a deep breath. "We better take action."

"Just tell me what to do," Susan replied.

Jessie surveyed her property. Having a fireman in the family had one advantage—she'd known to take precautions against the spread of fire. Her pile of cooking wood sat at the back of the lot away from any structure and she'd had the winter coal stowed in the coal cellar.

"Wet down the wooden sidewalk in the front. Ruby, you go in and close all the downstairs windows. I'll do the upstairs ones. That will prevent sparks from igniting the curtains."

Gripping the railing against the wild wind, Susan hurried to the side of the house to the outdoor faucet while Ruby and Jessie went inside.

As Jessie latched the attic windows, she gained a chilling view of the furious fires to the south. As she scurried down the staircase, Miss Wright called to her, "Jessie, is your mother back?"

Jessie halted in the doorway. "No, she isn't."

"Why are you closing all the windows?"

"A man from downtown said the fire's headed this way."

"Do you believe him?"

Jessie considered not worrying the woman, but decided against it. "From the attic, it looks threatening, but I can't believe it will advance this far."

"I'm getting up."

"All right, but don't come outside. A wind gust actually knocked Susan and me off our feet."

"I'll come to the kitchen."

"Fine." Jessie hurried out the front door.

For the next hour or more Jessie and Susan worked frantically, taking turns filling buckets and saturating the wood sidewalk, front, and back steps. The fevered radiance in the south flared and flared until the moon was eclipsed in brilliance.

As Jessie and Susan toiled, a trickle of refugees from the south started, increased to a steady stream, then finally a river at flood stage. The refugees carried a peculiar assortment of items: lamps, portraits, skillets, blankets, hatboxes, and valises stuffed so full they couldn't be latched. All of them were fleeing north, away from danger.

"That won't work!" a stranger yelled at them as Jessie helped Susan douse the house.

"The fire's too hot!" another shouted.

"Pack your things while you have time!"

"The fire's out of control!"

"Get out while you can!" The warnings called to Jessie and Susan became a litany of rising terror even as they tried to ignore the ever-expanding crimson glow to the south.

"What are you women doing?" A man dashed toward them. "Are you mad? Do you think you can fight a fiery, rampaging monster with a garden pail!" Soot had blackened the man's face. He'd lost his hat; his hair blew in all directions with the continuous tumult of air.

"We have to save our house," Jessie shouted.

"Don't you think we felt that way?" he demanded, pointing to the last of the refugees hurrying up the street.

"I'm a widow. This boardinghouse supports us!" Watching a shower of sparks dancing over the church steeple two blocks away distracted Jessie.

"You're in danger, don't you understand? People are dying!"

A jolt of terror shot through Jessie.

As the man retreated to the street, he yelled back, "For God's sake, woman, get out while you can!"

Susan turned to Jessie. "We gotta make sure Linc and your ma have a home to come back to, you hear?"

Jessie nodded, fighting the blasts of wind. Then another explosion rocked them. Screams shocked Jessie and she turned to see Mrs. O'Toole from her attic window. "It's only two blocks away! Dear God, save us!"

"Pack your things!" Mrs. Crawford from the front walk shouted to them. "The fire is nearly here!"

Jessie hurried to her. "Did Mr. Smith return to board with you? Do you know where he is?"

"I haven't seen him in the last few days. Mrs. Wagstaff, you must come with me. You are in real danger."

"But we'll lose everything!"

"Better to lose everything and save your lives. Don't delay!" Mrs. Crawford began to run to catch up with her son and daughter. "The fire is burning along the wooden sidewalks and streets and jumping from roof to—"

Her final words were blown away. The gust brought a shower of flaming sparks into Jessie's face. Susan screamed. Jessie raced back to her. "What!"

Susan pointed to the faucet. "The water stopped!"

Linc running away. Her mother not returning. The fire advancing, advancing . . . She wanted to run inside and hide under her bed like a little girl.

"Look!" Susan screamed.

A line of flames flashed up in the alley behind them. The leaping, orange flames began gnawing at her small barn and her fence. *It can't have reached us! My God, forgive my stubbornness! Help us! We've waited too long!*

"Susan, get Ruby to the front," Jessie shouted. "I'll get Miss Wright!"

Jessie found Miss Wright, calmly waiting inside the front door. "I'm ready to go. Here's your shawl."

"I must get—"

"I've gathered all your daguerreotypes and letters from Will in this satchel. You'll have to carry it." Both glanced around the foyer as though memorizing it.

"Jessie!" Susan screeched from the front walk. "Come out! The back porch gone caught fire!"

As Jessie helped Miss Wright through the door, she put Jessie's fear into words, "I hope we haven't delayed too long."

Terrified, Jessie led them out into the now empty street. The glare from the burning alley, overwhelming the night's darkness, cast a terrifying radiance over the faces looking to her. Embers, sparks, burning ash swirled around her in the blistering maelstrom. Ruby's dress caught fire. Jessie frantically beat the flames with her hand.

Jessie managed to lead them a block northwest, the two older women staggering between her and Susan. Then the wind shifted and, under her horrified gaze, outflanked them. It blocked the street in front of them. "We're hemmed in on three sides!"

Miss Wright pointed east. "We must get to the lake before we are surrounded and cut off. Hurry!"

Miss Wright increased her halting gait. Jessie took her arm, helping her to hurry. Susan helped Ruby.

The scorching fire crowded close. Its din crackled, filled Jessie's ears. The smell of burning wood overwhelmed her. The fire was a giant hand reaching out to pull them into its death grip.

"I shouldn't have waited!" Jessie moaned. The smoky air made her cough, but she didn't slacken pace. They were running for their lives. *God help us. Forgive me for staying too long. Please, Lord, these women depended on me.*

Suddenly Ruby collapsed in a heap. "I can't . . . go . . . on—" She coughed, wheezed.

Choking smoke roiled around Jessie. For a moment, she was paralyzed. The fire swirled just behind her. The wall of a nearby house crashed into the street. Flaming debris cascaded over them like a shower of flaming darts.

Susan shrieked, "Grandma, get up, the fire is right on us!" The young woman tried but couldn't lift Ruby. "Help me, Jessie!" Jessie ran to Susan.

"I can't go on," Ruby gasped, choked. "Leave me." But Jessie and Susan strained to get the old woman back on her feet.

Miss Wright's cane slashed down right behind Ruby, jolting them all. "Get up!" the old schoolteacher commanded. "Get up or we'll all die!"

"Leave me," Ruby implored.

The cane crashed down. "Get up! If you don't, you'll kill us all. We won't go on without you!" The cane slammed down again. "Now!"

Ruby lunged to her feet. Jessie and Susan grabbed Ruby under her arms. Overpowering heat roared around Jessie's hair, singeing, burning.

"Go!" Miss Wright ordered. She prodded Ruby with the point of her cane. "Go! I'm right behind you!"

Ruby leaned heavily on Jessie and Susan as they dragged her along between them. Exploding barrels, overexpanded by the overwhelming heat, the roar of the fire, collapsing walls, crumbling chimneys, all merged into a horrific din. Searing heat scorched Jessie. She panted for air and choked in black smoke.

She labored along with Susan to keep Ruby on her feet, her back breaking. Her lungs about to explode. But Miss Wright's cane prodded relentlessly.

"The beach!" Jessie gasped. They all stumbled across the last street onto the narrow sandy beach.

"Don't stop!" Miss Wright ordered. "The fire is right behind us. To the water!"

Jessie strained over the last twenty feet of the harrowing trek and waded into Lake Michigan. She shivered violently as her scorched body plunged into the icy October waves. She led the others out onto a shallow sandbar—as far away from the shore as possible. As one, they turned back to view the city.

"Oh, Lord!" Ruby cried out.

The whole western skyline flamed in brilliant orange and scarlet. Above the remaining skeletons of buildings, huge billows of black smoke surged, tumbled toward heaven.

The sight shredded the last of Jessie's self-control. "My son! Lincoln!" she screamed. "Mother! Lee! I've lost them all!"

Susan pulled Jessie to her and fiercely wrapped her arms around her. She shouted, "Almighty God, you save that boy and Esther and Lee. God, save my people, too! Caleb, Lord, keep him safe. He a stubborn man. You freed us. You can't leave us without hope. You saved us! You be our hope and salvation. Cover us with Your mighty hand!"

"That we should live to see such a sight," Miss Wright said to Ruby as they listened to Susan's pleas to heaven.

Ruby faced her. "Lord, have mercy on us."

Tears slid down Miss Wright's cheeks. "I don't know if I can bear to lose Margaret's only grandchild."

"The Lord will protect him," Ruby said, looking up at Miss Wright.

"He must. He must." Miss Wright put her arms around the other woman's broad shoulders and began to weep without restraint.

Ruby bent her own head and rested it on Miss Wright's breast and let her tears flow too. "Lord, have mercy on us. Lord, have mercy."

Chapter 16

October 10, 1871

The noisy crowded church-turned-hospital was momentarily peaceful. The afternoon sun sparkled through the stained glass windows in brilliant crimson, royal blue, gilded amber. Taking solace from the glittering display, Lee blinked his gritty eyes. Since the fire began Sunday evening, he had slept little. With the deluge of burnt and broken patients over the past two days, all the knowledge he'd thought he'd forgotten had come rushing back.

"Doctor?"

Yawning behind his hand, Lee bent to look at the plump volunteer nurse at his elbow.

"Have you set up the dispensary yet?"

"Yes, a tent outside has been organized."

"Excellent. We'll need a list of what is available. Distribute it to the other doctors."

"Certainly, Dr. Smith." The volunteer hurried away.

"Doctor?" The familiar feminine voice came, sounding surprised.

"Pearl!" Lee folded her into his arms. "You're safe."

Pearl stepped back to look at him. "So you're not a bartender, you're a doctor?"

"Yes, I'm Dr. Leland Granger Smith." Two days and two nights of raging fire had left its mark on his attractive, former employer, now soot-covered and disheveled like all the rest.

"I'm looking for my father." Her voice hoarse, Pearl searched his face, her hands knotted. "His block burned to the ground. I finally found a neighbor who said my father had been struck by a collapsing wall. This is the third makeshift hospital I've been to."

His heart aching for Jessie and Linc, Lee rested his hand on her shoulder. "What's his name?"

"Lorenz Schiffer."

Lee guided her to a small table near the pulpit of the church where he flipped through a stack of papers on the table. "He's on my list."

Pearl pressed her hands to her heart. "He's here?" Her voice broke with emotion.

Lee put an arm around her shoulder to brace her as he led her down the aisle, flanked by pews that now served as beds, back to the rows of blankets on the floor of church's foyer.

Surveying the tired, injured men lying there, Lee motioned Pearl to a pallet where an old man lay, bandaged but awake.

"Papa!" Pearl knelt beside her father and bent forward to hug him. "I've been so worried—"

Lee stepped back, not wanting to intrude on their reunion, one of many he'd witnessed over the last two days. Had Jessie, Linc, and everyone else come through the fire safely? Where were they? Did they need him?

At last, Pearl stood up. "How long will my father have to stay here?" She dabbed her moist eyes with a smudged hankie.

"All he really needs is good food and bedrest."

"You don't know . . . the worry . . ." She sagged. Lee caught her, holding her against him.

Her eyes fluttered open. "What happened? Did I faint? I never—"

"Over the past two days, we've all done things we normally don't do."

She nodded, her lips pursed. "How's your Jessie?"

Holding in the pain, Lee shook his head. "It's early yet. The fires only stopped burning hours ago. That made it hard to get news." He repeated the same words he'd comforted so many others within the past hours.

"The Workman's Rest is a total loss." She looked down at the toes of her muddy shoes.

"What will you do?"

She sighed. "Right now, I'm just glad we're all alive." She smiled suddenly; her usual teasing manner returning, "Are you going to tell me why a doctor was bartending for me?"

Lee recognized and appreciated her attempt to rally him from gloom. He grinned for her. "Sometime."

"You really *are* a doctor?"

Lee said in a mock serious tone, "Harvard Class of 1861."

She shook her head at him. "You never didn't fit my idea of a barkeep."

"Pearl, you never fit my idea of a bar owner. You know you *made* the best nickel lunch in town. Why not build a restaurant instead of a new saloon?"

"You may be right, Doctor." Pearl gave him a quick hug.

"Leave your address with the nurse. I'll want to check on him daily for a week."

"That suits me."

As Lee watched Pearl leave with her father, he thought how none of them could have prepared for this ordeal.

In the face of this tragic fire, he had responded the same way he had to President Lincoln's calling up of troops in 1860. On a street corner downtown, he'd told a police captain that he was a veteran army surgeon, new to Chicago. He'd, in effect, enlisted in this battle, the best way he could.

He'd been dispatched to this church with two other doctors to set up a temporary shelter for the injured. When he'd revealed his experience in field medicine, the other doctors had unanimously promoted him to director.

Though uneasy, he'd surprised himself by falling into remembered duties and procedures. The past two fiery days and nights had been a round of cleansing and bandaging burns and cuts, setting broken limbs, and delivering a baby. He'd searched the face of each refugee, hoping to see Jessie, Linc, Susan. But in vain. Now the awful terror of not knowing, of facing a future without Jessie and Linc, overwhelmed him.

Never to see Jessie again, in her crisp white apron in command of her kitchen. Or late in the afternoon when tendrils of her hair escaped from her tight bun and formed a light brown halo of curls around her face. The thought of losing her forever slid through him like honed steel, left him reeling. He slumped onto a chair at the back of the church. Yearning for Jessie and Linc swirled through his heart. *I can't live without them. God, Will was right. I can't survive this on my own.* Tears gathered in Lee's smoke-raw throat.

He recalled Will's face by campfire light on battlefield after battlefield. Will's low comforting voice came to him, "You must humble yourself. Every man must let God be God. We are not able to understand why God allows death. Such matters are too great for us to know."

"I know that now, Will," Lee whispered and slid to his knees.

God, I'm on my knees at last. I have resisted You all my adult years. Now I see Your hand in my life.

You fed my ambition to be a doctor and gave me the strength to defy my family. You led me into the war I hated. But some men lived because Will and I were there.

Now because of my war service, I was able to help people again.

Lee looked up. *I lost myself, but now You've let me taste life with Linc and Jessie. I can't face life without them. I can't believe You would take them from me now, just when I know what I really want in life. I don't deserve them. But have mercy on me—a sinner.* He stifled a wrenching sob.

The cinched-in feeling, which had gripped him more tightly over the last few days, but which had been with him since Will died, began to loosen. He took a free breath, testing the new feeling of freedom. He stood up.

"I thank You, God," he whispered. "I don't know if Jessie and Linc will be restored to me, but I know we're in Your hands. Henceforth, I want to be the best man, the best doctor You can help me to be."

"Smith!"

Lee looked up and exclaimed, "Huff, praise God! You're safe!" He took Hiram's hand and gripped it.

The fire captain's uniform was torn, burned, smudged with soot. Huff's blackened face was covered with blistered burns. "Smith, is it really you?" Huff's voice sounded gritty from a smoke-burned throat.

"Yes, it's a long story, but I'm really Dr., not Mr., Smith. Let me treat those burns on your face and hands."

Huff pulled back. "Have you seen Esther?"

"No, do you have any news about Jessie's neighborhood?"

"Burned to the ground. Even the chimneys were turned to ash."

These words slammed into Lee's gut.

"That devil wind swept the fire ahead of us. We couldn't keep up. We couldn't stop it!" Pain contorting his face, Huff looked near to breaking down.

"Let's get you some coffee and a sandwich."

"I've got to find her." Hiram shook with emotion.

"You will." Lee put his hand on Hiram's shoulder. "Coffee and food will help you keep going."

"It's all my fault. If I hadn't argued with her, she would have been safe at home with the twins." Huff coughed into a blackened handkerchief. "Our neighborhood wasn't touched. My fault. Mine."

Lee led Hiram out to the tent where Lee forced him to sit down on a rickety chair and take a cup of strong coffee. Motioning to one of the woman volunteers, Lee murmured to her, "Make sure he eats something before you let him leave. He's near collapse." She nodded.

An older, female volunteer approached him. "Dr. Smith, do you have a sister by the name of Eugenia?"

"Yes, is she here?"

"No, Mayor Mason has sent a call out to locate you for her."

"How is my sister? How did she know where to find me?"

The white-haired woman smiled. "She's safe. And she told the mayor you'd be found as a volunteer doctor at one of the shelters."

"She did?" Lee shook his head. Evidently Eugenia knew more about him than he did. "Please let her know I'm fine."

The woman nodded. "And, Dr. Smith, more injured have been brought in."

Hiram jolted to his feet, spilling his coffee. "Any women?"

"No, sorry. No women."

The chair creaked as Hiram let himself drop back into it.

Lee squeezed Hiram's shoulder. "I'll be here for the duration. If you locate any of our loved ones, let me know?"

Hiram nodded, his red-rimmed eyes nearly shut. When he brought the tin coffee cup to his lips, his hand trembled.

Lee left to join the other two doctors where an area had been set aside for examining the wounded. Before he reached them, Butch bounded up to Lee, yipping, leaping knee-high.

"Butch, where's Linc?" Barking, the pup surged away. The dog led Lee to a small boy huddled among battered and blackened men.

"Lincoln!" Lee swung the boy up into his arms. He couldn't speak, hold back tears. *Thank You, Father.* "Linc, where's your mother?"

"I don't know." Linc's voice vibrated with the force of his own tears. "I ran away. To find you."

As Lee stroked Linc's hair, rocking him in his arms, he gently examined the boy's arms, legs, and ribs and found only bruises and a few cuts. Lee looked around.

Linc clutched him. "Don't leave me!"

"I won't."

One doctor was swabbing the burns. The other, setting a dislocated shoulder, said, "We can handle these, Smith."

"Thanks." Lee turned to one of the nurses. "A weak solution of laudanum, please." Within minutes, Lee was coaxing Linc to swallow the nasty-tasting medicine and settling him onto a blanket. While waiting for the sedative to work, Lee asked, "Linc, how did you get so bumped and bruised?"

"Everybody was running. I was on the bridge . . ." His small voice started to quaver with more tears.

"Son, it's all over. There's nothing to worry about anymore."

"But, my mother—"

"It's late. We'll find her together in the morning. I'll stay until you fall asleep. Don't worry."

Linc rolled onto his side. "You won't let them take Butch away?"

"No, of course, not."

"I ran away from the other place they took me to. They wanted to take Butch—"

"Don't worry. He'll stay right here with you."

The boy, sighing, closed his eyes and fell asleep. Butch settled down on the floor beside his master, panting happily.

Soon Lee was engrossed in setting the wrist of a policeman. After that, nearly a complete company of firemen came in, led by the hand like blind men. It took the doctors over an hour to bathe their swollen, red, smoke-burned eyes and treat all their burns, contusions, and lacerations.

Lee tied the last bandage on the final firefighter needing treatment. "It's a wonder you men were able to walk here at all."

"We'd still be out there if it wasn't for Milwaukee sending practically their whole fire department by rail on Monday."

"They've been as dry as us. Hope Milwaukee gets rain, so they don't burn," another added.

Lee marveled at these men who'd fought the fire Sunday night through Tuesday afternoon.

One of the volunteers came to lead the smoked-blinded firemen away to a hot meal. They each put a hand on the shoulder of the man in front of him, then walked single file down the main aisle.

At the back of the church again, Lee stood over Linc, content just to watch him sleep. Butch had jumped up on the cot to lie with the boy. Scratching the loyal dog behind his ears, Lee gazed at the child he thought he had lost.

Thoughts of Jessie intruded. He prayed until a nurse bullied him into sitting down. Settling himself onto the creaky chair, he watched the gentle rise and fall of Linc's chest in slumber. His head drooped.

Startled, Lee awoke to see Jessie stride into the candle-lit room. Butch yipped nearby. Lee leaped out of the chair and rushed to her. "Jess!" At first, all he could do was hold her—feel the softness of her body against his, knowing she was real, not imagined. He buried his face in the crook of her neck, letting his cheek glory in the feel of her soft hair against his face.

Finally he looked down into her face. "Jess."

"Lee." Rising onto her toes, she gave him a tender kiss. Then she rested her hands on his arms and studied him as though memorizing him.

His words came out husky with emotion. "I was so worried."

She sighed wearily. "It has been the longest two days of my life." She ran her hands over his arms again, as though making certain he was real. "I feared I'd lost you."

Butch gave another yip from where he guarded Linc.

Jessie glanced at the pup. "Linc's here?"

"Yes. Come." He took her to the pew where Linc slept.

Jessie dropped to her knees, pressing her prayer-folded hands to her lips. "My son." With an angel touch, she examined his face, shoulders, arms, hands, chest, abdomen, and legs. She looked up, concern in her expression.

Lee dropped to one knee beside her. "He's bruised up and very tired. He said there was a stampede on one of the bridges when it caught fire."

Jessie moaned and laid her head on her son's chest. "It's all my fault—"

"No, I was the one who lied and caused Linc to run away—"

"But if I hadn't—"

Lee lifted her to her feet. "None of us could have predicted this fire." Again he had to hold her, had to know that she was really with him.

"Dr. Smith?" One of the other physicians cleared his throat. "The kitchen is just about out of food again. You haven't eaten since lunch and we insist you go to supper *now*."

Lee was touched by the genuine concern in the other doctor's voice. "Thank you. Dr. Cooledge, this is my very dear friend, Mrs. Wagstaff. The boy is her son, Lincoln."

The doctor greeted Jessie, then urged her to go with Lee.

"I don't want to leave Linc." Jessie hung back. "What if he awakes and I'm not here?"

"I gave him a sedative. He won't wake until morning," Lee assured her. "Besides, Butch is here to keep watch, aren't you, Butch?"

The little dog sat up and looked at Lee with serious eyes.

"See? Linc's safe. Jess, come on."

Outside, the day's light had waned to a faint glow over the bleak, burned-over horizon. "I can't believe what I'm seeing," Jessie murmured.

"It's still a miracle the fires are finally out. I have never experienced such wind in my life."

"It was horrible." Jessie's voice broke on the last word and she began to tremble.

Lee put his arm around her shoulders and drew her to a chair and table beneath a canvas canopy. Soon he returned with two tin cups of soup and hunks of warm, fresh bread. He sat down beside her.

"The thought of food makes me sick. I haven't been able to eat anything." She clenched her hands in her lap.

"What is troubling you? Are Susan, Ruby—"

"They're all safe, but not thanks to me. We should have left the house long before we did. I couldn't believe the fire would reach us." She bowed her head.

"You weren't the only one who thought that." He lifted her chin with his hand.

"But it could have cost us all our lives. Susan, Ruby, Miss Wright were depending on *me*. God sent warning after warning, but I wouldn't listen. I was going to save my house no matter what."

"Jess, how could you know how devastating this fire would be? We're only human. We don't, can't know everything. We're not God."

"*You* speaking of God?" She touched his hand.

He took her hand in both of his. "Yes, this fire burned away a lot of foolish guilt and pride from me, too. Now God's brought you safely here—you and Linc." He drew her hand to his lips and kissed it.

They sat a long time, knee to knee, hand in hand. Finally Lee came to his senses. "I insist you eat some of this before it's stone cold." He pushed the tin cup toward her and lifted his own. "You must eat," he coaxed.

"I can't. Not until I find my mother."

"You became separated from her?"

Jessie nodded, fresh tears beginning to fall. "She went to town to look for Linc. She thought he might try to find you at the Workman's Rest."

"Where have you looked?"

"Everywhere. Yesterday we were finally able to leave the beach. We had been marooned on a sandbar for hours—all through that damp night. Miss Wright and Ruby are suffering dreadful pain in their joints from it. When we left the beach, I found shelter for Susan, Ruby, and Miss Wright at a Lutheran church. I spent all today searching." She passed her hand over her forehead.

"Your stepfather was here, looking for her, too. I had forgotten . . . Seeing you pushed every other thought out of my mind."

"That man." Jessie's voice surged with anger. "Their neighborhood wasn't touched. If *that man* hadn't driven her away, Mother would have been safely at home! If anything has happened to Mother, I'll . . . I'll," Jessie's voice broke.

"Dr. Gooden was here, too. He's working with the mayor to keep cholera from breaking out in these conditions."

"I'm glad. But where's Mother?"

Lee moved so Jessie's cheek rested on his shoulder. Knowing he could do nothing to ease her heartbreak shook him. Minutes passed. Jessie finally was able to eat. "How about one more cup of coffee?" Lee suggested. "Then you can sit the rest of the night beside your son."

Jessie accepted coffee from the volunteer. Looking over Lee's shoulder, Jessie saw her stepfather. Rage shot through her like the thrust of a hot poker. The cup of coffee dropped from her hands. "You!"

Before she could say more, Hiram rushed forward and—for the first time in her life—wrapped his arms around her. Shock froze her.

"Jessie." Shaking with emotion, Hiram tried to catch his breath.

Sudden dread gripped Jessie. "Mother. It's Mother, isn't it?"

"Yes," Hiram gasped. Releasing Jessie, he gripped the back of a chair.

"Tell me." Jessie heard the shrillness in her plea. Hiram continued to struggle for words; she fought the urge to shake them out of him.

"The captain of the Coventry Company," Hiram said, "caught up with me at my station." He gasped again, drawing another ragged breath. "He saw Esther. He's sure it was Esther—"

"What happened? Is she at another hospital?" Jessie's control began slipping. "Where is she?"

"We've lost her. Dear God, she's gone." He began to weep in strangling gasps.

"No!" Jessie shook him by one of his shoulders.

"She was helping a family get out of their burning house. She went back in. Coventry Company tried to stop her." He struggled for breath. "The roof collapsed. She never made it out." Dry rasping sobs wrenched his body.

Jessie swayed. "No, you're lying. You're lying!" Voices buzzed in her ear. Lee gripped her, holding her up.

Hiram moaned. "If I hadn't argued with her, she would have been home safe with the twins."

Jessie wrenched herself from Lee. Her hands clenched and unclenched. She wanted to beat her stepfather, see him bleeding and broken on the floor in front of her. She wanted to hear him scream with anguish.

Hiram dropped to his knees in front of Jessie. "Dear God, forgive me. Jessie, forgive me."

Jessie half turned away from him, seeing his abject sorrow but unwilling to let it sway her.

Huff in his painful raspy voice went on, "I've sinned against God and man. Esther, Esther, I'm sorry. I always had to have my own way in everything. Forgive me." He buried his face in his hands.

Jessie took a step back from him.

"She said I'd never loved her. Oh, God, it's true. I loved only myself. Forgive me, Jessie."

His words made her sick. She wanted to leave him here in his misery. But the honest grief in his voice forced her to turn back to him. Pity for him reared up inside her. Fighting it, she brought to mind all the times he had forced himself between her mother and her. Then she pictured the day he had marched her to Margaret Wagstaff's back door and coldly left her there alone.

Margaret. She saw Margaret's sweet face. Margaret had taught her to love no matter what, no matter who. Then she recalled Reverend Mitchell's dying words, "Forgive. You'll never be free until you forgive." He had said the words to Caleb, but she had needed to hear them, too.

She hated her stepfather. *I can't forgive him. I don't want to.*

She heard Margaret's soft voice, "Forgive, Jessie, forgive." As if Will and Margaret stood one on each side of her, she felt bathed in their love for her; her love for them. Will and Margaret loved her and God. God didn't hate. He forgave.

Jessie closed her eyes. She heard people moving around them, speaking in quiet, troubled voices, near but apart. She tried to harden her heart against all Will and Margaret had taught her of love. She couldn't. She opened her eyes.

Feeling older than her years, she took Hiram's hands in hers. She tugged him to his feet. *This is because of you, Margaret, you, Reverend Mitchell, and you, Mother.* "I forgive you." Her voice was dead.

"Jessie, I don't deserve your forgiveness."

Jessie tried to say something comforting, but she felt numb, unable to respond. She felt alone, totally alone.

Her stepfather wept into his hands. "What will we do without your mother?"

Jessie averted her eyes. She mumbled, "We'll manage somehow."

She felt like a wounded animal. She wanted this man, whom she still hated to take his grief away. She wanted to mourn alone. How could God have let this hateful man live and let her beautiful mother die? Waves of anger tried to swell inside her. *I forgave him, Margaret. I'll do what I can.* She looked to Lee. Tears dripped from his eyes. But Jessie felt dry, flat, alone.

Then it came. . .

Soothing warmth poured through Jessie. Over the jagged shards of her shattered heart flowed a healing balm. Love, more wonderful than she thought possible, more healing than she could have imagined. Its intensity gripped her.

Strength . . . peace . . . joy . . . lifted her spirit—summer breezes fluttering through her cold heart. Love, God's unbelievable love for her became love for this man. It bubbled up within her, overflow-ing; its force stunned her.

"I forgive you," Jessie whispered and purifying tears washed her cheeks.

Lee saw Jessie's face softened, her embrace of Hiram lost its wooden quality. Reaching out, Lee laid his hand on her shoulder. The smile she gave him was the most beautiful he'd ever received, reminding him of a Renaissance Madonna, smiling down at the babe Jesus. Fleetingly he recalled the touch of his own mother's hand, the mother he'd lost when he was near Linc's age. "Jess," he whispered, his tears falling, too.

She stepped closer to Lee, releasing Hiram. The three of them stood like statues. Only their labored breathing and flowing tears betrayed them as human. They silently absorbed the impact of what had just taken place.

She'd learned of the miracle of grace, but she'd never experi-enced it so real before. Her tears washed away the last traces of the numbness that had gripped her. Her heart lived again. In the faces of Lee and her stepfather, she saw what she felt reflected back to her.

Finally Jessie spoke, "We have to take care of the twins. They'll need us the most, Hiram."

Wiping away his tears with his hands, her stepfather embraced her fiercely, then stepped back. "You're right. They need us. You must come and live with us until you can rebuild."

"I'll come to help you, but I have to stay with Miss Wright, Su-san, and Ruby—"

"I have room for them, too. Bring them with you."

Gazing at Lee, Jessie saw her own surprise mirrored in Lee's face. "Even Susan and Ruby? Do you mean that?"

"Yes, I've been a fool. All I sense now is that they need me and I need them. I can't explain it. I feel . . . changed. I'm not the same."

"I feel it, too." Jessie drew nearer Lee.

"I have to go break the news to the twins." Hiram spoke briskly, his usual take-charge manner returning. "The three of us will get ready for all of you. You, too, Smith, I mean, Dr. Smith." He shook hands with Lee, kissed Jessie once more, then hurried away.

Jessie and Lee stood, faced each other, then Lee said, "I can't believe what I just witnessed."

"I can hardly believe it myself. I can't explain it, but all my anger toward him left me—completely."

"This is a day of miracles."

Nearby only a few tired volunteers clustered at the back, drinking coffee and talking quietly. On the night breeze, the scorched stench from the burned-over land came to Lee.

"Jess, what about me? Has your anger toward me left you?"

"Yes, oh, yes." She stepped eagerly into his open arms.

"I can hardly remember the man I was that April morning when I walked up your back steps."

Jessie rested her head on his shoulder.

The powerful joy on her face almost made him weak at the knees. *I don't deserve her, Lord.* Lee murmured, "I'll try to be worthy of you, Jess."

"Don't talk about being worthy of me. Tell me what's in your heart."

"I love you, Jessie. You'll be my wife?"

"Yes." Jessie stroked his cheek. "Yes. God's given us time and love, gifts too precious to waste."

LOST IN HIS LOVE

January 20, 1893

Papa's shouting woke Cecy. She sat up in her bed. In the blackness, she clutched her favorite dolly. Would he come to her room and break things?

Mama's high voice climbed higher while Papa kept shouting. The loud voices fought back and forth. They might rush into her room. They might shout at her and break her china dolly's head. Cecy felt tears wet her cheeks. They might break her.

The door opened. Soft light glowed into the darkness. It was Nana.

"Nana!" Cecy cried out. She held up her hands.

"Hush, hush, sweetheart." Gently, Nana lifted her. "It's all right. I'm here. Don't cry."

"I'm scared," Cecy whimpered. Warm, soft arms closed around her. She heard Nana's soft words, but she couldn't stop shaking.

Nana carried her to the rocking chair, snuggling her close. The old chair began to move back and forth. Creak. Creak. She rested her head on soft Nana. Nana smelled sweet, like the powder Nana patted on Cecy after her baths.

From below, the voices shouted and cried, but Nana hugged her. Nana wouldn't let them break dolly or her.

Then Nana said the good words, the words that always let Cecy breathe easier. She closed her eyes to sleep. Nana whispered in her ear, "The Lord is my shepherd; I shall not want. He maketh me to lie down in green pastures: he leadeth me beside the still waters. He restoreth my soul . . ."

Chapter 1

January 1906

"They'll be preening like peacocks on a terrace." In a black bombazine gown, Auntie paced in Cecy Jackson's bedroom. "Men, they think they're in charge. But a wise woman always stays in control of herself. And of them."

Cecy stood very still while her personal maid lifted the ivory satin gown over her coifed hair and settled it carefully in place. Cecy had difficulty taking in air, her nerves as tight as her stays.

"Oh, Miss Cecilia," the chambermaid said breathlessly. "I never seen a dress this pretty."

"Pretty?" Auntie snapped. "It's an original by Paquin of Paris. I doubt any other young lady at tonight's ball will have as lovely a gown. You may leave. We have no further use for you."

Blushing, the maid blinked quickly as if beset by tears. Cecy felt her embarrassment as her own. As the girl left, Cecy murmured, "Thank you." The maid darted a look at her and fled, closing the door behind her.

Auntie glared at the door and then turned back, "Tell me, Cecilia, how does a woman stay in control of men?"

Cecy's mind raced, calling up her aunt's careful instruction. "I set the pace."

"Exactly. You make them dance to your tune, Cecilia. Not theirs."

As Cecy's personal maid buttoned the hundred or so buttons that closed the back of her gown, Auntie walked around as if viewing a statue at the Louvre. Then she halted. "Now that girl from New Orleans—what's her name?"

"Fleur?"

"Yes, the Fourchette girl. She's the only one who'll give you any competition."

Cecy's stomach clenched tighter.

"None of the other debutantes vying with you to be the Belle of San Francisco 1906 have a chance." Auntie's face rounded with a satisfied smile. "But the competition Fleur provides will make your victory all the sweeter."

Cecy swallowed, firming her resolve to outshine the Fourchette girl. "Yes, it will."

"You performed creditably at your coming-out party. Tonight however, you must set the tone for your entrance into society. You are my sister's daughter, a Higginbottom of Boston. You mustn't let these provincials, these Westerners, shine you down. You must not show any weakness tonight."

"I'll try—"

"Try?" Auntie halted. "You won't *try*. You will do it. I didn't waste all last year coaching you for social success just to let you falter at the post. A woman is nothing without social success."

Auntie lifted Cecy's chin and looked into her eyes. "You have your mother's features. It's unfortunate that you inherited your father's red hair, but it's not as bad now that you're older and it's become more auburn than carroty."

Her aunt glanced at the wall clock. "The hour is nearly here. Remember. You are immeasurably superior to any young woman you will meet tonight. Show no fear. If you do, they will take the lead and leave you behind in their social dust. You must shine. Let no one attract more beaus than you, do you understand? And keep the men dangling and uncertain. Then they and the other debutantes will respect you."

"Yes, Auntie." Cecy's voice quavered slightly.

Her aunt studied her and then turned away. "Just remember not to make the same mistake your mother did. Or you could end up just like her. I'll meet you downstairs when you are ready." Auntie left her alone with her maid.

Finally, the maid finished buttoning her dress and then began coaxing the first skin-tight white silk glove up Cecy's fingers, hand, and arm. "I'm sure you'll have a lovely time tonight, miss," the maid murmured. "It's a party, not a battle."

Cecy made no response. She didn't know exactly what had caused her mother's problems. But Auntie knew and Cecy had to do what Auntie said to avoid following in her mother's footsteps.

Tonight was going into battle. She'd do whatever it took to seize her rightful place in society and put her desolate past behind her forever. *Auntie's right. Show no fear.*

Linc Wagstaff got out of his brand-new Pierce Arrow in disgust. His new Chinese houseman, Kang, stood beside the vehicle, his hands folded. "Auto not good like horse."

"At this moment I'm inclined to agree with you." Linc stalked out of the old carriage house at the rear of his new home.

"What you do now, mister?" Kang hurried along a step behind Linc.

The ding-ding of a nearby cable car bell interrupted. Linc instantly picked up his pace. "I'll take the cable car!" Linc sprinted to the street, hailing the cable car. It lurched to a stop. Linc leaped aboard.

Invigorated by his run, he looked at his fellow passengers, some workmen and a few women. His evening dress had taken them by surprise. Despite the swaying of the vehicle, he made a half-bow. "Good evening, ladies and gents."

At his sally, most grinned at him. Linc flipped up his tails and sat down before he could unceremoniously lose his balance.

The cable car made its way up the next hill, straining and rocking. Over the grinding noise of the car, one of the workmen called to him, "Horses lame?"

Linc shook his head. "My automobile wouldn't start."

This announcement was followed by hoots. "Autos! Get a horse!"

This only made Linc grin more.

The old woman who sat beside him said, "Automobiles are of the devil. God made horses."

Accustomed to this attitude, Linc nodded politely, but without agreement. This new twentieth century was a mere six years old. Change, the possibility of even more progress, was what drove him tonight. The future could be better if only good men would try to make it that way. Gaslights wrapped in wisps of fog passed by as the car went up and down hills. Finally he recognized Nob Hill. "This is where I get off!" Doffing his silk top hat in farewell, he descended from the cable car amid friendly wishes.

He walked down misty, winter-darkened California Street toward his destination, the Ward mansion. After all the presentation parties held in the weeks following New Year's Eve, Mrs. Zebulon Ward always hosted the first formal ball.

Ahead, golden electric light radiated from inside the imposing, three-story stone Ward residence. Gleaming black carriages and motorcars lined up near the entrance. Arriving on foot would not add to Linc's consequence in the eyes of society. In the shadows of the high wrought-iron fence, he waited until the liveried footmen were busy helping two ladies from an opulent carriage. Quietly, he slipped from the shadows and followed the pair to the open double front doors.

He waited for the ladies to enter. When they had been relieved of their dark velvet cloaks, Linc stepped inside the huge foyer. The excited buzz of voices and bursts of laughter filled his ears. A footman relieved him of his cape and hat. He handed his invitation to another footman who carried it to the butler. The butler bowed, then read Linc's full name aloud to his hostess who headed the receiving line. "Mr. Lincoln Granger Smith Wagstaff."

Linc bowed over Mrs. Ward's pudgy gloved hand.

"Lincoln, I just received a letter from your dear Aunt Eugenia yesterday. I was happy to write back and say I would be seeing you tonight." Wearing a dog collar of glittering diamonds, Mrs. Ward went on to make the debutante next to her aware of Linc's distinguished Boston Back Bay connections. She finished with, "Smiths have been bankers in Boston as long as there have been banks in Boston!" Linc worked his way through the line which consisted of Mrs. Ward's protégé, a shy motherless girl whom kind Mrs. Ward was bringing out this season, and Mr. Ward. Linc smiled to himself—certain that the words "banker" and "Boston" had escaped no one. Wouldn't it be amusing if someone approached him about a loan? After all, his stepfather's family's reputation and distinctions had very little to do with his own life. And he'd never before traded on anyone else's credit. Doing so made him feel like a quack selling snake oil. But his purpose did include hobnobbing with the wealthy, the people he needed for success. His research into who owned what and how much in California had led him directly to the people in this ballroom—especially one redhead.

Accepting a glass of ruby red punch from a waiter, he strolled through the gathering of San Francisco's top two hundred families. Though he wore the latest in evening attire, the glittering rubies, sapphires, and emeralds and shimmering brocade dresses made him feel like a country rube. He drifted to a place near the receiving line where he could observe the assembly while watching for his redhead to arrive.

In front of him, a knot of young gentlemen collected. Linc idly listened to their conversations.

One gallant with brown hair and freckles intoned in mock seriousness. "The 1906 San Francisco marriage mart begins tonight."

"You marry, Archie? Who would have you?" The fair-haired man grinned at Archie.

"Sneer if you dare, Bower," Archie replied in a theatrical tone.

A rakish-looking man with straight black hair stepped closer. "Finally looking for a wife, Bower?"

"None of your affair, Hunt." Bower's words came out stiffly.

The obvious friction between the two men—Bower so fair and

Hunt so dark—piqued Linc's interest. He read the tension in the stiffness of their posture as well as the way they positioned themselves as though they were in a ring about to box.

Hunt asked in a snide tone, "Anyone you fancy in particular, Bower?"

Archie interrupted, "We all want to get another look at her. No mystery about that. They've kept the redhead under wraps for a year since her old man died—"

Redhead? So they wanted to see her, too? Would that interfere with Linc's plans for her?

"Died and left her a fortune. That should interest you, Hunt," Bower said acidly. "Some need a wealthy bride more than others."

Stung, Hunt took a hasty step forward. "What I do is *none* of your business."

"You trifled with my sister for nearly a year. I won't forget that."

Linc stirred uneasily. What kind of game was Hunt at? Any man misleading an eligible girl made himself suspect.

"I did nothing that I ought not. I didn't propose." Hunt paused to dust an invisible speck from his sleeve. "We just didn't suit."

The scornful edge to Hunt's words brought a faint flush to Bower's face.

"You two, stop it," Archie urged in an undertone. "Look!"

Linc obeyed, too. Across the long room, a beautiful brunette in a fawn-colored gown was receiving Mrs. Ward's welcome. Hunt gave a barely discernible wolf whistle in approval.

"Is that Fleur Fourchette—that Southern belle who's come to live with her aunt?" Bower inquired.

"Right," Archie replied. "She's from New Orleans, an old French family."

Linc admired the brunette's pretty face and petite form, but briefly. This brunette didn't figure in his plan.

The three fashionable young blades moved away from Linc toward the receiving line. A small orchestra, arranged at one end of the ballroom, quietly played a piece by Haydn. Humming the tune in a near whisper, Linc watched the lovely Miss Fourchette smile prettily as Archie approached her and motioned toward the dance card, dangling from her small wrist.

Linc judged Archie, Hunt, and Bower to be sons of men who'd made their money in the gold mines or railroads, now connecting the east and west coasts. Restless young men, finished with education and trying to find a place in the scheme of things, overshadowed by successful fathers. Why then did Bower accuse Hunt of needing a wealthy wife? Why had Hunt trifled with Bower's sister? Though none of this had anything to do with his reason for being here, Linc's newspaper reporter instincts stirred.

"Miss Cecilia Jackson." The words had not been spoken louder than any of the other names, but it was the name Linc had been waiting for. His eyes snapped back to the imposing entrance.

His redhead had arrived. He moved forward to observe her. Her careful boarding school training was plain in her bearing. She moved like a diva making her first stage entrance. When she and her aunt reached the end of the receiving line, Linc overheard her starched-up aunt's final instructions. "Cecilia, remember your breeding. You are a cultured young woman, not a ninny-hammer like most of the girls here tonight."

The debutante's gaze skimmed the dazzling room.

Electric lights blazed from crystal chandeliers. Bunches of pink roses dangled from the branches of the chandeliers above, making the room redolent as any rose garden in summer. Tall, rainbow-colored silk draperies hung between the columns that supported the mezzanine and ringed the grand ballroom on three sides. The setting was the perfect one for her loveliness.

And Miss Jackson's beauty hadn't been exaggerated. Her hair was that highly prized warm auburn; her white skin creamy and unblemished except for a tiny enchanting mole at the corner of her mouth. How many young men this night would dream of kissing that beauty mark? And her eyes weren't the expected blue or green of most redheads. Her eyes were a rich brown, the shade of brown sugar. Linc waited to see who would approach her first.

"Miss Jackson." Archie bowed to her. "I'm Archie Pierce. We

were introduced at your come-out. May I have a place on your dance card tonight?"

She hesitated, smiling prettily at him. "How could I say no to the first gentleman to ask? I'm so afraid of being left a wallflower tonight." As she said the words, she managed to smile demurely. As Miss Jackson rewarded Archie with his name on her dance card, Linc realized that, though young and inexperienced, her entrance had a studied, practiced flavor.

As Miss Jackson moved away from Linc, other men stopped her, obviously soliciting dances. Not invited to the presentation parties, Linc had expected Miss Jackson to be just another beautiful deb. But his redhead in the flesh disconcerted him. He went over the facts he'd gleaned about her. She was nineteen. She'd lost her father a year ago. Her mother was ill, so her Boston aunt lived with her as chaperone. She was the richest unmarried heiress in San Francisco.

He'd expected Miss Jackson to be a sweet pink rosebud, which he would help to unfurl. Instead, she was a full red rose with thorns. The other debutantes fluttered around the gaily decorated room like colorful but insubstantial butterflies. They tittered behind fans and tried not to be seen glancing toward the young men, seeking their favor.

Cecilia Jackson, on the other hand, moved through the gathering like an aloof lioness on the prowl. Linc watched the young bloods react. They couldn't take their eyes off her. Neither could Linc.

As the evening progressed, Linc watched a complex ballroom drama slowly build in intensity. If Hunt showed interest in one of the debutantes, so did Bower. Linc also noted after young ladies had danced with Bower, they'd often frowned at Hunt. Was Bower warning them away from Hunt? Sowing seeds of distrust? Had Bower decided to exact revenge on Hunt for slighting his sister the year before?

The rollicking polka ended. The jaunty schottische began. Miss Jackson was swept away by young Bower who appeared more pained than happy. Then Linc straightened up. Had Miss Jackson really made eye contact with him? At the meeting of their eyes, a shock like electricity had connected them for a split second. Then she glanced away.

"Hello, Wagstaff." A journalist from the *Examiner* whose name Linc couldn't remember grinned at him. "Didn't think I'd see you here."

"Likewise." Linc shook the man's hand.

"I'm the society editor tonight."

Out of the corner of his eye, Linc continued to monitor the redhead. She was bestowing Bower with winsome smiles and flirtatious looks. He whispered something into her ear.

Linc made himself look away. "A promotion for you," Linc quipped. "A nice easy beat to cover."

The reporter smirked. "The society column is the most bloodthirsty one in the paper and you know it."

Linc nodded, but eyed Miss Jackson with a sinking sensation. Over Bower's shoulder, she now cast flirtatious glances toward Hunt. Though dancing with the pretty brunette, Hunt grinned back at Miss Jackson, winking.

"Are you enjoying the unfolding drama?" the reporter asked.

"You mean the daring Miss Jackson?"

"Thanks for my lead." The man pulled out a stub of a pencil and jotted down a note in a small navy notebook.

The schottische ended. A number of gentlemen hastened to the lovely redhead to vie for the next dance, a quadrille. Hunt shouldered his way through. Bower didn't give way, but stayed right beside the redhead. The two men squared off with her between them. Where was her aunt? She should intervene before—

"You haven't been dancing, Lincoln," his hostess Mrs. Ward appeared at Linc's side.

Linc bowed but couldn't take his eyes off Bower and Hunt. Hunt had taken the redhead's hand. Bower crowded close to Hunt, speaking too low for Linc to hear. As the two men drew even closer, Miss Jackson pouted, but triumph glowed in her eyes.

Mrs. Ward stared at her now, as did others.

Across the room, the heedless redhead made a show of deliberating between Bower and Hunt for the quadrille.

Mrs. Ward took a step forward. "Does she have any idea what trouble she's causing?"

Bower and Hunt were now nose to nose. Ignoring Miss Jackson.

Mrs. Ward drew in a quick breath. "They'll be shouting before long. Oh, this is dreadful. A scene in my ballroom." Frantically, the hostess motioned for the musicians to start the quadrille.

Hunt tugged at Miss Jackson's hand. Bower took the other. Miss Jackson flushed pink, dismay flashing over her face. She tried to pull away. Was she just now realizing what she'd sparked?

In a split-second decision, Linc strode with poised assurance right into the eye of the storm, forcing Bower and Hunt to give ground and release her. Linc claimed Miss Jackson's hand. "Our quadrille begins," he said caressingly. "Let's not be tardy in joining our set."

Both Hunt and Bower objected. Linc didn't even glance at them. Miss Jackson let Linc lead her into the set.

Chapter 2

A firm hand drew Cecy away from Hunt and Bower. She was dancing the quadrille with the stranger who'd rescued her. Sensing curious eyes, she blushed. What had gone wrong? Who was leading her through the quadrille?

She glanced at the stranger and drew a sharp breath. Why, he was the man whom she had glimpsed during the schottische. She studied him. He wasn't a youth like her other partners tonight. His hair was dark blond and his eyes clear blue. Over six feet tall, he wore his stylish evening dress well. But who was he? And why had he rescued her?

Then the stranger looked into her eyes—wrenchingly. She felt as though he opened her heart and read it in a glance. Instantly, she looked away. He'd had that startling effect on her twice this evening. Her pulse pounded at her temples.

Expertly, he drew her into a quick spin. So near to her, only a whisper separated them. He smelled like warmed autumn spices. He possessed an indefinable air of assurance she envied. Did he know how she trembled inside? His warm breath feathered wisps of her hair at the nape of her neck. She shivered. No other partner tonight had evoked a reaction such as this from her. Why did all her senses soar at this man's touch? She felt as if she were losing herself to him.

The point in the dance came where the blond stranger released her to cross the square and dance with another partner. She stepped mincingly to the opposite corner of the set of eight. Summoning her courage, she smiled at the other man in their set who now faced her.

He nodded, no greeting in his eyes. The rebuff chilled Cecy like a splash of cold water. Hunt and Bower were responsible for this. How could they have forced a disagreement in the midst of a ball? She'd only done everything Auntie had told her. The fault was theirs.

The disapproving gentleman danced with her, then released her once more to the blond stranger who stepped to her side and led her in a sequence of steps. His powerful sway over her sensations, the general disapproval she felt—she wished the dance would end. Covertly, she glanced at the faces of the ladies in their set. Not one would make eye contact with her. Her spirit failed her. She made a misstep. Frantically, she looked to her partner. "I'm indisposed. Please lead me from the floor."

The stranger swept her into a waltzlike embrace. Restraining her, he increased his pressure at the small of her back. "Courage," he whispered.

His comment sparked her temper. She had strength. She gave him a furious glare.

He chuckled.

Oh, men were altogether contemptible. She averted her face. First, Bower and Hunt misbehaving and now this.

She tightened inside, marshaling her will to survive, to succeed. She smiled brilliantly at the dancers in her set. The other ladies still didn't meet her eye easily, but who were they to judge her? She'd show them, all of them. She gave her partner as charming a smile as she could.

He looked back unimpressed, amused.

Chagrined again, she held her smile in place. She'd teach him to laugh at her. "Who are you?" she purred into his ear.

"A friend."

Was he going to play hide-and-seek with her? She tamped down her irritation. Honey gathered more bees than vinegar. "Friends have names," she returned.

"I'm a friend of Mrs. Ward," he replied with maddening calm. "She knows my name."

His insult rendered her speechless. She tugged at his hold on her. He murmured, "Miss Jackson, please don't cause another scene within minutes of your first."

The injustice of what he intimated made her seethe. "I didn't cause the scene. And if I want your advice, I'll ask for it," she hissed.

"You don't seem to know enough to realize what you need."

She gasped, then lifted her chin. "I won't forget your high-handedness."

"No matter. I know you probably won't accept my advice, but I'm going to give it to you anyway. You don't have to conquer San Francisco all in one night. And don't be so obvious about competing with the New Orleans belle. She won't suffer from your actions, you will."

She gave him a startled look. "What do you mean?"

"You heard me, and I always say exactly what I mean." He spun her to the final four beats of the dance, then bowed. "Thank you for a lovely dance," he said loud enough for those around them to hear. Then he whispered, "But don't entertain San Francisco society with another scene tonight. Save something for the next ball." He grinned and walked away.

She swallowed down her hot reply. Her next partner approached her cautiously. She gave him a dazzling smile, but inside she rioted.

Shrill laughter of children exploded all around Linc as he, Meg, and Susan's grandson Del stepped off the horse trolley at the amusement park on Haight Street. For their Saturday afternoon treat, Meg wanted to see the wild animals.

"I see a lion!" Meg shouted, towing Linc forward by one chilled hand while Del held back on the other. "Hurry, Daddy!"

Linc felt like the linchpin of a seesaw. "Del, don't you want to see the lions?"

"No, That stuff's for kids. I'll wait here." Del pulled away and went to stand by a streetlamp.

For kids? Del was only ten, just three years older than Meg. But Linc couldn't halt Meg's enthusiastic plunge toward the amusement. "Don't stray, Del!"

His impetuous, determined daughter dragged him into the thick of the crowd.

"Look! It's a lion!" With gloved hands, Meg clung to the bars. A lioness paraded out of the lion house with the same expression as the audacious redhead. Last night, as he'd led Miss Jackson into the quadrille, she'd looked chastened, shocked at her own behavior. For those few moments, Linc had felt himself drawn to her. She'd seemed so innocent . . . but that hadn't lasted even as long as their dance.

Linc glanced backward. Del stood stolidly against the lamppost. Since the death of Del's parents, the boy and his grandmother, Susan, had lived with Linc's family. When Linc had decided to move to San Francisco, Susan had insisted on moving with them. No stranger was going to raise Meg, her best friend's only grandchild.

The move from Chicago hadn't seemed to bother Del at first. Lately, however, whenever they left their home, Del became silent and moody. Linc wondered whether his own sorrow over losing Virginia been communicated to the boy? He still felt homesick for the life he'd shared with his beloved wife.

Now Linc put mourning behind him. His daughter was seven years old. She needed to have her childhood. He bought Meg peanuts to feed the chattering, cavorting monkeys. Finally, chilled by the winter dampness, they walked back to Del.

"You missed it all," Meg said in disappointment.

Del looked at his feet. "I saw what I wanted from here."

"Let's go." Linc drew them to the curb to wait for the next trolley home. "Susan will have hot cocoa waiting for us."

The four of them sat around the square kitchen table in the quiet house. The new house still didn't feel like home. But Linc leaned back in his chair, drawing as much solace as he could from the warmth of the oven, the fragrance of beef roasting slowly, the sweet chocolate on his tongue.

He studied Del. The lad's glum face tore at Linc's heart. He recalled the summer he'd been given his first dog, Butch. Maybe the children needed a pet in this lonely time.

Susan gave Linc an inquiring glance over Del's head. Linc shrugged. Finally, Susan stood up. "Del, later you need to practice your piano. The tuner was here this afternoon. And I bought you that new sheet music you wanted."

"'Maple Leaf Rag'?" For an instant, excitement flickered on the boy's features.

"Yes, but I expect to hear more Frederic Chopin than Scott Joplin. Do you understand me?"

"Yes, ma'am." Del became sober again.

"Now, Meg, you come with me. You have to spend time today on your embroidery."

"But I don't like embroidery."

"That doesn't matter. Your mother, may she rest in peace, started you on that sampler and I'm going to make sure you finish it." As Susan stepped behind her grandson, she nodded at Linc, clearly telling him to talk to Del and find out what was wrong. Meg grumbled, but followed Susan out of the kitchen.

Linc stood up. "We'd better go out and see if we can figure out why my auto wouldn't start last night."

"All right," Del agreed without enthusiasm.

In the old carriage house, now the garage, Linc switched on the dangling garage lights and gazed around for a moment. Electric lights in a garage and his own automobile. He'd never get used to the wonders of this new century and the change in his living standard after the large inheritance from his stepfather. His stepfather's last request was for Linc to use his talents as a journalist to inspire others with wealth and influence. Linc's writing with his stepfather's money behind it could change lives for the better.

Del's unhappy face brought Linc back to the present. Mulling over how to help the child beside him, Linc lifted the hood and propped it open. The engine. This was when he really felt inept. He understood the theory of the spontaneous combustion engine, but theory didn't fix the car.

"Del, get that manual off the shelf and we'll go through the checklist again."

Del fetched the large black clothbound book. He began reading off the parts to be checked if the car wouldn't start: magneto, carburetor . . .

Linc paused, looking toward Del whose face was masked by the manual he held. "I want you to tell me what's bothering you."

The book slowly lowered, but still Del wouldn't look Linc in the eye.

"Whatever it is, we'll work it out."

"It's not something we can work out." Del looked up rebelliously. "We can't change our skin. I'm colored. You're white."

Linc wiped his greasy hands on a rag and recalled his own childhood and the names he'd sometimes been called. The closeness of his mother and Susan had made him a target, too. "Has someone been bothering you at school?"

"It isn't just at school." Del balanced the manual on the bumper. "Everywhere we go—when we're together, you and me or me and Meg, people *look* at me." Del wouldn't meet Linc's gaze. "Don't you see them *looking?*"

Linc leaned against the car. "Sometimes," he admitted, "but when I was your age in Chicago, people used to look at me the same way when I was with your grandmother."

"They did?" Del glanced up.

"Yes, because there were so few Negroes in Chicago right after the Civil War. But they just thought she was my 'mammy.'"

Del rolled his eyes at this.

Linc shrugged. "They would have looked shocked if I'd told them the truth—that Susan wasn't my mother's hired girl. Susan and mother ran our boardinghouse together as equals. They were best friends."

"But people didn't look at me funny in Chicago."

"That's because they knew of the long-lasting relationship between our two families. Not that they knew of the friendship between us. For your family's protection, we've always had to let people believe that your family were our . . ."

"Servants?" Del scowled.

"Yes, unfortunately. After your grandmother married and left us, people just thought we were good to your family. Trying to make people understand the truth held real danger for you. Your grandparents found out freedom didn't mean equality."

He knew it would be futile to tell Del that, in spite of prejudice, he was a fortunate child. So many children, black and white, lived in squalor and abuse. Photographs taken by a young Progressive, Edward Hines, still haunted him. Children with exhausted and hopeless faces atop shrunken, ill-nourished bodies. He couldn't get the images out of his mind. He had to change the images for the better.

"If I could change things for you, Del, I would. But this century is still young, change is coming. Remember, your grandmother was born a slave, but your grandfather and father voted in elections. You will someday, too."

"I don't like the way people look at me."

"God doesn't either, Del." Linc pulled the boy into a quick, rough hug. He could provide for Del, love Del, but he couldn't change the world for Del. Even at the beginning of a new century, he couldn't protect him from the consequences of being born dark-skinned.

Chapter 3

Attending Cecilia's aunt's first afternoon tea as a journalist, Linc stood in the Jackson mansion's vast ivory-and-gold drawing room. Satins and silks in jewel tones, large decorated hats, lacy white hand-kerchiefs—all created a heady montage of high fashion and higher privilege. Linc was impressed by the attendance by San Francisco's finest, the wives and daughters of the richest men in the city—the Big Four of the Central Pacific Railroad and the Bonanza Kings of the Comstock Lode. Cecilia's aunt, a newcomer, evidently had the right touch or maybe her drawing card was her broad Boston accent.

Near Linc, the pretty debutantes of 1906 had gravitated to two ivory-brocaded sofas that faced each other. In apricot silk, Miss Jackson sipped tea from her translucent cup. "Are you enjoying your visit in San Francisco, Miss Fourchette?"

"Why, yes, San Francisco is so different from New Orleans." The attractive brunette's soft Southern drawl contrasted sharply with the touch of Boston in Miss Jackson's voice.

Mrs. Ward's protégé, a little brown sparrow named Ann, leaned forward. "I hear that your family is one of the oldest Bourbon families in New Orleans," she said with obvious awe.

"That's somewhat true," Miss Fourchette said self-deprecatingly. "My family is descended from one of the original French colonial families, but not all Bourbons are."

"Really? Being raised in Boston, I know little of Southern society." With a trace of derision in her smile, Miss Jackson set her cup and saucer without a sound onto the inlaid rosewood table.

Miss Fourchette smiled, but said nothing.

"Smart girl," Linc silently commented.

The redhead had avoided him thus far. But he wasn't deceived. She'd taken the effort to discover his identity and have him invited as the freelance reporter to write up this tea. And in the midst of tepid debutante conversation, she was sizing him up.

"Oh, the photographer's arrived!" Cecy exclaimed. Out of the corner of her eye, she'd glimpsed that irritating reporter grin at her.

"Photographer?" Ann looked around dismayed.

"Yes, I'd like a photograph of the all debs who came out with me." She'd thought long and hard to come up with a truly distinctive, modern favor for her guests. "Each of you will receive a framed print." Cecy motioned them all to precede her, turning her back on *that man*.

Fleur smiled. "I'll treasure it."

As Auntie introduced the photographer, she gave her a reminding look. Cecy nodded, recalling Auntie's advice. She was to appear modest during the picture-taking, but make sure she was central in the photographs.

Cecy had spent her life trying to be unnoticed. Fortunately, after her father's death, Auntie had taken her to Europe, had shown her what life could be. She'd learned about lavish hotel life, operas, parties, balls, champagne, and flirtation. She wouldn't give up her freedom by marrying, but neither would she spend her life as a pitied spinster.

The photographer instructed, "Miss Jackson, will you stand beside the chair please?" She nodded and took her place, which would upstage all the other debs just as Auntie had planned.

When as a child she'd been banished to the Boston boarding school, she'd been robbed of this privileged life that should have been hers. Only once had her father provided her more than the others, extra music lessons. But Auntie was the one who'd requested them for her.

My whole life lies before me. I'll be the Belle of San Francisco. My reception for the Great Caruso during his visit in April will crown my social triumph. Then I'll be independent and get to know my mother.

She obeyed the photographer and tilted her head more toward him. She smiled for him, a real smile. For her future.

Linc looked on as the other guests called to the young ladies to stand up straight, to tilt their heads in different positions and to smile, smile. Linc worried that before the session ended, the beleaguered photographer would explode with one of his powder flashes.

Linc was aware of Miss Jackson's covert attention to him. Whenever she thought no one was looking, her gaze drifted to him. Was there some surprise she had in store for him? His mind worked on two levels: one watching and taking mental notes about the occasion for the article he'd write up for the *Bulletin*; the other leaped ahead trying to guess what Miss Jackson would say when she did speak to him.

The photographer shot his last negative, folded up his tripod, and escaped. The debutantes drifted toward the two sofas again. Linc followed them.

"What a truly original touch, Miss Jackson," Fleur said. "I only wish someone had thought of it during my New Orleans come-out."

Another deb, very scrawny and fair to almost colorless, said in catty satisfaction, "This is your second season too, then."

Linc tried to place the plain deb. Someone had pointed her out to him.

"Why, yes, I feel almost greedy enjoying a second season. But my aunt has no daughter and she insisted I let her sponsor me here."

"Oh, I wouldn't want to have to do two seasons in two different cities," shy Ann squeaked.

Fleur patted Ann's hand. "You've gotten off to a wonderful start. Mrs. Ward's ball was simply exquisite."

"And it had quite *exciting* moments." The plain girl grinned, her eyes straying toward Miss Jackson.

Recognition hit Linc. He'd done his society research. The plain girl was Clarence Bower's sister, the spurned Clarissa Bower. No wonder she sounded cross. Why would Hunt ever pay court to such a lanky and unprepossessing girl?

In response to Clarissa's jibe, Miss Jackson raised her chin, her eyes sparkling with unspoken wrath.

"Oh, you mean that silly little dust-up between those two gentlemen?" Fleur giggled. "High-couraged gentlemen can always be relied on to add a touch of drama to any evening."

Linc paused. Once again he was impressed with the lady from New Orleans. Did Miss Jackson realize the signal service Fleur was executing for her?

With a mischievous grin, Fleur went on, "Why at my first ball, two gentlemen threatened to duel over me."

Fleur gave her distinctive trill of laughter. "No duel took place. Though I suspect fisticuffs may have."

The debs tittered at this. The plain Clarissa frowned.

"The incident was none of my doing," Miss Jackson spoke up. "Men will be men, Auntie says."

Linc shook his head. Why hadn't she remained silent? Fleur had effectively closed the subject without bringing Miss Jackson into it by name and dredging up the fiasco at the ball.

"Did you hear? Victor Hunt has a new auto," Fleur again turned to a safer topic.

"Clarence got one, too," Clarissa said, still sounding grumpy. "They're planning a race through the streets of San Francisco."

Miss Jackson looked up. "An auto race. How exciting."

"They might be hurt." Little Ann sounded shocked.

"I doubt that." Clarissa pointed her nose upward.

"I'm buying an automobile," Miss Jackson declared. "I intend to learn how to drive it, too."

Did she? Linc was intrigued in spite of himself.

Ann gasped. "Drive a car?"

Miss Jackson chuckled. "Why not? Autos don't rear up at the slightest thing."

Interrupting them, Cecilia's aunt clapped her hands asking for attention. "Ladies, Miss Fourchette's aunt tells me that her niece is quite accomplished on the piano and has a lovely singing voice. Please help me encourage her to entertain us."

All the ladies clapped. Fleur rose with convincing modesty. She moved to the other end of the vast drawing room, sat down at the dark grand piano and began to play and sing in a pretty voice, "I Dream of Jeannie with the Light Brown Hair."

Observing Miss Jackson drifting to the buffet table, Linc met her there. He busied himself choosing an appetizer from among the rich array of food.

"Good afternoon, Mr. Wagstaff," Miss Jackson said in a quietly triumphant voice.

He casually bowed. "Miss Jackson." Then he turned back to the table.

"I found out who you are."

"I never doubted you would," he said, then popped a featherlight cheese puff into his mouth.

"It was I who asked Auntie to invite you here."

"I thought so." He spread caviar on a cracker.

She bristled. "Don't you want to know why?"

"I know why." With an urbane smile, he accepted a cup of creamy tea from the Chinese waiter tending the table.

"You are the rudest man."

He looked at her. "Do you really intend to drive an auto?"

"Yes, but—"

"I'll be happy to take you to the auto race." He walked on down the buffet table.

With a curt swish of her skirts, she pursued him. "Mr.—"

He interrupted her, "You're still competing much too obviously against Miss Fourchette. You're going to end up in everyone's bad book."

"If you're not careful about offending me, Auntie will make certain you're not invited to any more society functions."

He shook his head at her. "If you think that, then you don't really know who I am."

"Yes, I do." She sounded hoarsely desperate. "You're a journalist who's starting up a weekly society journal."

He chuckled. "Your sources aren't very reliable." He walked away from her.

She trailed him until they were partially hidden by several potted plants behind a sofa. She hissed, "Don't walk away from me."

At the other end of the vast drawing room, Fleur accepted applause, then agreed to sing another song, "Lorena." The mournful song settled over the room. Even Cecilia fell silent.

Two matrons sitting on the sofa in front of them leaned toward each other to talk. From behind, Linc could see only their hats. The one in a brown felt hat said, "I don't care how good a front she puts up today. She caused that dreadful scene at Ward's ball—"

The other lady in a mauve hat nodded. "To be fair, Hunt and Bower compete in everything and now more since Hunt insulted Bower's sister."

"Didn't Hunt's father insist his son marry Clarissa Bower or he'd disinherit him?"

"Never say so." The mauve hat bobbed. "Do you think he's trying to marry a different fortune and best his father?"

The brown hat bent. "That Jackson chit better watch out. Hunt is interested in her money, not her."

Uneasy, Linc watched Cecilia's stunned expression.

Mauve hat said, "She doesn't have a mother to guide her—"

"And why is that? Where is her mother?" the brown hat asked archly.

The mauve hat bent forward. "You know she's been ill at that sanitarium south on the way to Monterey for years."

Linc hated hearing such unsympathetic gossip. *Why is Cecilia's mother in a sanitarium?*

The brown hat tilted backward. "That's one way to say it. Neither her father's millions nor her mother's Boston background can blind me to the truth. Bad blood always comes out. Mark my words."

Cecilia stiffened beside him. Fearing she might actually respond, he steered her by the elbow to a convenient anteroom.

"How dare they?" Miss Jackson's low voice shook with temper.

"I tried to warn you not to push yourself forward—"

"Auntie said that," the redhead went on in a tone of dawning disbelief, "the scene the other night was merely a lack of tact by Bower and Hunt—a gaucherie."

"Your aunt is a stranger here. She overestimates the Boston connection. That might actually work against you."

Her eyes flashed with anger. "Who do you think you are? If you're going to succeed with your society paper, you need *my* good graces."

Giving her a bleak look, he shook his head. "You've been misinformed. My journal will be about *social issues*, Miss Jackson, not society news." He bowed and left her.

How did God expect him to use this young woman who was completely uninterested in anything beyond social ambition and seemed hell-bent on self-destruction? It had all seemed so plain to him in Chicago. Virginia's death had made him ready to leave. His inheritance had opened new opportunities for further social progress. And this redhead had fascinated him since he'd discovered her in his research. But had he gotten it all wrong?

Applause for Miss Fourchette's last song greeted him as he reentered the drawing room. Miss Jackson swept past him toward the piano.

Fleur stepped forward to meet her. "Are you going to sing for us now?"

Miss Jackson nodded imperiously.

"Would you like me to accompany you?"

Miss Jackson moved in front of the piano keyboard. "I'll sing a capella." Fleur left her alone by the piano.

Linc sincerely hoped Miss Jackson's anger hadn't led her into something foolhardy. Was her voice equal to the challenge of singing without piano?

She touched one key, sounding one high note. Then she faced them all, her eyes heavenward. Her rich voice soared above them all.

Linc recognized the aria from *Aida*, Verdi's tragic love story. When Aida discovers that the man she loves and her father will go into battle as enemies, she despairs, "Pity me, heaven."

Linc stood, transfixed. The lady's glorious soprano voice swept him beyond his surroundings. The deep misery conveyed through her rich voice etched his aching heart, reminding him of all he'd lost these last few years.

Still he couldn't take his eyes off Cecilia. In the late afternoon sun flowing down from the skylight, her hair flamed. Her creamy white throat vibrated with song. The aria swept on. No one whispered. No one looked away.

Her voice reached higher, higher until the final plea to heaven. She flung out her arms in a gesture of despair. Then with the last, wrenching note, she bowed her head. Silence.

The ladies surged to their feet, applauding. The virtuosity of the solo had been stunning, stirring. Linc shouted, "Bravo! Bravo!" Miss Jackson curtseyed.

He realized then in her singing he'd finally seen—for the first time—the real Cecilia. Grief, sympathy, tenderness—they'd poured from her lips. What had wounded her so, made her feel so profoundly? And why did she hide this depth?

A beautiful, young woman with a heart full of compassion would have been an irresistible combination, one that could have

San Francisco for the asking. Linc longed to tell her, "Cecilia, the woman you're hiding could shake San Francisco to its foundation. Take off the mask."

Linc walked up Market Street to the corner of Third where *The Call* and *Examiner* buildings stood on opposite corners. As a newspaperman, he knew all the stories of this brash city, famous for its newspapers. The *Examiner*, "The Monarch of the Dailies," was William Randolph Hearst's paper. Ten years before, *The Call* had been sold in an all-day auction for $360,000. The *Chronicle* stood across the street, its skyscraper clock tower reminding Linc to get to the *Bulletin* office to turn in his copy on the afternoon tea.

Hurrying on, he wondered if he'd succeed in the newspaper world of this city. The new Progressives were changing the East and South. But the complacent fashionable wealthy of San Francisco needed shaking up to use their means in bettering the future of America. The West needed a voice raised for social justice.

But was he that voice? Learning the real Cecilia Jackson hid behind a veil had shaken his confidence. He'd believed Cecilia was a merely spoiled, rich deb. A girl who flaunted her wealth and had no knowledge of what gaining that wealth had cost others. He'd been so sure he'd had her all figured out. He'd been wrong.

Entering the cluttered desks and listening to the ticker tape run in the *Bulletin* offices, he experienced a sharp jab of homesickness. Leaving the *Tribune* months ago had been like tying off an artery.

He walked back out into the chill evening, mist swirling up, his spirits floundering.

"Wagstaff?"

Linc turned to see a tall, raw-boned man with a walrus mustache in the *Bulletin* doorway. "Yes?"

"I'm Fremont Older, managing editor." He offered his hand.

Recognizing the name, Linc shook with him. Older, who'd started out as a "tramp" printer, was a big man in San Francisco journalism. So what did Older want of him?

"Got a minute?"

"Certainly," Linc said.

Older led him inside to his large office. The two sat down facing each other. "How'd you get the only invite to that Jackson tea?"

Linc looked up, amused. "Yes, it is a foggy evening."

"Eh?" Older glared at him.

"Sorry. Your directness startled me. I just endured an afternoon of genteel, ladylike conversation." But Linc'd heard some very un-ladylike conversation this afternoon—not only from the two hats, but from Cecilia Jackson, too.

Older's face cleared; he chuckled. "Not much of an assignment for a real newsman."

Linc nodded, unwilling to discuss why Cecilia had invited only him. He'd made the mistake of thinking she was still an innocent, not past her first youth like he was. He'd struggle writing a column of meaningless pleasantries. The hidden Cecilia Jackson was the real story. The one he couldn't tell.

"So what do you think of the daring Miss Jackson and her stuffy Boston aunt?"

Linc hated being less than candid, but he didn't want to further rumors. "I'm undecided," Linc replied. "I think I have her figured out, then she shows another side of herself." That was the truth— though barely.

"I'm trying to find out if she fits her family." Older steepled his fingers.

Linc's expression asked Older to go on.

"Her father, August Jackson, was the son of a German immigrant who didn't come to pan for gold. After taking the name Jackson, he set up shop extorting money from the forty-niners. One dollar for an egg—that kind of thing. When August came of age, he showed the same business shrewdness and greed. Instead of dissipating his father's wealth, he doubled it."

Linc wondered why Older was telling him this.

Older leaned back in his chair. "Her father's one talent and religion was making money. I'm not a religious man, but August Jackson violated at least nine of the Ten Commandments—more than once. Never heard him accused of murder. But he had a nasty temper."

The words chilled Linc. He'd never known his own father, who'd been a casualty of the Civil War, but his stepfather had been a true father to him. "Poor Miss Jackson."

Older shook his head. "I doubt she has much memory of him."

Linc gave Older a startled glance. "He died just last year."

"That's right. But his daughter grew up in Boston."

"I knew she went to school there, but I thought she was there for finishing school."

"No, she was sent away at seven."

"Seven?" Linc asked, shocked.

"This is the story. August was so bad, no girl in San Francisco would marry him, no decent girl. So he went back East, put on a good show, and married a Boston girl. Back in San Francisco, when the Boston girl finally realized what she'd married, she sent the daughter to boarding school in Boston near her unmarried sister. The aunt that came with Cecilia from Boston."

"Why didn't the mother just take the child and go home?" Linc asked.

Older shook his head. "Father disowned her for marrying Jackson."

"I've heard she's at a sanitarium in the mountains. Why?"

"No one knows for sure. Could be insanity or . . ." Older held up one hand. "Miss Jackson's a stranger in her hometown. Everyone in society is waiting to see if she'll turn out like her father."

Linc frowned. Cecilia Jackson was playing a daring game trying to impress society. Was she aware that people might be watching for signs of her father's bad blood. Just as in the gossip they'd over-heard?

"So how did you get the only invite today?"

Linc looked up. He couldn't tell the truth—that Cecilia had wanted to make him dance on the end of her string. "I extricated her from a minor unpleasantness at the Ward ball." Maybe he could talk to the aunt.

"Makes sense." Older nodded. "Are you likely to get more invitations?"

"Might." Grateful for the information Older had given him, Linc explained, "I've got Boston connections myself."

"I know. Boston bankers." Older grinned.

Linc nodded. Older had done his homework.

"The *Bulletin* will be glad to buy any more society articles you can get."

Chagrined, Linc nodded noncommittally. "I really want to get my journal operating."

"Heard you're a muckraker. You'll find a lot of muck to rake here, starting with Mayor Schmitz. A political puppet for the Reuf gang. Corruption is so thick and rich in this town you could cut it with a butter knife."

"Politics isn't my focus."

"What is?" Older leaned forward.

"Children and their welfare. Have you heard of the National Child Labor Committee?"

"Can't say I have."

"Well, you and the rest of this city's about to hear all about it."

Leaning forward in her seat in the darkened opera house, Cecy tried to lose herself in the melodious duet between deceitful Lt. Pinkerton and his trusting Japanese bride—Cio-Cio-San, or Butterfly.

Restless, Cecy couldn't rid herself of the images from her afternoon visit to the sanitarium. Her mother's pale face. Her listless eyes, nervous fingers. The year before at Cecy's father's funeral, her frail mother in the care of a nurse had collapsed and been returned to the sanitarium. Auntie had said her mother was too sick to leave the sanitarium and that the doctors discouraged visits, so they'd gone away to Europe. Cecy hadn't questioned this but should she have?

After the soprano's lilting notes died, the theater lights signaling the intermission came up to applause. Cecy pressed a lacy handkerchief to her eyes, wiping away tears that had nothing to do with the opera.

Her aunt in sedate gray velvet glanced around. "Gentlemen will visit our box. Be sure to give Miss Fourchette to our left a gracious nod. I'll keep a discreet watch to see if she receives more visitors than you."

"Yes, Auntie." Cecy struggled to keep a smile on her face. While the opera was being performed, she had tried to lose herself in it. Now her aunt demanded she perform on the social tightrope. But she'd show everyone she could attract and keep admirers who behaved as "gentlemen."

After being declared Belle of 1906, she wouldn't spend the rest of her life in the shadows, an unfortunate spinster like her aunt or a broken woman like her mother. If she chose not to marry, no one would dare say it was because she'd had no offers. But what had happened to her mother? Or what exactly had she done to spoil her chances, as Auntie always told her? Why wouldn't Auntie ever tell her the whole truth?

Hunt, handsome in black evening dress, stepped through the box's velvet curtains. "Miss Jackson."

Extending her kid-gloved hand, she wished she could turn away. Did Hunt actually think she'd accept an offer from someone as distasteful as he?

Arriving shortly after, Bower asked, "Will you be attending our masked ball?"

"A masquerade. How charming," she replied by rote.

The lights flickered. The men said their adieux and left. Cool relief whistled through her. Now she could be alone again with her thoughts about her mother.

Auntie's voice intruded. "Bower stopped at Miss Fourchette's box first. I don't like that."

And I don't really care. Today, mother had merely stared at them both—as though she didn't know them. Finally, Cecy hadn't been able to hold back, "Mother, Auntie and I are living in San Francisco now." Trembling, Cecy had taken up her mother's soft, limp hand. "We want you to get better and come to live with us."

Her mother had stared at her, looking expressionless but somehow frightened. Finally she'd whispered, "I'm not well." That was all. Cecy had craved so much more. They'd been apart so many years.

Then just before the lights went down for the next act, Cecy glimpsed that man, Wagstaff, across the theater. Handsome with his straight nose, square chin, and honey-colored hair, he drew her attention, but it wasn't his good looks. Gazing across at him, she tingled as his clear blue eyes connect with hers, piercing her, making her feel exposed.

Other gentlemen flattered her, begged for her favor. Not Mr. Wagstaff. Would he really take her to the auto race? Did she even want to speak to him again?

The opera went on. A stage cannon fired. Pinkerton's ship had arrived in the harbor. In awful irony, Butterfly rejoiced singing of her love and cherry blossoms. Tears ran down Cecy's face.

Linc shifted in his seat. Puccini's *Madame Butterfly*, the tragic story of an innocent girl who gives her love to a cad, paralleled too closely Older's story of Cecilia's parents. Did Cecilia know the truth? Should he try to warn her that her father's deplorable reputation placed her in social peril? Would she believe him if he did?

Linc watched Cecy's profile by the light from the stage. Dressed in a soft shade of pink, she matched the silk cherry blossoms on the stage. But her sadness showed clearly in the lines of her body: the dipping of her chin, the slump of her shoulders, the handkerchief dabbed at her eyes.

Linc longed to comfort her. The treacherous course she was on could bring more pain. *How can I get through to her?*

Then the opera ensnared him again. Butterfly sang, longing for Pinkerton to return. It unleashed his own impossible yearning for his lost love, Virginia. A knot of agony clotted in his throat. *Lord, I know she's with you, but I can't let go.*

Then on stage, learning of her husband's betrayal, Madame Butterfly sang in despair, "Goodbye, happy home, home of love." He looked up to Cecilia. As Butterfly's voice soared higher in anguish, steel bands tightened around Linc's heart. He recalled Cecilia singing as desperate Aida; her voice rivaled this soprano's.

Now that he knew the truth about Cecilia's family, Linc glimpsed her deep needs. A sudden urge to hold her in his arms and soothe her anguish with kisses and soft words rocked Linc to his foundation. He imagined the silky softness of her hair between his fingers . . .

Linc's chair began to sway. The stage curtains swished side to side as though a wind blew through the theater. Linc sat, petrified. On stage, the fake front of the Japanese house crashed down. The soprano screamed. Some woman shrieked, "Earthquake!" Linc leaped from his seat and raced toward the staircase to Cecilia's box.

Chapter 4

Barely keeping his balance on the undulating floor, Linc brushed through the curtains of Cecilia's box. Cecilia was swaying but motionless.

"Get the girl!" The aunt escaped past Linc.

Heart pounding, Linc swept Cecilia into his arms. The theater stopped its rocking. Linc halted. Nervous laughter rippled throughout the audience. The stage curtains swished to a stop. In midshriek, the soprano fell silent.

Linc looked down at the woman in his arms and murmured, "Cecilia." She smelled of spring flowers and her head rested on his shoulder. In spite of the corset, her womanly softness brought a rush of awareness that engulfed him. He pressed his face into the velvety fold of her neck.

Her dazed eyes cleared. "Mr. Wagstaff?"

"Just a tremor." He carried her back to her chair. Aware of the impropriety of their intimacy, he tried to set her down.

But she clawed at his shoulders. "Don't leave me alone."

The house lights went up. Linc didn't want people to see him embracing Cecilia even in these circumstances. He knelt, setting her on her chair, effectually hiding himself behind the sides of the box. "I won't leave you until you are recovered."

She clung to him.

"I promise." He captured her soft hands and tenderly drew them down. "It was just a tremor. Nothing bad is going to happen. It's over."

"I-I've never felt anything like that," she stammered.

"We're both newcomers here." Though breaking their connection pained him, he drew his hands from hers.

Her aunt hurried back into the box. Linc helped the distraught older woman take her seat.

"Auntie, are you all right?" Cecilia's voice broke on the last word.

Applause drowned out Miss Higginbottom's reply. The curtain rose. The lights dimmed. A few bars of the overture announced the resumption of the opera. Still shaken, Linc bowed to both the ladies and walked to the rear of the box.

"Mr. Wagstaff, thank you."

At the sound of Cecilia's voice, he turned. "My pleasure." The velvet curtains fell into place behind him. He meant to walk back to his seat, but the lingering sensation of Cecilia in his arms made it impossible for him to return to sitting quietly. He walked outside, going home to check on Meg, Susan, and Del. The haunting melody of the tragic heroine's aria followed him out into the clear, cool night.

February 12, 1906

On Montgomery Street on a clear, crisp day, the elite were on parade to see and be seen, the Saturday-afternoon promenade. Cecy slipped both hands into her stylish fox-fur muff. An emptiness squeezed inside her. What was so wrong with her mother that Auntie wouldn't discuss it? Did her mother have a fatal illness? Cecy half stumbled over uneven paving.

"Be careful," Auntie grumbled beside her.

As they strolled, Cecy nodded and smiled to acquaintances, yet she felt like a mannequin. Wearing beautiful new clothing every day, instead of an ugly school uniform, still delighted her. However, the burden of conquering society weighed more and more. Her aunt had advised her that she must be declared the Belle of her season. Otherwise, when she didn't marry, she'd be pitied as a failure or an oddity for the rest of her life. She wanted to get past her season. Then she'd be free to get to know her mother. Wouldn't Auntie tell her if her mother's condition might prove fatal?

Victor Hunt crossed the street directly to Cecy. A disreputable air clung to him and he often smelled of spirits. Cecy forced a smile, but inside she hissed, "I don't trust you."

Auntie began walking slower, letting Hunt draw Cecy ahead for a *tête-à-tête*. Cecy hated it when Auntie did that.

Just ahead of them, Fleur Fourchette alighted from a glossy black carriage with Clarence Bower's assistance. For once, Cecy was glad to see her, even in the company of the eligible Bower. With Fleur and Bower, Cecy would make their unwelcome twosome a foursome. Out of the corner of her eye, she glimpsed Mr. Wagstaff across the busy street. She recalled his embrace and prickles ran down her arms. Later when she'd come to her senses, she'd been shocked at her own weakness over a mere tremor. Like some weak Nellie, she'd clung to him. Yet for those moments, she'd felt secure, safe. But why had he alone come to rescue her last night? The man must want something.

As though reading Cecy's mind, Fleur said, "Miss Jackson, wasn't that tremor just shocking? I told Auntie I just don't know how y'all live where there might be an earthquake any time."

Across the street, Mr. Wagstaff paused and glanced her way. An intriguing new thought about how this man might be useful to her came to her. As though the earth tremor hadn't disturbed her at all, Cecy smiled. "Don't you have hurricanes in Louisiana, Miss Fourchette?"

"But the two can't be compared." Fleur held on to her rose-red felt hat against a gust of chill wind.

Auntie caught up with them. "Mr. Bower, I called your mother and accepted the invitation to your masked ball."

Cecy turned the new idea about Mr. Wagstaff over in her mind.

"Normally I wouldn't allow Cecilia to attend. Some masquerades become routs. But your mother's assured me that you young gentlemen will keep the line."

"Of course, ma'am," Bower and Hunt replied.

An uncomfortable silence fell over the group. Her large hat brim flapping in the wind, Cecy pushed her hatpins in deeper. Mr. Wagstaff threaded his way through the parading carriages across the street toward her. Could she persuade the newsman to help her once again?

Hunt drawled, "Well, Bower, have you finally decided what day you'd like our auto race to take place or are you going to admit defeat?" The contrast between the lazy way Hunt said the words and the dark intent in his eyes startled Cecy.

"I hear you've been wagering heavily on our race. Can't you afford to lose—" Bower began.

Fleur interrupted, "Oh, you men. What does it matter who has the fastest car?"

Cecy spoke up with forced pertness, "Auto races are exciting. Auntie and I witnessed one in Monte Carlo."

"Miss Jackson is more daring than I." Fleur smiled. "She even owns an auto and plans to learn to drive it."

Hunt half bowed to Cecy. "I'd be more than willing to take you out for a spin and teach you a few things."

Aunt Amelia frowned at this clumsy double entendre.

Desiring to put Hunt in his place, Cecy waved to Mr. Wagstaff. He nodded, then strode toward her. Mr. Wagstaff was a reporter and reporters knew how to find out things. Now she needed information.

"I've seen Mr. Hunt drive and he appeared to be more interested in speed than style," Bower spoke with a touch of steel in his tone.

Hunt's jaw hardened, but his words came out smoothly, "Bower, Miss Jackson can ask your sister just how exciting a drive with me can be."

Bower took a step toward Hunt. Fleur touched his sleeve.

Mr. Wagstaff reached their group. "Miss Jackson, how may I be of service?"

His calm voice halted the tense exchange. Cecy was positive this man could find out the truth about her mother's illness. She grinned as she asked the question that would confound Hunt and create a way to talk privately with the journalist. "Mr. Wagstaff," she improvised, "I just wanted to remind you of your offer to teach me how to drive."

She was pleased to see how chagrined both Hunt and Bower looked. That would teach them not to cause these unpleasant scenes.

The newspaperman bowed. "Anytime, Miss Jackson."

Cecy beamed. The man was intelligent enough to go along with her. He hadn't offered her lessons, merely to take her to the auto race. But Hunt's stiff expression pleased Cecy.

At Bower's masquerade, in an Elizabethan costume rented from Goldstein's, Cecy was certain no one recognized her behind her mask and red wig. Tonight Cecy sought Mr. Wagstaff. He could find the truth about her mother. She just hoped the condition wasn't something shameful that he might write up as news. But how could she recognize him? No dance cards. Identities remained secret until midnight when the masks came off.

A masked and hooded medieval monk took her hand and led her into a merry polka. "I did not know monks danced," Cecy said in a husky version of her voice, trying to get the monk to speak and reveal his identity through his voice.

"My child, are you tempting me to break my vow of silence?" he demanded in a scratchy, false voice.

Cecy knew she'd danced with this man before. As she stepped and hopped to the bouncy music, she scanned the crowded ballroom. She glimpsed a Musketeer with a blue-plumed hat over blond hair that might be Mr. Wagstaff. The polka ended. She curtseyed her thank-you, then drifted away.

Auntie said her father had sent Cecilia away. Now that he was dead, why didn't her mother want to come home so they could be together? A horrible new thought came—what if her mother suffered mental instability and that was why Auntie wouldn't tell her.

"Your majesty, would you favor this poor Musketeer with a waltz?"

Cecy turned to the courtly Musketeer. Maybe she could figure out his identity as they danced. "I find you worthy, kind sir. Let us waltz."

He swept her into his arms. She tried to decide if this blond Musketeer danced with her the same way Mr. Wagstaff had. No. Clarence Bower? Then nearby she heard Fleur's distinctive trill laugh. So Fleur was Marie Antoinette. She caught her partner's eye.

He winked.

Perhaps she could take the night off from competing with Fleur. She toyed with the idea of just enjoying the evening. But at midnight, the masks came off. Everyone would know Cecy had been Queen Elizabeth. So the English queen must triumph over the French.

A tall Little Bo Peep danced by with the monk. The monk leered at Cecy as he went by, reminding her of Hunt. Her partner stiffened. Why? Bo Peep reminded her of someone. She was tall enough to be Bower's sister, but Cecy couldn't be sure. If her partner was Bower, he'd dislike Bo Peep dancing with the monk whom might be Hunt.

If only she could find Mr. Wagstaff and arrange her first driving lesson. An open car would preclude the need of her aunt's chaperonage yet give her the privacy she needed to discuss her mother with him. The waltz ended. Cecy regally swept away.

"Your Highness." A Harlequin, a jester wearing a hat with tassels, stopped her. She wanted to ignore him, but he'd just part-nered Marie Antoinette. Cecy swallowed her irritation, smiled, and let him lead her into the schottische. The Harlequin answered her with nods and smiles. But she'd smelled his spicy scent before. Mr. Wagstaff? But how could she ask him that before the masks were removed?

At the end of the dance, she turned to find the monk. He kissed her hand. The next dance, the galop, started. Cecy didn't want to dance with the monk; she was certain it was Hunt. But she must not be seen standing alone without a partner.

The electric lights went out. The orchestra cut off in ragged peeps and screeches. Cecy's own exclamation was cut off by a hand clamped over her mouth. Her assailant roughly dragged her through the French doors and out into the garden. In the cool night air, she struggled trying to free herself, trying to see who this was. But his strength overpowered her. The moonlight lit the garden, but her assailant had her clutched with her back to him.

"Help!" Cecy screamed silently into the hand. She clawed the arm that held her. The hand at her mouth lifted. She gasped, "Help!"

He struck her temple. Her senses swam. Suddenly released, she pitched forward, her head reeling. "Oh . . . oh . . . ." She slumped onto the wet ground. There were sounds of a struggle. A man loomed over her.

Chapter 5

Linc lifted the limp Cecilia. He wanted to pursue the vanishing figure but couldn't leave her unprotected. One, two, then more pinpoints of light shone from inside the French doors. With Cecilia secure in his arms, Linc shoved his way back inside. He tried to call the alarm, but the deafening hubbub inside swallowed his words. *Who had doused the lights and tried to make away with Cecilia?*

While the servants brought in candelabras and lit more and more candles, the would-be kidnapper had gotten away. Linc's jaw clenched. Cecilia stirred in his arms. She was so frail, so young. He wanted to chase down the culprit, punish him. Leaning close to her ear, he said, "Cecilia, who was it?"

"I couldn't see him." She gasped, struggling with tears.

As candlelight quelled the darkness, the festive mood around them bubbled up again. Through the dimness, Linc finally located a sofa and set Cecilia on it. She wouldn't let go of his shoulders. "Don't leave me."

"Cecilia," her aunt snapped, drawing close to them. "Release Mr. Wagstaff at once," she hissed, "before anyone sees you."

Linc straightened, withdrawing reluctantly from Cecilia's hold. But she clung to one of his hands. Linc leaned closer to the aunt. "A man tried to abduct her. The police must be summoned—"

"No!" The older woman flared up. "You're mistaken."

Cecilia sobbed. "He dragged me outside, Auntie. I couldn't get away—"

"Hush!" The aunt leaned closer. "Think of the scandal."

Linc touched the older woman's arm. "Some man tried to carry away your niece. Doesn't that concern—"

"Not another word." She glared at him, then lowered her voice. "Just a prank. High spirits at a masked ball."

Linc longed to shake the woman. Cecilia was in danger. *Father, what should I do?* Wrestling his outrage under control, Linc bowed. "May I be of further assistance?"

Cecilia sat up. "Don't leave me."

Her piteous tone squeezed his heart.

"You're indisposed, Cecilia. We're going home." Miss Higginbottom snapped. "Mr. Wagstaff, will you escort us to our carriage?"

"Yes, I will, and I'll follow you home, too," he insisted.

Widespread, loud laughter drowned out his last words.

The aunt smiled sourly. "Thank you, but you must speak to no one about this prank. I should have known better than to attend a masquerade."

Linc bowed once more. He wouldn't say anything now, but this wasn't over. Thank heaven, he'd been at hand.

Linc led Cecilia down the rear steps toward her carriage house. Both of them wore auto coats, long buff-colored dusters. The cool breeze played with the veil of Cecilia's large hat, flaring and lifting its ends. Even in the drab driving garb, she was beautiful.

Linc hated keeping his true concerns hidden. The danger Cecilia had been exposed to the other night still made him seethe, but her foolish aunt had tied his hands. He'd finally decided that it most likely was Hunt who'd tried to kidnap Cecilia. He'd probably decided to compromise this innocent's reputation and then the families would cover it up as an elopement. But how could he persuade Cecilia or more to the point convince her unwise aunt? Setting these worries aside, he walked around the gleaming, dark green runabout. "Electric?"

"Auntie said I couldn't possibly crank the starter—"

"She's right. There's always the danger of a backfiring engine and a broken arm." *Or being abducted.* He looked at her unable to hide his concern any longer. "Are you recovered from your shock?"

"What shock?"

He hardened his tone. "The shock at end of the masked ball." With the open car between them, he watched her. Anxiety tightened his midsection. Would she be honest with him?

"Oh, that." She wouldn't meet his eyes. "Auntie said it was just due to high spirits." Cecy pointed to the car. "Now what do I do first?"

Take what happened at the masquerade seriously. "You don't have a chauffeur?"

Her voice stiffened. "I intend to drive myself."

Linc tamped down his agitation. "If you don't intend on employing a chauffeur, does that mean you will maintain the car your-self?"

"Maintain it?"

"This morning did you check your brake rods, steering connec-tions, springs, and tires?"

She stared at him.

"They must be checked every time you plan to go out for a drive or you might as well stay home—*unless* you're in the mood for a hike."

"No need to use sarcasm." Lifting her chin, she moved closer to him at the front of the vehicle.

Intensely aware of her light floral fragrance, he opened the hood and began pointing to the parts and naming them. Perhaps truth would open her eyes. "Hunt was dressed as a monk at the ball. A little out of character, don't you think?" He caught a flash of fear in her eye.

"Clarence was the musketeer, right?" she asked, ignoring his question.

Linc nodded. "Bower told me someone cut the electric wires into his house."

Turning away, she pointed to the engine. "What is that part again?"

"The steering connection." Why did she keep changing the sub-ject? He had to make her realize the flirtation she encouraged was much more complex than she guessed. What would Cecilia say if he told her Hunt still flirted with Clarissa when he thought no one was looking, that he probably had gone farther than hold hands with Clarissa Bower? But one didn't discuss such lurid topics with an innocent like Cecilia. But then how could he warn her? Frustra-tion tightened Linc's jaw.

"Can we drive now?" she asked abruptly.

He nodded, then opened the driver's door and helped her in. Taking his seat beside her, he slid his goggles into place.

Cecilia positioned her oversized goggles, then tied her large off-white veil over her face, a study of intense concentration. It tugged at his heart: Cecilia, so young, so intense, so lost. *Father, how do I help protect her?*

He rested his hand on the tiller, which jutted out from the red leather dash between them. "Do you understand how this tiller works?"

"Not really."

"Just lightly move it in the opposite direction you want to go." He'd been feeling as though an unseen hand had been turning him from his purpose in moving to San Francisco. He'd tried to go forward establishing his weekly newspaper. But he kept getting steered back toward this beautiful young redhead. She slipped into his thoughts all too often, worrying him. While Bower was beginning a promising law career, Hunt was a gambler who spent time in the brothels of Chinatown. Many Barbary Coast bartenders told Linc he was a mean drunk. The story about Hunt's father insisting his son marry Clarissa was true. The older Hunt thought marriage would settle his wild son down. Linc didn't agree. It would just make for an unhappy wife tied to a profligate husband.

She obeyed his instructions. "Oh, I see."

Her perilous campaign to be the most sought-after deb had interfered with his plan to show her photos of ragged four-year-olds working barefoot in Louisiana shrimp processing plants, eight-year-old miners with blackened, desolate faces. But she needed his maturity, his guidance, since flirting with social disaster seemed to be her favorite past-time. Or was it her aunt's imprudence?

At Linc's okay, she flipped the switch on the dash. The vehicle moved forward. "Oh!" She trod hard on the brake. Both of them lurched forward.

"I'm sorry." She blushed with obvious embarrassment.

He wished she was always so open to instruction. "I did the same the first time I stepped on my brakes. Now just ease up a little on the brake pedal."

She cautiously obeyed. The car rolled forward.

"Now push the tiller gently, very gently toward your left and we'll drive around in a circle a few times before we venture out on the road."

They made several wide circles in the large open area of the stable yard. "You might as well drive out onto the street now." After she'd driven tensely several blocks, she smiled. "I knew it this would be fun."

"Always remember: be aware of the vehicles, horses, and people around you, you could hurt someone and yourself seriously."

For once she didn't argue but nodded soberly. Maybe he could bring her to her senses about leading on Hunt and Bower any further.

Linc cleared his throat. "Are we still headed for that auto race this afternoon at Golden Gate Park?"

"Yes."

He let a few minutes of silence pass. "Your aunt was wise about your driving an electric auto. It runs so quietly it won't startle horses nearby."

She nodded, intent on the tiller.

He drew a deep breath. "I wish your aunt was as concerned about your safety at the masked ball. No one can convince me you weren't nearly abducted two nights ago."

"But Auntie—"

Linc couldn't hold back. "Your aunt shows poor judgment about the true danger you stand in."

Cecy made herself show no reaction. Auntie had told her to refuse to discuss the incident with Mr. Wagstaff. But Cecy couldn't free herself from remembering those awful moments of fear and helplessness. She glanced at him from the corner of her eye. "What danger do I stand in?"

"I've thought of two motives for someone kidnapping you—"

"I could think of only one, ransom. What other reason could there be?" Her pulse beat a quick tempo.

"Have you thought someone might want to compromise your reputation, so you would have to have marry him?"

"I—I don't understand." His words buzzed in her mind. Stopping, she let a startled pedestrian cross in front of them.

"You would disappear for a night. In the morning, your reputation would be in tatters."

Cecy tightened her hold on the tiller and herself. Primitive fear made it difficult for her to breathe. "Everyone would know he took me against my will."

Linc shook his head. "Miss Jackson, unfortunately the world would prefer the man marry you quietly and cover his sin and scandal. Once a young woman's reputation is tarnished, she is shunned. It isn't fair, but that's the way of the world."

Cecy clenched her jaw, reliving those terrifying moments in Bower's garden . . . Her hand shook.

Mr. Wagstaff put his hand over hers. "I'm sorry to have to upset you like this, but I'm worried about you."

Many young men had touched her hand in the past month. Not one had touched her the comforting way this man did. His calm, sure strength flowed from his hand to hers, making the contrast between his confidence and her own uncertainty clear.

If she could only confide in him, she'd reveal that she wasn't interested in either of the gentlemen, just a way to reunite with her mother. But she knew only this man's family connections and his career. He was a stranger, after all, a question mark.

She willed herself to relax. "I'll be fine. No more masked balls for me and I'm going nowhere without my aunt. And you're coming to my opera party tonight?"

He nodded.

"I'm planning a surprise treat for my guests." She forced a lighter tone. "Now let's get to the race. Won't everyone stare to see me drive up?" She cast him a tremulous smile, laced with bravado.

Driving had benefits more than show. The sanitarium was within the range of her electric car. In a few days, she'd just invite Mr. Wagstaff out for a spin and they'd merely drive to the sanitarium. She'd speak to her mother privately and her doctors. Mr. Wagstaff wouldn't need to know the particulars. Since everyone already knew her mother was in a sanatorium, he'd have no new gossip.

She drove through Golden Gate Park where mothers and nannies strolled with buggies and children. A fashionable crowd had gathered along at a small lake in the park. Cecy waved her free hand.

"Miss Jackson! Is that you?" Many young ladies and gentlemen greeted her, their attention a balm to her ragged spirits. In his calm, no-nonsense way, Mr. Wagstaff instructed her how to park the auto. She drew back her veil, pulled off her goggles and driving gloves and tossed them onto the car seat.

"I am quite impressed." Fleur smiled at her.

Cecy looked away, searching the crowd. "Are the racers here yet?"

"I'm here." Bower appeared at her elbow in a driving coat.

She wanted to draw back from him. This was Mr. Wagstaff's fault. Whoever had tried to kidnap her had either been a stranger seeking ransom or a young man merely carried away by the rowdiness of the masked ball as Auntie said. Mr. Wagstaff's idea of social ruin and a forced marriage was too farfetched.

"Mr. Bower." Cecy smiled, gazing at him from under lowered eyelashes. "I've been waiting for today—my first driving lesson, this race, then my opera-company party. Three exciting events on one date."

Bower kissed her hand. "The daring Miss Jackson."

She savored this name society columnists had given her. She'd be known as a modern woman, a woman who'd been courted by many, but who had disdained marriage.

"Miss Jackson." Hunt appeared and shockingly kissed her cheek.

So unexpected, Hunt's kiss stunned her. Then she boiled with indignation. How dare Hunt try to mark her publicly as his? Everyone around her looked shocked. Except for Clarissa who paled. Cecy wouldn't let Hunt show her disrespect. "Sir, you've overstepped—"

Bower pushed in front of her. "Hunt, you've gone too far—"

Hunt took a step forward. "Who asked for your interference—"

"There are ladies present." Linc raised his voice.

His words shut both men's mouths. A few tense moments passed in silence.

"Ready to start, Bower?" Hunt sneered the words.

Glaring at Hunt, Cecy took Bower's arm.

Bower placed his hand over hers. "I'm ready to best you, Hunt."

The two angry men strode to their autos—Hunt's REO and Bower's Pierce Arrow. Linc stood near the front of their vehicles, waiting for the assistants to crank the starters. Bower and Hunt donned their goggles and driving gloves. The Pierce Arrow surged to life. Then the REO engine caught. The assistants leaped out of the way. Linc raised the white flag.

"Wait!" Cecy shouted over the engines roaring. She'd teach Hunt to make free with her reputation. "My champion must wear my favor into battle!" She ran to Bower and tied her driving veil around Bower's neck. Standing on the running board, she flashed Hunt a daggerlook. Cecy stepped down, her heart racing with her own audacity.

"Ready, set, go!" Linc slashed the flag down.

Hunt and Bower surged forward. Bower's Pierce Arrow took the lead. The cars were to race three laps around a loop of paved road, circling Spreckels Lake. As the racers passed Linc the first time, he flashed the flag and shouted, "One!"

Cecy was breathlessly caught up in the excitement.

Bower's longer, more powerful car outclassed Hunt's REO. Finishing another lap, the two drivers sped toward Linc again. "Two."

On the last lap, Hunt sped up and edged close to Bower, crowding him, endangering both. Bower leaned forward obviously flooring the accelerator and moved another yard ahead of Hunt.

Cecy danced on her toes. "Mr. Bower! You can beat him!"

The two autos widened at the turn and raced on, Hunt still trying to edge ahead, but to no avail. Bower drove through the tape hastily strung up across the starting line. The young audience burst into applause and cheers.

Cecy rushed forward to congratulate Bower. He drew both her hands in his and kissed them. "Dear Miss Jackson."

Cecy cast a triumphant look at Hunt. He glared back at her. She froze. She'd heard of looks that could kill. Now she knew how one felt.

The tinkling laughter, dancers swirling around the polished floor, and the fragrance of vanilla-scented candles filled Linc with dread. Cecilia's long-awaited opera party was in full swing. He felt like he was at the city's Cinograph Theater watching a movie depicting the lavish French court before heads rolled in the Revolution.

Cecilia, dressed in an extravagant light green satin gown, floated through the gathering with her constellation of admirers, mainly Bower. In addition, Cecilia's novel touch—the principals of the opera cast of *La Bohème* still in costume—mingled with San Francisco society.

Hunt made his dashing entrance and went directly to the beautiful Mimi, the soprano of the opera cast. Linc observed his flushed face. Could Hunt be inebriated already? Linc's somber mood deepened. Who knew what that kiss this afternoon might provoke?

"Mr. Wagstaff?"

Linc glanced down into Fleur's pretty face. "Good evening, Miss."

She smiled, but her eyes held worry. "May I speak to you?"

To forestall speculation about their conversation, Linc led the lady into the dance. The bouncy two-step tempo contrasted with the young woman's serious expression. Finally she glanced up. "You and I are both strangers here, so perhaps we are aware of things others more familiar overlook."

"What are you trying to tell me?"

"Miss Jackson should flirt less." The Southern belle looked away. "Mr. Hunt is not a boy to be trifled with. I don't think she comprehends . . ."

"The stakes are higher than she realizes?"

"I fear they are," the lady murmured.

The two-step ended. Linc bowed, thanking Miss Fourchette for the dance and her concern. With renewed purpose, Linc spotted Cecilia and headed for her. Just then the small orchestra struck a chord for attention. Everyone quieted.

Cecilia's aunt stood beside the orchestra leader. "As part of this evening's entertainment, our friends from the opera company will periodically sing a brief selection from *La Bohème*. Monsieur Rodolfo and Mademoiselle Mimi, if you please?"

The tenor and soprano who portrayed two of the four poor young "bohemians" in Paris drew in front of the orchestra.

The music had no power over Linc now. He had to prevent the imminent disaster. Moving through the crowd, he approached Cecilia's aunt. Though he faced forward so none would know he talked privately with her, he whispered, "Miss Higginbottom, are you aware that Hunt kissed your niece today at the auto race?"

"Kissed her?" Her tone could have frozen boiling water.

"Yes, Bower and he nearly came to blows over it."

"I had entrusted Cecilia to *your* care, sir."

Linc acknowledged this with a nod. He had done his best, but Hunt had crossed the line. "I cannot control a man who isn't in control of himself. Are you aware of Mr. Hunt's poor reputation with women?"

"Cecilia didn't inform me of Mr. Hunt's latest affront. But I have persuaded her to depress that man's pursuit of her."

The woman's words didn't reassure Linc. The duet ended and was greeted with applause, and Cecelia's aunt went forward to thank the singers. Linc approached Cecilia and saw Hunt toss down another whiskey at the bar. He had to make her listen to him. "May I have a word with you, Cecilia?"

"Just for a moment." She accepted the arm he offered her.

Leading her away from the center of the room, he longed to shield her from the menacing undercurrents in her own ballroom. "This afternoon I believe you saw a side of Victor Hunt you've been blind to before."

She gave him an exasperated look. "Is that what you wanted to talk about?"

He nodded. "You are a gently reared young lady, so I cannot be plain about this. Hunt has a very bad reputation—especially with women."

She shrugged. "Hunt's outrageous kiss was too much. I don't need or want that man's attentions as he will soon learn—"

Bower approached them. "Dear lady, this is our dance."

With profound resignation, Linc bowed. Cecy walked away on Bower's arm. Soon they danced the new ragtime one-step.

Clarissa was pursuing Hunt who made sure to keep his distance. The man looked unsteady—how much had he drunk before arriving? Were Linc and Miss Fourchette the only ones here who were thinking clearly?

Gliding through the slower Boston waltz, Cecy couldn't remember ever feeling so blissful. Her daring decision to include the visiting opera company's young attractive singers as guests, not merely entertainment, had added a definite éclat to the whole evening.

Hunt danced by, holding the soprano tightly in his arms. Cecilia would put him in his place once and for all. But more important than that, she had a surprise for everyone, her own personal triumph. Her longed-for link to the opera would be forged this evening. As a lady, she could never sing professionally. But as a generous supporter of the opera, she'd vicariously live the musical life. After tonight she'd never again be alone, cast out, or ignored.

The clock struck two o'clock. Cecy glowed with anticipation. Her moment, her triumph had come.

Always the gentleman, Bower led her to the orchestra, bowed, and left her. She would reward him with a chaste kiss this evening and tell Hunt she'd rejected him. Rodolfo joined her. The orchestra began to play the pensive music from the final scene of *La Bohème*, the scene where recalling their first meeting, Mimi dies in Rodolfo's arms.

Aware of the surprise in the faces before her, Cecy bowed to the gathering. Then she sang to Rodolfo, "I've so many things to tell you, or one thing—huge as the sea, deep and infinite as the sea . . . I love you . . . you're all my life."

Cecy's exquisite voice and passion tugged at Linc's emotions once more. Her voice had the power to lift him out of himself to see life in all its fullness. God had given Cecilia the gift to touch hearts, make them feel pity and draw them to a sensation of glory, of human love. If she only knew of God's love and showed it to others.

Cecilia's voice soared with pathos, tragic love, then death. Many women dabbed at their eyes. The orchestra fell silent. Cecilia, as Mimi, sank into Rodolfo's arms. He cried out in agony, "Mimi! Mimi!"

In the echoing silence, Hunt lunged forward. "You sing like an angel." He went down on one knee. "Dear lady. Be mine."

Cecy straightened up, pushing away from him. "You forget yourself, sir."

Hunt stood. He pushed the tenor who was trying to shield Cecilia away. "I love you. Be mine."

Bower, Archie, and Linc rushed forward. Behind them, Clarissa shrieked, "No! He loves me!"

Archie turned back, took hold of Clarissa, and drew her away. Bower grabbed Hunt by the shoulders. "You're a disgrace. How dare you address a lady when it's obvious you're stinking drunk?"

Linc tried to thrust himself between Hunt and Bower as Rodolfo dragged Cecilia aside. Hunt swung at Bower. The two men struggled. They crashed into the assembled orchestra, scattering the musicians clutching their instruments. Ladies screamed.

Father, help me stop them. This could destroy Cecilia. Linc pursued Hunt and Bower. He had to end this embarrassing scene before someone got hurt. He circled the two men exchanging punches. Bower answered each of Hunt's blows. But Hunt's drunken state started slowing him. Linc edged around them waiting for a chance to help Bower subdue Hunt.

Bower delivered what should have been a stunning blow. But

Hunt dodged it. He reached behind himself, then flashed a knife in Bower's face.

Chapter 6

The glitter of honed-steel stunned Linc. Bower caught Hunt's wrist. Linc jumped back—fearful of interfering, of causing more harm than good. Hunt's knife reduced fisticuffs to a barroom brawl. The two men struggled; the knife their focus. Their grunts and tortured expressions cast a common horror through the stunned, silent audience.

Linc broke free of the nightmare. He edged forward, waiting for the moment he could help Bower.

Hunt tripped Bower and Bower stumbled forward. The knife flashed up, slicing Bower's cheek. Cecilia sailed past Linc. She threw herself on Hunt—shrieking, "Stop!" Shocked, Hunt sprang back, dropping the knife.

Linc rushed to Bower. He pulled out his handkerchief and pressed it to Bower's face. "A doctor!" he shouted, but his voice was drowned by Cecilia's.

"You worthless men!" she screamed. "You've ruined everything!"

Hunt, looking dazed, objected, "But—"

"Do you think I'd marry you? Either of you!" Her voice vibrated with vitriol. "I will never marry! I hate you!"

To stop her from doing more harm to herself, Linc grabbed Cecilia's shoulders and shook her violently. A shocked gasp echoed through the crowd. "She's hysterical." Cecilia collapsed against him, white-faced and sobbing. "Someone summon a doctor!"

The assemblage remained frozen. Then Bower's mother rushed to her son's side. "My son!"

As though awakening, Hunt turned and pushed his way through the throng, releasing the audience from its stupor. Voices of condemnation, panic burst forth.

Still burdened by Cecilia, Linc shouted, "Stop Hunt!" But it was too late. The rogue had escaped.

Cecilia struggled vainly in Linc's arms. "Oh, let me go. They've ruined everything."

Cecy looked down into her coffee cup. Instead of creamy coffee, she saw bright red blood, dripping down Bower's starched white shirtfront. She covered her face with trembling hands and closed her eyes. And she couldn't help but remember the other scene, two days ago—the Saturday promenade on crowded Montgomery Street.

Cecy, walking beside her aunt, had marched down the avenue. Auntie's plan was to face society after the "dreadful scene" and turn popular opinion in their favor.

"Auntie, maybe we should have waited until more time has passed before appearing in public."

"Nonsense. No one can blame you for what happened the other night."

The knife fight had made the front page of every newspaper. Headlines like SWAINS FIGHT DUEL OVER LADY LOVE, DASTARDLY FIGHT AMID THE HIGH LIFE still made Cecy cringe. "But the papers—"

"Journalists always revel in lurid detail. No genteel person will pay any attention to such disgusting sensationalism."

Mrs. Ward and her protégé, Ann, approached them.

"Mrs. Ward." Auntie smiled sweetly. "Good day."

The lady barely glanced in their direction.

"Cecilia—" Ann began.

Mrs. Ward quickened her pace, pulling Ann along with her.

Ice shards pierced Cecy's heart, nearly making her cry out.

"Well," Auntie huffed. "In Boston that woman wouldn't figure in society at all. Her father was a buffalo hunter for the railroads, for goodness sake."

People, strolling or riding by in carriages, ignored both of them. Each step took on a more hideous quality. Cecy began to shrivel, fade, become invisible.

Fleur Fourchette, beside her aunt in her carriage, did look at Cecy. But with such pity. Humiliation clogged Cecy's throat like bitter coffee grounds. After that, each averted glance, each snub sizzled into her heart like a hot iron.

At the end of the block, Aunt Amelia motioned for their coachman to pick them up. In the bright mocking sunshine of early spring, they'd driven home in agonizing silence. Then Auntie had taken to her bed and hadn't permitted Cecy into her room since.

Now the smell of buttered toast and eggs brought Cecy back to the present, nauseating her. She shoved back her chair. She lurched past the butler and fled to the conservatory at the rear of the first floor. In the past three days since the opera ball, Cecy'd found refuge amid the plants there. From the glass dome above, the pale light of morning hung like a pall over the room. She sank into a chair beside a drooping fig tree.

Waves of panic rippled through her. The silence of the huge mansion pressed in on her. The servants spoke in whispers and crept around the house as though someone were dying. Maybe they were right. She'd faced much in her life, but how could she face ruin, social death? Even her ability to feel anger at Hunt had waned. In spite of the agony it caused her, she'd read each day's papers because of her concern for Bower.

Was he recovering? She stood up abruptly and hurried to the library where a phone was. Picking up the ornate receiver, she waited for the operator's voice. "Please connect me with two-three-six."

The connection was made. A formal voice said, "The Bower residence."

"Hello . . ." She almost gave her name, but decided against this. "How is Mr. Bower, Clarence Bower?"

"Mr. Bower's condition is stable. Who may I say is calling?"

"Just a friend. Thank you." Slowly, she put the receiver down. At least, the man who'd come to her assistance was mending. *But what am I to do?* For a second the thought of appealing to God flickered in Cecy's mind. She snuffed it. Even if God were here, He didn't care anything about Cecy. He proved that years ago.

She paced the Aubusson carpet in front of a wall of leather-bound books. With each step, the injustice of the rejection she was suffering swelled inside her. "I did nothing wrong."

"Miss?" Her butler stood in the doorway.

"Yes?"

"Your aunt would like to see you in the foyer."

"Foyer?" Why was Auntie there? Cecy brushed past him and sped down the hallway and grand staircase.

In a black traveling suit, her aunt faced her. Valises, hatboxes, and a trunk surrounded her. The appalling sight checked Cecy. Why had Auntie packed everything? Why hadn't any of Cecy's luggage been packed, too? "Auntie, what's wrong?"

"Cecilia, I have decided it's time, past time for me to visit your grandfather in Boston."

Cecy reeled as though she'd been slapped. "Boston?"

"Yes, I leave in an hour by train—"

"Leave?"

"Yes, I must wish you farewell for a time." Auntie pursed her lips in a chilling grin.

Clutching the railing, Cecy gasped. "You can't mean you're leaving me."

Auntie's mouth spread into a flat, frigid smile. "You've established yourself here now, so I feel I can leave—"

"Established? That's a lie." She ran down the steps.

"Cecilia," Auntie checked her sternly. "You must learn not to let your emotions run away with you."

Cecy stopped on the bottom step. "You can't go. Everything's awful! I need you!"

"You're exaggerating." Looking away, the older woman pushed one of her jet hatpins in tighter.

Cecy felt as though the hatpins were being jabbed into her skull. "Then I'll go back to Boston with you—"

"That's not possible." Auntie scowled. "You force me to be unkind. You'll be as socially unacceptable in Boston as you are here." Her aunt's voice chilled further with each word. "This isn't fifty years ago. There are telephones, the telegraph. Everyone in Boston knows of your disgrace by now."

"Europe then," Cecy pleaded.

Glaring at Cecy, her aunt shook her head. "I had high hopes for you. We could've had a good life together. But you have proved to be a complete disappointment." Auntie's voice rose shrilly. "After all my efforts, you managed to spoil everything just like your mother."

"There must be some way we can repair—"

Ignoring her, Auntie adjusted one of the buttons at the wrist of her black glove. Her voice hardened. "There is no longer any connection between us. I warned you about the lot of a spinster in society. I must be absolutely scrupulous in my social connections."

"Auntie." Cecy choked on panic, pain, shock.

"Goodbye, Cecilia." Her aunt turned her back and marched to the door. The butler and footmen carried her luggage outside. The door shut. Cecy sank to the carpeted steps. She held her head in her hands and moaned without words. She couldn't stop shaking.

Finally, she dragged herself into her room and collapsed onto her bed. The curtains were drawn; the room lay in shadow—just like her life. Thoughts, words, and images spun out of her control. Her life had ended. Auntie, the only family she'd ever known, had abandoned her. Tears oozed from her eyes. How could she still have tears? Was the supply endless? Moaning hoarsely, she buried her head in her feather pillow.

Her aunt's heart-crushing words pounded her down into total

despair—"Just like your mother." No. Hopelessness suffocated her. She flung herself off the bed, striking her head against the wall. Slumping to the carpet, she felt as though bony hands were dragging her down into a swirling black abyss.

"Miss Jackson?" a timid voice whispered hours later.

Cecy opened her eyes. The room was dark.

"Miss Jackson?"

It was her maid. "Go away," Cecy muttered. Her mouth was dry and tasted bad.

"Cecilia."

At the sound of a man's voice, she shrank back. "Go away!"

Firm, heavy footsteps shuddered from the floor through her as he crossed the room. Mr. Wagstaff bent, gathered her up into his arms.

"No," she whimpered.

He spoke to the maid: "Please pack her a bag for an overnight stay."

Cecy gasped. "What do you mean an overnight stay?"

He ignored her feeble struggling and carried her out the door. "I'm taking you home with me."

Chapter 7

Cecy was barely conscious of Mr. Wagstaff wrapping a coat around her and carrying her outside into cool air. She couldn't focus on the dim sights and vague sounds around her. She could hardly hold her head up.

"Just lean on my shoulder." Linc drove her away.

The rasping motor and its shuddering woke her a little. Unable to question him, she slumped against him. After days of loneliness, she nestled against his shoulder—so warm, solid, comforting. After a time, the car stopped and he lifted her again. "Where are we?" she whispered.

"Home."

Then a door opened. Bright light and warmth enveloped her. This made her weep again.

"Susan, here she is."

A woman with a strong voice answered him, "I'll put her to bed after some warm milk."

Cecy glanced around. A silver-haired black woman followed them up a staircase. "I shouldn't . . ."

"Susan will stay with you all night for propriety's sake and tomorrow we'll get a more suitable chaperone," Mr. Wagstaff said.

Too deep in despair to argue, Cecy let Linc lay her down on a featherbed. What did propriety mean to her now? She was ruined. He began unbuttoning her shoes. He shouldn't, but she couldn't bring words to her lips.

"I'll do that," the woman objected. "You go get that warm milk from Kang. I'll have her in a nightgown when you get back."

"I don't like milk," Cecy muttered.

"Nobody asked you that," the old black woman said kindly, but firmly. "You'll drink your milk or else."

Cecy gave in with a sigh, feeling wobbly lying on the soft bed.

"When was the last time you ate a meal?" The old woman nudged her as she unbuttoned the many buttons at Cecy's back.

"Can't remember."

Feeling her corset be loosened and then pulled away forced a deep sigh from Cecy. Her eyes drifted shut.

"Don't go to sleep on me. I'm too old to lift deadweight. You roll over when I tell you to."

Cecy thought she nodded.

Cecy followed directions and soon she was dressed in a very loose, soft flannel gown.

A tap on the door. "Come in," Susan ordered.

Cecy opened her eyes. Linc walked in with a steaming cup on a small silver tray. "Here's your milk."

"Meg and Del are waiting for you to say prayers with them," the older woman said. "You go on. I'll get Miss Jackson all tucked in."

"Good night, Cecilia." Linc touched her cheek. "Everything will look brighter in the morning." He walked out closing the door behind him.

Cecy whispered in her mind, "He called me Cecilia." Tears came again, but they were warm tears of gratitude.

The old woman propped Cecilia up against several pillows. "You'll feel better when you drink your milk."

Her head seemingly stuffed with cotton wool, Cecy accepted the cup and sipped the warm, sweet milk.

The old woman sat in a chair beside the bed and hummed an old spiritual Cecy recognized, "Swing Low, Sweet Chariot." The melody quieted Cecy. Then tears of shame slid from her eyes down to the soft flannel gown.

"Don't go letting sadness take over. Linc won't let anyone hurt you. You're not alone."

Cecy didn't have the strength to argue. Her tears flowed, unchecked—inexhaustible.

"Okay. You're all buttoned up." The black woman said from behind Cecy. "Breakfast is waiting on us downstairs."

I can't face anyone. "I'm not hungry." Cecy frowned.

A little girl with brown braids popped into the room. "I smell bacon, don't you?" Without ceasing to chatter, the little girl took Cecy's hand and led her out the door. "I think we're having pancakes today, too."

"Who are you?" Cecy looked down into the cheerful, freckled face.

"I'm Meg Wagstaff. My papa is Linc Wagstaff. He's your friend. He brought you here because you're sad because your aunt had to go away. You're Miss Cecilia Jackson. I read about you in the articles Papa wrote—"

"You're Mr. Wagstaff's daughter?" Cecy hadn't ever given a thought to this man's personal life.

The child stopped, looking up in surprise. "I just told you that."

As Meg led her down the steps, Cecy felt a little unsteady and gripped the railing. Cecy smelled bacon, melted butter. Her stomach growled.

Meg giggled. "See—you sound hungry."

"Don't talk like that to your elders." The older black woman had followed them downstairs.

"Sorry, Aunt Susan," Meg recited.

Cecy's memory brought up the singsong response that she and the other boarding school girls had recited: "Yes, Miss. No, Miss." But this happy child made her reply sound pert and teasing, not beaten down and hopeless as she and the others had been. Cecy smiled at Meg. "I do sound hungry."

The little girl wrinkled her freckled nose, grinning.

Aunt Susan slid open the pocket door and ushered both Meg and Cecy into a small dining room. Meg let go of Cecy's hand and ran to her father. She threw her arms around him. "Papa, I brought her down. See?"

Standing at the head of the table, Linc hugged his daughter. A small black boy at the table stood also.

"Good morning, Cecilia," Linc said. "Del, will you please help Miss Jackson take her seat?"

Cecy waited, silenced by seeing Mr. Wagstaff in these new surroundings. Wearing a serious expression, the boy came around the table and pulled out the chair to Mr. Wagstaff's right. Linc made the introductions. "Cecilia, Del is Aunt Susan's grandson. Del, this is Miss Jackson."

Nodding, Cecy sat down and shyly smiled her thanks at Del. The boy nodded soberly, then returned to his place across from her. Meg took the seat beside her while Linc seated Aunt Susan at the foot of the table.

Cecy looked at the faces around the table. She'd assumed that Aunt Susan was Mr. Wagstaff's housekeeper. But housekeepers weren't seated at the table by their employers. What were the relationships of the mixed group around the table?

The door from the kitchen opened and a Chinese houseman walked in carrying a huge platter of scrambled eggs, bacon, golden pancakes, and fragrant maple syrup.

Cecy's appetite leaped to life.

The houseman set the tray on the sideboard. "Good morning. I see the lady has come down. Lady, you drink tea or coffee for breakfast?" He pinned her with a bright, questioning look.

The mention of coffee brought back the memory of trying to drink a cup the morning before and the dreadful vision of blood. "Tea," she murmured.

Meg tugged Cecy's sleeve. "Are you going to be here when Del and me—"

"Del and I," Aunt Susan corrected as she stirred cream into her cup of coffee.

Meg grinned. "Are you going to be here when Del and I get home from school, Miss Jackson?"

Cecy couldn't reply. Where would she go now? She was ruined. Auntie had left her.

Mr. Wagstaff cut her frantic thoughts short. "Miss Jackson will stay with us a day or two while she makes plans for the future."

"Good." The little girl stared up into Cecy's eyes. "I want to show you my dollies and the new dollhouse I got for Christmas—"

"Meg," Aunt Susan reminded, "you better get busy eating breakfast, so you don't get to school late."

Mr. Wagstaff asked a blessing for the day. "And, Lord, we thank You for Your word, sorrow endureth for the night, but joy cometh in the morning."

As he prayed, Cecy tried to make sense out of the unexpected family she found herself in. But she couldn't.

The houseman put a pot of tea on the table near her. Cecy waited to see if he would sit down with the family, too.

"Anyone need anything else?" the houseman asked.

"No, thank you, Kang. Another excellent breakfast," Aunt Susan replied. The Chinese man smiled, bowed, and went back through the door for the kitchen.

"Do you like pancakes?" Meg asked Cecy again as she offered Cecy the blue-and-white china serving plate.

"Yes." Cecy took the plate of pancakes from the child. Her hunger made her feel lightheaded and slightly nauseated. She forced herself to fill her plate. She had to eat to have a clear head to think.

Cecy watched as Meg looked back and waved, then skipped around the corner toward school with Del at her side. Meg took all the gladness of the spring morning away with her. Cecy folded her arms around herself, chilled.

Linc pulled out his pocket watch. "Please fetch your driving coat, gloves, and hat. We're leaving right away."

Cold fear bathed her. "Where?"

He touched her arm. "Later I'll take you to meet Mrs. Hansen, now I'm taking you to my office."

"Why?"

"Because we have work to do." He gave her a long look. "Now, be a good girl. Go up and get your things."

She wanted to argue, but how could she? Her only plans had been hiding in her room and crying. Upstairs, as she reluctantly donned her auto duster, hat, and gloves, she realized she'd be unrecognizable under this automobiling garb.

Heartened, she joined Linc in the drive beside his Pierce Arrow. Within minutes, they chugged up, then down the hills of San Francisco toward busy Market Street. There Mr. Wagstaff helped her out of his vehicle and into an imposing office building. A few men glanced at her, but without interest. Relieved, Cecy preceded Mr. Wagstaff into the elevator and let him usher her into a nearly empty office.

"Where's the rest of your furniture?" she asked, looking around.

"We'll discuss that later." He pulled a spindly chair close to his desk, which occupied the middle of an otherwise bare, large walnut-wainscoted room. Then he sat down in the only other chair and faced her. "Now let's discuss where you go from here." He took her hand. "You've been cast as the culprit in a very nasty scandal. Yesterday your aunt left town—"

Her pulse sped up. "How did you know that?"

"A friend called me. I'm trying to come up with a way out of this scandal."

A sob tried to work its way up and out, but she fought it under control. "Why do you care?"

He released her hand. "I wanted to warn you that your father's bad reputation put you in a precarious position socially." Leaning forward closer to her, he rested his elbows on the arms of his chair.

"I don't under—"

"Tell me what you know about your father."

She wiped her moist eyes with a lacy handkerchief and looked away. Of all the unpleasant topics he could have brought up this was the worst. "I don't want to talk about my father."

"Cecilia, don't you know by now you can trust me?" His voice didn't coax her. He merely spoke the truth.

"My father sent me away."

He nodded. "Most of San Francisco doesn't think highly of your father because of how he treated your mother and everyone else. They were waiting to see if you would take after your mother. Or your father."

Auntie's final words echoed in her mind: "Just like your mother." Cecy burst into tears.

Without a pause, he took her hands pulling her up. "Cecilia, I'm not trying to hurt you. We've got to figure out what you're going to do."

She knew she should push away from him. She didn't want any man to hold her. But in the past few days, too much had transpired. And his embrace was so reassuring and strong. *I'm so alone—again.* She pressed herself deeper into his embrace. Was he going to kiss her? Why didn't he think her shameless, too?

The scent of her perfume, a profusion of spring flowers, filled Linc's head. She was warm, close, so wounded. He bent his head, tempted to brush her lips with his. He whispered her name like a prayer.

His hold around her tightened, but only to prevent her from pressing nearer. He understood her need to be physically close. But he wouldn't take advantage of her vulnerability. How could he be attracted to this woman when his heart still belonged to his sweet, lost Virginia?

He continued to hold Cecilia, but he tried to hold her as he would have held Meg. But holding Meg was nothing like holding this vibrant, enticing woman. Still, if he abruptly severed their closeness, she'd feel rejected. But being this near and not giving into the desire to kiss her became torture.

He yearned to tell her so much, but having a heart-to-heart talk didn't seem to be what Cecilia needed to pull herself together. He wanted to convince her of God's love and purpose for her. Everyday, he walked in his own grief, a suffocating fog. Still he knew God waited—willing to heal and guide him. But Cecilia wouldn't understand this. Yet.

She stopped crying. Linc urged her back on the other chair and cleared his throat. "We better get busy doing what we came here to do."

She eyed him, dabbing at her tear-stained face. "What was that?"

"I need you to go shopping with me for office furniture."

"Shopping?" She stood up. "I couldn't."

"Where we'll be shopping"—he rose and took her hand—"you won't meet anyone you know."

Soon Cecy walked beside Linc through the vast furniture warehouse near the Embarcadero. Only a few customers, salesmen, and workmen shuffled through the narrow aisles. Cecy and Linc stopped to look at an assortment of leather chairs.

Linc asked, "Do you think I should go with the red leather or brown?"

"The red looks more imposing," she replied in a flat voice. She didn't care a fig about furniture. She longed to have him hold her again, make her feel safe, wanted. But what did she know about this man? "Is Meg really your daughter?"

"Does it surprise you that I have a daughter?" He sounded amused.

She still couldn't put the bubbly little girl with this man, who was always so serious. Listlessly she stroked the back of a Queen Anne-style chair. "Where's your wife?"

"After our son was stillborn, Virginia died in childbirth about eighteen months ago." He looked away. "How many chairs do you think I should buy?"

Cecy didn't like the way he said his late wife's name with near reverence. While he'd held her in his arms, had he thought of his late wife? "Who's Susan?"

"Susan was my mother's best friend."

She stared at him, open-mouthed.

"That surprises you?" He raised an eyebrow, throwing her on the defensive.

"I never knew black and white people could be best friends. How did they?"

"My mother was a Civil War widow who ran a boardinghouse with Susan's help." He sat on the arm of a wing-back chair.

"Then how did you become related to Boston bankers?" She stood in front of him.

"Through my stepfather."

She nodded knowingly. "Oh, your mother married well the second time."

He shook his head and grinned. "My mother would have said she married well both times. She adored my father."

Doubtful, she ran her fingers over the top of the smooth cool leather of the chair he sat in. No doubt some love matches existed. Anything was possible. "Who's Del?"

"Susan's grandson. When he was five, his parents died and Susan and he came to live with me."

"I like Meg."

His face lit with a brilliant smile. "She's my treasure."

An ache, an old one, clenched within Cecy. Her father hadn't treasured her.

"Your father should have treasured you."

At hearing her own thought said aloud, she shied like a frightened filly. "I don't want to talk about him." A salesman approached them. Cecy glanced away, regaining her composure.

Linc ordered the four red leather chairs Cecy had preferred. Then the salesman led Cecy and Linc to a section of smaller desks and left them. "Cecilia, did your aunt tell you when she'd be coming back?" Linc asked close to her ear.

"I don't think she's coming back." He'd forced this admission out of her. Cecy went on comparing wood grain with her finger tips.

"Your aunt didn't give you good advice. Now she's abandoned you."

The anger in his voice startled Cecy. Had Auntie misled her?

He stared over her head. "You'll stay a few days with me, but it's imperative you go back to your own house as soon as possible."

"I'm sorry to be an imposition," she answered stiffly. She wished she could say, "I'll go home today." But she couldn't face that empty house and silent servants.

"You're not an imposition." He glanced down at her, his brows drawn together. "But Susan isn't an adequate chaperone in the eyes of society."

Society. The word stung.

"You'll sleep at Mrs. Hansen's until we find you a chaperone." He touched her shoulder and changed topics. "Do you like this?"

"It's fine." She scarcely looked at the desk.

"It could be yours."

"Mine?" She stared at him.

"I'm offering you a position on my weekly journal."

"Me? A journalist?"

"You don't need to make it sound like an exotic tropical disease." He opened and shut a desk drawer, grinning at her.

"After the newspapers've made my life miserable spreading this scandal, you think I'd want anything to do with them?" She turned her back to him.

"The newspapers didn't make Hunt pull a knife at your ball."

She wouldn't look at him.

"You need to take action to repair your reputation."

"I can't talk about that now." Though she spoke with bravado, she began shuddering inside.

"I've wanted to interest you in my work since we met. You could do a great deal of good. Plus your writing for a social-issues magazine would show society they've no power over you. They've consigned you to that dismal mausoleum of a house for a life sentence."

These words brought to mind the grim image of her mansion, all hooded windows and gray stone. Mr. Wagstaff had described it and her situation too accurately for comfort. But become a reporter? No matter the scandal—a well-bred lady working as a journalist? The idea was shocking.

"First, we need to find you an adequate chaperone."

Thinking of a chaperone brought her mother to mind. If her mother were well, she could come home and serve as chaperone. But her mother wasn't well enough, was she? Or had Auntie misled her about that, too? She'd wanted to go to see her mother to find out the truth, but how could she face her mother after the scandal? But perhaps her mother would understand. It seems she had a scandal of her own.

He rested his hand on her shoulder. "We have a few days before we must act. But no more."

After ordering desks and chairs, Linc drove Cecy home and then walked past just-budding yellow daffodils into the front hall.

Cecy was untying her veil when Susan stepped out of the parlor. "Miss Jackson, you have a visitor in the parlor."

Cecy turned to bolt.

Linc caught her by the arm, stopping her. "Who is it, Aunt Susan?"

"It's I."

The soft Southern drawl made Cecy strain against Linc's clasp on her shoulder.

Giving Cecy a stern look, he said, "Miss Fourchette, we're happy you came."

Cecy wanted to run up the stairs. She couldn't face her triumphant rival. But her rigid boarding school training leaped to her rescue. She pasted a brave smile on her quivering lips. "Fleur, how kind of you to call."

Susan beckoned them into the parlor. "I'll get tea." Linc went to stand by the fireplace.

Drawing off her gloves, Cecy settled on the nearest chair, sitting as straight as if a poker had been jammed up her spine. So Fleur had come to pity her.

"Are you well, Miss Jackson?" Fleur asked.

"The other night was a dreadful shock, of course." Cecy had no trouble looking sad.

"I've been having dreadful nightmares, too. And Mr. Bower's recovering. He's so sorry that you've been—"

"Blamed?" Cecy snapped.

"It is unfair," Fleur agreed without hesitating. "When Mr. Bower recovers, he intends to do what he can on your behalf."

"Is he better?" Cecy asked, seeking reassurance.

"Yes, they permitted me to see him today. When I told him your aunt had left—"

"How did you know that?" A hot flush burned upward from Cecy's neck.

"Miss Fourchette alerted me that your aunt had left," Linc said.

"Your aunt drove by my window with all her valises and trunks piled at the back of the carriage," Fleur explained earnestly. "I'd been so worried about you."

"You shouldn't have worried." Cecy's throat tightened. "Until I find another chaperone, I'm staying with a neighbor here." Cecy took a deep breath. "And Mr. Wagstaff's offered me a position on his weekly journal. He's reminded me that there are more important things in life than parties." Cecy watched for Fleur's reaction. "It's time I turned to more serious pursuits."

"Is that so?" Fleur asked with a bewildered expression.

Good. Cecy began to feel more like herself. She couldn't let herself be a weak Nellie. But she still needed a proper chaperone to gain respect again. Cecy drew back her shoulders. "I'm hoping my own dear mother is able to join me at home. Mr. Wagstaff has offered to take me to ask her."

Chapter 8

In the creeping shadows of early twilight, Cecy perched on the edge of the featherbed in Linc's guest room. Cecy had resisted Susan's insistence she nap, but as soon as she had laid her head on the down pillow, she'd fallen asleep. Now the softly ticking bedside clock said it was almost evening. The hours since breakfast felt more like days. Where was Linc?

Linc? She'd never thought of him as anything but Mr. Wagstaff, a man who alternately irritated and protected her. She remembered his sweeping her into his arms the night before, his strong fingers on her ankles as he'd unbuttoned her shoes. Earlier, Linc had held her in his arms and she'd wanted him to kiss her. A week ago that would have been unthinkable. A week ago she'd been Miss Cecilia Jackson, heiress and debutante. Who was she now?

Why did Linc always turn up just when she needed him? Why had he offered her a job? What did he want from her? *I don't want to need him. Or anyone else.* The image of her aunt, all in black, marching out the door, flickered painfully in Cecy's memory. If she couldn't count on her aunt, the only relative who'd visited her every week all those years since she'd been sent away to Boston, whom could she trust? No one.

Restless, she began pacing on the braided rag rug. San Francisco society had consigned her to lifelong seclusion and shame. Who did they think they were? Because one San Francisco man had no breeding whatsoever, *she* was to be blamed. Could she become another of the few women journalists in America, women like Annie Laurie or Ida Tarbell? Was there a possibility that Cecy, too, could reap that kind of reputation and influence?

After father's funeral, Auntie had counseled that since Cecy never wished to marry—never wished to be under any man's thumb—that Cecy must at all costs be acclaimed a "belle."

Auntie had explained that a woman who had achieved social success, who could have married well, but inexplicably chose not to, would not be scorned like other spinsters. Often society conjured up a rumor of an impossible love to explain the belle's not marrying, which only added to the unmarried beauty's mystique. She could even indulge in eccentricity and be socially sought after

With the flash of his knife, Hunt had killed the possibility of Cecy being proclaimed a "belle." But being a career woman might serve her ambition to be free of male interference and yet be respected. Hearing a motor, she looked out the white-curtained window. Linc drove up with Susan, Del, and Meg. Wasn't it late for the children to come home from school?

She hurried to the side window to watch Linc pull up to the carriage house in back. As soon as the car stopped, Del jumped out and ran toward the house. Cecy heard the side door open and slam, then furious feet pounding the wooden floor downstairs. Within seconds, she heard agitated voices. Cecy moved to her door to listen. Meg was crying. Who had hurt Del, Meg? Cecy opened her door just a crack.

"Sugar," Susan said down in the first-floor hall, "I know you're upset, but you're going to make yourself sick. Come. I'll wash those tears off your face."

Meg tried to answer, but started hiccupping.

"I'll go to Del." From below, Linc's voice sounded disturbed. That surprised Cecy. Even when she'd been nearly kidnapped, he'd sounded unruffled like the calm center of a storm. Not wishing to be caught eavesdropping, Cecy stepped back. Susan huffed and Meg clattered up the steps.

"I don't like that school." Meg hiccupped.

Susan wheezed as she climbed, her each step slow. "I don't either."

"I'm not going there any more!" Meg declared.

"Your father and I need to talk that over—"

"I won't!" Meg cried hysterically.

Cecy sucked in her breath, fearing she'd hear a sharp slap. At school, seeing others slapped for impudence, she'd never once spoken out of turn.

"Sugar, we'll talk about that when you're calmer. Your papa won't let anyone hurt you."

"They hurt Del. But I punched them—"

"You're just getting yourself into a state." Susan's voice sounded firm, but gentle. "There will always be mean people in this world. You did right to fight them. But you have to calm down or you're going to be sick. Please."

"I feel sick." Meg sobbed.

"Come into the lavatory. I'll wash your face and hands, then we'll put a cold cloth on the back of your neck."

"All . . . right," Meg choked on her words, then sobbed between hiccups.

Cecy longed to comfort the little girl, longed to thank Susan for being so kind. But she was a stranger in this house. For just a second, a soothing voice, similar to Susan's whispered, in her memory. Had it been her mother's? Cecy turned back to the exchange she'd just overhead in her mind. Who had hurt Del? She listened to the sounds of Susan soothing Meg.

Quickly, Cecy smoothed her hair and dress, then slipped outside her door. Her curiosity over Del and what had gone wrong at their school propelled her silently down the steps. She heard Linc's voice immediately. He was in a room toward the back of the first floor. She tread cautiously down the hall and drew close to the door, which stood open just a fraction.

"I hate them." Del repeated, "I hate them."

Linc replied in a steady voice, "Why didn't you tell me things were getting out of hand at school?"

"I don't care about that. I hate them."

"You mean you're just like them?"

"I'm not anything like them!" Del shouted.

"If you hate them, then you are just like them—"

"You don't know how I feel!" The boy began weeping.

A pause. Cecy's heart went out to the child. She'd felt just the same way after the opera party. Hunt had dealt her a death blow. She hated him. Why shouldn't Del hate his tormentors?

Linc said, "Perhaps not. But I do care how you feel. I love you."

Silence, except for the sound of the boy crying.

Cecy backed up and tiptoed into the parlor. Linc's words, "I do care how you feel. I love you," echoed in her mind. She sat down, pondering Susan and Linc and their love for two very fortunate children. A presence, a memory, nibbled at her conscious mind but remained elusive. Someone had loved her once.

The rosy spring dawn radiated over the green hills of San Francisco. Cecy perched on the front seat of Linc's Pierce Arrow as they drove out of the city to her mother's sanitarium. Cecy's nervous stomach objected to the wide turning Linc made around a mountain curve.

"Cecilia, what did the doctor tell you over the phone?"

"He said that Mother could see me if she felt up to it." Her voice betrayed her by quavering on the last phrase.

"If she is able to come home, Susan said she'll come and stay with you until you hire a nurse for your mother."

Cecy cleared her thick throat. "That's very thoughtful."

"Susan is angry with your aunt. She says family stands by family—no matter what."

Cecy gave a mirthless laugh. She'd thought her aunt had been the only one in her family who wouldn't disappoint her. Tears threatened, but she steeled herself against them. *What if my mother can't come home?*

Glancing sideways, Linc confounded her again by saying, "I'm sure your mother will *wish* to help. But she might not be well enough."

"I know." *I have to try.* Something, a little like hysteria, ignited in the pit of her stomach. What if her mother wouldn't come? Having to hire a stranger as a chaperone—humiliating. *I won't do it. I'll defy convention and live alone.*

Linc's even voice called her out of the vortex of emotion. "Did your mother ever visit you in Boston?"

An arrow of pain pierced her. "My father wouldn't let her at first. He said I should adjust to school before she visited me." Adjust to being abandoned.

"And then?"

"And then she was too sick to come." Desperate in her loneliness, Cecy had written many times over the years, inviting her mother to school events, begging to come home for the summer. In all those years, no one but Auntie had ever come. Her father had paid her school, clothing, music, and summer camp fees, but she'd only received civil replies from his lawyer. Why had her father hated her so? She closed her eyes trying to block out all she'd endured.

"The sanitarium's just around this bend."

She opened her eyes, forcing the past back, driving it back into its cage. "Yes, I recognize where we are now."

After they drove through the gate, the gatekeeper swung the

black wrought iron gate closed behind them. Its clang resonated through Cecy's every fiber.

Linc looked uneasy. "I take it this is one of those exclusive hospitals for the very wealthy?"

"Yes, the security is very good here . . . Auntie said." For a fleeting second, she yearned to rest her aching head on Linc's broad shoulder. Would her mother even see her?

At the impressive carved, double oak door, a staff doctor welcomed them. He led them down an empty corridor to his office, their careful footsteps echoing. They sat down by his desk and he faced them.

Cecy drew herself up, clutching at the shreds of her tattered courage. "Is my mother well enough to see me?"

"Yes, I think she is." The doctor, an earnest-looking young man, steepled his fingers and gazed at her over them. "I explained to her earlier this morning that you and Mr. Wagstaff would be coming. You mentioned that you hoped she might be able to come home with you for a visit?"

She nodded.

He eyed her warily. "May I be frank, Miss Jackson?"

"Please." The word scraped her throat like a nail file.

"The last time you visited, your mother seemed so much more agitated. But this time when I said only you and a gentleman were coming, she seemed much calmer. Miss Jackson, has anyone told you about your mother's condition?"

"No." Why had she quietly accepted the polite phrases with which Auntie had covered up her mother's illness?

"Please tell me doctor. My aunt was not open with me about my mother's condition, but I'm very concerned about her."

He leaned his chin on the back of his hand. "Your mother's illness is a combination of things, but primarily she is, or was, an inebriate."

Cecy gasped. "What makes you say that?"

"I'm new here, but I went through her file thoroughly."

Nodding woodenly, Cecy couldn't take her eyes off him.

"Nearly a decade ago, I think your mother was admitted here because of delirium tremens."

"What is delirium tremens?" she asked haltingly.

The doctor exchanged glances with Linc. "When a person imbibes alcohol too liberally over a long period of time, the alcohol takes its toll on the mind—"

"My mother is unbalanced?" Cecy nearly rose.

"No. Delirium tremens ends as alcohol consumption decreases. The mind usually recovers its natural tone."

Thank God. Cecy felt weak.

Linc leaned forward. "How is she physically?"

"She's very frail due to liver damage, common to inebriates."

"Is that why she has stayed here?" Linc persisted.

The doctor fingered papers on his desk. "I believe Mrs. Jackson preferred staying here to going home. Was your parents' marriage a troubled one?"

To say the least. Cecy didn't reply. "But she could go home now if she wants to?"

The doctor pinned her with his gaze. "Yes, but I insist she lead a very quiet life. I warn you too much change might trigger her returning to alcohol, which could begin the damaging cycle again."

"Quiet would be no problem." Cecy wouldn't meet his gaze.

"Very well. I'll take you to your mother." He ushered them out into the hall. The atmosphere was hushed, but not repressive. No matter the outcome today, she'd discover if she and her mother could become a family again.

The doctor left them in a spacious sunroom at the end of the hall. Cecy sat down on a wicker chair. Linc settled nearby. She wished he'd sat nearer.

Within minutes, a nurse dressed in a white uniform and cap entered with a thin woman.

Cecy stood. "Mother." The nurse walked away.

"Amelia isn't with you, Cecy?" Her mother's voice was barely a whisper.

Cecy's heart raced. Would her mother be angry with her over Aunt Amelia leaving? "Auntie has gone back to Boston."

"When will she come back?" Her mother's gaze pierced Cecy.

No more secrets, no more lies. Cecy forced herself to tell the plain facts. "She's washed her hands of me."

"She won't be back, then?"

"No."

"What a relief." Her mother shut her eyes, then opened them. She smiled. "Now I can go home."

Later, alone with Linc in his cozy parlor, Cecy cupped a mug of warm tea with both hands. Her fledgling confidence flowered like the pink blossoms on the almond trees, budding all over town.

She glanced at Linc as he read the evening paper. Before she'd been so busy flirting, she'd thought of Linc as just another suitor. But he was different. Would it be possible to love a man, to love Linc? For a second, she fantasized that she and Linc were husband and wife. *Foolish thoughts.*

Linc closed his paper. "Tomorrow we'll hire a nurse for your mother."

For the first time since Cecy was seven years old, she and mother would live together. Joy and fear leap-frogged inside Cecy. What had gone so dreadfully wrong that her mother had preferred a sanitarium to her own home? Why was her mother so relieved that Aunt Amelia had gone back to Boston for good? Old whispers and secrets rustled all around Cecy.

Pushing these aside, she asked, "What happened to the children at school?"

He frowned. "The children are having some problems adjusting to their new school. Children can be cruel."

Cecy's own school days had been filled with taunts and slights. Children unerringly picked out the weakest to torture. *I'm not weak anymore.* "I'm sorry to hear that."

"Susan and I've decided to teach them at home."

She didn't like the hollow, sad sound in his voice. But what could she do to help?

"You'll be busy for a few days getting your mother settled, but then I want you to begin accompanying me on a few interviews."

She set her cup onto the doily-covered table between them. She recognized his effort to bolster her confidence.

Susan slid open the pocket door. "Miss Jackson, Meg wants you to say prayers with her."

"Would you mind?" Linc asked.

"No, but . . ."

"She's waiting." Susan folded her hands over her ample girth.

Cecy went upstairs, but hesitated at the open door to Meg's room.

Standing beside a doll-sized cradle, Meg hugged her porcelain-headed doll. "Time to sleep, Matilda. Don't you worry. You won't have any nightmares." The little girl tucked her doll into its cradle with a small hand-stitched crazy quilt.

Cecy drew close. "Meg, Susan said you want—"

"I want to say prayers with you." Meg tugged Cecy over to her high bed. "Because I like you. You talk nice and you're pretty." Meg knelt and pulled Cecy down beside her. The hardwood floor brought the reality of the moment to Cecy.

Still a genuine smile lifted the corners of Cecy's mouth. Yet Cecy dreaded hearing the chant, "Now I lay me down to sleep. I pray the Lord my soul to keep. If I should die before I wake, I pray the Lord my soul to take." She'd been forced to recite these awful words aloud at school. "You say the prayer, Meg."

"Dear Father in heaven," Meg began. "I love you. I'm trying to like it here in San Francisco, but it's not easy. Please make people here like Del and me."

Cecy floundered. This cozy conversation was prayers to Meg?

The little girl continued. "Bless Papa, Susan, Del, and Miss Jackson, my new friend, and her mama. Hug my mama in heaven and tell her I still miss her." Then she began to recite, "The Lord is my Shepherd I shall not want . . ."

The Twenty-third Psalm. Cecy had heard it thousands of times. But hearing it in this child's voice released a memory from deep in Cecy's misty past.

Before she'd been sent away, someone had held her close and prayed this over her many times. But the voice Cecy heard in her memory wasn't her mother's. Whose was it?

Chapter 9

As the afternoon sun waned, the butler held the door open. Cecy waited for her mother to precede her, but the lady froze, staring up at the stone house.

Cecy murmured, "Is something wrong?"

Her mother slowly crossed the solid brass threshold.

The butler closed the door behind them. "Miss Jackson, I took the liberty of ordering tea for you in the conservatory."

Cecy took her mother's arm. The older woman looked around as though she'd never seen the house before. The ride home had been an agony of uncomfortable silences and forced pleasantries. *This is my mother, the person I should feel the closest to in all the world.* They were strangers.

The conservatory filled with luxuriant, fragrant plants overcame the emptiness of the mansion. Cecy wished she could ask her mother about the hazy memory Meg's prayers had triggered. Instead, she asked, "How are you feeling?"

"I'm tired." Still, her mother sat very straight, not letting her spine touch the chair back. Just like Cecy had been taught by Auntie.

The butler entered bearing a tray with tea and sandwiches. Cecy smiled her thanks and he withdrew. "Did I tell you that I'll be writing for a new journal?" More important questions wanting answers simmered deep inside her. *Why did you marry Father? Why did you let Father send me away?*

"Do you like to write?" Her mother's gaze met hers.

This question hadn't occurred to her. "I suppose. "

"Your plants are beautiful."

Why did you turn to drinking spirits? Did Father drive you to it? "I come here when I'm troubled." *Will you ask me what's troubling me now, Mother?*

Her mother lifted her translucent cup. As the light in the room shone through the cup, Cecy wished her past, and her mother's, could be that transparent.

"Cecilia, who's your business advisor?"

The question startled Cecy. "Mr. Edmonds."

"Have you spoken to him regularly?"

Cecy tried to read her mother's bland tone and emotionless face. "No, I've been preoccupied."

"You should see him soon."

"Oh?" *Why, Mother?*

"A woman, even a journalist, should never assume men are watching out for her where money is concerned."

Cecy hid behind her teacup. What had prompted this advice?

"Are you seeing anyone?" Her mother didn't meet Cecy's eyes.

"No." Cecy gave the pat explanation she'd already used with others. "Becoming a journalist will be more satisfying than being a debutante, don't you think?"

"I never thought of you pursuing a career."

Neither did I. Linc said Aunt Amelia gave me bad advice. Could you have warned me? Why didn't you?

The butler ushered Susan and Meg into the conservatory. Cecy's mood lifted just seeing Meg's face brimful of suppressed excitement. "Meg, hello."

"I brought a present for your mama." The little girl skipped over to the lady.

"Who are you?" Cecy's mother asked.

Cecy touched one of Meg's red-ribboned braids. "Meg's Linc Wagstaff's daughter." Cecy motioned toward Susan. "This is Susan, Mr. Wagstaff's family friend. She's spending tonight with us. Susan, this is my mother, Florence." Smiling, Susan lowered herself into the chair beside Cecy's.

"Want to see your present?" Meg leaned closer.

Florence framed Meg's rosy face with her fragile white hands. "What a sweet face you have."

From her red spring coat, Meg drew out a tiny, gray-striped kitten. "Want to hold it?"

"Oh, my," Florence breathed.

"It's a girl kitty." Meg gently laid the tiny ball of fur into the lady's hands. "You pet it careful like this." Meg demonstrated by stroking the kitten's head with one finger. "She's very little."

Florence stroked the kitten, too. The furry baby mewed and rubbed against her hand, begging for more attention. "Cecilia, may I keep the kitten?"

The childlike question pinched Cecy. "Mother, this is your home. You can have whatever you wish."

Florence smiled, her drawn face showing new color and life.

"Last night our neighbor brought them over for me and Del. I got a girl kitty and Del got a boy."

"Who's Del?"

"He's my grandson," Susan spoke up with a smile.

"What are you going to name her?" Meg stared up at Cecelia's mother's face.

"What do you suggest?" the lady asked.

Wearing a sailor blouse, Meg swished herself side to side, making her navy blue pleated skirt swirl. "Something for a real little kitty."

Florence tapped Meg's nose. "When I saw you walk in, I thought, what a pretty little miss. Why don't we call her Missy?"

"Yes." Meg clapped her hands.

Missy cringed and meowed piteously.

"Don't be afraid, Missy," Florence crooned. "I'll take care of you."

Over-sensitive emotions rolled and swirled inside Cecy. Why did she feel like crying? Meg petted and cooed to the kitten. Susan cleared her throat. "Ma'am, you need a nap."

The lady sighed. "I am tired."

"Mother, your room is all ready." Cecy stood, unsure whether she should accompany Susan or not.

"Thank you, dear. Coming home . . ." Her mother suddenly appeared near tears.

Cecy felt the same way. "If you need anything, Mother, just let us know."

Treasuring her kitty in the crook of her arm on her way out of the room, her mother paused. "Seeing this sweet little girl brought Millie Anderson to mind."

"Millie Anderson?"

"I suppose you don't remember Millie. She was your nanny. It would be lovely to see her again."

Cecy stood, stunned. She recalled the image and voice that she couldn't place. "Did she recite the Twenty-third Psalm to me?"

"Every night."

Her mother's simple words rocked Cecy. As Susan led Florence from the conservatory, Cecy shut her eyes, holding back tears.

"Don't cry." Meg hugged her.

Tears streamed from Cecy's eyes. *Nana, I remember you. You loved me.*

In his Pierce Arrow, Linc saw Cecilia's hands were clenched in her lap. Was she nervous about accompanying him to an interview? Or was it her mother? Susan had let him know how tentative relations were between Cecilia and her mother.

Linc parked the car at red brick Fire House Number One, where Fire Department chief, Dennis Sullivan, had his office. As Linc escorted Cecy inside, she gripped his arm. He'd brought her along to inspire her with a desire to write, to interview. Originally he hadn't meant to have Cecilia write for his journal. He'd merely wanted to influence her to take action against child labor. She had the right business interests, money. He hoped his new plan for her worked. The human stakes were high.

After the introductions in the office, Linc and Cecy sat down side by side, facing Sullivan at his desk. Linc took out a notebook and pencil. Cecy followed suit.

"Which paper did you say you were writing for?" Sullivan asked.

"The article's for my weekly journal, *Cause Celebre*."

"Haven't read that one."

Linc grinned. "This interview will appear in the premiere issue later this month. *Cause Celebre* will tackle issues other papers avoid."

Sullivan snorted. "So that's why you're here. I've tried to interest the *Examiner, Call,* and *Bulletin* in my worries and they all say a story like mine is bad for circulation. Nobody wants to think about a possible earthquake."

"Do you think there will be another earthquake?" Cecy glanced at the slender man with graying temples, her interest caught.

"Hel . . . I mean, heavens, yes." Sullivan grinned sheepishly.

"So tell us what needs to be done—if and when another earthquake strikes." Linc poised his pencil over his paper.

Cecy wrote "Earthquake Measures" on her page.

"It's impossible to predict when an earthquake will hit," Sullivan began. "But let's be realistic. San Francisco has seen them before and will see them again. That hasn't changed, but our population density has increased. And now everyone has gas piped into their houses. Even if they've hooked up to electricity, most people cook with gas now, not wood. Cracked or broken gas pipes are an open invitation to fire."

Cecy hadn't expected interviewing the fire chief to be interesting. But this was riveting.

"In 1860, the city fathers showed more foresight than the jokers today. Back in the sixties, they constructed large underground cisterns throughout the city to fight fires. But these need to be repaired and reactivated. The biggest problem in fighting any large-scale fire is getting water. If gas pipes break, the water pipes will break, too. If water pipes break—"

"You can't get the water to fight the fires." Linc scribbled on his pad.

"Give that man a cigar." Sullivan nodded.

"So why aren't the cisterns being reactivated?" Cecy asked. She waited to jot down the man's answer.

Sullivan grunted. "Money, of course. The Reuf gang that got Schmitz elected is too busy siphoning off municipal funds to be concerned about a little thing like the safety of the citizens."

"Graft?" Linc demanded.

Sullivan's concern was clear in the tautness of his posture and in his grave expression. "If they won't give us water, we need to purchase high explosives to fuel firebreaks. But they nixed that, too."

"Firebreaks?" Cecy glanced up from her notebook.

He looked at her. "Yes, a trained fire department can devise and explode a series of firebreaks, lines of very dense high rubble that serve as a barrier to the spreading flames."

The vision of sweeping, unchecked flames abruptly halted Cecy's pen. *Could this actually happen?*

"Pretty tricky business," Linc muttered.

"You can say that again." Sullivan's face flushed with irritation; his voice grew more gruff. "If it isn't done right, the explosives just provide more fuel for the fire. Spreads the fire. But when I ask for money to bring in professionals to train my men, all I get are excuses. No money. They're fools, every last one of them. Fools."

Linc pulled away from curb. "What did you think?"

"I think the people of San Francisco should be told what their fire chief needs for their protection." She spoke with a passion that startled her. The images of an earthquake and flames had fired her imagination. "I can't believe the municipal government won't give him the money he needs."

Linc grinned. "See I told you, you have what it takes to be a journalist."

"I may care about the issue, but that doesn't mean I can write about it." She doubted her sketchy notes would be sufficient.

"Writing is something you can learn. Caring about inequities and abuses of power and wanting them to change for the better can't be taught. That must come from the heart." He smiled at her.

His approval warmed her. But why did she want, need his approval? Everyone she'd ever trusted had let her down. Everyone, except perhaps Millie Anderson.

Her mother said her former nanny had insisted on traveling with her to Boston, but father had dismissed her and hired a new nurse to take Cecy across country to Boston. Her father's need to isolate her from anyone who loved her didn't make sense. What could Cecy have done at such a tender age to make him hate her?

Hesitantly, Cecy glanced at Linc. "My mother would like to locate someone."

"Who?"

"My old nanny Millie Anderson. How does one locate a person?"

Linc swerved to miss a startled horse. The hack driver shook his fist at them. "Often employment agencies keep track of people throughout their many job changes. And we can always advertise in the classifieds."

"My mother wants to see her again." *Just as I do*. Perhaps Millie could answer questions from the past, save Cecy from chasing after answers on her own.

Linc drove up to Cecy's house. "In a couple of days, we'll tour a cannery. I told the manager we just wanted to do a story about how a cannery works. But really it will be a story about working conditions there."

"I see." Cecy dreaded going back to face her mother. Not being able to ask her mother all the questions she needed answers to made finding Millie even more pressing.

Linc parked and came over to help her out of the auto. Feeling warm, she unbuttoned her coat while the butler let them in the front door.

The butler smiled. "Miss, your mother and the nurse are in the conservatory with Susan, the child, and kittens."

Cecy and Linc walked to the conservatory. Susan, Meg, and Florence were teasing Missy and Meg's kittens with a ball of blue angora yarn. Linc looked around. "Where's Del?"

Susan frowned. "When we were ready to catch the cable car, I couldn't find that boy."

Had there been more trouble with Del? Cecy nearly asked, but the butler appeared, announcing a call for her. Cecy stepped to the phone and picked up the receiver. "Hello."

"Cecilia Jackson?"

"Yes, who's this?"

"This is Clarissa Hunt calling."

The new combination of names jumbled in Cecy's mind. "Clarissa Hunt?"

"Mrs. Victor Hunt. Victor and I just returned from our elopement."

"You eloped with Hunt?" A weakness snaked through Cecy. She clutched the telephone table.

"Yes, now you know he loved me, not you," the woman gloated. "He was just pursuing you to give his father a hard time. Victor didn't like being told whom to marry."

Clarissa believed that drivel? "He stabbed your brother because of his pride?"

"Victor would never hurt my brother. You pushed between them. You're the one responsible."

I didn't bring the knife. Every bad thing she'd learned about Hunt rushed through Cecy's mind. This woman was in danger of suffering like Cecy's own mother. "Clarissa—"

"I just wanted to tell you myself, go back East—"

Cecy broke into the stream of spiteful words. "*Clarissa*, if you ever need help, call on me, *please*."

"What? I've married the man I love and who loves me. Just stay away from my husband."

Cecy's anger flared. "Isn't he too much in love with you to be tempted by me?"

Clarissa slammed down the receiver in Cecy's ear.

Cecy hung up slowly.

"Who was that?" Linc asked.

"A fool, a stupid little fool."

Cecilia's crushed expression brought Linc to her side. He took her arm, walking her to the cover of the lush green plants and tall, potted trees. "Who was it?"

"Mrs. Victor Hunt." Her voice dripped with sarcasm. "Clarissa Hunt called; she's married to the man she loves. And she said I should leave town." She turned her face away.

He tugged her closer. Her vulnerability drew him. He wanted to pull her into his arms, run his fingers through her feathery-soft hair. *No.*

She turned back to him. "Linc, nothing will change what has happened—"

His hand pressed her soft lips together, stopping her words. Then his hand slid over her smooth skin to cup her cheek. "I'll lead you into the future."

She leaned into his shirtfront. "I have no future."

"I'll show you you're wrong." *Don't kiss her.* But his lips refused to obey him. Leaning down, he kissed her fragrant, auburn hair.

She leaned her head back to kiss him in return.

He gently slid his lips from hers. *Oh, Cecilia, what am I going to do with you?*

Chapter 10

The sky threatened rain as Linc and Cecilia set out down Market Street for a Saturday-afternoon promenade, very different from the fashionable Montgomery Street one. After Clarissa's nasty call, he'd decided a good way to cheer Cecilia was to introduce her to the avant-garde of San Francisco. Now he had qualms.

He'd learned from childhood how to mix with all classes, colors, and types of people. His parents with their wealth and zeal for social issues had led the way. Both of them had also shocked other Christians with their involvement with "undesirables."

"Who are these people you want me to meet?" she asked. Would Cecilia be able to see these people as they were or only as the personas they showed in public? "The artistic community parades down Market Street on Saturday."

"While the hypocrites, who think Hunt is a fine young man, walk Montgomery Street?" she snapped.

"This afternoon is just to widen your experience. Miss Fourchette said both she and Bower would help."

She waved his words away. "Hunt is Bower's brother-in-law now. They'll all close ranks."

Linc tightened his grip on her arm. Her cynicism grated on him. "Don't always assume the worst about people. Have I ever failed you?"

"I trust you more than anyone else in San Francisco."

How deeply had this troubled young woman worked her way into his heart? Too deeply. He took a painful breath. "If that's the best you can do."

"Sorry." Her chin dipped low. "Your daughter shows what a good man you are."

Before Linc could react, a handsome man with a shock of blond-gray hair, Ambrose Bierce, a noted writer, walked up to Linc. "Wagstaff, you've brought the scandalous Miss Jackson to the rogue's promenade." Bierce bowed over her hand. "How do you stand Wagstaff? He's so upright he makes my teeth ache."

Looking bemused, Cecilia curtseyed.

Linc groaned. "Just because I don't want to drink with you all night on the Barbary Coast—"

"Hey, Wagstaff!" another man hailed them. "How's that rag of yours going?"

Linc introduced Cecilia to McEwen, an editor of another avantgarde paper.

A lady—rouged and sporting an outrageous pink feather boa—swept up to them. "Lincoln, introduce me to my rival."

Linc bowed. "Miss Jackson, Miss Bonnie LaRoux, a lady of the stage."

"Oh, you're the scandalous redhead. Delighted, I'm sure." The actress touched gloved hands with Cecilia, then turned to Linc. "I've gotten a part in that new play opening at the Alhambra."

Cecy felt her spirits lift as the five of them promenaded together, greeting others who all—shockingly—laughed over her scandal. Who would have dreamed Linc had friends like these?

The five of them ended up at Delmonico's for an early steak dinner. Daringly, she ordered champagne for everyone—in spite of Linc's frown. The champagne bubbles tickled her nose and she giggled. The electric lights and gilded rococo mirrors dazzled her eyes. The tart, witty conversation flowed around her. The words weren't important. Being a part of a group again was.

After her third glass champagne, the actress eyed Cecy. "So how wealthy are you, dear?"

Cecy nearly choked. No one had ever asked her that question before. And she didn't know the answer. Her mother's advice came back to her. Yes, she would talk to her business advisor. Soon.

"Bad taste, LaRoux." Bierce shook his head. "The oppressed never ask the oppressor how much she has in the bank—especially before the check's been paid."

Cecy looked around warily. Had she offended them in some way?

"They're both just showing their lack of breeding," McEwen apologized. "Socialism is in vogue."

"According to Marx," Bierce supplied, "each man should put in what he is able and take out what he needs."

"Which sounds good, but isn't very realistic." Linc rested his elbows on the white damask.

"Why, Lincoln?" the actress asked as Bierce lit the cigarette she held in a long ivory holder.

"Because, the poor can be just as greedy as the rich. Being poor is no virtue," Linc said.

"But isn't your rag intended to do exposés?" McEwen demanded.

Exposés? Cecy frowned into the pale champagne in her glass.

"Yes, the poor read all about the rich in *every* evening newspaper," Linc said. "But the rich know *nothing* of the poor."

"Oh, let's talk about something amusing." Miss LaRoux waved her boa. "The poor are a bore."

After the flamed dessert, Linc stood up. "Miss Jackson and I must be leaving."

Cecy rose, a little wobbly. "I enjoyed meeting you all."

Bierce winked. "You'll find you have much more fun as the scandalous redhead."

Outside mist floated on the night breeze. Linc helped her into a hack. Sighing, Cecilia leaned her head back. "What fun people."

"They're fun—this early in the evening," he cautioned her.

Cecy couldn't make sense of his answer, but she floated lighter than air like the bubbles in the champagne.

Soon the hack let them down at Cecilia's home. Knowing that gossips were probably at their windows, Linc tried to quiet Cecy who was giggling. The butler opened the door. Linc almost carried Cecilia as he hurried her into the foyer.

"Cecilia?" Her mother, dressed in a lavender flannel wrapper, stood at the top of the curved staircase. "You said you'd be back much earlier."

"I'm sorry, Mother." Cecilia clung to the post at the base of the balustrade. "We had dinner with friends."

The nurse behind the lady touched her arm. "Well," her mother began, "as long as you're—"

Cecilia stepped forward and tripped somehow. She gave a trill of a giggle. Linc caught her before she fell. But when he looked up, he glimpsed Cecilia's mother's white, stricken face.

With Del in the middle, Linc sat in the front seat beside Cecilia, who controlled the tiller of her electric runabout, motoring them to the *Bulletin* office. Inquiring at the employment agencies about her old nurse Millie Anderson hadn't paid off, so Linc had told her to place a classified ad.

As they drove past trees, budding white, along the street, he made himself face forward. Cecilia glided in and out of his thoughts. Her rich brown sugar eyes, that little mole beside her upper lip . . .

"Is this the turn?" She grinned at him with a saucy glint in her eye.

He nodded. "You're in a good mood."

"I am." She grinned again. "Mr. Bierce called me about getting up a theater party. Would you like to come along?"

"I'll consult my extensive social calendar," he replied dryly. Linc's mood lowered. He'd hoped glimpsing bohemian life would cheer Cecilia, not ensnare her. Had he led Cecilia, already so dear to him, into the path of temptation?

All last night he'd poured his heart out, begging God to take away his attraction to this lovely young woman. But his grief over losing Virginia kept intruding. The same, old empty feeling filled him.

Cecilia interrupted his thoughts. "I can't wait to go out again."

"I understand." A young, vibrant woman needed to be out having fun. On the other hand, he was a widower with children to raise. Very aware of the sullen child sitting beside him, Linc pondered how to help Del. Cecilia parked in front of the newspaper office. Inside, Linc escorted her to the Classifieds Desk. "I'll leave you here. I want a word with Fremont Older." With a hand on Del's shoulder, Linc guided the boy to Older's office doorway.

Waving them in, Older said a few more words into the phone, then hung up. "Hadn't seen you for a while. How's the heiress?"

Linc sat down and gave a half-grin. "Please don't beat around the bush." He pulled Del close to his side. The boy glanced at Older, then stared at his feet.

"Did the papers tell the truth about her?" Older leaned back.

"The papers didn't get much right."

"And who is this young fellow you have with you?" Older nodded toward Del.

"This is Del, my housekeeper's grandson." He felt the same twinge he always felt when he couldn't speak the plain facts about his true relationship to Susan and Del. But rarely did anyone understand even after detailed explanation. Susan never even tried to explain.

Older stared at Del. "Need a job, son? I could use another messenger boy."

Del looked startled.

"No, thanks," Linc replied. "Del has schoolwork to do."

"He can read a little, can't he? Count to a hundred? What else does he need?" Older asked.

Irritated, Linc gripped Del's shoulder. "Del's father and grandfather were both educated at Howard University. I expect him to follow in their distinguished footsteps." Linc had hoped visiting a large newspaper office might catch Del's interest, not bring up again the whole matter of how the world looked down at him.

"You don't say?" Older glanced curiously at Del. "So when's your rag coming out?"

Linc wished he knew how Del was reacting. "I plan to get the first issue out in late March."

"Still muckraking?"

"I interviewed the fire chief, how he'd fight fires in event of a major earthquake."

"The public won't thank you for it. They don't want to know—"

"I want to know," Linc insisted. Remembered images of leaping flames—roaring, crackling—froze Linc inside. "At eight years old, I survived the Great Chicago Fire."

"Sorry."

"I don't want my daughter going through something like I did."
God, keep us safe.

Older considered this with a grim expression. "That interview might be good idea. Shake people up—especially our do-nothing, pretty-boy mayor."

In early morning darkness, Linc drove along the coast by the glow of a full moon. Cecilia napped beside him. Hearing the slap of waves, he followed the uneven dirt road toward a huddle of waterfront buildings. The scene was anything but romantic. Crude shanties, dilapidated storefronts—weathered and splintered from salt spray—hugged both sides of the road. The stench of fish and saltwater hung in the air.

He recognized the cannery and parked in front. A lone dog barked in the stillness. Linc folded up his collar against the damp chill. It was for this day that God had called him to San Francisco, the day he'd planned for, the reason he made his foray into San Francisco society to meet Miss Cecilia Jackson. Today he would measure the true size of her heart and the mettle of her spirit. Making up for lost sleep, he closed his eyes and dozed.

A keening, screeching whistle woke Cecy. She sat up in Linc's front seat. Bleak kerosene lights flickered in a string of buildings. The maddening whistle continued. The rank odor of rotten fish hit and, half awake, she gagged.

Linc awoke. "We're at the cannery across the Bay." He helped her out and they entered the drafty warehouse-factory, open on one side to the sea. The whistle broke off.

Linc spoke close to her ear. "Remember. I'm here to do research for an article, maybe a book. Keep your eyes and ears open and remember everything."

A tall, cadaverously thin man in a canvas slicker loomed over them. "You two ain't here to work the catch. Who are you?"

"I'm Linc Wagstaff and this my assistant." He offered his hand. "I have permission from your boss, Mr. Boynton, to observe how a cannery works. Are you the foreman?"

"Yeah, but what-cha want to know what we do here for?" The man spat tobacco out of the side of his mouth.

"Maybe I'll write an article in the paper or a book about it," Linc said.

The man rubbed his stubbled chin. "Ya don't say? You're sure you talked to Mr. Boynton?"

Linc nodded.

"Okay, just don't get in the way. We got a sardine catch to work."

"On an article like this, I usually work along with everyone so I can get a feel for the job."

Cecy was distracted by people, no doubt from the shacks around the cannery, who had begun streaming in. The fish stench kept Cecy's stomach churning.

"Won't-cha get your good clothes dirty?" The man objected.

Linc shrugged. "These are my work clothes."

"Swells, huh?" He tossed Linc a dirty long oil-cloth apron. "Wear that. Follow me."

Linc shrugged on the apron and hurried after the foreman.

Cecy struggled with her revulsion. She wanted to escape to the auto outside, but a dreadful rumbling, groaning came from the seaside opening and swallowed up her words. In the din, she hurried to keep close to Linc. Visiting a cannery had sounded so inoffensive. Now inside the cannery, reality hit her from all sides—the horrific noise, the filth-encrusted walls, the grinding of crushed shells and debris under her feet, the wretched stink. Catching up with Linc, she snagged his sleeve. She tried to make herself heard over the noise, but failed.

He shook his head, then followed the foreman toward the sardine boat unloading its catch.

Cecy hung back, watching the fishermen on the boat deck scramble to send the silvery run of wiggling sardines down a huge funnel into a kind of small boxcar. As each was loaded, men appeared and trundled the wheeled cars farther back into the cannery.

She turned her head to watch the contents of the carts being dumped onto long metal tables. Instantly, swarthy unkempt men and gaunt women and children—who stood on rickety crates—pulled out short, fine knives and began slitting the small fish and flinging fish entrails to the floor.

Cecy retched and retched, but thankfully her stomach was empty. Finally, she closed her eyes and leaned back against a rough beam. She would have fainted, but the thought of touching the filthy floor made her fight for consciousness. Something tugged her skirt. Her eyes flew open. She glanced down.

A small, wailing child, still in baby skirts—grimy ones—clung to the fold of her dress. The child held up its arms. Cecy looked around desperately for a mother seeking a child. No mother looked up from the work of gutting sardines.

Confused, she frowned down at the toddler. What was a baby doing in this awful place? And the baby was barefoot. She snatched the child off the filthy floor. *That can't be healthy*. She carried the baby over to the nearest table. She leaned close to one of the women. A slimy blot of fish insides landed on Cecy's cheek. She exclaimed, flicking it off.

More horrific noises descended from the floor above. Cecy couldn't make herself heard above the din. The women at the table all motioned her back toward the middle of the room.

Queasy, she put the child on her hip and picked her way through the crowded room, filled with tables and frantically laboring men, women, and children. In the center of the room, a stove had been stoked and feeble warmth hung around it. Boxes had been set around the stove—away from the chill seaside drafts.

She glanced down into the boxes. Babies? Babies wrapped in tattered blankets slept in the boxes. A dilapidated pram stood to one side with two babies. A lone wooden chair sat by the stove. Had they just dumped their babies here? With no one to care for them? Bewildered, Cecy sank onto the rickety chair.

Within seconds, more sleepy, shoeless toddlers in soiled dresses crowded around her. Each grabbing a piece of her skirt, they clung to her, leaning against her, knuckling sleep-crusted eyes. Some crying; some sober.

Poor children. Her heart was wrung. She clumsily patted a dark-haired child whose tears ran down dirt-lined cheeks. "There, there," she murmured into the surrounding maelstrom. The child looked up at her solemnly and used Cecy's dress to wipe its eyes and nose.

A warm wetness oozed over Cecy's lap and down her legs. The toddler sitting on her had no diaper. She closed her eyes in resignation. Surrounded, she couldn't move without disturbing, distressing the innocents further. She felt their abandonment. Their eyes pleaded, "Why doesn't mama hold me? I need her." Cecy stroked another small, downy head.

Cecy wanted to escape, but how could she abandon these little ones? They'd been deserted just as she had in faraway Boston. Left to cry all alone.

Hours later, Linc found Cecilia sitting by the stove. Her hair had come loose. She had fish guts smeared down one cheek and dirty fingerprints on the other. Her white collar was grimy. In her arms, she held a swaddled Chinese baby. She'd never looked more lovely to him. "Cecilia."

"Linc," she said the word with what sounded like heartfelt relief.

A short Chinese couple stopped beside Linc, bowing. The woman lifted the baby from Cecy and said something in Chinese.

The husband translated, "Wife say thank you hold baby. Our first son. One week old."

"Congratulations." Linc shook the man's hand, then pulled a dollar from his pocket. "This is for the baby." The couple smiled, bowed and then straggled out. Noise still rattled and groaned above them.

"We've been here forever." Cecilia stood up and stretched.

"Eleven hours."

"Please can we go?" Her hair slid completely down to her shoulder as he led her outside into the sunshine. Cecilia paused beside his auto.

"What's wrong?" He held the door open for her.

She looked down at herself. "I'm too filthy to sit in your car." She started to cry in little gasps. "Why did you bring me to this awful place?"

He stared into her eyes. "Have you ever been filthy before?"

"What has that got to do with anything?"

"Everything. Have you ever been filthy?"

"I've never even been allowed to be smudged."

"Exactly. How else could I make you understand how awful it feels to be filthy?" He motioned around him. "Did you imagine a cannery being anything like this?"

"I imagined men doing something with fish—"

He pressed her. "Not the children, not the babies—"

"No!" Gazing, she turned around in a complete circle. "Why do people let awful places like this exist?"

Free to voice his passion at last, Linc gripped her shoulders. "That's why I must write. God has called me to shout for justice for the helpless. This is why I came to San Francisco. People must understand this. It's bad enough for the men and even the women— but what about the children, the babies?"

She gazed into his eyes. "I'd like to meet the man who owns this disgusting place. And tell him *just* what I think of him."

Chapter 11

In one of her new "journalist" outfits, a severe, brown gabardine suit, Cecy sat behind the imposing oak desk in her father's office, a room in her house that she'd previously avoided, awaiting her business advisor. After she'd called his office for three days, he'd finally returned her call. Miss LaRoux's question remained—how rich was she? And why was Mr. Edmonds avoiding her?

And who owned sardine canneries near Monterey? That day, she'd come home, stripped off her clothing, told her maid to burn them, then she'd scrubbed herself clean with a brush. If the heartless factory owner didn't change the filthy conditions there, she'd expose him in Linc's journal. For the first time in her life, she found herself passionately concerned about something besides music.

Her butler said, "Miss Jackson, your business advisor."

In a starched white shirt and black suit, Mr. Edmonds marched in. "What's this all about? I'm a busy man."

She smiled, but kept him standing, reminding him he worked for her. "What is the extent of my wealth?"

He bristled like his stiff, broomlike mustache. "Your father left you and your mother secure. Business is too weighty a subject for a woman."

"I want a detailed list of my stocks, property, and where all my cash is deposited." She waited, serenely composed like photographs of Queen Victoria.

A red flush crawled up his neck. "You don't need to get your nose into my business—"

"Now, why are you behaving as though you don't want to give me information about my own finances?" She gave him a narrow look.

"I have nothing to hide." The red flush suffused his bulbous face now.

"When may I expect to receive a complete accounting from you?"

"Next Monday."

"Fine. Oh, another matter, would you look into who owns sardine canneries north of Monterey?"

He looked as though he were about to ask her why, then changed his mind. "If you wish."

"Until Monday, then."

He left.

I did it. I'm taking charge of my life. She stood. Thinking about finances had not been a part of her life before. Rays of light were piercing the darkness in her life. Millie Anderson would come forward soon and she might, at last, have more answers about the past. In the hall, Cecy met her mother.

"Cecilia, what did Edmonds say?"

Cecy stroked the silky kitten her mother carried everywhere over her arm. Cecy lowered her voice, "Is there any specific concern you have about our finances that I should know about?"

For once, her mother didn't look away when asked a direct question. "Cecilia, money is power and freedom. Men know that. That's why they keep it from us. Never forget that."

The words nearly brought tears to Cecy's eyes. It was the very first real exchange of ideas with her mother. "I won't forget. I'm going to see Linc now."

Her mother's face brightened. "Please invite Susan and Meg to tea again."

"I will." Cecy felt heartened by her mother's cheerier expression. For the past few days, she'd seemed depressed again.

Her mother looked into her eyes. "Have you had any answer to your advertisement about Millie Anderson?"

"Not yet. Linc says these things take time."

"You'll be home this evening, won't you?"

"No, I've made arrangements to attend *The Mikado* with friends, followed by dinner."

A shadow of concern clouded her mother's face.

"Linc will be my escort. Don't worry." Cecy smiled.

The lady turned to join the nurse. "Just remember a lady must guard her reputation jealously."

Cecy winced at this blow. Everyone had agreed to protect her mother by remaining silent about the scandal. "Don't worry about me, Mother." *I've already lost my reputation, thanks to Hunt.*

"Miss Cecilia." Meg opened the red front door and grinned. Cecy stepped inside, warmed by the child's welcome. Meg frowned. "Del left without asking permission."

"Good day, Miss Jackson." Susan had walked up behind Meg. "I'm sorry but Meg can't miss her study time."

"But Del's not here," Meg grumbled.

"That's Del's problem." Susan turned Meg by the shoulders toward the dining room.

Linc came jogging down the walnut stairs. "Cecilia, I'm sorry I have to go out now."

"I'll come along." Cecy smiled her challenge. "My car's right outside."

Linc hesitated on the bottom step, resting a hand on the curved balustrade. Linc gave the deepest frown she'd ever seen on his face. "Older called me. He saw Del at the Barbary Coast."

He opened the door to show her out. "You can't—"

"I'm driving." She marched out to her shiny green car, past the pink azaleas along the drive.

"I can't let you drive to the Barbary Coast. Your reputation—"

"Is quite ruined already." She positioned her driving goggles.

He put his hands on his hips, flaring both sides of his drab driving coat, then got in. "Go! I haven't time to argue with you."

Triumphantly, she secured her veil and headed down to the waterfront, the notorious Barbary Coast. A rush of forbidden excitement coursed through Cecy. Whispered phrases about Mickey Finns, Shanghai-ed sailors, opium dens, and ladies of easy virtue flitted through her mind. But by daylight, the Barbary Coast disappointed her. Derelict buildings, scruffy-looking men with black hats pulled low, slatternly women in bright garish dresses, and sneaky-looking mongrels slunk in and out of alleyways. "This isn't where Del should be."

"Del's been confused since our move here." Linc looked at her as though testing her. "He can't understand why his color makes him count for less in the eyes of the world."

Before she could answer, she glimpsed Del and stomped on the brake. "Del!"

A large group of black boys milled around at the head of a dark alleyway with Del at the center. Linc leaped out of the car. "Del!" The boys ran away headlong into the shadows. His buff-colored coat flaring behind him, Linc chased after them.

Cecy sped around the corner to head them off at the other end. Ahead, the first boy in tattered denim overalls broke out of the alley. She surged forward to cut off the runaways. A couple thudded against her car door; all yowled in shock.

Linc sprinted ahead and grabbed Del by the shoulder. Without a word, he yanked Del to the car, unceremoniously tossed him in next to Cecy, and then got in.

"Hey! You can't grab him!" A few boys threw stones at the car.

Cecy pressed on the gas. Why would a boy so loved want to run away to the company of young toughs?

"I don't want to go home," Del blustered, almost in tears, pushing against Linc.

Linc pressed Del back into the seat. "You're going home."

Cecy tried to soothe the boy. "Del, you're worrying your grandmother. Why?"

The boy wrapped his arms around himself and stared at his feet.

"Answer us," Linc demanded.

On the drive home, both the sulky boy and Linc sat silent and gloomy. She'd barely stopped at their side door when Del vaulted over the seat and darted down the drive.

Linc jumped out of the car. "Del!"

Cecy watched Del disappear from sight. "Shall we go after him?"

Linc looked skyward. "God, I don't know what to do. He's so gifted musically. So much potential to waste. But You'll have to make the difference. I can't."

Linc stood there as though he actually expected to receive an answer from God. Discomfited, Cecy didn't know where to look.

"Cecilia, you're still set on going to the operetta tonight?" He looked and sounded grim.

She eyed him warily. "I can go without you—"

"No. I'll pick you up about seven."

Not knowing what she should say, she drove away.

Gripped by powerlessness, Linc stood a long time in the empty drive, dead-sure Del was on his way back to the Barbary Coast. The same helplessness he'd felt when Virginia died filled him. He'd failed Del. "God," he whispered, "I can't see my way. Help me."

Cecy's smile began to pinch at the corners of her mouth. In the darkened Tivoli Opera House around her sat Linc, Miss LaRoux, Bierce, and McEwen. *The Mikado* made everyone else laugh, but flashes of *Madame Butterfly* and that first earth tremor bobbed in her memory. Finally, the maroon velvet curtains swung closed; its gold tassels swaying; she nearly sighed aloud with relief.

Linc glanced at her. "You said you'd made a reservation at the Palace restaurant?"

She nodded. Outside, she wanted to ask him about Del, but Miss LaRoux, McEwen, and Bierce occupied the rear seat of the Pierce Arrow. The chic Palm Garden Restaurant at the grand Palace Hotel was the crown jewel of the downtown with its glass dome and six tiered stories opened onto the palmed court.

At their table, Cecy nodded to the head waiter. Pink Chablis, the first of seven wines for the various courses, flowed into their glasses. Cecy sipped the piquant wine. When she'd attempted to scale the heights of society, she'd needed a clear head. Now as the scandalous redhead, she could let this wine take away the worries about her mother, and troubling memories of the helpless babies at the cannery. By the light of the many electric chandeliers, she admired Linc's good looks. He was different, special. His clear blue eyes looked out on the world, seeing the truth without flinching.

Everyone laughed. Not hearing the joke, she forced a chuckle to fit in. Why did Linc keep frowning at her so?

When the waiter came to fill Cecilia's glass of champagne too soon, Linc waved the man away. After doing this twice, the waiter held back until Cecilia demanded her glass filled.

Not wanting to cause a public argument, he hid his worry. Certain families were prone to certain sins. Her mother had ended up in a sanitarium with delirium tremens. *Dear God, how can I stop this from happening to Cecilia?*

The evening finally ended near two A.M. Gripping her elbow, Linc guided Cecilia out to his Pierce Arrow in the cool night breeze. Her exaggerated gestures, giggles, and missteps broadcast her condition. Eager to go home, he parked outside Cecilia's mansion and escorted her to the door.

"Why are there so many lights on?" Cecilia bumped into Linc.

He steadied her. "Perhaps your staff decided to wait up for you."

"Mother . . . Mother might be ill." He helped her mount the steps. The butler opened the door. "What's wrong?" Cecilia asked.

Linc blinked, adjusting to the bright lights in the large foyer.

"Cecy!" A warm, female voice rang out. "Cecy, my precious!"

Cecilia looked up, mouth wide.

Linc watched a gray-haired woman of generous proportions envelop Cecilia in her arms.

Cecilia gasped, "Nana. Oh, Nana."

Chapter 12

Cecy's heart leaped. She buried her tearful face against Nana's ample bosom, recognizing Nana's sweet scent.

"My sweet Cecy, my precious . . ." Nana's soft words, spoken only a breath away from Cecy's ear, fell like a dew of blessing.

Finally, Linc's voice filtered through the warm cocoon of Nana's embrace. "Let's move to the library; it's more comfortable."

Wiping her face with her hands, Cecy drew Nana away to the sofa. Her mother took the wing-back chair. Linc sat beside Cecy. A fire warmed the room.

"I knew you'd be happy." Her mother's smile embraced Cecy.

Linc quietly introduced himself. "Did you read our ad?"

"I'd just returned to my room at the boardinghouse and my landlady pointed it out to me. I couldn't believe you remembered me after all the years."

"I had forgotten, but . . ." How could Cecy explain how Meg's reciting the Twenty-third Psalm had brought Nana back to mind?

Nana squeezed Cecy's hand. "I've often prayed for you, Cecy. I suppose I should call you Miss Cecilia now—"

"Call me Cecy." Now Cecy knew where she'd gotten her secret name for herself she'd never shared with anyone else. But why hadn't she remembered this woman who'd named her that, loved her so? Her mother's presence stopped her from asking. Would Nana answer her or hesitate to stir up the murky past?

Nana edged forward on her seat. "I should be leaving."

Cecy caught her by the arm. "Mother has a nurse, but she needs a companion. Will you come live with us?"

Nana's smile burst over her face. "If you really want me."

Cecy experienced a joy like reaching the high note of a difficult aria.

Florence asked, "Can you stay tonight?"

"I must." Millie chuckled. "I've stayed away too late to go home without disturbing my poor landlady."

Linc stood up. "Then I am the one who must leave."

Glad to have a moment with him, Cecy rose. "I'll walk you to the door." Away from the others, Cecy murmured, "Linc, I . . . how could I have forgotten Nana all these years?"

He gave her his arm. "Perhaps being separated from her was too painful for you to bear."

"A person can't control her own memory like that." Cecy tightened her grip on his sleeve.

He tugged her closer. "I had a conversation with my stepfather once about his experiences as a Union army surgeon. He said often soldiers would forget the circumstances of their wounding. His explanation was they couldn't bear to remember."

They'd reached the entry hall. He picked up his black top hat and white silk scarf.

She yearned to slip her arms around his neck and kiss him. Breathing in his scent of warm autumn spices, she could almost feel his lips coaxing hers. She resisted. After their good-nights, Cecy closed the door after him. She turned to go back to Nana, Mother, wondering why, how this man—out of all the others—had the power to move her.

Linc had put in a heavy day's work at his newly furnished office. Nearing the waterfront, Linc parked under a streetlight, then caught the trolley that descended to the Barbary Coast. Only a fool would leave a car unattended on Battery Street after dark. At the breakfast table, Susan's hands had rattled her cup. Kang had burned the toast. Meg had refused to eat. And Linc knew he was the one who had to find Del. *I've lost Virginia, Father. Please don't let me lose Del, too.*

Cecy's new friends deemed rubbing shoulders with the habitués of the Coast daring fun. They let themselves be fooled by the frantic laughter, garish colors, and the loud ragtime. But Linc heard tubercular coughing, saw the dawning of syphilitic madness in dilated eyes, the sunken sadness of those bound to opium. Sin gave pleasure for a season, but it was an exceedingly short season on the Coast.

Clutching his walking stick, he stepped off the trolley. Night fell. Rats screeched down dark alleys. Ragtime burst from the doorway of the first saloon where Linc looked for Del. He wasn't at the Blue Moon or the Last Chance or the Golden Slipper. Linc found him at Oscar's, playing jaunty ragtime with a drummer and horn player in a three-piece band. In the dim light, Linc slipped along the wall until he was near the band and sat down at a table. The syncopated music gave the cheap saloon atmosphere a cheerfulness it lacked on its own. Ordering a beer he didn't plan to drink, Linc waited, motionless, until Del glanced his way.

The boy froze, except for his fingers, which somehow kept up the beat. The drummer and horn player looked at Linc with edgy curiosity. The song ended. The drummer stood up signaling a break. Del glared at Linc. "Why'd you come here? I'm not—"

The drummer cuffed Del, silencing him. "Okay, mister, who are you?"

The man's touch had been light, fatherly. Rising, Linc offered the man his hand. "I'm Linc Wagstaff. I'm Del's guardian."

"I'm Long Jack and that's Freddie," the tall horn player said indignantly. "Your boy said he was an orphan."

"He is, but his grandmother lives in my home and cares for my daughter, Meg." Linc spoke to Del, "Your grandmother's so worried she can't eat."

Del hung his head. The drummer, Freddie, shook the boy by the shoulder. "I don't like it when people lie to me, boy."

Del reared his shoulder. "I hate it there."

Freddie shook his large-knuckled finger in Del's face. "If this man was mean to you, you'd be scared, not mad."

Linc smiled at the man's simple wisdom.

The drummer solemnly considered Linc. "Can he stay till the night's through? We need him or we don't get paid."

Linc debated with himself. "I'd enjoy listening." He sat back down. He paid the waiter for another beer and offered the two glasses to the musicians. They nodded their thanks. A few sips and the "strutting" melody enlivened the dark saloon again.

Linc sat listening, watching how the two men treated Del. He'd come to take Del home. But would Del just run away again and perhaps into worse company? He'd gotten a good feeling about Freddie and Long Jack. At two A.M., Linc approached the band. "Where's the boy staying?"

"He bunks with me and him." The drummer jerked his thumb at the horn player. "We could tell he been brung up proper. He don't swear."

Linc hid a grin. A sudden idea, one which shocked him, would shock Del, came to him. *Thank you, Lord.* "I think it's best the three of you came to lunch tomorrow. Del knows the way. See you about noon."

Linc waved farewell and walked out. Maybe a few days of working for a living for strangers would teach Del more than he could in their snug home.

Once again her business advisor stood before Cecy in her father's office. In a prim navy suit, she perused the ledger sheets. Though she knew very little about stocks, bonds, real –estate, and the businesses listed in Mr. Edmond's secretary's neat handwriting, she took her time reading the entries. Finally Cecy tapped the sheets together on the desktop. "Did you find out about the ownership of the canneries across the Bay?"

"Didn't you see them on page three?"

The blood drained from her head. "Page three?" She shuffled through the sheaf of paper.

Edmonds leaned over and pointed to the neat notations. "You own all the canneries there."

"Did you know?" Birds chattered in the leafy maple nearby when Cecy confronted Linc at his front door. Not waiting, she pushed past him. When she came face-to-face with Del and two black men, she came up short. "Del, you came home?"

Linc followed her. "Cecilia, this is Long Jack and Freddie. Del's been playing ragtime with them."

Glancing over her shoulder at Linc, Cecy felt her mouth drop open, surprised by the news and by Linc's calm tone. With his forefinger under her chin, Linc closed her mouth. Susan stepped forward. "We're just going into lunch. Will you join us, Miss Cecilia?"

"I think Cecilia wants to talk with me first. We'll join you in a moment." He took Cecy by the elbow into the parlor and pulled the pocket door closed.

Cecy propped her hands on her hips. "You knew I own every sardine cannery across the Bay, didn't you?"

"I didn't know you owned *every* one."

"Why didn't you tell me?"

He had the nerve to grin. "The way you said, 'I'd like to tell him just what I think of him,' I knew you'd ferret out who the owner was."

"What am I going to do, Linc? Those poor people, those children—babies." She leaned toward him, his strength drawing her.

He rested his hands on her shoulders. "What do you want to do about them?"

She tried to ignore the effect he was having on her, holding on to the thread of her thoughts. "How can I write about the canneries? *I'm* the guilty owner."

"We're all guilty. All have sinned and fallen—"

"Don't quote the Bible to me." She plumped down the sofa. "I can't own such a place." She looked to him. "What am I to do?"

Linc rejoiced. *Oh, Lord, how wonderful are Your ways. I never guessed she would so quickly turn from disgust to action.* Energized, he paced. "You need to decide how to change the conditions at the canneries while still making a profit."

"Profit? I'm worth millions. I don't need to worry about profits."

Linc shook his head. She was so beautiful to him now—her eyes afire—her face flushed under that ridiculous driving hat and veil. "To start and keep a business growing, one needs profits, profits you can use to help your workers. Those people want and need higher wages and better working conditions, *not* a closed cannery and handouts."

She stared at him, wide-eyed. "What should I do?"

"The canneries belong to you. You can *do* anything you want." He wanted to sweep her up and dance around the room. And laugh. "Have you heard of Jane Addams's famous Hull House in Chicago?"

She shook her head. "But I want to right the conditions at my canneries." Her voice rose. "I can't bear it when I think of those babies, those little children."

"So what would you like to do?" he asked, holding his breath.

"They should be in their mother's or a good nanny's care in a clean place."

"Yes."

She grinned. "And after I've done that, I'll visit all my factories and mines and make more improvements."

"Yes." Unable to stop himself, he drew her up and held her as though preparing to waltz. "I'm at your disposal." Glancing down into her lovely face, he paused. "That is, if you want me."

She stood straighter. "I do."

"Cecilia, you're wonderful." He jerked her forward, making her driving veil fly backward, and soundly kissed her.

Now that he had her firmly in his arms, he found he couldn't let her go. He saw himself loosing her hair, letting it flow down her back like burnished spun copper. Then he would brush it aside and press soft kisses into the hollow behind her ear . . . Closing his eyes, he prayed for strength to stop his thoughts from going further. He released her gently.

She gazed at him, looking dazed.

"We should go into lunch." Careful not to touch her and tempt himself again, he helped her off with her driving coat and hat. What had he been thinking? He arranged her wrap on the hall tree, then led her to the dining room. But these mundane motions had nothing to do with his true feelings. An awful realization rammed him hard. He could barely breathe. *Dear God, I'm falling in love with this woman.*

Cecy noted Linc frowning again. The same group they'd seen *The Mikado* with had come to see Bonnie's friend Effie Bond in *Little Princess.* Now in her cluttered dressing room, Effie stepped behind a trifold black Chinese inlaid screen. When Effie began discarding clothing over the top of the screen, Cecy couldn't believe she was undressing with them all standing around. "Bonnie," Effie called. "Come back and help me with these buttons."

Bierce offered his help and was rebuffed. A little shocked, Cecy grinned. The past two days had been so serious, so dark—though in a way strangely satisfying. But tonight she could look forward to another lovely night of laughter and champagne. "Everyone," she announced, "I'm officially now a journalist. Today, I finished my first article."

Everyone applauded. Bonnie LaRoux stepped from behind the screen. "If I were filthy rich like you, I'd eat bonbons all day and dance all night."

Bierce lifted his glass to Cecy. "I'm proud of you. What's the article about?"

"It's an exposé of a sardine cannery and the terrible conditions. Linc and I worked there a day last week."

"A sardine factory?" Effie exclaimed, still hidden. "Why would you go to such a disgusting place? You journalists are insane."

Linc said nothing. It wasn't the time for a stern lecture about social responsibility. And guilt over kissing Cecilia and betraying his love for Virginia tangled around his heart.

Cecy held her glass up to be refilled. Linc nearly snatched it away from her. He'd helped her grapple with the conditions at the cannery and write about the changes she'd already thought up. But that didn't give him the right to dictate to her.

Effie stepped out, dressed in a low-cut blue gown studded with rhinestones. "So, darlings, where are we off to for supper?"

"Why not Cliff House?" Bierce's wicked smile glinted.

Linc held Cecy's fur wrap and helped her into it. The Cliff House was a notorious restaurant that had a particularly unsavory reputation. Linc would bind and gag Cecy and carry her home before he let her go to such a place. "I made reservations at the Poodle Dog."

"Let's be off." Cecy drained her champagne glass.

Feeling grim, Linc gave her his arm. Unable to help himself, he leaned close to her ear and whispered, "Go easy on the champagne or we'll go home early."

Cecy giggled. "Go home if you wish. I'm off to 'see the elephant.'"

"Seeing the elephant" was the San Francisco term for touring its nightspots.

Outside, the March breeze blew deceptively warm around Linc's ears. In front of the theater, Linc arranged everyone in his Pierce Arrow, but inside himself, he fumed. Miss Cecilia Jackson was going home after supper—if it was the last thing he ever did.

When he walked into the Poodle Dog with Cecilia on his arm, the restaurant rang with tipsy laughter. The head waiter barely seated them before Cecilia ordered more champagne. Over the past few days, Linc'd been so impressed with Cecilia's desire to change her canneries for the better. Why hadn't these meaningful experiences satisfied her instead of champagne?

Struggling not to glance at his watch, Linc couldn't think of anything more boring than watching other people get tipsy. He'd get Cecilia so busy she'd have no time for any more of these "champagne" evenings. Finally, the crème brûlée had been consumed over a discussion of the great Caruso, who would appear in San Francisco in less than a month. Cecy invited everyone to dinner after Caruso's performance. Linc's head ached. Cecy sipped the last of her champagne. Linc summarily signaled away the waiter who'd come to bring another bottle of champagne. He pulled out his watch. "Cecilia, it's nearly three A.M."

"And I have a matinee and an evening performance tomorrow." Effie rose. "Will you drop me at my hotel please, Lincoln?"

Linc could have kissed the blonde.

Bonnie stood also. "I have an early rehearsal, too."

"So you won't be going to 'see the elephant' tonight, Cecilia?" Bierce asked in a taunting tone.

Over my dead body. Linc steamed.

"If you've seen one elephant, you've seen them all." Effie waved her hand.

Gratefully, Linc squired the ladies to his car and drove them each home in the cool of early morning. Finally, as he helped Cecilia up to her door, he vowed this would be the last "champagne" evening—if he had to lock her up.

The butler admitted them. Nana waited at the top the staircase, dressed in a plain white flannel wrapper. "You're home at last."

Linc heard the relief in Nana's voice. Cecy walked unsteadily up the stairs. Nana came down and met her halfway. Taking Cecilia's arm, she led her upstairs. Since the first nurse had quit, Nana now had to contend with Cecy as well as Florence.

He bid them a gruff good night. Outside, Linc gazed at the flickering stars. The stars glinted knowingly, almost mocking him—"You're in love with her." *Virginia was enough for me. I don't want another love.*

Ring. Ring. Linc surfaced from the deep sleep. He hurried downstairs to the phone. "Yes?" he mumbled.

"Linc!" Cecilia cried out. "Come, quick."

Chapter 13

Through the shadowy foyer and up the curved staircase, Linc jogged, side-by-side with the butler. The butler opened Cecilia's mother's bedroom door but remained outside. Linc stepped into a darkened room. Florence lay perfectly still. Was she even breathing? Wearing a forbidding expression, a gray-haired doctor stood beside the rumpled bed, Millie at his side.

In the low lamplight, Cecilia, deathly pale, stood opposite the doctor. Her auburn hair flowed around her unbound. The giddy young woman she'd been earlier had vanished. "Linc." Cecilia's voice quivered near hysteria.

Millie spoke up loudly, "Mr. Wagstaff, thank you for coming. Mrs. Jackson took too much of her sleeping tonic by accident. I must have poured out the amount twice without realizing it."

Cecilia wrung her mother's limp hand.

His voice and expression distinctly suspicious, the grim doctor cleared his throat. "Your mother will live, thanks to her quick nurse's action, but she should not be left alone."

"She won't be." Cecilia lifted her mother's hand.

The doctor made a strange disapproving noise then gathered up his bag, bowed stiffly, and left.

Cecilia started to speak, but Millie, with the shake of her head, silenced her, evidently not wanting the doctor to overhear anything. Still in the middle of room, Linc waited in suspense. What had gone so wrong since he brought Cecilia home?

Within moments, the butler returned. "The doctor is gone." He withdrew closing the door behind him.

Cecilia flew into Linc's arms.

He caught her and the temptation was too much. He pressed her to him, willing his strength to her. Her sobs ripped at his heart. He kissed her hair as though that could blot out her suffering. Even as he calmed her, his awareness that only a fine silk wrapper separated them alarmed him. He forced himself to concentrate on her misery, letting his sympathy increase, overwhelm his longing. *Father, help me say the right words.* Leading Cecilia to a love seat, he eased her down. She wouldn't release his hand, so he sat down beside her. "Millie, please explain what has happened."

Millie collapsed on a bedside chair, twisting her hands together. "Since the nurse quit, I've been giving Mrs. Jackson her sleeping medication. Tonight, I couldn't sleep. Tried to ignore it, but the prompting came over and over that I should check on her." She lifted the small amber bottle from the bedside table. "Thank God,

I obeyed. When I came in, I found this empty. I filled this back up with water, so the doctor wouldn't see it was empty. If it leaked out that your mother had attempted . . ." The woman fell silent as if the dread of what had taken place sealed her lips.

Linc let the awful truth sink in. Attempted suicide. Cecilia wept into her hands, hiding the tears.

Millie continued in a flat tone: "I was able to wake her enough to force her to be sick, then she fell unconscious again. I summoned the doctor. Thought he might be able to do more."

"But why did she?" Cecilia choked on her words.

Millie gazed at Cecilia. "The truth, the facts are hard, but you need to hear them." Millie paused to wipe her eyes with a handkerchief. "Cecy, you don't remember much about your parents, do you?"

Cecilia shook her head. "I've wanted to ask you, but I didn't want to hurt . . . mother."

Linc's anxiety inched higher.

Millie bowed her head. "I should have told you." She sighed. "But I hated to stir up the ugly past. Now I must do so to prevent more happening." She looked into Cecilia's eyes. "Tonight, your mother tried to take her life because she was afraid you are following her sad path to alcoholism."

Linc, proved right, regretted it. Cecilia crumpled in his arms, her sobs vibrating against him. *I put her in temptation's way*. He tasted acid regret.

Cecilia lolled weakly against Linc's shoulder. He held her. "Tell me, Nana," she begged in a whisper. "Please"

Linc nodded. *Put an end to this*.

Millie perched on the end of the tapestry love seat, her face drawn in the low light. "Your mother confided only in me and I kept her trust all these years. It all started when your father went to Boston to find a wife."

Linc's mind went back to the *Bulletin* editor, Fremont Older, who'd told him one version of August Jackson's life.

"Your father became fascinated"—Millie paused to blink away tears—"with your Aunt Amelia."

Cecilia sat upright. "Aunt Amelia?"

Cecilia's tone echoed his own disbelief. Had the two sisters been romantic rivals?

Millie nodded. "Your aunt was quite striking in her youth. But very headstrong. Even though strongly attracted to one another, your father and aunt fought—constantly. Then they had one huge argument and broke up.

"To make your aunt jealous, I think, your father turned his affections to your mother. Your mother was being pressured by her father to marry his wealthiest friend—a man nearly seventy-years old." Millie drew in air, sounding defeated. "Your mother, only seventeen, accepted your father's proposal instead and eloped with him. I've always thought she married just to get away from the elderly suitor, her father, and bitter envious older sister." Millie drew in a shivering breath. "Then you were born only eight months after their wedding." Millie frowned as in pain. "Your father used this against your mother."

"What?" Cecilia trembled against him.

Linc tucked her nearer. "He accused her of being pregnant by someone else when they married?" Linc asked, well aware of the implications of this and how powerless a woman would be in this situation.

Millie nodded. "It wasn't true, of course, and he knew it. Anyone could see the resemblance of Cecy to her father."

"I wish I wasn't anything like him!" Cecilia cried out.

"Was that the reason Cecilia was sent away?" Linc asked as he fought the urge to hate Cecilia's father. A man who'd turn against his own child.

Millie continued, "By then, Mrs. Jackson had given in to despair and numbed herself with alcohol. Your father was a violent man. They had dreadful arguments."

Cecilia nodded against Linc. "I remember," she whispered.

"Was the short pregnancy his only reason for his ill treatment of his wife and daughter?" Linc asked, trying to understand the twisted logic.

"Was it, Nana?" Cecilia's voice quavered.

Millie pursed her lips. "I think he regretted marrying your mother. After all was said and done, I think in his way he'd loved Amelia but had been too willful and stubborn to suffer a woman who wouldn't knuckle under to him. He despised your mother for the very reason he married her, her compliance."

Linc shook his head.

Millie said, "He used your mother's attack of delirium tremens as an excuse to rid himself of both his unwanted wife and his daughter. He telegraphed Amelia and she arranged for Cecy to be sent to the Boston school."

Cecilia gasped. "My aunt?"

Millie's faced turned darker. "She took revenge on your mother for stealing her love by helping to take her daughter from her. Truly, your aunt would have been a match for your father. Both evil."

Linc nodded grimly, recalling all the times he'd wondered about the aunt's motives himself.

Wiping away tears, Millie sighed. "Your mother was sent to the sanitarium and I was dismissed. I thought my heart would break when I had to leave you." Millie choked back a sob. "But I had no money, no legal way of stopping your father. I only had my prayers. And I've prayed for you every day since your father wrenched you from me. Oh, why didn't I tell you the truth right away?"

A tap at the door startled Cecy. She'd been completely immersed in the agonizing past. Linc went to the door and Nana drifted back to Cecy's mother's side to check her pulse again. Cecy wrapped her arms around herself, missing Linc's warmth.

After speaking to the butler, Linc turned back to face her. "I've a phone call." He left and returned within minutes.

"What was it?" Cecy leaned toward Linc, her hair falling forward. She tossed it back over her shoulder. "Is something wrong at home? Del?"

"No, but I have to leave—"

"Don't." Feeling herself begin to gasp for air, she held her arms to him in silent appeal.

He grasped her upper arms, urging her to stand up. "I wouldn't go if it weren't absolutely necessary. I'll come back as soon as I can."

His strength had eased the anguish of hearing about her past. Why couldn't he stay and hold her until her mother woke? Mother might still die. But seeing his resolve, Cecy repressed a bone-deep shudder. "You'll come back?"

"As soon as I'm able." He hesitated, then bent to kiss her on the lips. She threw her arms around his neck and clung to him. All the effort she'd put into starting a new life was slipping through her fingers like silk thread. Only Linc seemed able to guide her. She hated needing anyone. She forced herself to let go. "I'll be waiting."

Giving her his unspoken promise again, he left.

Feeling as though all the life had been drawn out of her, Cecy crept over to stand beside Nana who put her arm around Cecy's waist. Cecy stared down at the limp form on the bed. Would she wake? Why had she feared probing the truth? "If she'd only spoken to me . . ."

"She's led a solitary life for so long . . ." Nana shook her head. "I wish you'd seen her when she was so young, so pretty."

Cecy took a calming breath, bringing air in slowly and pushing out anxiety. When she'd come into her inheritance here in San Francisco, she'd thought her powerless days were in the past. But money couldn't help her now. The worst outcome, though, had been averted tonight. Her mother had been saved by Nana. "No more secrets. My father. My aunt. My grandfather—they'll never touch her life, my life again." Saying the vow out loud gave her strength.

Some tight knot in Cecy unfurled, then dissolved. She took another deep breath, pressing down the last trace of her panic. "Nana, you were right. The truth has set me free."

The story of twisted evil Linc had listened to made him ache. Many in this new twentieth-century scoffed at the existence of evil. *Fools.* Parking on deserted Market Street, he charged into the *Bulletin* building, unusually bright for the hour, nearly dawn. Would he be able to scotch another scandal?

The door to Older's office was open. His heart pounding in his ears, Linc stepped inside. Looking back at him were Fremont Older and the other San Francisco managing editors, one each from the *Examiner, Call,* and *Chronicle.* He'd come to know them over the past months.

"What's all this about?" the *Examiner* editor, a slender young man with spectacles asked.

Linc began, "You've all been contacted by Dr. Kemper?"

The rumpled *Call* editor leaned back in his chair. "Let me guess, you don't want us to run the latest chapter in your favorite red-head's scandal?"

"It's news. We print news." The spectacled *Examiner* editor shrugged. The gray-haired man from the *Chronicle* kept his silence like Older.

Showing a confidence he was far from feeling, Linc leaned against Older's filing cabinets. Cecilia's reputation—what was left—hung by a strand. The scandal of attempted suicide outweighed every-thing else. Suicide was a shame which couldn't be washed away. The worst of it was—Cecilia would be blamed. He imagined a headline: WILD HEIRESS DRIVES MOTHER TO SUICIDE. But keeping the attempted suicide from the papers wouldn't be easy. What could he tempt them with?

Linc prayed for a persuasive argument, for God to move the hearts of these men. "First I think you all owe Cecilia Jackson an apology. Every one of you here knew the truth about Victor Hunt and you still painted her as the villain."

"Is she really writing for your muckraking journal?" The young editor peered over his round spectacles.

Linc knew then what he had to offer them. "Yes, and in my first issue out in a week, she exposes the disgusting conditions of can-neries across the Bay—"

"Canneries? What kind of punch does a story like that have?" The rumpled *Call* editor sneered.

"Miss Jackson wrote an exposé of the horrible abuses of the

workers—men, women, and children in the canneries owned by"—he paused dramatically, then made himself grin—"Miss Cecilia Jackson."

"What?" the rumpled editor unfolded himself.

"Why would she do something like that?" The bespectacled editor looked amused.

Linc spread his arms in a what-could-I-do gesture. "It was her decision. She went with me and worked a sardine catch there."

The young editor grinned. "A young lady of quality worked in a sardine cannery?"

Linc nodded. "She lasted the whole eleven-hour shift. The experience changed her. Her article not only graphically describes four-year-olds gutting fish while their mothers work nearby. She also outlines the changes she has already set in motion."

Older spoke up for the first time: "What changes?"

Linc glanced at him. Later he'd thank Older for calling to warn him of the doctor's revelation. "First of all, in voluntary compliance with the new Pure Food Act, she's ordered all the canneries across the Bay to be scrubbed spotless."

"Since I eat sardines on toast, I'll thank you not to tell me just how dirty they were," Older quipped.

Linc smiled at him. "Next, she's commissioned a mechanical engineer to improve the machinery design for safety and increased efficiency."

The *Chronicle* editor finally spoke: "I'm sure all this is interesting, but I have better things to do."

Linc ignored this. "She's already signed construction contracts for a large a settlement house across from the cannery. It'll include a nursery, an infirmary with a nurse, a day school, a bath house, and a laundry for all cannery workers."

"Something like Jane Addams's Hull House?" The young editor looked thoughtful.

"A cross between that and a company town—only a good company town. The workers will be required to report to work clean and in clean clothing to meet new sanitary standards. No children under the age of twelve will be hired. All children and infants will be left at the nursery and day school while their parents work." Linc studied the men trying to gauge their reactions.

The *Chronicle* editor asked, "How does she plan to still make a profit with all these new expenses? Lower wages?"

Linc proudly shook his head. "The cleanliness changes would be necessary in themselves since the passage of the Pure Food Act, so money would have to be spent in any case. But she has *doubled* her workers' wages and will still be able to make a healthy profit." Linc smiled. "She believes the newly designed machinery will increase productivity and keep her cannery in the black."

The young man admitted, "I'm quite impressed with what you've said, Wagstaff. But why should we hush up the scandal?"

Linc crossed his arms over his chest, sending up one final prayer. "Number one, would you like your doctor calling the paper to tell about your ailments? And which is more likely to make a better story? A near suicide or the reclamation of my scandalous redhead? If you run the suicide story, it will overshadow and weaken the story of Miss Jackson's reclamation, which will give you many more opportunities for copy. Let me remind you, she has lots of factories. And she has plans for them all."

The *Chronicle* editor rose. "Are you sure this isn't just a set-up to get publicity in all our papers for your *serious* journal?"

Linc shrugged. It stung giving his scoop up to other papers, but Cecilia was worth more.

"Here's my two cents. I don't like Hunt," Older drawled. "If Wagstaff's heiress is writing for Linc, that makes her one of us."

The editors absorbed this and left. Linc closed the door after them and turned to face Older. "I can't thank you enough for warning me." He wrung Older's hand.

"Don't mention it. Bring your redhead in sometime. I'd like to meet her."

"She'll want to thank you herself. Do you think I convinced them?"

"Time will tell. Either the scandal will run today or it won't."

* * *

After the meeting at Older's office, Linc hurried back to Cecilia. He stood at the door to her mother's bedroom. Cecilia drooped beside the bed, holding her still-sleeping mother's hand. Should he warn Cecilia another scandal was brewing?

He strode over the thick carpet to stand behind her. He gently cupped her shoulders with his hands. "Where's Millie?"

"I sent Nana to get some rest," Cecy whispered, pointing to the cat curled up beside her mother. "See, Mother's kitten came out from underneath the bed."

She stroked the cat. "I'm hoping the kitten senses everything is okay." Her voice quavered. "But I'm still afraid my mother won't wake up." A tiny sob escaped on her last syllable.

Linc stepped around Cecilia and took her mother's pulse. He leaned close to her face and felt her shallow breaths against his cheek. "Your mother is merely sleeping peacefully. When the drug wears off, she will wake up with a slight headache. Her appetite will be dulled."

"You sound confident." Hope lit her eyes.

"My stepfather was a doctor, remember?" Her dawning hopefulness tightened his fear for her. Another scandal might come with the evening papers. How would she take it? "Now you're going to get up and go freshen up."

"No."

He coaxed her to her feet, reluctantly releasing her hand. "When your mother awakes, she'll feel more reassured if she sees you looking fresh."

She buried her face into her hands. "It's all my fault."

He took her into his arms but held himself in check. Everything about her soft form without corset stays against him, her disheveled beauty, tormented him. She needed him, but she was vulnerable now. This was no time to hint at love, especially love he wouldn't act on. Too much separated them—age, wealth, faith. "All this started years before you were born. I blame myself for introducing you to bohemian life—"

"It's not your fault. It's mine."

He forced her lovely chin up. Her brown eyes pooled with tears. Her lips parted in silent invitation. "Cecilia, for over a year now, I've held on to my guilt over my wife's death."

Her eyes asked him why he'd brought this up now.

"Our second baby came with complications and was stillborn. When Virginia died just hours later, I wanted to wrap myself around her lifeless body and go down into the grave with her."

"Linc," her surprise came as a strained whisper.

Just speaking about Virginia's death brought the scene back to life. A room much like this. A still body in a rumpled bed. Grief twisted around his neck like a hangman's noose. "I know it's unreasonable, but I've blamed myself over and over." He gripped her by the shoulders. "Let go of the guilt. Just promise that you'll never again repeat the behavior that hurt your mother."

Her eyes widened. "I'll never take another drink."

He wrapped his arms around her. *Dear God, keep me strong against temptation.* "We'll fight guilt together." He allowed himself to experience the joy of holding Cecilia. He brushed her forehead with his lips, then made himself release her. "I'll stay with her till you return." He pushed her to the door. "Put on your prettiest morning gown for her, so she'll know you are happy to see her." With many backward glances, she went, closing the door.

Linc eased his tired body onto the stiff-backed chair. A night of shock, worry, and a bare two hours of sleep had left him feeling hollow. An old spiritual, one Susan had sung a million times, played in his mind, "I'm gonna lay down my burden, down by the river side . . ."

He gazed at the frail, sleeping woman. "Madam, I love your daughter. And I don't know what to do about it."

Chapter 14

In an ivory morning frock, Cecy lingered by her mother's bedside. Just hours earlier, Cecy had teetered on the brink of losing her mother one more time, this time forever. Now as she watched her mother blessedly breathe in, breathe out, she clung to Nana and Linc's reassurances.

The earth beneath Cecy's life had shifted. Aunt Amelia, the one in her family she'd thought she could count on, had secretly despised her. No wonder her mother wouldn't come home while her sister stayed here. In her carefully planned revenge, Auntie would have reaped all the advantages of her former beau's wealth and also the vengeance of standing as Cecy's parent while Cecy's own mother remained hidden away and alone at the sanitarium. Only with Cecy by her side and with Cecy's millions, could Auntie live the high society life she'd evidently wanted, the one she would have lived if she'd married Cecy's father. And her father's hatred of Cecy helped her aunt. Why had her father rejected his only child without a reason? Had he known anything of love?

What do I know of love? I love my mother. I love Nana. And little Meg. Recalling Linc's embrace and kisses from the early morning, she pressed her hot cheeks with her cool hands. If it had been possible, she would've stayed within his arms. With his effortless strength, his calm authority, his clear blue eyes, which saw deep inside her, he'd stood as her friend. *Oh, Linc, stay close. But I can't love you.*

Then her mother's eyes fluttered open. "Cecy?" The lady's voice sounded thready, unbelieving.

Cecy sat on the bed and gathered her frail mother into her arms. "Oh, mother, I thought I might never see you again."

"I'm sorry." The lady began to cry weakly.

"No, *I'm* sorry." Cecy kissed her mother's drawn cheek. "I know everything and I'll never drink another drop of alcohol. And *you* must promise never to try to leave me again."

Her mother's soft gray eyes filled with tears.

"I just couldn't face seeing you end up like me."

"You and I are together at last. Aunt Amelia, father, and grandfather will never hurt us or separate us again."

"You know the truth?" Her mother whispered with a shaking voice. "Everything?"

Cecy nodded, triumphant. "Yes, Nana told me and I love you more now than ever before and nothing will ever come between us again."

The lady touched Cecy's hair. "Dearest daughter, my own sweet girl. I prayed for us to be together without secrets, then despaired. Even so, God brought it to pass."

Though Cecy nodded, she didn't know if God or Linc Wagstaff were responsible. Then a thought stunned her. *Victor Hunt did me a favor.* Hunt's actions had set her free from her aunt by making her flee from the scandal. They had reunited Cecy with her mother, and made Cecy willing to let Linc show her more of the world. *But what would I have done without Linc?*

"Thank you for coming." Linc led Cecilia into the parlor. Why had Linc called her here so urgently? Cecy went to the fireplace and held her icy hands in front of the fire.

Approaching her, Linc took her hands. "I've done everything I could, but there's a chance . . ."

"What?" Clinging to his strong, warm hands, she wanted to seek protection within his embrace once again. Inwardly, she took a step backward. *I can't depend on Linc. I have to depend on myself.*

"The doctor called the city papers this morning and told them about your mother's suicide attempt." She sagged against him. "Don't despair. The matter was handled better than I'd hoped."

"How?" Hating her weakness, she took in small breaths.

He settled her into a hearthside chair and faced her from its hassock. "This morning when left you, Older, the *Bulletin* editor, called the other three city editors to his office to meet with me. I tried to persuade them not to print the story. I told them about your changes at the canneries to show that you have become a new woman."

She leaned forward, her hands clutched in her lap. "What difference will that make to them?"

"It might be enough to remind them that now you are one of them, a journalist."

She sat back. "I hadn't thought about that."

"Anyway the editors handled it much better than I thought they would." He lifted a stack of papers from the floor beside his chair. He read from the *Examiner*.

Mrs. Florence Jackson, widow of the late San Francisco businessman August P. Jackson, was suddenly taken ill early this morning. Mrs. Jackson had returned from a sanitarium to be with her daughter, Miss Cecilia Jackson, after the recent scandal. It is unfortunate that some groundless rumors have been spread about Mrs. Jackson's illness today.

Evidently, Miss Jackson's experience of forsaking the city's social life has imbued her with a new, more serious purpose in life. She herself has embarked on a new venture into journalism. Read tomorrow's *Examiner* to learn more of her new social progressivism north of Monterey.

"But it didn't say anything about suicide, just rumors," she objected.

"What if the doctor continues spreading the rumor? Often men don't like having their word called groundless rumors. For that reason alone, I had to bring you here to warn you."

She rubbed her forehead. *Can't anything ever go right?* "What should I do?" she murmured.

"Perhaps your mother should go back to the sanitarium."

"No!"

He held up his hand. "If your mother is under the care of physicians at the sanitarium again, her illness will be seen as a relapse related to her previous stay. That should weaken any gossip the doctor might spread."

She buried her face in her hands. "Is it necessary?"

"It will only be for a few days. I wouldn't urge you to do this unless I thought it were absolutely necessary. Millie should go with her. By the time Florence comes back, your new career as a social progressive will have been launched." He smiled at her. "This will all be forgotten."

He made everything sound so reasonable. How could she doubt him? Her emotions seemed all used up. "If you think it's really for the best." She straightened in her chair. "But I'm going to go ahead with my work on your journal and on changing matters at my factories. Whether San Francisco loves me or hates me, I can't stand by and not change such . . . evil."

"Yes, but you must go slow and make well thought out improvements. As a woman, if you make mistakes, others will use them against you—saying you are incompetent to handle such weighty matters. What did your business advisor think of what you've done north of Monterey?"

"He didn't look pleased. Why should I care?"

"If you take time to persuade, things will go smoother. You'll be well thought of. I want you to have the kind of freedom I have. I associate with the intelligentsia as well as the fashionable and humble."

"I don't believe I will want to associate with society. My aunt is well respected in Boston and we know the truth about her."

Linc shook his head. "My Aunt Eugenia is well respected in Boston, too. I'm going to send her the first issue of my journal. When she reads what you've done here, all of Boston will hear of it. My aunt may be a snob, but she has spent her life working to lift up the poor."

"Unlike my aunt."

Susan slid the pocket door open. "Linc, Del's home."

Linc stood up and slid the papers onto the side table. "He's in the kitchen with Kang." Susan folded her hands over her waist. Linc strode out the doorway.

Cecy had a physical reaction of loss to his leaving her. Her thoughts strayed again to Linc's embrace and kisses this morning.

Susan opened her arms. "Miss Jackson, I have a hug with your name on it."

Cecy walked into the large woman's arms and rested her head on Susan's cushiony-soft breast. "Oh, Susan, I never want another day like this."

Susan hugged her. "Some days live on in our memories." Susan released Cecy. "Meg wants to see you."

Cecy brightened. "I'll go right up with you."

"Good. I think I'll just sit down in here and rest some."

"You're all right, aren't you, Aunt Susan?"

Susan shuffled to the chair nearest the fireplace. "I'm an old woman and those stairs are getting me. Why this San Francisco have to be such an up-and-down place? Everywhere I go, I got to walk either steps or hills. Chicago was nice and flat."

Cecy chuckled, then felt the wonder of hearing herself. After all that happened today, she could still laugh. Cecy ran out into the hall and up the flight of stairs to Meg's room. Before she could speak, Meg scrambled to her.

"Miss Cecilia, how are you? Your mama's sick."

Taking Meg's hand, she let the child lead her into the room. "My mother's going to be fine."

"I'm glad. I wouldn't want you to lose your mama, too."

Cecy smoothed Meg's dark hair off her sweet, rosy face. This child must favor her mother. This thought caused Cecy a moment of disquiet. *Linc's life with Virginia has nothing to do with me.* "I'm not going to lose her, but she's going to go away for a while for a rest."

"Aunt Susan needs to rest a lot, too."

"Oh?" Cecy heard the worry in the child's voice.

"Yes, she has to stop all the time on walks. And she cries, but she says being tired makes her eyes water." Meg looked up into Cecy's eyes with a serious face. "Del doesn't live here anymore. I think that makes Susan cry." Meg looked ready to cry herself.

Recalling Nana's sweet ways, Cecy sat on the rocker and coaxed Meg onto her lap. Holding a child in her arms was a new experience. "You mustn't worry, dear." How nice to have someone to call "dear." "Your father will find a way to persuade Del to come home." If anyone can, Linc would.

"It's because the kids at school called him names because he isn't white like me. People don't like you if you have dark skin. I hate that."

The child only spoke the truth. Cecy could imagine how cruel the children at school had been. Her mind went back to Clarissa Hunt's phone call. Adults weren't much kinder. "Don't worry, Meg."

"Aunt Susan says faith is the victory," Meg said.

"Well, Susan would know more about that than I would." Then Cecy indulged herself by hugging Meg close, rocking her. How blessed Linc was to have this sweet child as his daughter.

Linc watched Del neatly "putting away" a stack of pancakes and a rasher of bacon. Kang poured Del a second glass of milk. Del looked sideways at Linc. "I'm sorry I ran away. That was bad."

Linc nodded, wondering what was coming next. Had letting the boy see how the other half lived worked? *God, is he ready?* Or had Del just come home, driven by an empty stomach?

"But I like it down on the coast. Nobody picks on me."

Kang stepped forward and waved a spatula in Del's face. "Nobody pick on you here."

Linc glanced with surprise at Kang. The houseman hadn't ever come forward with an opinion about the family before. Del looked startled, too.

"You do bad, treat father with disrespect," Kang accused.

"Linc isn't my father," Del objected.

"He give you home, food, send to school."

"I can take care of myself now," Del blustered.

Linc thought Del's milk "mustache" cost him some credibility, but

Linc kept his peace. Maybe Kang could make Del listen to reason.

"You get mad at school. Kids call you name because you colored. You think you the only one? They call Kang—'stupid Chinee. Hey, dumb Chinaman.' Kang no run away. Kang work and help family. When father die, he say, 'Kang take care of mother and sisters. You good son.'" Kang put his hands on his hips. "Even dog know better than you. Dog do good to one who feed him."

Del stood up. "I don't have to listen to you."

Kang pointed at the table. "Sit. Eat. You still full of foolishness. Someday you be sorry you show disrespect to father. Someday."

Linc stood by his desk in his office. Electric lights gleamed against the shadows of dusk. Cecilia removed her gloves and tucked them into the pocket of her matching cape. "Should we get started?"

"Very well." With the beautiful redhead in it, his office felt very small. He found it harder to breathe. Moments before he'd been alone—but not at peace. His thoughts had been a snarl of worry about Del, excitement mixed with dread over the launching of his new journal, and of course, Cecilia.

He scanned his cluttered desk and picked up the sheaf of papers. He handed her a pencil, taking care not to touch her elegant fingers. He imagined turning her hand over and kissing her palm. *No.* He said in a businesslike tone, "Lightly circle any mistake you find."

"Shouldn't I check my own articles?" She glanced up at him.

"No, you're less likely to see your own mistakes. Your mind fixes things automatically before you see them."

A tap at the outer door interrupted. Linc rose and opened it.

Shocked, Cecy stood. "Fleur? Mr. Bower?"

Fleur took both Cecy's hands in hers. "How've you been?"

Cecy looked to Mr. Bower. "Very well. But, sir, I have been so concerned for you."

"I'm much better. Please call me Clarence."

Cecy couldn't take her eyes from Bower who stood a little behind Fleur. The emotions from that awful night rushed back through her. "I'm sor—"

"Now, it wasn't your fault." Fleur stepped aside, so Clarence could bow over Cecy's hand. "We know you're completely innocent."

Linc quickly arranged four chairs into a cozy circle.

"I've wanted to visit you before this," Clarence said with his hat balanced on his knee. "But I wasn't well and my parents insisted I take no action until my sister's elopement had been accepted by society."

Cecy was shocked by his frankness and couldn't reply.

"You've heard that Hunt married Clarissa?" Fleur asked gently.

Cecy remembered Clarissa's nasty phone call. Clarence's frankness made her brave. "Do your parents approve of the elopement?"

"They have no choice. Clarissa would have been ruined if her marriage weren't accepted."

Linc spoke, "What can we do for you?"

Glancing sideways toward Clarence and Linc, Cecy compared the men. Clarence was still handsome in spite of the vivid red welt on one cheek. But Linc's face showed strength and wisdom.

Tugging off her pale kid gloves, Fleur replied, "We've been reading about what you've been doing at your canneries. It's wonderful—exciting."

Cecy couldn't hide her pleasure. "For the first time, I feel like I'm doing something important with my life."

Clarence edged forward on his chair. "And we want you to know that we're going to do everything we can to smooth your way back into society—"

Cecy's heart jerked in her breast. "I don't—" Fleur leaned over and touched Cecy's hand. A large diamond ring on Fleur's caught her eye. "You're engaged?"

Fleur blushed. "Yes, Clarence did the honor of proposing to me."

Linc cleared his throat. "Congratulations, both of you."

"Yes, I wish you both happiness." Cecy meant the words.

Clarence nodded. "We came to ask you to be Fleur's maid of honor."

Chapter 15

Cecy gripped the leather arms of her chair.

Clarence lifted his chin. "Fleur and I hope it will further your acceptance back into society."

Cecy noted Fleur had lowered her worried brown eyes. "But shouldn't your sister be matron of honor?"

His handsome face tightened. "She'll be near the end of her confinement by then."

Cecy felt ill. Victor Hunt, a father? *No.*

Bridging his hands in front of himself, Linc leaned forward; his voice calm. "I understand your generous motive to help right the wrong done to Cecilia, but you may do a lot more harm than good. Why not wait until your sister recovers from her confinement? Passing over Clarissa for someone your sister views as a rival may cause hard feelings that could linger for years."

"Linc's right. And we all know what kind of man Victor is." Cecy didn't want Clarissa cut off from help as her mother had been. "Your sister will need your support . . ." Discretion stopped her.

"I've already warned Hunt I'll visit my sister often." Clarence gave her a look filled with meaning. A few more moments of polite conversation, then the happy couple left. Cecy stood next to Linc at the office door, watching the elevator doors close. "I didn't believe you when you said they would assist me back into society."

"I was proud of you just now." He rested one hand on her shoulder. "Your first thought was for Clarissa."

"I pity her. I pray she doesn't suffer from her poor choice." Her tone spoke of her own pain.

Linc touched her cheek. "You don't have a very high opinion of marriage."

She reacted to his soft touch, her breath catching. "Would you if you were me?"

The coldness of her tone pierced Linc, an icy needle through his heart. Did she doubt him, too? He'd started letting go of his guilt over losing Virginia. Could Cecy ever let go of her distrust of men? His voice dipped lower as emotion expanded inside him. "What if someone fell in love with you?"

She faced away from him and with a harsh imitation of worldly wisdom said, "No one will ever love me—except for my money."

Under the sarcasm, he heard the deeper pain. Just as he'd clung to his own grief, she didn't want to believe she was lovable. He stepped nearer. The creamy skin of her nape glowed in the light. His words came out hoarse and low. "My own inheritance is more than I'll ever need."

She didn't turn to him.

Leaning forward, he let his own breath caress her neck, just below her ear. He drew her shoulders back to him. The wool of her suit sensitized his fingertips. He whispered into her ear, "I love you—you, headstrong, passionate, innocent woman. You're too young for me and I vowed never to forget my wife, but I love you. I believe in God and the work He's given me. You have no faith beyond yourself. Yet I . . . love . . . you." He turned her by her shoulders—fraction by fraction. Then his lips brushed hers.

Cecy felt lighter than air—as though she might drift away from the earth. She slipped her arms around his neck, then she lifted herself on tiptoe so she could return his kiss. His enthralling kiss. She felt him loosen her hairpins. Her hair slid free.

With one arm, he cradled her head. With the other, he drew her hair forward over her shoulder. "You always smell of spring flowers." Lacing his fingers through her silken hair, he turned his head and kissed her parted lips.

Linc, Linc. All the jagged, sharp edges of her shattered emotions cried out for his restoring touch. His insistent lips wandered down her neck. Each tender kiss, each feather-soft caress soothed, healed her.

She floated on the warm tide of the sensation. All the operas she'd ever sung had glorified love, passion. Was this what Madame Butterfly experienced in the arms of her American officer? Was this love, temptation? Was this what brought joy, then tragedy?

She pulled back, her hands pushed forward fending him away. "No. I want no man's love."

"Even mine?" His gaze held her motionless.

"Even yours." She turned her back to him and gathered up her wanton hair, twisting it back into place. "I will never marry."

"And I never thought I could love again. I've changed. You've changed."

"Don't love me, Linc."

He stared at her back, stiff and resolute. "Please forgive me. It won't happen again." Each polite word cost him.

Without a backward glance, she sat at her desk.

Linc stared at her. *My love for you must come from God. I never sought it. I love you, Cecilia, for better or worse, for richer for poorer, until death do us part. Just as only death parted me from Virginia, my first love, not my last.*

In the brightly lit, crowded restaurant at their table for four, Cecy couldn't take her eyes off Linc, devastatingly handsome in evening dress. Fleur sat to her left; Clarence to her right. Lucchetti's, done in red, white, and green, the first-ever Italian restaurant for Cecilia and Fleur, had been Clarence's choice for their dinner date.

After the last round of gossip over her mother's illness and her own new profession, Cecy hadn't wanted to appear in public with Fleur. Both Effie Bond and Bonnie LaRoux had called to give her sympathy and encouragement. She'd felt their concern was genuine, not society's insincere show. Perhaps she could have that kind of easy entree into every level of society as Linc. Still, Linc's kisses haunted her day and night.

"Cecilia." Fleur touched her hand and nodded discreetly to the side.

At Fleur's hint, Cecy glimpsed Mrs. Ward and Ann sitting down at a table to their left. Cecy's pulse sped up. She glanced forward, knowing she'd find Linc gazing at her. When she recalled his fingers lacing through her hair, she felt thankful that her hat's veil hid her blush.

Linc experienced a stab of regret, longing. The woman he loved sat across the table from him—unreachable. She might as well be standing on the other side of the Pacific. *Life and love are so fragile in this fallen world. Let me love you, Cecilia.*

"Both of you, we'd still love to have you come to our wedding." Fleur glanced at each of them in turn.

Linc waited to see what Cecilia said.

Cecy took a sip of her tea. "I'll see how my mother is."

With a flourish, the white-aproned waiter brought a large wooden bowl of lettuce, tomatoes, and green onions and tossed their salad at the table. Taking her first bite, Cecy savored the tangy dressing. She turned to Fleur. "Are you going to hear Caruso sing?"

"Oh, I would love to." Fleur nodded.

A motion to Cecy's left froze her in place. *Oh, no.*

Linc glanced up to see Mrs. Ward and Ann approaching their table. Why did they have to come here tonight of all nights? He rose politely.

"Miss Jackson, we thought that was you." Mrs. Ward's piercing voice cut through the hubbub of the restaurant.

Clarence stood; Linc clutched his napkin like a weapon.

"Good evening, Mrs. Ward, Ann," Fleur greeted them.

Cecilia remained frozen.

Mrs. Ward gushed to Fleur, "Are you celebrating your engagement with Miss Jackson and Lincoln?" Mrs. Ward offered Clarence her hand. "Lincoln, I just received a letter from your dear Aunt Eugenia. She's so excited. Everyone in Boston's read your first issue."

With a swirl of ostrich feathers, the lady turned back toward the table. "But your article, Miss Jackson! Your description of those poor babies brought tears to my eyes. Didn't you agree, Ann?"

Ann nodded. "I think you're wonderful, helping people—"

"Yes, such good work," Mrs. Ward finished for her. "Cecilia," the matron lowered her voice, "I'm so sorry your mother had a relapse."

Cecy nodded woodenly.

"When she is home feeling better, I'll call. I'm sure she'd love to join our embroidery circle."

Cecilia barely nodded once more.

Mrs. Ward leaned close to Linc's ear in a flutter of ostrich feathers. "Tell Cecilia her aunt didn't receive a warm welcome in Boston." The lady turned to her protégé. "Ann, I think we should go back to our table now. Archie will be joining us—Oh! There he is. There may be another engagement announced soon." She tittered, then waved, returning to her table in a flurry of feathers and well-wishes.

Linc and Clarence took their seats. Fleur whispered, "Such a sweet lady, but she *does* talk so." Clarence laughed out loud. "Hush," Fleur hissed, "I declare you're embarrassing me."

Linc glanced across at Cecy. Had she heard what the lady had said of her aunt? He caught Cecy staring wistfully at Fleur.

"Rats." Cecy hit the leather dashboard of her runabout with both her hands. Around them the city hurried about its business under the clear April sky. Rain appeared imminent. "I could spit nails."

Linc agreed, but grinned at her colorful phrase. "You know what's happening, don't you?"

"Someone warned them." She turned to him. "Who?"

"Who do you think?"

"Edmonds." She slapped the dashboard again.

"You win." He should have warned her not to let her business advisor know the day she planned to begin her factory inspections. This was the second factory they'd visited. Both factories had resembled ghost towns. Edmonds obviously had decided Cecy couldn't expose anything, if nothing was in operation.

"What can we do?" She glanced sideways at him.

"You're the boss, lady," he said wryly.

"That's right. I am." She stared straight ahead. Flipping the starter switch, she backed out into the traffic. "I'll go to the warehouse I remember seeing on another list."

Linc frowned. "If we can't find any of your factories in operation today, maybe we should wait a day or two."

"Not on your life. I won't put up with this." She swept around a corner making two men jump back onto the curb. "If Edmonds bucks me any further, I'll fire him. I'll fire everyone and start fresh."

He grinned. Many things about Cecilia had changed, but her determination to have her own way had not. *August P. Jackson, this is your daughter. Too bad you didn't value her as you should have. But perhaps God wants the strength you endowed her with for His glory.*

Within a few blocks, Cecy pulled up to one of many seedy warehouses along the South End district.

"Cecilia—"

"Linc, I really don't like that name."

"You mean Cecilia?" He tried to gauge her mood.

"Yes, will you call me Cecy?" She lowered her chin.

"You mean like Millie does?"

"Yes, please. I've never liked my name. Cecy is who I've always thought of myself as." Her voice sounded gentle like it did when she talked to Meg. Was she softening to him?

He turned toward her. "Why do you think that is, Cecy?"

"Cecy is . . . Cecy is separate from my father, from the Boston school, from my Aunt Amelia. Cecy is myself connected to Nana."

"You still plan to call her Nana, not Millie?"

"Yes, she'll always be Nana. She's really the only one to successfully oppose my father."

"How do you mean?"

"She protected me, shielded me from him. That was her victory."

She prayed for you, too. "You've thought deeply about this."

"Everything I believed about my life before the night of Hunt's attack wasn't true. My aunt had fed me lies, so she'd have her revenge. But she failed."

Thanks to God.

Cecy took off her goggles and untied her driving veil. "I'm going to have the life I want my way."

Not God's way? But he sensed this wasn't the time to speak of the possibility of God having a plan for her life. "What does that life include?" *Does it include me?*

"I'm not completely sure yet. Right now I'm going to clean up my businesses and do what I can to learn to write well."

"Good. But you aren't leaving open the door for love?" He couldn't have stopped himself from asking this question if he'd tried.

"Love." She thrust open her car door and stepped outside with a decided swirl of her skirt. She faced forward, only giving him her profile.

Exiting the car, he bent forward resting his wrists on the top of the shining green door. He studied her as she struggled with this inner conflict.

Over her shoulder, she glanced at him, then threw her driving veil back over her hat. "You are my best friend, my first real friend in my whole life." She leaned her hip against the car. "The other night I was thinking about what my life would have been like if I had been born lucky like Meg." Her gaze connected with his again. "If I'd been loved and kept at home, not sent away, I think love could have been a part of my life."

"You think it's impossible for you to love?" He could barely speak. His mouth was so dry.

"Linc, do you know what I felt when you asked if I couldn't leave the door open for love?"

"What?"

"Panic. The urge to run and not to stop running."

He wanted to reach for her. He didn't move a fraction. "Love isn't always cruel, Cecy. Just because your mother—"

She pinned him with a ironic expression. "This is me, Cecy Jackson, we're talking about. What do I know of love? In all my life, only Nana and my mother loved me, but I lost them both when I was seven years old. Do you know what that feels like?"

How could such a lovely, young face look so desolate? He longed to comfort her, but forced himself to stay on his side of the car. "I've known loss. I lost my father and a son I never got to know."

"And Virginia."

He looked away and sucked in his breath. A faint echo of his guilt screeched like a circling seagull over the warehouse. "Virginia is with God. I am free to love again."

"But I don't think I'm capable of loving any man." She faced him, her brown eyes overcast with suffering. "All I know is that the thought of trusting, loving someone, makes me sick with fear."

"Perfect love casts out fear," he murmured.

"Nothing is perfect in this world." She grimaced. "Don't preach to me." She straightened up and turned away from him again. "You said I was a changed woman and I am. After all I've gone through in three short months, I'm finally able to see my way. I'm going to live a good life, doing work I care about. Nothing will stop me now. And love isn't part of my plan."

He straightened, but he suddenly lost energy. How could he shake her out of this cynicism? "Shall we go in?"

"Wait." She held up her hand. "You go in the office and keep the manager busy while I look around in the back."

"Cecy, no—"

"Don't argue." She motioned airily and lightened her tone. "It's my factory. It's my story."

Grimacing, he headed for the door with the word "Office" printed above. Cecy walked around the other side of the dusty warehouse looking for another entrance. This time she was determined to glimpse what was really going on here, not what Mr. Edmonds wanted her to think was going on. She turned the corner of the building and came upon what must be the loading area. A gray-haired man was snoozing on a chair propped against the wall at the top of a short flight of steps. Running lightly upward, she passed by the sleeping man. Had Edmonds closed down the operation here or was this just a time between shipments?

Inside the warehouse, only dim natural light shone through high, grimy windows. Cecy walked quietly across the littered cement floor, looking up at the second-floor landing.

Farther along the upper landing, an opening door slammed back against the wall. "I told you get outta here!" The voice was a roar and markedly slurred. Was someone drinking on the job?

"But you owe me three days wages," a child's voice whined above. "I can't go home without it. Ma said."

Running toward the voices, Cecy rushed up the steps. Just as she reached the top, a burly man with a tight grip on a child's shirt met her at the top of the steps, his back to her.

The scruffy child bit the hand which held him.

"You little—" The man struck the side of the child's head. The boy screamed.

Cecy launched herself forward. "Stop!"

The man swung around toward her. His elbow hit her hard, right at the breast bone, just above her corset. She gasped one torturous breath.

Her own momentum multiplied the blow's force. She flailed frantically. Backward. The stairs! She was falling backward— screaming.

Her head struck a step. Blinding agony. Her back scraped. Tumbling over and over . . . toward the cement floor. "Linc! Help!"

Chapter 16

The late-night routine of nurses and patients went on around Linc as he kept his vigil. Cecilia, his own dear Cecy, lay unconscious in the darkened room for the second day.

The white bandages around Cecy's head stood out in the feeble light from the hallway. Hidden by the shadows were the black and purpled bruises that surrounded both her eyes and down the side of her face and chin. The doctors had told him her body had suffered bruises all over and two cracked ribs. The doctors surmised the repeated blows to her head must be responsible for her continued unconsciousness.

He glanced at the newspaper in his lap, which now proclaimed Cecy a tragic heroine and tossed it away. His back aching from sitting, he paced at the foot of her iron bed.

Dear God, this young woman has become a part of my life, my journal, the work You sent me to do. This young woman, the woman I love, was injured while protecting a child. You were there. You'd let her fall. Why?

A memory from his past surfaced: the image of Virginia clinging to life in the hellish hours after their son's stillbirth. He sat down, weakened. *I can't lose, Cecy, Lord. Please.* Holding his head in his hands, tears leaked through his fingers. *My faith feels like a mist, no longer a firm foundation.*

Linc leaned down and kissed Cecy's drawn cheek. "You must wake up and drink and eat soon." The vivid memory of hearing her screams from the back of that warehouse turned his veins to ice. He'd nearly throttled the drunk who sent her down the steps. It had taken two men to pull him off. His own rage had shocked Linc. At last, fatigue conquered him. Leaning back in the stiff chair, he fell asleep.

A moan.

Linc blinked in the subtle light of dawn. He sat up, shaking off sleep. He cleared his throat. "Cecy?"

He watched her lick her dry lips. Seizing her hand, he leaned forward. "Cecy, wake up." Hope flared.

"Oh, where am I?" She groaned. "Everything hurts."

Thank you, Lord. His voice shook. "You took a fall. Don't breathe too deeply. You've got two cracked ribs."

"Oh, I ache so . . ." She touched the bandages around her head.

He kissed her hand. "You're badly bruised. Now you're awake and everything's going to be all right." His heart beating a triumphant chorus, he rose to summon the nurse.

"Why is it so dark? Turn on the light. I can't see you."

Her fretful words froze him where he stood. In the early morning light, he turned back and looked into her eyes. Slowly he passed his hand in front of her eyes, knowing they should automatically track this movement.

They didn't.

The floor felt as though it were spinning beneath his feet. He clutched the cold iron railing on the bed.

"Turn on the lights, Linc," she repeated, agitated. "I'll feel better just seeing where I am."

He passed his trembling hand in front of her face once more. No response. Turning, he stumbled to the door. He shouted, heedless of the other patients and the early hour, "Nurse! Call the doctor. I need him—now!" Then he stood gasping against the door jam, too shaky to move, to pray.

The budding pink azaleas along the house mocked Linc as he walked slowly up the steps to his side door. Kang opened it for him. "Mr. Linc, we got good news for you."

Linc dragged his hat from his head. "What did you say?"

"Del come back last night."

Linc halted. "Del? Home?"

Kang nodded. "Aunt Susan sing all morning."

"Good." Linc leaned against the wall.

"You need coffee. I make fresh."

Linc let Kang lead him to the kitchen table. Linc lowered himself to the chair. Beaming, Susan walked into the kitchen. Her obvious joy made his anguish seem darker, weigh heavier. He tried to feel relief over Del's return. *I feel dead.*

"Linc, what's wrong?" Susan put her hand on his forehead as she had done so many times when he was a child.

"She can't see." Linc's voice ground low in his throat.

Susan sat down. "Lord, have mercy."

"They had to sedate her with laudanum." Her remembered shrieks enveloped his mind. "I came home to get some sleep. I have to be there when she wakes again." He covered his face with trembling hands. "Susan, I can't see my way. I was so sure the worst was over for Cecy. How much can one person bear?"

Susan touched his sleeve. "You're in love with her."

"My love only led her into harm's way." His voice broke.

"What exactly did the doctor say?" Susan took his hand.

"An eye specialist said the blindness must be from striking her head repeatedly as she fell. Her eyesight could return slowly or not at all."

"Miss Cecilia's blind?" Meg's shocked voice made Linc look up. Meg and Del came in together.

"Yes, Meg." He choked on the words. He opened his arms.

She ran to him. "I don't want her to be blind!"

Meg's tears wet his neck. A subdued Del crowded close to Susan's side. "Home for good, Del?"

"Yes, sir," Del said solemnly. "I won't ever run away again. I don't belong on the Coast. I guess I don't belong anywhere, but Freddie said I should stick with my family."

"I think Kang mentioned that also." Though the boy's unhappiness was clear, Linc gave the shadow of a smile. Kang nodded but did not show much satisfaction.

His spirit dragging in the dust, Linc breathed in. "I should have been there to break her fall."

"Seems to me that's exactly what you been doing ever since you met her." Susan looked at Linc. "Maybe it was time for her to hit bottom."

But I've hit bottom with her.

Feeling as though he dragged bags of cement behind him, Linc entered Cecy's room.

"Who's there?" she asked anxiously.

"It's Linc." He walked to her bedside. Her bruised and cut face stabbed his conscience.

"You left me." Her accusing voice heaped burning coals on his head.

"Not until you fell asleep." His hand inched over the coarse muslin sheet close to her arm, but stopped just before touching her.

"They drugged me."

"You were hysterical."

"Go away." Her tone was petulant. One tear slid down her right cheek.

"I won't leave you."

She rolled away from him in obvious pain, showing him her back.

He sat down beside her. "I won't leave you."

"I . . . don't . . . want . . . you." She swallowed sobs in between words.

"I love you and I won't leave you."

"Go." Her voice was absolutely cold.

Perhaps silence would be best. He bowed his head to pray. But no words came. His sorrow, shock, were too deep for words.

In the corridor, nurses passed by in their starched white uniforms and caps. Later, a nurse marched in. An orderly carrying a tray of food followed her. "I'm here to feed Miss Jackson."

"Take it away," Cecy ordered, her voice muffled by the pillow.

"I have doctor's orders." The nurse moved purposefully to the bed.

Linc startled the orderly by taking the tray. "I'll see she eats."

The nurse grimaced, then looked at the watch pinned to her breast. "Five minutes." She marched out.

He set the tray on the bedside table. Time to get Cecy thinking about more than herself. He knew she had a tender heart. "I spoke to your mother—"

"Oh, no."

"She had to be told. I told her you were temporarily blind—"

"You lied to her."

"You are taking the worst view—"

She went on heedlessly, "I don't want to go on."

"You must eat. Your mother can't lose you." He coaxed, "She's lost everything else. Will you abandon her?" He waited.

Slowly she rolled back toward him.

Relief overwhelmed him. By the time the nurse returned, Linc had Cecy sitting up with a large white napkin protecting her gown. The nurse waited sternly with arms crossed.

Linc picked up the bowl and plain spoon. "Looks like chicken broth, Cecy." He carefully piloted the spoon to her mouth. Cecy opened and swallowed. The nurse walked out of the room. Linc watched helplessly as tears rolled down Cecy's cheeks. He spooned another swallow for her. He had no comforting words for her. His own anguish defied words.

"I know you mean it kindly, but I'm not up to visitors." When she'd heard Fleur's voice, Cecy had rolled away. Having felt the bandages on her face and being painfully aware of the stitches that had been taken along her chin, she couldn't bear for anyone to see her like this. Cecy heard the scrape of a chair on the floor.

A gentle hand touched her shoulder. "I can't ignore you, Cecilia."

"Fleur, I can't face anyone. Please." Cecy choked back tears.

"You don't have to face me, honey. At home when neighbors have trouble, we sit with them."

Cecy lay still. "Sitting with me will do no good."

"I'm staying to feed you lunch. Ann is coming tomorrow."

"No." The idea of people coming in to look at her like a freak show—no.

"You have friends and we won't abandon you."

Cecy couldn't speak. Every minute—day and night—impenetrable blackness clung to her. Her hands moved. She couldn't see them. She felt as though she'd become a shadow, a ghost in an endless night. Bleakness had slipped deeply inside. *I don't want to live if I must depend on others.*

"Cecy, I talked to the doctor this morning. The longer you stay in bed the weaker your legs will become."

The thought of leaving the safe haven of her bed made her shake inside, but she knew she didn't have a choice. Sliding to the edge of the bed, she swung over her feet.

"Here's my arm."

Cecy stood. An image flashed through her mind, another day when she'd been too petrified to take a step—Aunt Amelia leaving her on the doorstep of the Boston school years ago. She froze, waves of fear washing over her.

"Just take one step."

She grasped Linc. Terrified, she took a step. "I hate this," she whispered.

Though the morning sun warmed her face, Cecy clung to Linc's arm as he led her through the endless midnight to his door. "Take me up to my room," she murmured to Linc. The safety of his guest room drew her like a magnet.

Linc helped her inside. "I couldn't bring the children into the hospital to see you."

She wanted to whirl away from him. But his home presented itself as a terrifying maze of objects to fall over, to bump into, to break. How could she make her recollections fit this dreadful murkiness that never knew dawn?

"Miss Cecilia!" The clatter of a child's footsteps warned Cecy to brace herself for Meg's hug around her waist. Cecy let go of Linc. Her hands skimmed over Meg's soft face.

"Come on." The little girl threatened to pull her off her feet.

"Wait." Cecy reached out to Linc who led her to the parlor chair, and, after feeling for it, she sat down. Meg put her kitten into Cecy's lap under her hands.

This simple act brought an avalanche of remembrance—Meg bringing her mother a kitten. *I'm an invalid now, too.*

A small hand on her cheek startled her. She jerked in her chair. The cat jumped down with a thump. "I was just wiping away your tear," Meg said.

Susan spoke up: "I told Linc he's wrong. You should go to be with your mother at the sanitarium."

The news of her accident and blindness had caused her mother to relapse. And at the sanitarium, Cecy'd be safe from prying eyes, too. Cecy tucked the handkerchief into her pocket. "Del, are you here?"

"Yes, Miss."

The boy still sounded unhappy. "You won't run away again, will you?"

"No, Miss, I won't."

"Good." She wished she could let him know how fortunate he was. But who was she to tell him to be happy?

"I want to read you an article about Caruso," Linc said. Cecy listened in pained silence. She'd looked forward to hearing the great Caruso sing for months. Now while the rest of San Francisco society thrilled to the world famous tenor, she'd sit alone. In the dark.

"Tomorrow night we're going to hear Caruso sing," Linc announced.

Cecy gasped. "No. I don't want anyone to see me like this."

"No one will notice you. Effie Bond has arranged with the stage manager at the Grand Opera House to have you enter by the stage door. I've purchased seats where we won't be seen. We'll go early—"

"*No.*" She stood.

Linc took her hands. "You're not missing Caruso. You're blind, Cecy. Not dead."

She pulled away from him, then stopped—afraid she might fall without his help. *I might as well be.*

Grimly, Linc sat beside Cecy in their seats at the Grand Opera House. A heavy black veil covered her face. Even with house lights up during intermission, their seats had been in the shadows. He'd tried to take her hand in the darkness, but she'd put up a barrier of polite coldness.

Onstage, Caruso and a formidable soprano sang in the final act of *Carmen*. Linc knew the opera's story of obsessive love well. In the Spanish mountains, the temptress, Carmen, played cards with her smuggler friends. She drew the card of death. Carmen laughed and sang "You can't avoid your fate!"

Linc glanced at the silent woman beside him. He was as blind as she. He'd thought he was seeing clearly, had a plan, but no more. Not all his pleading had changed Cecilia's intention of joining her mother at the sanitarium. Tomorrow he would rise early and drive Cecy to her mother. Would he ever get her to return? Even if she returned, would she ever be the same? The final musical note echoed and faded. Applause vibrated throughout the opera house. Roses, red roses cascaded from the balcony and private boxes onto the stage—bow after bow.

Throughout it all, he and Cecy sat still—a quiet island in a thunderous sea. At last, the Grand Opera House was empty and Linc escorted her out of the theater, to his home. Their only communication being his murmured directions to guide her along the way. He parked in front of his garage. He rested his hands on the steering wheel. They would leave early in the morning. "Cecy." He cleared his throat.

"Are we home?"

"Yes, but before we go in—"

"Everything has been said already. I'm going to the sanitarium."

"That's not the question. The question is will you return . . . to me, give me a chance to persuade you we have a future together?"

"Linc, I've told you I'll be no man's wife."

"Cecy, you must learn to walk by faith, not by sight."

"No more platitudes. I'm tired. Take me in." Her flat tone left him nothing to say. She opened the door and stood waiting for him to lead her in. Defeated, once inside he handed her over to Susan who led her away to the guest room.

Linc loosened his tie and shrugged out of his evening coat. Tired, but restless, he walked softly into Meg's darkened room. The moonlight shone over his beautiful child. Standing over her, he recalled donning the same evening wear for the first ball in San Francisco.

That night he'd been grieving for Virginia. He'd thought he'd suffered his greatest loss. Tonight he loved a girl so different from him, wrong for him, he'd barely admitted loving her even to himself. Now she'd suffered everything but death and he was going to lose her, too. He sank to his knees beside Meg's bed. Burying his face in the blanket, his soul cried out, *Dear Father, I've lost my way. Show me the way, Your way.*

Chapter 17

April 18, 1906

"Linc, wake up," Cecy's low, coaxing voice called Linc up from deepest slumber. Groggy, he sat up in bed and ran his fingers through his hair. In the bleak predawn, she stood in the doorway of his room. "Let's leave now."

Tilting his bedside clock to pick up the glow from the window, he said, "It's only a little after four A.M."

"Now," she insisted.

He swung his bare feet to the floor. After a short, restless night, he wanted to beg for more sleep. But he'd an afternoon meeting with Sullivan, the fire chief, and Brigadier General Funstan from the nearby Presidio garrison to discuss the army and city combining efforts for training in use of explosives for firebreaks. City graft had siphoned off the funds for the first attempt. The need to prepare for a large-scale fire had been goading Linc the past few days. Probably childhood memories of Chicago's fire kicking in at a stressful time. But he didn't want to miss the meeting.

Yawning, he blinked. "I'll dress. Please wait in your room." He ignored the lead weight in his gut. He didn't believe she meant to return. Today he'd lose Cecy, just as completely as he'd lost Virginia.

Ten minutes later, he helped Cecy on with her drab auto garb. Then they walked out the side door into the dewy morning. Spring fragrances, lilies, and lilacs floated in the air. Purple bougainvillea cascaded over his neighbor's fence. Drops of crystal clear dew dripped—drop, drop—from the lower petals. The beauty mocked him. Linc seated her in his car, casting a glance at his daughter's window. He'd left her sleeping peacefully, her kitten curled up at her feet. He shoved his hands into his coat pockets. "Won't you stay with Meg and me?"

She faced straight ahead. "No."

He stripped away the last of his pride, his voice raw. "My love means nothing to you, then?"

"I don't doubt you think you love me. But after all that's happened to me since we met . . ." She made a sound of disgust. "Let's go. My life is as good as over and we both know it."

Feeling a deep weariness that had nothing to do with the gloomy hour, Linc cranked the auto and drove them away from the life they could have shared. Loving Virginia had been as natural and uncomplicated as breathing. Loving Cecy was a circle of thorns wrapped around his heart.

Up and down nearly deserted streets, out of the city, they mounted the spring-green hills and left San Francisco behind. "Cecy—" A rumble from deep in the earth interrupted him. Crows overhead screeched. In fascination, he watched the leafy maple trees farther down the road sway and jump, flapping their branches like a chicken's wings. The car began to rock and shake.

Like someone swirling oil on a griddle, the world whirled. The deep groan moaned louder, closer. The wheel in front of him spun recklessly this way and that. Ahead an old roadside fence rippled like a flag unfurled in the wind. Cecy was pitched over the side of the car. Helpless as a rag doll, he was thrown over the other side. He tried to grab hold of something stable. Nothing was stable. The insane vibrations continued. He heard himself shouting, "Stop! Oh, God, help!"

The world stopped. He lay facedown, panting on the dirt by the side of the road, wild grass up his nose. Once again the earth felt solid beneath him. He didn't trust it. Slowly he got up on his knees and looked around. A gaping two-foot-wide fissure separated him from his car. The dancing maple trees lay uprooted across the road. Finally as though some force activated his ears, he heard Cecy calling, "Linc! Are you all right? Where are you?"

He staggered to his feet, still unsteady, jumped over the fissure, and scrambled around the car. On the ground Cecy writhed. He knelt beside her and lifted her into his arms.

"Linc! Thank God!" She collapsed against him. He scanned her, but found no blood, only a few scratches. "Nothing hurt you?" She threw her arms around his neck.

"It was an earthquake. Are you hurt?"

"I don't think so. Hold me."

For a while that's all he could do. *God, God, God.* He couldn't pray further than that. Finally he could think again. "We have to get back to town. Meg and Del need me."

"What about my mother and Nana?" Her arms tightened around his neck like a stiff collar.

Prying her hands apart, he looked at the trees blocking the road toward the sanitarium. "Meg and Del are children. And Susan is not in good health."

"I want my mother, Nana."

Her tone moved him to pity. "My family's in more danger in a city than your mother is at the sanitarium." He lifted her and without opening the door, dropped her into the passenger seat.

"How do you know that?" she pleaded.

"Your mother will be fine—"

"She has to be! I can't protect her. I hate this blindness." Cecy's voice rose to a shriek, "I'm helpless!"

Linc gripped her shoulders. "Everyone's helpless in an earthquake."

Cecy keened, "You'll leave me! Everyone leaves me! I can't see. I'll die!" Her words became frantic, nearer to wordless cries.

Linc crushed her in a fierce embrace. He spoke emphatically, "I—won't—leave—you. I—won't."

"You will!" she raved.

With all his strength, he pinned her against him. He shouted in her face, "I love you! I will never leave you!" Then he kissed her, forcing her into silence.

He felt her relax against him. Slowly he released her. "Now, we have to get going. We're about an hour out of the city. We'll go back and get Kang, Susan, Del, and Meg and we'll all go to the sanitarium. We'll be safe there."

"But the earthquake might have been worse where mother and Millie are." Cecy still swallowed tears.

"There's nothing we can do now about the earthquake." He put the car into gear. "I won't sugarcoat this. You interviewed Sullivan with me. There is a special danger in the city after an earthquake. We've *got* to get the children out."

"Fire," Cecy murmured.

"Fire." He pressed down hard on the accelerator. The word, short and easy to say, sent a chill from his past through Linc. Scenes from the Great Chicago Fire, forever etched on his memories, sprang to life. Only eight that night, he'd run away, so he'd faced it alone. Stampeding people—shouting and shoving—chimney's exploding from intense heat, showers of stinging golden red sparks. Cecy sat hunched against him as though fearing attack. He understood. He'd been terrified during the quake and he had his sight. Her new blindness had already pushed her into insecurity. Would she recover from this new blow? *Oh God, protect my family. Bring us safely to them.*

The formerly smooth macadam road was now fraught with lumps, deep depressions, and cracks. A force strong enough to break apart the earth boggled his mind. Finally, Linc turned a bend. As the city below came into view, he stopped the car.

"What's wrong?" Cecy shivered against him.

"Smoke." The word rasped his throat. "Fire." The ominous words clanged in his mind like a frantic fire bell, a death knell. On the skyline over the harbor, plumes of dark gray smoke ascended in the roiling columns. *It's begun.*

Grimly Linc drove his way through the littered streets. Bright April sunlight mocked him. All around him lay scattered proof of the savage earthquake. Tall maples, oaks had crashed across intersections. Windows had shattered across roadways. Water gushing down curbs spoke of broken water mains. Downed live electric wires shimmied and twisted, hissing like vicious snakes. Stopping to move debris or detour around it, he pressed on, yard by yard. People in robes and nightgowns strolled the sidewalks aimlessly, carrying things they'd grabbed as they ran from their homes—bird cages, framed pictures, coffeepots. A few stepped in front of his car as if unaware of it. *They're in shock.* His hold on the steering wheel became a death grip. *I have to get Meg and Del.*

In a macabre way, the billows of smoke downtown became his compass as he navigated the broken city. Closer to home, he saw the once-proud skyscrapers downtown. Their brick and stone shaken off like snakeskin, the tall buildings had become skeletons. The columns of black-gray smoke billowed wider and darker, obscuring his view. *I'm coming, Meg.*

Linc turned a corner and then screeched to a halt. A squad of soldiers blocked the road; they were tossing bricks from a shattered house, littering the street. One soldier motioned to Linc. "You there! Get out help us!"

"But—"

"Martial law has been declared. We have the right to impress citizens to clear rubble from the streets."

"But—"

The soldier swung his gleaming new rifle toward Linc. Instinctively Linc's hands went up. His heart pounded.

"Now!" The soldier barked.

He obeyed.

"Linc?" Cecy called.

"He has a gun. Stay down." He left her clinging to the steering wheel. The soldier's rifle gave him no choice. Linc began tossing rubble onto the curb with the other civilians and soldiers. When the path had been cleared, he hurried back to Cecy.

"Hey, you're not dismissed!" the soldier shouted.

"She's blind. I can't leave her." Linc slid behind the wheel. "We're trying to get home to the children."

"All right, but remember—the army is in control of the city. No alcohol can be bought or sold. Looters will be shot on sight."

"I don't drink! I don't steal!" Linc drove away with haste. Martial law hadn't been declared during the Chicago fire. "Things must be worse than I thought. I have to get home and get us all out of the city," he muttered to himself. He sped down the street heading for home. Cecy clung to his arm, making it throb painfully, but he said nothing. He turned another corner and came smack into another group of soldiers. Most looked too young to shave, much less be in uniform.

The soldier at the rear turned and ordered, "Halt! Out of the car!"

Linc stared at the man. "What?"

"Out of the car!"

"Why? What did I do?"

The soldier fired his rifle overhead.

"Don't shoot him!" Cecy screamed. Linc leaped out and dragged her from the vehicle. He held her close to his side. She quieted against him. "Are you hurt?" she asked with tears in her voice.

Linc called to the solder, "She's blind. We're just trying to get to the children." Linc stayed by the car, but scanned the surroundings for cover.

"Sorry. I've got orders to confiscate autos for the use of the city and military government."

"But you can't just take my car. It's private property."

Two soldiers climbed into the car, rendering the dispute null and void. Linc's Pierce Arrow was driven away—while he stood gaping in shock.

"Come with us." The soldier waved his rifle at Linc, motioning him to join the line of soldiers and volunteers. "All able-bodied men are needed to clear streets."

Incredulous, Linc shoved Cecy behind him. He faced the soldier. "I told you she's blind. I cannot leave her defenseless in the midst of earthquake and fire. You can shoot me if you want to, but I'm not leaving her!"

The soldier stared at them. "Lady," he barked, "are you really blind?"

"Yes!" she shrieked.

The soldier ordered his squad to march on. Looking back, he shouted, "Refugees are gathering at Golden Gate Park and the Presidio. Get your wife and kids there—pronto!"

Delayed fear hit Linc's stomach, making him queasy. Soldiers firing rifles in the streets? Impressing civilians? Confiscating private property? "Come on—before someone shoots us for looting." He set off on foot with Cecy trying to keep up with him. He judged they had about a mile to go to reach his home. He sensed Cecy's hesitation to move so quickly, sightless, but he couldn't help hurrying her anyway. He was rattled. She must be terrified. But she bravely kept up with him. He murmured, "Not far now."

"Linc, the children will be fine."

In gratitude, he kissed her temple, then hurried her on. Finally he found his street. What was left of it. He halted.

"What's wrong?" Cecy gasped, huddled close to him as though he were a warm hearth.

"My house is down."

"Down?"

"Yes, its roof has slid onto the drive and the house is leaning on its side. The front porch is hanging over the sidewalk," Linc said the simple words, but couldn't believe them. Almost three hours ago, his house had been whole, now it hung and listed, a battered wreck.

"Hurry," Cecy urged. "They might still be in there."

Her words moved him. Pulling her with him, he pelted down to the hulking remains of his house. Leaving her at the curb, he circled it, trying to locate a firm place to enter. But all the bricks and boards were cracked, broken at angles.

"Susan!" he called over and over. "Del! Meg, are you in there?" No answer came. He hesitated to venture inside for fear being injured and unable to care for Cecy. At last, he fell silent, baffled, unable to think.

"They're gone," a feeble voice called from across the street. "I saw what happened." It was Mrs. Hansen, who lived across the street and who'd let Cecy stay with her. The white-haired grandmother, still dressed in her frayed print nightgown, stood in front of her leaning red-brick house.

Linc raced to her. "Where did they go?"

Mrs. Hansen paced the crumbled sidewalk. "Everybody went off to Golden Gate Park. Don't they know—"

Linc interrupted, "Did you see my daughter and the others?"

"They went with everyone else." She motioned vaguely toward town. "I saw your colored woman run out with a child in each hand. Into the street. Things were falling—"

"But they were all right?" Linc wanted to shake the answers out of her. But she already looked as frail as a leaf.

She nodded. "You lost your Chinaman."

"What?" He whirled about and tried to detect any sign of his houseman.

"Your Chinaman ran out the side door. The roof came down right on him. I yelled, 'Wagstaff's Chinaman is under the roof!' The men tried to move it, but couldn't. They called and called. He didn't answer."

Disoriented, stunned, Linc turned to go, then paused. "You want to go with us?"

"No. I'm not leaving my home over some earthquake."

Though the woman chattered on, Linc hurried back to Cecy. "Did you hear?" He pulled her up by both hands and hugged her. Just touching her bolstered him.

"Yes, she said they are safe. But Kang's dead." Her voice broke.

Linc tried to think of what do if it were true that Kang indeed lay dead under the roof. But Linc's normal emotions had deserted him. *I suppose I'm in shock, too.* He looked into Cecy's face. What was she thinking, suffering? But he couldn't ask. They had to survive. They would talk later after . . .

"What are we going to do?" Raising her head, Cecy felt along his arm until she found his jaw, then cupped it with her hands.

He leaned his forehead against hers. "We'll go to Golden Gate Park. That's where people are headed—"

A terrible groan rippled through the air. The street under their feet began to roll again. The houses swayed, creaking, moaning, howling in protest. Linc threw his arms around Cecy. The old woman screamed. The rolling stopped. Bricks crashed to the pavement and rolled down the hill. Choking dust billowed upward. Linc was afraid to move. Would it start again? Was it just an aftershock or the prelude to another full-blown quake?

"Help!" Mrs. Hansen called. "Oh!" Her hands on her breast, she collapsed.

Pulling Cecy with one hand, Linc dashed to her side. She was gasping and pressing down on her breast.

He let go of Cecy and held the woman. He felt her stiffen, then go limp. He felt for her pulse. There was none. "She must have had a heart attack. And died." He lowered Mrs. Hansen to the pavement. Gone. "Stay here," he told Cecy. He ran into her precariously listing house, spotted a gray blanket over a chair, swept it up and ran back to Cecy. Kneeling beside the woman, he gently draped the blanket over her. He rose, bringing Cecy up with him. He bowed his head. "God, I commend to Your care Mrs. Hansen and our dear friend, Kang." He forced out each painful word. "Amen."

He took Cecy's arm and headed down the hill. With every glance at the towering "smoke stacks" downtown, he felt his anxiety surge again, again.

"Are we still going to Golden Gate Park?" With her free hand, Cecy pushed ineffectually at the fly-away hair around her face. Her off-white driving hat had fallen backward and hung by its ribbons around her neck, bouncing with each step.

He wished he could shield her. Danger lurked only a heartbeat away—armed soldiers, fire, and aftershocks. "Yes, I just hope they are there." He hugged her; then they set off. An explosion. Cecy cried out.

In the distant downtown below them, a scarlet flash of fire and a new spout of smoke ascended. The sight hit Linc like a mallet. "Dear God, they're dynamiting."

Wild gold-red fire raged along Market Street. Hot wind, ash, and sparks whirled high on scorching updrafts. Hearing soldiers coming, Linc towed Cecy to a gap between two buildings, not yet aflame. He pressed a hand over her mouth. The soldiers marched closer. He pushed Cecy into a doorway and froze.

"Hey, you!" A voice boomed in the street behind him.

Oh, Lord, don't let it be me he wants. But Linc didn't move a fraction of an inch though Cecy shuddered against him.

"Come out of that building with your hands up. Or we'll shoot."

A man's heated denial. A volley of shots. Crackling flames muffled the sounds. Boots marched away. After several moments, Linc eased out of the doorway though he still pressed Cecy into its shelter. A quick glance told him the soldiers had passed.

"Let's go." Then he halted as a stream of squealing rats, the size of alley cats, raced just inches from their feet. The Barbary Coast and Chinatown were famous for underground passages and their inhabitants, these rats. Now they were fleeing just like the humans. "The army should be shooting them. There's sure to be plague."

"What?" Cecy asked, her teeth chattering audibly. Her blindness must be doubling, tripling her fear. Leading her away by hand, he thanked God she couldn't see the fresh corpse of the poor looter lying in the street. In fact, her blindness had been an unexpected protection. She hadn't been forced to witness bodies lying lifeless in the streets or tossed like debris into fires. Life was cheap today in San Francisco. This day in San Francisco anything could happen. He fought the foreboding that crouched at the back of his heart and mind.

Now when dynamite was detonated, the past and present fused in his mind. In Chicago, the firemen had known how to use dynamite to create firebreaks. Linc knew for a fact the firemen here didn't. Why was Sullivan allowing this? With one eye on the smoke, he trudged along leading Cecy to Golden Gate Park. Would Meg, Del, and Susan be there? Inside he repeated, "Keep them safe. Keep us safe."

He'd never felt so removed from divine care. Shouldn't he feel closer to God now—when he needed Him so? His fear grew despite his prayers. *I believe, Lord. Help, Thou, my unbelief.*

Skirting Union Square, Linc and Cecy stopped. Refugees in all types of dress and undress loitered around an informal soup kitchen. The orange sun, though obscured by the smoke, dust, and flame, had begun its descent in the western sky.

"Is that coffee I smell?" Cecy asked in a wondering tone. "I'm so thirsty."

And just like that, his hunger and thirst came alive. He led Cecy to the line.

"Hello, lady and gent, how about a cup of coffee? And some bread?" His face blackened by smoke, a man tore pieces from a long loaf of bread.

Linc gladly accepted two tin cups filled with the muddy brew and two large hunks of bread. "We haven't eaten anything today."

"Don't mention it. This won't last much longer. Fire is getting close."

"Thank you," Cecy said as Linc led her to an open spot on the curb. Linc settled Cecy at his side. The strangers around them sat silently eating and drinking. It was eerie. *We're all sleepwalkers in a nightmare.*

When they finished, Linc helped her to her feet. "Not too much farther till we get to the Park." Boom! Another explosion. Glaring, red flames shot skyward only blocks away. Fiery sparks and cinders, some the size of silver dollars, showered down, dispersing the panicked crowd. Linc ran with Cecy holding his hand. Up ahead, he saw another squad of soldiers. To avoid them, he rushed down a side street. "I never thought I'd be running from U.S. troops."

A huffing man running beside them gasped out, "They're not all regular troops. Some are National Guard—just young college kids pressed into service for the emergency." Since Linc had to run slower because of Cecy's still hesitant gait, the man sped ahead of them. Seeking shelter while they caught their breath, Linc led Cecy behind a destroyed storefront. He gasped for breath.

"Linc." Cecy pulled his coat. "I hear something."

"What?"

She held her finger to her lips. A faint sound blew to them on the wind. "I think it's a child crying."

Linc strained, listening in spite of the steadily increasing roar of the approaching fire. He could barely hear it. But it was real. "Come on." He picked his way through the wreckage, keeping Cecy behind him. The sound, insistent but faint, led them to a house whose roof had caved in. "The sound is from in there."

"Go see what it is," Cecy urged.

Linc hung back. Cecy, blind, had missed the ghastly sight of hands and legs protruding from under wreckage which he had seen all that day. He fought revulsion. With the consuming flames advancing, he didn't want to abandon some helpless soul trapped beyond human help. He couldn't face it. The pitiful whimper beckoned again.

"Go!" She pushed him.

"Stay here." He picked his way through the shattered wood, plaster, broken glass. Then he saw her. A young woman was pinned under a beam. crushed, lifeless. *Dear God.* The whimper came again.

He knelt and looked under a nearby heap of smashed boards. A cradle turned on its side had formed a protection. The whimper was an exhausted infant's cry. The poor baby must have been alone since the early morning quake. Pity wrung his spirit.

In the cramped quarters, he got down on his belly. Reaching cautiously, not to disturb ravaged beams and make them shift, he snaked his arm along the floor. Shards of glass, pushing up under his sleeve, scored his arm. Gritting his teeth, he touched a corner of a blanket with his thumb and index finger. He dragged it. He saw the baby, not more than a few months old, on the blanket. Slowly, slowly he inched the blanket until the child was within his grasp. Rising to his knees, he reached in through the gap and lifted the babe to himself.

"Thank God!" he breathed. The little heart still beat under his hand. Linc stood up. "I've got it!"

"Drop it or I'll shoot!" a harsh voice commanded. "Turn with your hands in the air."

Linc swung around. A rifle shot.

Chapter 18

Cecy shrieked, "Stop! He went in to save a baby. Linc!"

"Baby? What are you saying?" Rough hands shook her shoulders.

She pounded the stranger with her fists. "We heard a baby crying. Linc went in . . " Screams frothed up from inside her. She pressed her hands over her mouth, holding them back.

The stranger dropped her shoulders. Hasty footsteps. The man's voice rose in panic, "It is a baby! What have I done? Here let me help you up, sir."

Linc gasped, "Take care. Think you hit my collarbone. I couldn't drop the baby—"

"When you spun around so quick, I thought you were going to shoot." The young soldier helped Linc stagger out of the wreckage, still clutching the wailing baby. "They told me to shoot anyone who was looting. I'm so sorry."

Linc fought faintness and gritted his teeth against the searing pain. "Cecy, are you all right?"

Her hands, outstretched, reached for him. "Don't die, Linc."

"Soldier, give her . . . this baby. She's blind."

"I shot a blind woman's husband." The soldier cursed himself.

The man folded Cecy's arms together like a nest and lay the baby there. "Linc, what should I do?" Cecy begged as she clutched the wet, crying baby.

Unable to respond, Linc pressed his hand to the wound, staunching the stream of bright red blood flowing from his shoulder. He slid down on the curb. "You'll . . . know . . . what . . . to . . . do. God . . ."

"Linc?" He didn't answer her.

Within minutes, she heard a motor squealing to a stop, felt the swoop of air. Hands took her by the arm and hurried her into a car. The young soldier explained, "I'm taking both of you to the military hospital at the Presidio."

"Linc?"

"Passed out. I laid him in the backseat. Dear God, don't let him die on me."

Abandoned in her blackness, Cecy sat on a hard hospital bench, cradling the whimpering infant close. Hysteria simmered inside her. Periodic distant explosions reminded her of the flames devouring the city. Would it drive them into the Pacific? *Linc, Linc.* The baby in her arms mewled more and more weakly. Would they let the child die? She heard a woman's footsteps, lighter with tapping heels, coming near. She reached out with one hand. "Please, I'm blind. Help me."

"What's the problem?"

In spite of the peculiar hospital odors, Cecy recognized the scent of rosewater. A lady. "Please I need food for the baby, diapers."

A soft hand touched her arm. "Aren't you able to nurse?"

"No, we found the child beside its dead mother. The child is growing weaker. Please—"

"A military hospital doesn't stock infant supplies."

Cecy pressed her hand forcefully over the woman's, detaining her. "Could you find a wet nurse?"

"I'll try." The woman squeezed Cecy's hand, then her purposeful steps clicked away.

"Please bring help," Cecy whispered, biting her lower lip, holding back tears. *I can't give in. If I let go, I'll start screaming and I won't be able to stop.*

"Ma'am?" A deep voice addressed her. "I'm your husband's doctor."

So deep in misery, she hadn't heard him approach. She looked toward the voice.

"Your husband lost a lot of blood, but we removed the bullet and set his collarbone."

Oh, Linc, dear one. She swallowed with difficulty. "Linc was shot—"

"I know, by mistake. I'm terribly sorry. But we're full to bursting already. As soon as your husband comes to, we'll have to move you both out to a tent. Have faith." A strong hand squeezed her shoulder; then left her in the darkness alone. A man screamed. She'd never heard men scream until today. Her shaking intensified. *Have faith?*

"Missus?" a quiet, feminine Chinese voice asked.

"Are you talking to me?" Cecy turned toward the voice.

"Yes, I wet nurse."

"Thank God." The child had fallen silent. Had help come in time? "Hurry please."

Small hands took the child from her. The woman sat down beside her, smelling of burned cloth.

"The fires?" Cecy's trembling voice revealed her fear.

"You need water."

Cecy clutched the woman's cotton sleeve. "Feed the baby." Then the baby began suckling loudly. Weak with relief, she bent her head into her hands.

Lighter footsteps coming toward her, then the familiar scent of rosewater. "I see the Chinese woman found you."

Cecy rose, reaching out for the hands of the kind woman. "Thank you."

The woman held Cecy's hands. "The doctor told me your husband is about to be brought out on a stretcher. An army nurse will check on him at least once tonight." She pulled her hands from Cecy. "We're short of morphine. I'm afraid he'll have a rough night. But President Roosevelt has ordered the Red Cross on its way."

"Missus need food, drink," the Chinese woman said.

The woman touched Cecy's shoulder. "See that she gets food. I must go."

Cecy reached out into the empty air. "What time is it?"

"After dark. God bless."

"Bless you." Cecy found the wet nurse's shoulder and squeezed it. "My name's Cecy. Thank you."

"I Kai Lin. I happy to feed baby. My baby die in quake."

"I'm so sorry," Cecy whispered.

"Very sad day." The woman's voice quavered with grief.

A thud of heavy, measured footsteps came toward Cecy. "Ma'am, if you will follow us."

"Missus. The stretcher here." The Chinese woman tugged at her arm.

"Linc?" Cecy held her hands out in front of her.

A stranger answered, "Yes. Follow us."

At the sound of the man's voice, Cecy let Kai Lin lead her away. "Linc? Can you hear me?"

"Yes." In the dark void, Linc's voice sounded faint and weak.

Panic hovered over her, threatening her calm. "Where's your hand?" She held out both her hands into the nothingness. "Please . . . I need to touch you."

"Hold up," a man ordered. "Lady, we've got him wrapped tight, both arms pinned down, trying to lessen the pain and not move him. Lower your hand. That's the stretcher. Do you feel it?"

"Thank you." The mere contact with the canvas and wood of Linc's stretcher reassured her. She followed along outside.

The stretcher halted. "Ladies, here's your tent. Wait outside while we go in and settle him on the cot."

The stretcher was pulled from Cecy's hand. Cool night air closed around her. Now everyone was in darkness just like she. With her remaining senses, she tried to take in her surroundings. The smell of burning was everywhere. Many voices, some high, some deep, rose and fell in the background. "Are there a lot of people here?" Cecy asked Kai Lin who pressed close beside her as though afraid they'd be parted.

"Yes, Missus, many people, many tents."

Cecy heard the men moving about in the tent, then they were back. "He's out again, but breathing. There are two blankets for you. Be sure to get in line for food—quick. They're about out of everything." The men moved away, wishing them well.

"Missus? You bend, please." The Chinese woman led her inside the low tent.

Cecy held out her hands feeling around for Linc.

"Here, Missus." The woman took her hand and put it on Linc's cot.

Cecy knelt by the cot, sliding her hands over Linc's form covered by the scratchy wool blanket. "How is the baby?"

"Baby fine. I go get us food now?"

"Yes, there is no chair?"

"No chair. Just one cot, two blankets."

"Could you give me one of the blankets to sit on?" Cecy let Kai Lin help her sit down with a blanket around her. The Chinese woman put the baby into Cecy's arms. She left with promises to return soon.

With the baby on one arm, Cecy felt on top of the coarse blanket again until she found Linc's hand underneath. Carefully she covered his hand with hers, the blanket between them.

How had they survived the day? The fear she'd lived with for ten days since she had awakened blind had been crushing, oppressive. But today, her terror had grown to monstrous proportions. Now she leaned her head on the hardwood frame and canvas of the cot. "Linc, can you hear me?" No answer. Only voices outside. A dog barked. A baby cried out. A little girl yelled, "I want my mama!"

The baby whimpered. Cecy let go of Linc's hand. The baby's cheek was wet with tears. "You'll be all right." But then she recalled that the baby was perhaps an orphan now. She knew the pain of estrangement, abandonment, loneliness. "Don't worry, little one. I'll never let you be lonely." She kissed the tiny palm, counting the chubby little fingers. *But how could I take care of a child? I'm blind.* She couldn't even take care of herself.

Linc moaned in his sleep. What had that woman meant when she said there wasn't enough morphine? *Linc, please sleep. Don't wake to pain.* What if the nurse didn't come? What if he needed something and she didn't know what do? What if he died tonight? Tears coursed down her face.

The canvas flap swished. "Is that you Kai Lin?"

"Yes." A piece of bread was pressed into one of Cecy's hands and a cup of coffee in the other.

Cecy drank the coffee and forced down the bread, hearing the baby nurse again. Cecy sensed Kai Lin sitting very close. After eating, Cecy kept one hand on Linc. He lay very still. That worried her. He moaned and that worried her. *I don't know what do. I do love you, Linc. Why I didn't see it . . . ?*

Tense and unchanging hours crawled by. She touched Linc's fevered forehead. The day had stripped her raw. She clutched the blanket around her.

A deep groan shuddered beneath her. A tremor. She screamed. The aftershock rocked on, startling the camp. She and Kai Lin clung to each other, Linc, and the baby. Finally the earth settled again. But the hysteria outside their tent clamored on. Too many souls pushed beyond their limits. Each noise shivered through her, rasping her nerves, stirring fresh panic.

From outside, over all the chaos, came the sound of one forceful baritone voice singing, "Rock of ages, cleft for me, let me hide myself in Thee." He sang the opening phrase again and again until the outcry around calmed, stilled. Then he sang on, "Let the water and the blood, From thy riven side which flowed . . ." Voices, then more and more joined the chorus, "Could my tears forever flow . . . All for sin could not atone . . ." Cecy pressed her hands to her breast holding back loneliness, paralyzing fear. *I'm alone. Linc may die.*

The song around them swelled louder and deepened with emotions. "Lord, Thou must save, and Thou alone. . . ." Mother, Nana, Meg did they need help?

"Nothing in my hand I bring, simply to Thy cross I cling . . . Rock of ages, cleft for me . . . let me hide myself in Thee."

Her teeth chattering, Cecy felt Kai Lin move against her side. "I'm so afraid, Kai Lin."

Kai Lin spoke next her ear, "Earthquake and fire take everything from Kai Lin, not just baby, family, husband, everyone."

Cecy leaned her face closer until it rested against the woman's soft cheek. "Oh, Kai Lin."

"Lord give, Lord take away. Nothing we can do. But pray." The simple words did not hide the woman's raw pain.

Their heads touching, Cecy felt their falling tears mingle. "I've not prayed for a long time. Not since I was little girl." *When I prayed to stay with Mama, Nana.*

"I pray. God, help us."

Outside, the hymn ended. The camp stilled at last.

A lone woman's voice began to recite the words, the good words which bound Cecy to Nana, to Meg. "The Lord is my shepherd. I shall not want." Again more voices joined in. "He maketh me to lie down in green pastures. He leadeth me beside the still waters. He restoreth my soul." Soon, the words of the psalm swelled until the prayer surrounded their tent.

As she listened to Kai Lin saying the psalm in her own tongue, Cecy silently mouthed the blessed words that Nana had taught her, "Yea, though I walk through the valley of the shadow of death, I shall fear no evil . . ." Today, death had prowled all around her. Even blind, she'd sensed it as though she crept through a dark forest alive with deadly peril.

The psalm outside ended with heartfelt Amens. She heard other women weeping. How many women tonight would keep vigil over loved ones? Grief surrounded her, permeated her. Inside, she could only say, "Dear God. Dear God."

She was praying. The shock of this realization dazzled her like a blazing illumination she experienced even without sight. She heard again Linc's voice, "Go ahead and shoot me, but I'm not leaving her!" He'd sworn he loved her. In the midst of earthquake, fire, and death, he'd protected and defended her. "How could I have doubted him?" she whispered.

Lord, You brought me home to San Francisco, to my mother, to Nana at last. You gave me Linc who loves me more than his own life. I cannot believe that You will part us now. But even if Linc dies, I'll know he truly loved me and that shows You love me. Free me, Lord, from my father and my aunt's hatred. I choose Linc. I choose Your love.

The words uncapped a deep spring of fresh, healing joy that surged through her. All the beautiful music she'd ever heard or sung intertwined, vibrated through her, a mighty chorus of joy, a stirring prelude to new life. Her hands searched the darkness and found Linc's face. She placed a hand on each of his cheeks. "I love you, Linc." Tracing her hands lovingly over Linc's form through the blanket, she kissed Linc's hand. *I love you, dearest of all.*

Though she huddled on bare, cold earth in an army blanket with the night chill around her, a warmth grew—not from outside, but from the inside. Love was warming her. She whispered, "My father didn't win. Heavenly Father, I put my trust in You."

April 19, 1906

"Cecy?" Linc's scratchy voice woke Cecy.

Her heart pounding, she moved to her knees and reached for his hand. "We're at the Presidio garrison. You were shot." With one hand, she felt her way gently up to his forehead. But his fever hadn't broken.

"Baby? Children . . . found?"

"The baby's fine, but . . . the children . . . no, not yet." Speaking of the children clogged her throat with emotion. She focused on Linc to gain control. She reached toward Kai Lin, who was still slept beside Cecy, and touched her hair. "Is it morning yet, Kai Lin? Please go get us some coffee."

"I go quick."

Cecy heard the rustling of the woman leaving the tent.

"Who?" Linc's voice sounded like a rusty hinge.

She laid her hand on the side of his face. "Kai Lin. She came to nurse the baby. How do you feel?"

"Hurt. Hot." His voice came out in forced gasps. "Children?"

"I described them to the soldier who shot you. He promised to look for them. We'll find them." Cecy pulled a crumpled handkerchief from her pocket and wiped his forehead.

"Fires?" he asked.

"Yes, fires still burning," Kai Lin's voice replied. "Here coffee."

Cecy accepted a cup. "Linc, can you sit up?"

"No," he moaned.

"I brought spoon. I do it."

"I feel . . . weak," he murmured. "Thanks. So thirsty."

Cecy listened to Linc sipping and swallowing the coffee. She brought her own cup to her lips. Her hands shook. Maybe today the fires would stop. Maybe today.

Linc asked in his weak voice, "What does it look like outside?"

"Big smoke over San Francisco. Color red over city, show through bad black smoke."

Cecy asked, suddenly sniffing the air. "Is something burning close by?"

"Tent burn! Look up!" Kai Lin exclaimed.

Reflexively, Cecy did look up.

"Sparks," Linc said with despair. "Water—quick."

"Isn't anywhere safe?" Cecy half rose, but Kai Lin pushed the child into Cecy's arms and ran out.

Soon, Cecy heard men's loud, hurried voices and footsteps outside the tent. The sound of water being splashed and a faint spray from overhead told her that the sparks were being put out. She gripped Linc's free hand again.

"The children," Linc murmured.

"They are in God's hands." Saying the words gave her comfort, a new sensation. Cecy closed her eyes and prayed aloud for the thousandth time for Meg, Del, and Susan.

"You . . . praying?" He squeezed her hand weakly.

"Last night God was all Kai Lin and I had left." She waited for his reaction.

Cecy felt Linc's smile. How could that be?

"I love you, Cecy. Thank you, Lord." Linc's voice, though thready and weak, sounded confident. "Children . . . God . . . send someone."

Cecy bowed her head until it touched to Linc's hand. How dear he was to her. He wouldn't die. The children would be found. Softly she sang the words from an old school hymn, "God has led us safe this far. And He will lead us home."

The second day passed like a month. The baby, now fed, quieted—even gurgled when Cecy tenderly rocked him in her arms. But Linc's fever rose. The nurse brought aspirin but to no avail. Using a small basin and cloth, Cecy bathed and bathed Linc's burning face. Kai Lin continued to douse the tent against showers of sparks.

Explosions punctuated the long hours. Rumors that Nob Hill had been demolished saddened Cecy. Were her servants safe? The remembered image of her mother, Nana, Susan, Meg, Del, and Linc all together in the lush conservatory made her heart ache. *I don't care if I never see again, Lord. I can live with blindness, but I can't live without my family.* The odor of burning flesh came on the wind. She realized parts of the city had become pyres for the dead. Fleur, Clarence, Little Ann—even Victor and Clarissa. Were they safe?

Every once in a while, a woman would wail out in shock and grief. All other voices would fall silent. The wailing would drop into moaning, the other voices would start up again louder, discreetly shielding someone's grief. Less often came shouts of welcome, of reunion. Loved ones found. Cecy recited the Twenty-third Psalm silently and clung to Linc's good hand. He lay still, too weak to talk, almost too weak to swallow broth.

April 20, 1906

"Papa! Papa!" Meg's voice.

Feeling a shock of joy, Cecy sat up from where she'd slumped asleep on the cold ground. She held out her arms.

"Meg, thank God," Linc's frail voice spoke in the darkness. "Del? But where is . . . Susan?"

"Oh, Papa." Meg began crying and must have bumped the cot. It moved. Linc moaned.

Cecy held her hands over Linc on the cot protectively. "Meg, dear, your father's shoulder is hurt." She held out her arms reaching for the child. "Don't touch his sling."

Del mumbled, "Grandma died."

Cecy's heart hurt.

"How did it happen?" Linc's feeble voice showed strain.

"We got out of the house," Meg whimpered. "Then we started walking and then Aunt Susan had to sit down. She couldn't breathe. We tried to get someone to help—"

"But no one would listen to us," Del added.

"Then she had to lie down and she couldn't get up." Meg began to sob.

Cecy's searching hands connected with Del's arm. She pulled

him close to her. Susan gone. She hugged Del and whispered her love for him.

"They made us leave her." Del's stark words reverberated with raw pain. "They said she was dead. Kang died, too."

Cecy stroked Del's moist cheeks and kissed him. "You're safe now."

Meg went on tearfully, "They took us away. They said we had to go to Oakland. We ran away. But they found us again—"

"Who?" Linc asked.

"The army," a man's voice replied.

Linc looked to the entrance of the tent. He hadn't noticed the soldier who'd wounded him stood there.

"I found them, sir. They were at Golden Gate Park."

"Thank you."

"The fire is dying and it looks like rain."

Cecy asked, "Have you found out about my mother?"

"Ma'am, from all the information I've been able to glean, your mother's sanitarium wasn't affected much. She should be okay."

"Thank you." A lump of cold dread in her middle dissolved. *Mother, Nana are safe.* Cecy wept for joy.

The soldier doffed his hat and left without a word. His debt paid in full.

Linc tried to believe what the children said about Aunt Susan, but he couldn't really take it in. In his memory, the faces of his mother Jessie and Susan captured for one moment in time. They stood side by side on the back porch of the Chicago house before the fire. They were laughing. *Oh, Mother, she's with you now.* Linc let his eyes close. "Lord, we commend our beloved Susan to Your care. She has fought the good fight. Bless us. Make us strong again. Heal our pain."

"Papa?" Meg bent her head and laid her cheek beside his. She pointed to Kai Lin. "Who's she?"

"She is Kai Lin, our new friend," Cecy replied, dabbing at her eyes.

Linc glanced at the sad, young Chinese woman who sat on a drab army blanket holding the smiling baby in her slender arms.

"Whose baby?" Del asked.

Cecy found and stroked Del's curly hair. "The poor child is an orphan. Meg, let me touch you, dear. I need to hold you."

Linc closed his eyes remembering the mother lying dead. The baby left all alone as the deadly fire had drawn nearer and nearer. Tears slid down the sides of his face. *Thank you, God. Over all the noises, Cecy had heard the baby's cry.*

After Meg kissed and hugged Cecy, she drew near the baby. "Can we keep her?"

"It boy baby." Kai Lin smiled wanly.

Cecy spoke up: "We've named him Shadrach because he came through the fire. If we don't find his family, we'll adopt him."

"I'm an orphan now, too." Del looked close to tears.

"As long as we live, you have family," Cecy said, reaching out, drawing him close again.

The words were exactly what Linc would have said. He gazed at her.

Sitting on the bare ground, still wearing her driving hat and coat, Cecy smiled. Her beautiful face was smudged with dirt and smoke, her driving coat torn, and her auburn hair bedraggled. So weak he still couldn't lift his head, he saw clearly Cecy had changed. Her lovely brown sugar eyes had no sight, but she looked at peace, even in the cramped tent.

Drawing a shaky breath, he felt like a flattened flour sack. But they'd made it through the crucible. "We won't be afraid anymore," he stated. Speaking took so much energy, but healing words needed to be said. "The six of us are family now. If you agree, Kai Lin?"

The Chinese woman nodded through tears. "We come through fire. We family."

Linc touched Cecy's hand. "You know God's love is true now. Do you believe I love you, too?"

"Oh, yes." She ran her hands over him till she found his face. She kissed him.

He kissed her in return. Del and Meg knelt on either side of Cecy. She whispered the words that had brought healing and had come true. "Surely goodness and mercy will follow me all the days of my life. And I will dwell in the house of the Lord forever. Amen."

ECHOES OF MERCY

Chapter 1

New Orleans
January 2, 1920

Voices shouted, "Police!" Del reared up in bed. A fist caught him in the eye. The lightbulb dangling from the ceiling exploded into blinding light. Three uniformed policemen crowded Del. One gripped him by the throat. One pointed a gun to his head. One was pawing under his mattress. "Well, look at this." He waved a thick wad of greenbacks. "And here's the gun."

Del gawked. The officer who had Del by the throat dragged him off his bed. Del clawed at the fingers on his neck. *Dear God, are they going to kill me?*

Another blow like a brick. Another. Light flashed in front of his eyes. He scrabbled at the fingers around his throat. Pain shot through his head. Blackness.

Cold water doused Del's face. "Why'd you kill Mitch Kennedy?"

Del ached. His arms were bound behind him to the hard chair he sat on. He shook his head, trying to come to.

"We're gone get a confession outa you or else. Hear me, boy?" A hard fist crashed into Del's jaw, bringing an unwelcome memory . . . Red-orange flames. German shells bursting, reverberating through his bones. He'd fly apart if it didn't stop!

"Why'd you shoot your boss?" Pain zigzagged through his head and face. The voice faded . . .

* * *

Gabriel St. Clair, New Orleans Parish Attorney, hated the dirty, drab anteroom to the city jail. The prisoner blinked, but his head lolled to the side. "Delman Dubois?" Gabe repeated.

Delman looked up. The sight of the black prisoner's battered face, one eye swollen shut, lacerated lips, and a swollen jaw, turned Gabe's stomach. "Rooney, you've got to keep your men from roughing up prisoners so badly."

"He resisted arrest," Deputy to the Chief of Police Rooney said; his lips twitched in a nasty grin.

"Delman, do you know the charges against you?" Gabe asked.

"No."

Gabe grimaced. Even a colored deserved to have his charge explained to him and a dog would have been treated better. "You've been arrested for the theft of two hundred dollars and the murder of your boss, Mitch Kennedy."

"Mitch's dead?" The prisoner licked his lips.

"You know he is." Rooney reached to strike again.

Gabe caught his arm.

Rooney glared at him, but pulled back.

"Delman, can you afford to hire counsel?"

"Afford a lawyer?" Rooney snorted again. "He's just a cheap piano player."

Gabe studied the prisoner. Beating a helpless man made Gabe sick. But what could he do after the fact? And legally, there was so little he could do for this boy. The money and the gun had been found in his room. An easy conviction. Just another cheap, nasty crime in Storyville.

The prisoner's head sagged forward. He jerked it up again, pain etched on his bruised face. "Sir, . . . you in France?"

"You served, too?" Gabe stirred just saying these words. The man's question about France brought back instant memories. Sweat beaded on Gabe's palms and he couldn't turn down another soldier, another survivor.

"Telegraph . . . please, Linc Wagstaff, 143 Cal . . . fornia Street . . . San Fran . . . cisc . . ." Delman passed out.

Gabe gazed at him. "See that he gets a clean bed and a doctor. I'll check on him tomorrow."

Rooney scowled. "That's the problem with lettin' blacks serve as soldiers. He'd never thought of shooting a white man here if he hadn't shot white men over there."

Gabe was familiar with the sentiment, but didn't believe it. "He faced death for his country." *And worse.* "He gets a bed and a doctor."

Rooney nodded sulkily.

Straightening his stiff white collar, Gabe walked away. He repeated the San Francisco address to himself. Despite his attempts to focus on the task at hand, more war images crowded into his mind—flying over trenches teeming with soldiers huddled under enemy fire; bodies slowly rotting in no-man's-land; the rush of adrenaline, panic when an enemy plane came into sight, then range . . .

His heart pounding, he closed his eyes, willing them away. He'd send the blasted telegram and get busy. Keeping busy was the only antidote now.

San Francisco
January 3, 1920

In her red silk robe, Meg Wagstaff sat in the darkened nursery and rocked Kai Lin's infant son. Though Kai Lin and her husband kept house for her parents, they were more like family. Home from war-ravaged Europe for only three months, Meg still suffered sleepless nights. Rocking the almond-eyed infant was the only sedative that worked.

She bent her head and breathed in the scent of baby powder and innocence.

The front door bell chimed through the sleeping house. Who'd rung their bell at nearly four in the morning? Meg heard the front door downstairs being unlocked. She carried the baby into the darkened upstairs hallway, where she met Kai Lin's husband coming up the stairs.

"Telegram for Mr. Linc." The man, in a blue cotton Chinese robe, exchanged the baby for the telegram. Meg walked to her parents' door. "It's Meg. A telegram."

Her father opened the door and took the yellow envelope from her. Suddenly feeling chilled, Meg moved into the room and onto the high bed, beside her blind stepmother, Cecy, who felt for Meg, then pulled her satiny blanket over her. "You're chilled, dear. Linc, good news could have waited until dawn."

Meg nestled close to Cecy. Under her arm, Meg felt Cecy's pregnant abdomen stir. *Little dear one, did we wake you too?* "Who's it from, father?"

"A Gabriel St. Clair in New Orleans." Her father opened the telegram.

"That's where Del is." Meg watched her father's face widen into shock. "What is it?"

"Del's been charged with murder." Disbelief laced her father's voice.

"No!" Cecy reached out for her husband and Linc hurried forward to catch her hand.

Meg stood up. "Read it."

Her father took a labored breath. "Delman Dubois arrested for murder. Stop. Being held at the New Orleans City jail, awaiting arraignment. Stop. Signed, Gabriel St. Clair, New Orleans Parish Attorney." Father looked at Meg over his reading glasses. The worry in his eyes shook her out of denial.

"Del wouldn't murder anyone," Meg said.

"I warned him against going South." Linc scowled. "Lynchings have exploded since the war—"

"He was at worse risk in France," Meg snapped, then felt ashamed. "Sorry."

"That's all right, sweetheart." Handing Meg the telegram, he took both of his wife's hands.

Meg stared at them, her father's graying blond hair next to her stepmother's auburn beauty. Their love for each other and concern for Del radiated in the dark room.

"We should call Fleur Bower," Cecy said. "Maybe she knows the St. Clair family in New Orleans."

"What difference would that make?" Meg bit out, then was ashamed again of her sharp tone. "I'm sorry, Cecy. I don't know why I can't seem to keep my temper lately."

Neither of her parents spoke a word, but their worried faces said much.

Meg looked away. She hated wounding them, but she would never again be the naive twenty-year-old girl who had put off law school to go to France. And no matter how much they loved her and she loved them, she couldn't fit back here as though she hadn't changed. "What are we going to do?"

"Linc," Cecy urged, "you'll have to go—"

Her father looked sick. "I can't leave you! You could go into labor any day."

Resting a hand on her large abdomen, Cecy replied calmly, "That can't be helped. Del needs us. We're the only family he has."

"We'll get him legal help. The best. But I can't leave you. Don't ask me to." Her father's face, though harassed, was determined.

Meg understood why he couldn't leave Cecy. Though Meg had only been five when her own mother had died in childbirth, she had vivid memories of her father's wrenching grief. Now, finally after fourteen years of marriage and two miscarriages, Cecy was carrying a child to term. But the doctor was worried and visited weekly. Meg crushed the telegram in her hand.

"As soon as it's light outside," he said, "we'll call the Bowers. Fleur knows New Orleans and Clarence will know what to do legally."

Cecy wiped away a tear.

Meg nodded, then left her parents. Feeling oppressed by the appalling news but oddly distanced from it, she walked to her room to sit and watch the sun come up. She knew exactly what she'd do. Only one of them must go and she would be the one.

The next morning Meg stood beside her luggage at the San Francisco train station. The sound of steam building in the locomotive engine filled the air. People, dressed warmly against the January chill, hustled along the crowded walkways between tracks. Negro and Chinese porters pushed carts of luggage along briskly. Everyone hurried.

Aunt Fleur and Uncle Clarence rushed up in the bleak early-morning light. "Oh, we're in time." Aunt Fleur stood on tiptoe embracing Meg. "I brought you the letter of introduction to my cousin Emilie. If you need anything, just call on her. I wish you would stay with her. I telegraphed and she'd love to have you—"

"I'll be happier at a hotel." Meg smiled to soften her refusal.

"Oh, these modern girls!" Aunt Fleur exclaimed. "Cecy, I can't get used to girls rushing off places without chaperones. We're quite old-fashioned now." She affectionately tucked her arm into the crook of Cecy's elbow.

Meg's father pulled her close. He whispered fiercely into her ear, "I wouldn't let you go if there were any other way."

"I'll be fine," Meg assured him. He was so dear, so good.

"I'll be praying every minute," he continued, "and I'll come as soon as I can leave your stepmother—"

"I'll be back before you know it." She spoke these words with another smile, but she didn't feel any confidence in them. After helping Del, she might go back to New York City. She hadn't felt quite so desperate there.

She itched to be on the train and away, but leaving was hard. She hugged her parents, showing her love without words, then her honorary aunt and uncle, and finally her younger adopted brother.

The strident train whistle and the conductor's "All aboard!" released Meg from the parting. She ran up the metal steps, following the black porter struggling with her bags. When she reached her Pullman compartment, she looked out the window. Meg waved as the train pulled out. With her straight, thick brown hair bobbed and her drab brown eyes, Meg always felt her lack of beauty compared to her mother and aunt. The two women, though fashionably dressed, still kept their skirt hems barely above their ankles and neither had yet parted with their old-fashioned long hair and large hats.

Meg dragged off her close-fitting cloche hat and ruffled her bobbed hair. A French officer in Paris had once told Meg she was more than a beauty, she was a striking woman with an air of mystery. Since he'd been trying unsuccessfully to seduce her at the time, she hadn't taken him seriously. How shocked her mother and Aunt Fleur would be if she told them that story. Since her return from France, the gulf between her and her parents left her feeling isolated and alone.

Sighing, she crossed her silk-stockinged legs and leaned back into the seat. She swung her ankle with the increasing clickety-clack of the metal wheels speeding away from San Francisco, her hometown. Where she no longer felt at home.

Dismal rain was streaming down the train window when Meg arrived in New Orleans. The old city looked gray, dilapidated, and depressing just after dawn. The porter knocked and entered. With a smile, Meg handed him three dollar bills. "One is for you. One for James in the dining car. One for the redcap to take my bags."

"Thank you, Miss. I'll take care of it." The porter smiled sincerely.

She tugged her ruby red cloche hat over her hair, then glanced at her compact. She powdered her nose and put on fresh lip rouge. "Make sure I get an honest cabby, please."

"You'll have the best in New Orleans, Miss." The way he pronounced the city's name, it sounded like, "Nawlin's."

After two days and two nights in the swaying car, Meg left her tiny compartment, feeling crumpled and grimy. *If I could only sleep*.

Soon she was stepping out of a yellow cab in front of the hotel Aunt Fleur had recommended. Under her black umbrella, Meg scooted through the pouring rain into the imposing white frame

building with ornate black wrought-iron balconies. Inside, she folded her umbrella, letting the stream of water drain down its point.
Damp and drowning in fatigue, she sauntered to the desk and
placed a hand on its smooth wood.

A clerk approached her. "May I help you, miss?" he asked in a
thick southern accent.

"I'd like a room with a bath, please."

The clerk's mouth primmed up. "Will your husband be joining
you?"

"I'm single." She sighed. "Where is your guest register? I've been
on a train for two days."

"You are traveling alone?" His tone was icy.

Meg finally looked the man directly in his frosty face. "What is
the problem?"

He folded his hands. "Here at Hotel Monteleone, we're not in
the habit of registering young *painted* females without escort."

Good grief! Young painted female because she powdered her
nose and rouged her lips? Meg mockingly folded her hands, too.
"Please ask the manager to give me a moment of his valuable time."
The clerk began to object. From under the low brim of her cloche,
Meg stared him down.

Within a few seconds, Meg was ushered into the manager's office. The impeccably groomed manager stood just within the door,
poised to give her a quick denial. Meg brushed past him and made
herself comfortable in the commodious green leather chair in front
of his desk. Forced to give ground, the manager sat and eyed her.

Meg sat back, nonchalant. "Your desk clerk has extremely outdated notions about women who travel alone."

"Our policy has always been not to allow unattended young
females—"

"Are you saying you think I'm a prostitute?" Meg's incisive tone
contrasted with the garbled reply the manager stuttered out.

Meg opened her red leather bag and pulled out a letter, which
she tossed to him. "This is a letter of introduction from my Aunt
Fleur." She said no more, but watched the manager as he read. The

change in his expression would have been amusing if Meg had been in the mood to be amused.

Without a word, she took back the letter and stood. Soon, she was bowed into a large luxurious room by the manager himself and she locked the door with a click.

Undressing as she went, she headed across the thick maroon carpet straight for the rose and white bathroom's claw foot tub. She twisted its ornate brass knobs. Hot water pounded against the white porcelain bottom. She dropped in paper-packaged bath salts. Steam rose. She shed her black silk teddy and slid into the rose-fragrant, frothy bubbles.

Bitterness welled up, a sour taste in her mouth. "They really know how to make a lady welcome in New Orleans. The parish attorney will be a treat, no doubt." She closed her eyes, letting the hot water relax her stiff muscles. "Del, why didn't you stay in Paris?"

After trying to eat a breakfast of slimy eggs, spicy sausage, and something lumpy and white called "grits," Meg took the short taxi ride to the courthouse. Wearing black except for her red cloche, handbag, and heels, she'd added her ruby earrings and solitaire ring. A discreet show of wealth might make her path to Del easier.

She mounted the courthouse's worn marble steps as the insistent rain pounded down. Still she maintained her habitual mask: calm, in control, so at variance with the restless, dissatisfied feeling she strove against every waking hour. A quick perusal of the list of names on the board and she walked up another flight of marble stairs to enter the parish attorney's office. A pale young man with prominent ears greeted her.

"Mr. St. Clair, please." She handed the young man her gilt-edged card, then waited while he took it in. Overhead, one lone lamp, dangling from the very high ceiling cast a ghostly glow over the outer office paneled in dark wood. The door to the inner office opened. She glanced up.

It appeared to be St. Clair, tall with black hair and a handsome face. He'd telegraphed, but would he help her? He returned her scrutiny, holding her card. "Miss Wagstaff," he read from it. "How may I help you?"

She longed to say, "Just give me Del DuBois and I'll go away and leave you alone." But, of course, that was impossible. She had to play out her role. Just as she had in France. "I've come to inquire about Delman Dubois. What is the status of his case?" To her own ears, her voice sounded too careless.

"Delman Dubois?" No recognition touched his cool gray eyes.

"Yes, you sent my father a telegram?" She watched the man's face. He had a small red scar along his jaw.

"*Oh*, that telegram I sent for the piano player who robbed and shot his boss."

"*No.*" With her index finger, she prodded him right beneath the knot of his black tie. "The *innocent* piano player you've falsely charged."

He caught her hand and gripped it. Her gloved hand tingling within his grasp, she tried to pull free.

He held tight. Scorching him with a glance, she tugged once more.

He released her. "Miss, I don't understand your interest in this case. That telegram went to Delman's people. You obviously aren't his family."

She wanted to shock him with the truth, that, though they were of different races, Del was like a brother to her. But the truth could be of no interest to this starched-up Southerner. Didn't antebellum males go out with the bustle? "Del's grandmother raised me." She forced out the words. "When she died, my father became Del's guardian."

Her explanation appeared to take the edge off his opposition. "Why didn't you say that in the beginning?"

"Would you please tell me the status of his case?" Meg asked in a measured tone.

"Where is your father?"

"What?"

"I sent that telegram to your father."

He's still sparring with me. Why? "And my father sent me to see what Del needed, to get this matter cleared up."

"In that case, I'll give you a list of local attorneys—"

"Thank you." She held on to the shreds of her frayed temper. "But won't you tell me what's taken place in the three days since the telegram?"

"Criminal law is no fit topic for a lady."

Tempted to hit him with her dripping umbrella, Meg stared at him. "I can't believe you said that with a straight face." She'd finally nicked him. He flushed red. Pent-up words flowed out of her lips. "Haven't you heard down here in Dixie that the Nineteenth Amendment is about to become law? I will be a voting citizen soon. Furthermore, for your information, I've been accepted at Stanford University law school for the fall term. If I intend to be a lawyer, law is a fit topic for me. *Now*, I'd like to know the status of Del's case. I'd like to visit him and then hire local counsel." She stared at him daring him to insult her again.

With a hard jaw, he met her stare.

Chapter 2

Meg stared at St. Clair. "Why are you behaving this way?"

"In what way? Your old nurse's grandson needs legal counsel and that's the only help I can give you."

"You're being helpful?" More furious words bubbled in her throat. Realizing animosity wouldn't get her anywhere, she substituted, "Fine."

"Won't you come into my office, then, and wait while I make

out the list?" He ushered her into his neat, masculine office. With unnecessary ceremony, he took her black umbrella and damp coat and seated her in a comfortable dark leather chair. If his former behavior hadn't shown his lack of respect for her as a woman, this wouldn't have offended her. But this man was the prosecuting attorney. She couldn't indulge herself by telling him off. Del was depending on her.

As he jotted the list, he kept up, in a rich southern accent, a soothing flow of inconsequential chatter. Meg doubted he would have noticed if she'd even disappeared. The self-absorbed southern gentleman—handsome, sleekly-tailored, and completely maddening, didn't realize he was a relic, the last of a dying breed. Viewing him as a museum exhibit made it possible for Meg to sit quietly. He'd never have survived in France. The rigid ones cracked, then broke.

Standing, St. Clair handed her a half sheet of yellow paper. She rose and accepted it. Even though her hands were gloved, the brush of his strong fingers on hers set a tingling racing through her palms. Had he done that on purpose? Did he have enough nerve to flirt with her?

She smiled at him from under fluttering lashes. If she flirted with him, would he actually think his gentlemanly behavior had reminded her of "her place"?

She glanced at the paper. Only four names and addresses. "I didn't realize there would be so few lawyers in New Orleans."

"I'm afraid very few lawyers will be interested in such a cut-and-dried case."

"Especially for a black man?" she asked disingenuously.

He nodded. For a moment, he looked as though he might say more, then went to open the door for her.

Burning with unspoken outrage, she allowed him to show her out with every courtly courtesy. Outside, she murmured, "You'll rue this day, Mr. St. Clair."

She rode away in a black-and-white taxi. When the taxi passed the building marked, "Jail," tears of frustration stung her eyes. Del, so alive, so good, was in there caged up away from his music. *Del, what are we going to do?*

In the distance, an imposing cathedral spire caught her eye. She tapped the cabby's shoulder and directed him to take her there. She hurried into the shadowed French colonial church.

The sound of the splashing rain on stone steps lingered by the open double doors. Meg closed her eyes, letting the peace of the cathedral seep inside her heart. She felt transported back to France where every city, and even some villages, boasted a medieval church. How many times, either in the midst of battle or on leave had she stolen into the back of a church and listened to the murmur of prayers and felt warmed by the glow of candles?

Sliding into a rear pew, she knelt on the padded kneeler. Closing her eyes, she bent her head to the top of the worn wooden seat in front her. She wanted to pray for Del, ask God for guidance. She couldn't. All her life, she'd been taught to pray. But now, inside, she felt parched, empty.

Stop this. If I can't get this cleared up, Del's life could end. She sat back into the pew, wiped her eyes, and drew in a few deep breaths. Two black-robed nuns entered, their white wimples glimmering in the murky light. St. Clair had made his opinion against Del clear; she couldn't trust the man. Meg glanced at the list. They might be the worst lawyers in New Orleans. To make her own judgment, she'd have to go where lawyers were, see them in action.

She walked out into Jackson Square, a park bound by a wrought iron fence. The rain had softened to a mist. Ahead at the river's edge, she glimpsed the French Market, street vendors under dripping awnings. Hailing another taxi, she ordered, "Take me to the county . . . I mean, parish courthouse please."

Marie is alive. Gabe couldn't get Paul's letter out of his mind. The bleak sky outside the courtroom cast almost no natural light through the tall windows. Someone coughed. Lonely globes of light dangled from the high ceiling. Gabe felt like he was waiting in a funeral parlor. He'd opened Paul's letter right after that Yankee woman had left. *Marie, oh, Marie.*

"All rise," the bailiff called, bringing Gabe back to his surroundings. Just another numbing day of initial appearances where he announced charges against prisoners. Petty theft, prostitution, first-degree murder . . . *I shouldn't have left France.* Gabe put this aside as white-haired Judge Simon LeGrand gaveled the court back into session.

Gabe stated charges against a thin man who had been caught pick-pocketing, then a black prostitute in a wrinkled blue dress who had strayed from the Storyville red-light district. Both in turn pleaded not guilty and bail was set. Then Delman DuBois was led to the desk facing the judge's bench. Someone behind Gabe let out a shocked gasp.

Gabe glanced around, then looked at the prisoner more closely. Three days had improved the boy's appearance though a white bandage stood out starkly on his dark forehead. The Yankee woman intruded on his confused thoughts. Miss Wagstaff would be worth a second look, if a man could overlook her naggy voice. What kind of man sent his young daughter alone to take care of a murder charge?

Gabe's conscience prodded him: *Why wouldn't you tell her that Delman's initial appearance was before the court today?*

Because it would only upset her. Even I was disgusted by his battered face. I couldn't expose a lady to something like that.

His conscience pressed harder: *You mean you felt guilty, not disgusted, don't you? A bound prisoner had been beaten.*

I can't be held responsible for others' crimes. Worse happened in France. I sent the telegram, checked to make sure the boy received a clean bed and medical attention.

The Yankee woman's extraordinary face, framed by that ridiculous scrap of a hat and full bangs, emerged again in his mind. *I can't change the way things are. I'm just the prosecutor.*

The ancient judge straightened a few papers in front of him with blue-veined hands. "What are the charges against the prisoner?"

Gabe replied, "Theft and murder in the first degree."

"How do you plead, Delman Dubois?" The judge peered down at the prisoner.

"Not guilty, Your Honor." Delman stood tall in spite of his rumpled clothing.

Then Gabe noticed the judge's gaze straying from both him and the prisoner to a point behind them. Unwilling to behave unprofessionally by twisting his neck around, Gabe waited in a silence that settled over the courtroom.

"Miss," the judge asked in a polite tone, "is there a reason for your standin' in the aisle of my courtroom?"

"Yes, Your Honor."

It couldn't be. Gabe stiffened as he recognized that voice. The Yankee had nerve, he'd give her that. He forced himself to keep his eyes on the judge. He wouldn't allow her audacity to draw him into ungentlemanlike behavior. Why did this woman have to push her way where she didn't belong . . . and today of all days.

"Would you care to give the court your reason?" the judge continued with exaggerated courtesy.

"If I may."

Her sweeter-than-sugar tone aggravated Gabe. She hadn't sounded that way in his office. She might fool this old judge, but not him.

"You may if you'll do so quickly." The judge motioned for her to come forward.

Her high heels clicked on the hardwood floor. Each tap made Gabe's irritation mount. "Thank you, Your Honor. I just wanted to let Del know that I'm here to help him—"

"Meg!" Delman swung around.

She hurried down the aisle past Gabe.

In the stark courtroom, Gabe took in the sight of her. Red hat, red purse and shoes, and rouged lips, she flaunted herself like an exotic tropical bird. She reached for Delman's hands. His wrists were shackled, but he caught her hands in his and bent his head over them.

Gabe averted his eyes, uncomfortable by the show of emotion inappropriate between them and in a courtroom.

"What did they do to you, Del?" She cast a blistering glance at St. Clair.

Gabe wanted to clear himself of her suspicion, but she had no business standing in judgment over him. He had matters of life and death on his mind. Marie's sweet face slipped through his thought, disrupting his concentration. How had she survived?

"Counselor, would you explain what happened to the prisoner?" The judge stared pointedly at Gabe.

Holding tightly to his self-control, Gabe gave a cramped smile. "Delman resisted arrest."

The prisoner straightened up and let go of the lady's hands.

She stared at St. Clair and in an undervoice demanded, "Is this why you wouldn't tell me about the status of Del's case?"

Before Gabe could reply, the judge asked, "Mr. St. Clair, do you know this young lady?"

"Yes, Your Honor. She visited my office this morning. I gave her a list of lawyers who might represent Delman." Men went to court, not ladies. And her showing up here now shouted an immodesty that no real lady would ever display.

The judge asked her what her relationship was to the prisoner. She gave the judge the same answer she'd given St. Clair. The judge looked sympathetic. "Young lady, we can't hold up this proceeding any longer."

"I'm sorry, Your Honor. But could I ask one question, please?"

Her flustered expression was very convincing. St. Clair gripped the back of the chair next to him, fighting the urge to hurry her out into the hall and give her a piece of his mind.

The judge nodded, obviously enjoying a lovely distraction in a boring, gray day.

She tilted her head shyly. "Is this a case where bail would be possible? Bail is the right term, isn't it, Your Honor?"

Her bewildered tone didn't fool Gabe. A woman who said she'd applied to law school knew something about bail.

"Mr. St. Clair," the judge asked patiently, "has the defendant obtained counsel?"

"Your honor," Gabe replied in a measured tone, "I wrote her a list of names—"

"Yes, he did, but I'm a stranger here," the woman put in sounding earnest. "How do I know how to judge which one to hire?"

Her helpless-sounding explanation made Gabe clench his jaw, so he wouldn't let a rash word slip. This judge was a stickler for decorum. And obviously a sucker for a well-turned ankle, which this woman definitely, unfortunately possessed.

The judge spoke again: "It would have been better if a male member of your family had come, Miss."

My thoughts exactly, Judge. Gabe fumed.

"My father couldn't leave my stepmother. She's at the end of a very difficult confinement."

"That is unfortunate. But the question of bail will have to be postponed until Delman has obtained counsel. Mr. St. Clair, I will order a continuance for this case for two days while this little lady seeks counsel for him."

"Thank you so much." Her voice dripped with honeyed relief. "Your honor, are prisoners allowed visitors?"

"You'll have to talk to the bailiff about that, Miss."

"Thank you again." She touched the prisoner's shoulder, then he was led away. As she turned to saunter to the back in the courtroom and sit down again, the blasted woman had the nerve to smile sweetly at him.

Gabe continued his duties. All the while, he felt her eyes burning into the back of this head. Women and law didn't mix. She'd just proven that. But Gabe's mind strayed back to what was more important. What was he going to do about Marie?

Shaking inside with outrage, Meg made her way out of the courtroom. In the hallway, she asked the bailiff about visiting Del. He told her she could see him at the jail tomorrow at four in the afternoon. She walked back out to the street. The rain had stopped, but dismal clouds obscured the late afternoon sky.

Seeing the evidence of the abuse Del had suffered had more than shocked her. Her father had never sheltered her from the nasty side of life. At fifteen, she'd started doing interviews for her father's issues magazine, the *Cause Celebre*—striking workers outside factories, suffragettes, children picking fruit twelve hours a day for pennies. Then in France, she'd witnessed wholesale carnage and unimaginable suffering. But this was Del, practically her brother and one of the finest men she knew. She'd yearned to slap the prosecuting attorney's smug face.

Another taxi took her to the telegraph office where she struggled to compose a confident message. "Dear father, arrived safely. Stop. Spoke to parish attorney. Stop. Have seen Del. Stop. In process hiring counsel. Stop. Love to all, Meg."

Soon she returned to her hotel lobby and requested her key. An envelope awaited her, a pink gardenia-scented one. Upstairs in her room, she slit it open with her nail file. It was an invitation to dine with Aunt Fleur's cousin, Emilie. Meg tossed it onto the soft bed and lay down. Dinner? She should be starving, but all she wanted was to storm the parish jail, free Del, and shake off the must and mold of this dreadful town.

Del's situation was more serious than she'd thought. The only way she could help Del was by arming herself with all the information she could find, not only about law but about this city as well. She needed to know where power lay here and who had clean hands. Cousin Emilie could introduce her to people of influence. She'd need influence to free Del. He didn't merely face a false charge. He faced unabashed racial prejudice.

She phoned Emilie who was just thrilled that Meg was in town, couldn't wait to meet her, and who would send her car to pick Meg up at 7:30 P.M.

The evening mist masked the moon and stars. Dressed in a sleek ebony wrap, Meg stepped out of Cousin Emilie's car. Feeling nearly invisible in the gloom, she was greeted at the door by a white-haired black butler in tails. She'd guessed correctly, then. This would be a formal dinner. A footman received her evening cape and she was announced to a drawing room dotted with about ten people. The ivory and green room had a faded elegance.

Cousin Emilie, a petite graying widow, came forward with arms outstretched. "Meg, honey, we are so happy you could join us. Fleur has often mentioned you in her letters over the years."

Meg murmured polite responses while being drawn to a grouping of chairs around a fireplace. A generous fire flickered behind a brass screen and chased away the damp chill of the January night. Emilie seemed honestly glad to see her and that soothed Meg's frayed nerves. Maybe she would find help for Del here.

Emilie introduced the assembled party: her daughter, son-in-law, and her teenage granddaughter, Maisy. All three women showed a family resemblance to Fleur—all petite, attractive brunettes. A blond cousin, Dulcine Fourchette, about Meg's age, affected the pouty look of film star Mary Pickford.

When Meg was introduced to the other guests, Mr. and Mrs. Sands St. Clair and their teenaged daughter, her interest perked up. Mr. St. Clair, still a handsome man with graying temples, sat in a wheelchair. His wife sat beside him plump and pretty in a china-doll way. Could they be related to Gabriel St. Clair? She didn't ask. She didn't think that, at this moment, she could be civil about Gabriel St. Clair. Besides she hadn't gathered enough facts to come up with a strategy to free Del. On no account did she want to make the wrong impression or to embarrass Aunt Fleur. She banked the fire in the pit of her stomach. Meg needed these people and what she could learn from them. Taking the place Emilie indicated, Meg lounged back against a wicker chair and smiled politely.

"I just love your dress, Miss Wagstaff," Emilie's granddaughter, Maisy, gushed.

"Thank you. I brought it back from Paris." Meg had chosen to wear a black silk Charmeuse that skimmed over her slender form. Meg noted the cousin, Dulcine, surreptitiously weighing and measuring her.

So Meg reciprocated. Dulcine, her long blonde hair pulled low in a neat bun, wore a long blue satin skirt. Did Dulcine think Meg intended to be her rival? How amusing.

"You've been to Paris?" Maisy asked, excitement lighting her eyes.

The girl's innocent reaction made Meg feel at least a century old. "Yes."

Emilie exclaimed, "Meg was one of our brave young American women who worked at YMCA canteens sustaining our gallant doughboys."

Both young girls looked at Meg as though she'd just been crowned queen. But Mrs. St. Clair cast a worried glance at her young daughter.

Meg was used to this reaction. *Don't worry, madam, the war is over.*

The raven-haired St. Clair girl, appropriately named Belle, breathed, "How exciting that must have been."

Why did young women still react like this? Hadn't enough truth about the war reached the States? "Sometimes the work got a little too exciting," Meg commented dryly. "You can't believe what it was like being one of only three women when a hundred soldiers came to dance."

Her two young admirers looked a bit daunted.

"My, that *does* sound like a sacrifice," Dulcine slipped in.

"You're too modest, Meg." Emilie made a deprecating motion with her hand. "Why, Fleur wrote me that you were injured at the Somme."

Meg smiled and pushed away her dark memories of the Somme.

"You were?" Belle squealed. "How?"

"Belle," Mrs. St. Clair admonished, "Miss Wagstaff is a lady and a lady never discusses physical problems."

"Well," Maisy announced, "being in Paris didn't hurt you. Your dress makes us all look frumpy by comparison."

Dulcine shot a razor-sharp glance at Meg.

Meg shrugged. "Most of us bought Parisian designs to help the designers get back on their feet. The war decimated the French economy."

"That was indeed charitable of you," Sands St. Clair put in.

Meg caught the hint of irony in his tone and laughed. "And, of course, the temptation to come home with the thoroughly modern look was irresistible."

"Personally," Mrs. St. Clair said with a disapproving moue, "I don't understand what the Paris designers are thinking. How much skill does it take to drop a sack on a woman?"

Meg could detect all too clearly the likeness in outdated ideas between the prosecuting attorney and this woman.

"Mother!" Her lovely daughter with her long black hair coiled at her nape blushed with embarrassment. "Miss Wagstaff will think us dreadfully old-fashioned."

Meg laughed again. "My father wasn't too happy with it either. My skirts are much too short." She smiled warmly at the little brunette.

"I think you're the cat's meow."

The butler announced dinner and Cousin Emilie led them to the dining room. Meg was given the place of honor next to her hostess. Meg noted one seat unoccupied. This day of extreme emotions had begun to tell on her. With so much on her mind and heart, how would she endure polite conversation?

"Everyone, enjoy the wine." Emilie lifted her glass to salute her guests. "That dreadful Prohibition is only weeks away."

Meg raised her glass to her hostess, but didn't take a sip.

"Emilie," Sands St. Clair spoke up, "you needn't fear losing your right to drink your own wine in your own home. Prohibition only regulates the sale and distribution of liquor."

"But my wine cellar cannot hold a lifetime supply," Emilie countered.

"Those foolish Yankees pushing such a ridiculous law down our throats." Mrs. St. Clair frowned. "Why can't they understand that dinner without wine is like a rose without its fragrance?"

A murmur of agreement flowed around Meg. This woman, who

evidently wanted no change in the still-new century, must be Gabriel St. Clair's mother.

"It is a foolish law," Sands said with quiet authority. "How the U.S. government expects to enforce this law with the vast borders of our country and without spending money on a sizable enforcement fleet, is beyond me. It is not only a foolish law. It is a bad law."

"You speak like a lawyer," Meg commented.

"Until my riding accident before the war, I had an active law practice."

Meg nodded. "My father, though a teetotaler, says bad laws make honest men criminals and law-breakers rich."

"Well said," Sands agreed.

From the dining room doorway, the black butler announced, "Mr. Gabriel St. Clair."

Hearing the name brought Meg instantly alive. St. Clair strode in, wearing impeccable evening dress. The phrase, "devastatingly handsome," slipped through Meg's mind. He bowed over his hostess's hand, then glanced up.

Concealing the shiver of recognition, Meg lifted her water glass to him. Round three was about to begin.

Chapter 3

Forced to smile, inside Meg flared with animosity. Of all the people in New Orleans, she'd be eating dinner with Gabriel St. Clair!

"How dreadful you had to work late again, son," his mother said.

He turned and bestowed a light kiss on her unrouged cheek. "Sorry. I'll make it up to you and Emilie."

From her place at the head of the long damask-covered table, Emilie waved gaily to him. "Gabriel, I must present to you Miss Meg Wagstaff from San Francisco."

Meg read no sign of recognition on his face. He wouldn't deny meeting her earlier, would he?

But unbelievably, he greeted her as though he'd never seen her before and took the chair beside his mother.

"Gabe," his sister claimed his attention, "Miss Wagstaff was in France."

"Very interesting," was his only comment.

Dulcine greeted him. Although the young blonde betrayed no partiality, Meg sensed the other woman's interest in him as clearly as a spoken word. *Dulcine, you're welcome to him.*

St. Clair chatted with his mother, Dulcine, and teased his sister about a beau. If he intended his denial to put her at a disadvantage, he'd failed. Meg toyed with the idea of embarrassing him by recounting his refusal to help her, but she couldn't put her hostess in an awkward position, and in the end, it would do Del more harm than good.

The highly polished silver gleamed in the candlelight. The gilt-edged china was obviously old but treasured. Emilie certainly knew how to set the mood of elegance and ease and Meg's own deep fatigue threatened to take the edge off her alertness. She pondered the enigma of Gabriel St. Clair. Finally, she decided to stir the simmering situation and see what floated to the top. She leaned against the table. "Mr. St. Clair?"

Both men looked at her.

She smiled. "Yes, I might as well address this to both of you. I'm looking for a good defense lawyer." She observed St. Clair closely, but he didn't show a flicker of recognition.

"Why do you need a defense lawyer?" The senior St. Clair appraised her with a sharp glance.

Emilie replied before Meg could, "That's why I invited you,

Sands. I thought you and your son might advise her. She's come to get her old nurse's grandson out of some trouble here."

Meg nodded. "Yes, after being mustered out of the infantry, Del decided to come here to learn more about New Orleans jazz."

Mrs. St. Clair murmured in a disapproving tone, "That awful jazz."

Ignoring this, Meg leaned forward, folding her hands under her chin. "He's been arrested for robbing and murdering his boss at the nightclub where he played piano."

Dulcine paused with her fork above her plate and smiled archly. "Not a very appetizing dinner topic, Miss Wagstaff."

"No, indeed," Mrs. St. Clair agreed.

"I agree, but I need to find Del counsel. He's obviously been framed and I need someone who can prove that in a court of law."

A lull came over the table as though everyone waited for a response to Meg.

"A most unfortunate incident," Sands murmured. "Are you positive he's innocent?"

His question didn't anger Meg. He didn't speak condescendingly. "Del's no murderer."

Sands accepted her answer by nodding.

Gabriel leaned back in his chair and challenged her with his glance. The flickering shadows of the candlelight wavered over the contours of his face, giving him a mysterious quality. Meg resisted the pull toward him from deep inside her. He was just the kind of man she couldn't respect. He had no social conscience.

"What if you're wrong? Do you know what evidence there is against him?" His blunt words weren't unexpected, but they hit Meg hard.

His mother spoke up, "Perhaps you could call on Gabriel tomorrow for advice. Let's talk about the social season. After all, this is Belle's year to come out."

Maisy, Emilie's granddaughter, exclaimed, "Miss Wagstaff, you've come to New Orleans at just the right time. It's Carnival!"

Meg tried to look interested.

"Carnival starts each year with January's Twelfth Night Ball and ends the night before Ash Wednesday. That's Mardi Gras," Gabriel said, watching her.

Emilie smiled. "Yes, you must come to our cocktail party tomorrow evening. I'll be one of the first hostesses in New Orleans to give one! A pox on Prohibition!"

The facts of the New Orleans social season were of no interest to Meg, but she made a polite rejoinder. With any luck, she and Del would be long-gone before Mardi Gras. Out of the corner of her eye, she noted Belle's young face. The girl looked close to tears. Why would talk of parties depress a young debutante?

Meg sat back as the remainder of the evening flowed by. Beneath her unruffled surface, dangerous currents swirled and eddied. She must find a willing and competent lawyer, then visit Del at the jail. Recalling his mangled face, she gripped the arms of her chair.

Later, at Emilie's request, Gabriel offered the Yankee his arm, escorting her to his Franklin touring car to drop her at her hotel. The air was thick and chill. He watched his parent's car as their chauffeur drove them away. His sister's underlying unhappiness had been evident to him. He drove down the short lane to the street, glancing at Meg from the corner of his eye.

Beside him, she lay back against the seat. Her sensuous posture mocked him. "So why didn't you want anyone to know that we had met earlier?"

Her mocking tone scraped his taut nerves. "I have better manners than to discuss legal business at dinner. Ladies aren't interested in law."

She had the nerve to chuckle. "Where do you get these Gothic notions?"

He tamped down his rising irritation. This woman may have popped up three times in his day, but she wouldn't last in New Orleans for long. She'd find out all too soon she couldn't wrap every man she met around her little finger even with her "come-hither" look. "My mother has always requested that my father not discuss legal matters at dinner."

"Why doesn't that surprise me?" The ivory lace of her collar shone in the darkness, casting faint light onto her face.

Her implied criticism galled him. "My mother is a wonderful woman—"

"Your mother is a wonderful *nineteenth-century* woman." Languidly, she pushed her bobbed hair behind her ear.

Her presence worked on him even as he resisted it. "Well, isn't your mother?"

"Heavens, no."

"I don't expect you to understand our ways," he asserted.

"Yes, I'm just a Yankee." She stretched like a cat. "Now why didn't you let on that we had met earlier?"

He gave no answer. Reading Paul's disturbing letter about Marie, then tedious hours of courtroom detail and duty. After an hour of trying to get a phone call through to the American Embassy in Paris in vain, to find her at the table in the midst of friends . . . He'd been through too much today.

Meg ran her fingers through her bangs. "You're angry with me because I wouldn't do what you told me to do."

His exasperation burst. "You are the type of modern woman I dislike the most. You say you are the equal of men, but you don't hesitate to use feminine wiles to get your own way."

She taunted him by angling her body toward him using all her feminine attraction to mock him. "If you're honest with yourself, you'll recall I was frank with you until you began acting like a medieval lord. If you don't fight fair, I don't feel compelled to either."

How dare she tell him how he should behave? "You don't know what you're talking about." *You don't know me at all.*

She sniffed audibly.

"That boy is guilty. The evidence proves that."

"Boy?" she retorted. "Del's a man, a good man and he's innocent. You and your vicious police have made a mistake. All I need is a good lawyer to prove it."

"Fine. Some people have to learn everything the hard way."

* * *

Today if Meg survived the search for a lawyer to represent him, she would finally get to visit Del. In the early afternoon, Meg smiled at the legal secretary, the fourth one she'd met that day, the last lawyer on St. Clair's list. A night of worry had brought her no new ideas on how to find counsel for Del. Though outdated and narrow, St. Clair might be honest. If nothing else, she would eliminate the four names he'd suggested, then go on.

The secretary showed her into the lawyer's office. A white-haired man stood to greet her. Facing Del today without a lawyer would crush them both. "I'm interested—"

"This is about that black boy charged with murdering Mitch Kennedy?" the man interrupted.

This frankness threw Meg off her stride. "Oh?"

"I'm afraid I'll have to give you the same answer I've heard others have. I just don't have the time to take on another case right now."

The room felt as though it was growing warmer, much warmer. Meg stood up abruptly, afraid she might begin to cry. Outdoors, she stood on the street corner, wondering what she could do now. The judge's continuance gave her only today and tomorrow to obtain counsel for Del. How could she give Del hope if she couldn't even hire him a lawyer?

She knew a great deal about law, but not Louisiana law and she'd be no help to Del without a New Orleans lawyer. Hiring counsel shouldn't be so hard. Del's arrest had been a dreadful mistake. A good lawyer could unravel it and she and Del could get out of New Orleans. This thought fired her frustration twice as hot as the day before. She marched back inside the same office building. She scanned the list of lawyers and notaries public on it. An hour later and more rejections, she walked across the narrow street and into the first law office there. This office held no secretary. A very young lawyer greeted her himself. Interest flared in the man's eyes. Using her most convincing helpless-female tactics, she told him she was a stranger in New Orleans and needed legal advice.

"Please, Miss, do take a seat. Now how may I help you?"

"I have a friend who needs a lawyer."

"What is the charge against him?"

Meg was so weary of explaining, but she had to keep trying. She kept her eyes downcast demurely. "I'm afraid it's murder."

"You mean that black boy?" The young man's tone hardened.

"Yes, Del Dubois." She looked him in the eye.

"That's not the kind of case I'm interested in." The man literally hurried her out of his office.

What was going on here? First, she'd thought St. Clair had given her a list of the worst attorneys; then she decided to try his list. Finally, she'd gone hunting her own and been turned down by everyone she asked. Was it Del's race? Was it the crime he was charged with—a black man killing a white man? *What am I missing?*

Dread gnawed at Meg's empty stomach. In 1917, she'd gone overseas plump. She'd come home without an ounce of fat. She barely ate at all these days. Food never seemed to be what she needed to satisfy her. Now, as she walked down the dingy corridor with others who had come to visit a friend or a relative at the Orleans jail, she was glad her stomach was empty. The scent of disinfectant, body odor, and cheap perfume sickened her. How could she face Del and tell him she had failed? Her knees weakened.

Along with the others, she halted and listened to the deputy's gruff practiced speech: "When you enter the room, go to the table of the prisoner you wish to visit. Sit down and put your hands on the table. Keep them there or you'll be asked to leave. Are there any questions?"

Aware of covert glances from the other visitors, Meg felt like replying to the unasked question that hung in the air around her: "That's right. I don't belong here and neither does Del."

The deputy unlocked the door and began letting them in one by one asking for the name of the inmate from each. Meg's turn came. She murmured Del's name. The deputy touched her arm halting her. "Who?"

She repeated Del's name.

The man's expression made the hair on the back of her neck prickle. "You'll be sitting on the colored side of the room." So Jim Crow lived in jail, too.

Everyone watched her as she crossed from the area of white inmates to the black. As she negotiated a path around the many square wooden tables, her heart beat in her ears like the bass drum in a marching band. She sat down, placed her hands on the scarred tabletop, then looked at Del. The swelling had gone down from the day before, but Del still looked haggard. She longed to take him out of here to a doctor, a hot bath, and a good meal.

He attacked without preamble, "Why didn't your father come?"

"He couldn't leave Cecy so near the end of her pregnancy."

Del nodded, but his expression stayed stormy.

Even under normal circumstances, he hated waiting. Now he had to kill time, powerless to get this sorted out. She wanted to touch his hand, to tell him she was taking care of everything, but she could do neither. Pointing out his helplessness would only make him feel more desperate. Her own failure caught in her throat. Finally, she said, "Tell me what happened. How did you get mixed up in this?"

He hung his head. "You were right. I should have stayed in Paris. But I thought I could lose myself in playing jazz here." He sighed. "I was wrong. This was the last place on earth I should have come."

"Because of the racial unrest?" Fear crouched inside her as she recalled stark newspaper headlines. The KKK was riding high even north of Dixie.

"Black men serving in the war and returning home in uniform has upset the racial apple cart. We need to be reminded of *our place*. But the KKK didn't get me arrested."

"Who did?" Her mouth went dry.

"I decided to head north to Chicago. That's where everyone's going—Kid Ory, Jelly Roll Morton, Louis Armstrong. Jazz was born here, but the music is too free to prosper here. In Chicago and New York, they're paying big bucks and even recording good bands. A few guys decided to head north with me. The boss didn't like it."

Del never could leave anything alone. She pursed her lips. "He's the man you're supposed to have robbed and . . . ."

"And killed?" he supplied. "Yes, the four of us should have just left, but he was holding back our last two weeks' pay. We couldn't leave without it. So I asked him for it. We had words."

The last three words were spoken with deadly emphasis. Meg cringed inwardly. *Oh, Del, the crusader and defender. Couldn't you for once have avoided confrontation?*

"What happened then?"

"In the early hours of the next morning, the police broke down my door, found cash and a gun under my bed, and arrested me." He looked down. "Somebody must have put something in my last drink. When the police questioned me . . . it was like swimming up from deep water."

An awful dread sparked in Meg's middle. "You were drugged and someone planted the evidence in your room while you slept?"

"That or they planted it before I got there, but I didn't notice. I remember being really tired when I got to my room and fell asleep immediately."

Meg gazed at him. If Del had it right, someone had set him up. Ice slid through her veins. How could she tell him she hadn't even found him a lawyer? And what if she couldn't get a lawyer? She needed more information. Maybe a good private investigator could help. Too often in the past, Del had tried to protect her from the truth. He didn't want her to worry about him and he might hold back facts she needed now for the same reason.

She looked at him narrowly. She'd try to get enough out of him now to get an investigator started with. "Who were you playing with?"

"Tommy Willis, LaVerne Mason, Pete Brown. Why?"

"Where were you playing?"

"A hole-in-the-wall in Storyville."

"Storyville?" she asked.

"Yes, it was the district for legal prostitution before the war. But the police don't make much of an effort, even now, to stop it if the girls stay in Storyville. It's where all the clubs are."

Recalling the prostitute in court the day before, Meg nodded. "What's the club's name?"

"Penny Candy . . ." He paused to give her a worried look. "Meg, you stay out of there."

"Del, I need to talk to people—"

He cut her off: "Meg, I don't even want you here in New Orleans."

"What?"

"Get me a lawyer and then get out of this town." His words struck her as fatalistic, not like Del at all.

"Why do you say that, Del?"

"Just get someone to represent me, then go home."

"I won't leave until you're free." She stared at him.

He scowled. "Meg, I know the Wagstaff is a family of reformers. But this is New Orleans. It's a dirty city. Just give me a fighting chance. That's all I can hope for."

His plea struck a raw nerve. How could she tell him that so far she hadn't even gotten him that fighting chance? "Del—"

"And this city won't tolerate anyone who crosses the color line. Do you understand me?"

She gripped the edge of the rough table. She'd already crossed that line when she'd walked to this table. "They all seem to buy my story that I'm concerned because you're the grandson of my old nurse. It's true—"

"If you show too much concern for me, it will get you into trouble." His voice became rough. "I mean it."

All through their life together, their contrasting colors had perplexed Meg. Why did the surface of their skin make such a vast difference to people? No answer had ever satisfied her. "We've dealt with this our whole lives, Del. We can't let it separate us now."

"You're alone. I can't protect you."

This sounded like the Del she knew. "I can take care of myself. I got through a war, if you recall."

He gave her grim smile. "Both of us know it was by the skin of our teeth."

"That's the only way anyone comes through a war." She lifted her chin bravely.

The deputy's nasal voice cut through the buzz of voices. "Time's up. Everyone, stay seated. I'll dismiss you table by table."

Meg suddenly felt close to tears. They'd only had minutes together. The deputy started tapping visitors one by one signaling them to leave.

"I'll come tomorrow," she said. Surely she'd have a lawyer by then. She'd call her father. Maybe he'd found some link to an attorney here.

"No, don't. Coming every day is too much. I'll see you in court with my lawyer."

Meg felt the tap on her shoulder.

"Ma'am, stand up, fold your hands together, and walk to the door."

She wanted to drag Del from his chair and make a run for it. But she obeyed. Leaving Del in this dreadful place squeezed her heart, making it hard to breathe. Again, she couldn't bring herself to pray. Why had God made the world this way? Her white skin and her family's money always protected her, but Del always stood defenseless before the world. Now neither their money nor influence could shield him. *Del, I won't leave you to face this alone. What do I care what these people think?*

As Del watched Meg go, he wondered if he should have whispered what he feared had caused all this. A feeling of impotence gripped him. Helpless to protect her, he knew, unfortunately, that she could be depended upon to stir up the delta muck. *Meg, be careful. Please.*

Feeling like an empty shell, Meg stepped out of the cab and walked up to Cousin Emilie's door for the cocktail party. Tonight the large house was ablaze with lights. Laughter and the hum of voices greeted Meg as she let the footman take her cape. The butler showed her to the door of the drawing room where people in evening dress stood talking to one another.

"Meg, honey!" her hostess greeted her warmly.

Cousin Emilie led her around, introducing her to people who were dressed for the after-cocktails opera. Silks, velvets, satins glowed in the light of the electric sconces. The men looked like stuffed penguins in their black-and-white tuxes. Among these, there must be lawyers and there must be at least one attorney in New Orleans who would represent Del. One of these people might know him.

Across the room, Meg glimpsed Dulcine in a rose jersey dress tight at the waist, then flowing to the floor. Dulcine was flirting with two successful-looking men, but Meg noted that Dulcine's glance darted back to the doorway often. Was she looking for Gabriel St. Clair?

"Good evenin', Miss Wagstaff."

Turning, Meg found the senior St. Clair in his wheelchair. "The same to you, sir."

"Who did you find to represent that young jazz musician?"

Loud laughter made her bend over to answer him. "I talked to over a dozen attorneys today and no one was interested." She tried to keep her voice unperturbed. Not easy to do.

St. Clair spoke: "My son has arrived."

Meg nodded, observing Dulcine turn away as though masking her obvious interest in the young lawyer.

When Gabe approached his father, Meg offered him her hand.

"Miss Wagstaff." He shook her hand.

She murmured a polite nothing and drifted away from them.

"Miss Wagstaff, please let me know whom you engage in your friend's case," Sands St. Clair said after her.

For the next half hour, she went from group to group chatting. In each group, she let it be known she was seeking a lawyer for a friend. Finally, Meg had made it around the room. Not one person had taken the bait, though two of the men had been identified to her as lawyers. What else could she do? Glum, Meg walked the hallway to the room where ladies could freshen themselves. Stepping inside, she found Belle St. Clair weeping in front of the mirrored vanity. "My dear, what's wrong?" Meg asked.

"No . . . thing," the girl stammered.

Meg shook her head.

Belle's pretty face crumpled. "I want to die."

Chapter 4

For one moment, Meg flirted with the idea of offering to summon Belle's mother. With Del in jeopardy, she had enough on her mind. But she squashed this selfishness. If any girl needed a friend, Mrs. St. Clair's daughter did. Meg took both Belle's soft hands. "Whatever has happened to you?" Belle's tears flowed down her flushed cheeks. "Someone else might come in." This last phrase appeared to reach Belle. She breathed deeply.

Meg dabbed the girl's pretty face dry. But Belle still showed telltale signs of tears—reddened eyes and a pink nose. Within minutes, Meg thanked Emilie's butler as he closed the door, leaving them alone in a cozy den. Meg sat down by the fireplace where low, orange flames flickered, warming them against the damp delta chill. Belle sat opposite her. "Now, what has upset you?"

"I'm a thankless daughter." Belle twisted her damp hankie.

Meg suppressed a chuckle. "What caused your mother to say that?"

"I don't want a season." Even weeping, with her raven black hair coiled at her nape and perfect olive skin, Belle made an attractive picture in an elegant white satin dress.

Meg answered in a light tone, afraid of fostering more tears, "I went to Europe instead." Suddenly Meg pondered the anxiety her parents must have experienced when permitting her to travel, alone, to another continent in time of war. "Tell me what you would rather be doing."

"I'd rather stay in high school." Belle stared at the toes of her white satin slippers.

"Why can't you?"

"Because," Belle explained with an earnest expression, "women in my mother's family *always* have a season at seventeen, and make a brilliant marriage—"

This repressive attitude fit what she'd seen of Belle's mother. "Why don't you have your season next year after you've graduated?"

"I told you—"

Meg held up one hand. "I want you to explain to me *why* what other women in your family have done *in the past* has anything to do with you."

Belle stared at her as though Meg spoke a foreign language.

"I wouldn't suggest you disobey your parents if you were planning to . . . say . . . elope with someone unsuitable. But what is unreasonable about your wanting to graduate from high school?"

Belle blinked. "Mother says men don't want overly educated women for wives."

Meg gave a crack of laughter. "This is the twentieth century. I plan to attend law school this fall. That certainly won't put off the kind of man I intend to wed."

Belle fussed with the folds in her skirt, shimmering pale in the low light. "I want to go to Newcomb College here in New Orleans."

Meg wondered why any mother would object to such innocuous plans. But she had been raised by progressive parents who'd assumed she'd have a career, an attitude still advanced for 1920. "Go on."

"Then I'd like to train to be a nurse." Belle stared at Meg, half-defiant, half-scared.

"Why not?"

Belle blurted out, "Mother absolutely forbid me even to think of such an unladylike idea."

Meg smiled at the foolishness of that instruction. "What does your father say?"

A line creased Belle's forehead. "When I ask him about things, he always says, 'What does your mother say?'"

Meg frowned. "Why not try? Your father seems to be intelligent and reasonable." *Unlike your mother.*

Staring at the fireplace, Belle said, "What if he says no, too?"

Meg stood up. She had pressing goals to accomplish tonight. "Tell him everything—high school, college, and nurse's training. He'll take you more seriously if you let him know all your ambitions."

Belle grumbled, "No one takes me seriously."

"That means you have some work to do." Unfortunately, Meg suspected Belle's older brother would be no ally to his young sister. Not Mr. Antebellum.

Belle rose, smiling uncertainly. "May I sit with you at the opera?"

"I'm not attending the opera tonight." This delay prodded Meg to action. "I'm going to a club, Penny Candy." Meg slipped out her white gold compact and studied her reflection. She fluffed her bangs and freshened her scarlet lip rouge.

Wordlessly Belle requested Meg's compact and examined herself, frowned, then handed it back. "I've never heard of it."

Meg slipped the compact into her black beaded bag. "Let me know what your father says."

"I will and thank you."

Meg smiled and went off to bid her hostess good night.

Storyville differed from Emilie's cocktail party as hell differed from heaven. In the hip pocket of the French Quarter, Storyville reminded Meg of the notorious Barbary Coast. Black prostitutes dressed in skimpy bits of shiny red or blue lingered at each streetlamp. From the cab, Meg shivered with vague fear. "This is the place, driver."

"Miss, are you sure this be where y'all want to go?"

She handed him a silver half-dollar. If Del's life didn't depend on it, she would never come to a club like this unescorted. But she had no choice. "Yes."

"I see swells come down y'here after society parties, but ladies don't come without no gentlemum." He took the half-dollar and handed her change.

"I won't be staying long. Keep the change."

"Thank you, Miss. I'll stay in de area and come back around a few times."

"Fine, but don't feel compelled to pass up fares for me. So far the nicest people I've met in New Orleans are the cabbies."

The man chuckled and thanked her again. Meg clutched her purse as she got out. She couldn't let anyone snatch it tonight, not with what she had in it.

Inside Penny Candy, rich jazz enveloped Meg, making her blood spring to life. She strolled past the club bouncer, letting her eyes adjust to the dark interior. In a haze of cigarette smoke, candles on each table glowed as points of light. On a tiny jammed dance floor, couples, many in the latest evening dress, danced the new fox-trot. Three black musicians, a pianist, coronet player, and saxophonist, blasted out the lively rhythm Del had taught Meg to love.

She chose a small empty table and perched on a hard café chair. A waiter stepped to her side. "What will it be, lady?"

A card on the table announced: "No cover. Minimum: three drinks." She didn't want to order a drink, but to sit in the chair she had to pay for at least three. "Bourbon." He nodded and left. She eased back. Soon the waiter set a short glass of amber liquid in front of her. She paid him, then motioned him to lean closer. "When the musicians take a break, I'd like to thank them with a round of drinks." This ploy would let her speak to them without rousing suspicion. He nodded and left.

Meg slid her glass aside. Eyes shut, she allowed the music to take her back to the little clubs on the Left Bank. Jazz's syncopated beat and spirited songs overpowered war-torn France's pervasive misery. Listening to ragtime let one forget. . . .

Colin took her hand, then kissed it. "I don't know why you've come all this way, my dear. But I'm so glad you did." Meg straightened up, her heart racing. The memory had been vivid, undiluted by time. She'd felt his caress.

She nearly reached for the glass of bourbon. No. She'd seen too many soldiers in France try drowning pain in alcohol only to sink into utter disintegration. She'd no time for her private sorrow. Del's life depended on her.

The song ended; couples drifted from the dance floor. Meg clapped, adding her praise to the noisy applause. Meg's waiter delivered a tray of drinks to the band, then gestured toward Meg. Her pulse beating a rapid six-eight rhythm, she approached the musicians.

"Thank you, Miss," the saxophonist said amid the raucous voices.

"Don't mention it." She raised her voice, "I'm Meg Wagstaff, Del Dubois's friend."

Guardedly, all three introduced themselves: Tommy the saxophonist, LaVerne the horn player, and Pete on the piano. Their eyes kept sliding away from hers.

"Del gave me your names. Perhaps you could give me more information about what happened."

No one replied. She noticed, from the corner of her eye, a young black woman, wearing a stylish red dress and standing alone, staring at her.

The unmoved silence of the three musicians irked Meg. Perhaps reminding them that Del had been willing to stick his neck out for them might prompt them to help. "Del explained you four had intended to go up north together."

LaVerne, a serious-looking man, spoke up, "Del's a great guy. We told him we'd hitchhike north or ride the rails. Not to make a big deal—"

"It wasn't fair to hold up our wages, but Mitch would have paid us eventually," Tommy who had a round, boyish face added.

The slender girl edged toward Meg. "Do you have any idea of who might have set Del up? Did Mitch have any enemies?" Meg itched to shake them. *Help me. What are you holding back and why?*

"Everyone's got enemies, Miss," LaVerne said. "We don't know nothin' about what happened to Mitch or why Del had the cash and gun in his room—"

"Good evenin'." A tall man in evening dress drew alongside Meg. Near the end of her rail journey, Meg had glimpsed alligators slither in and out of the swamps or bayous near New Orleans. This man moved like an alligator sliding into the water to watch and wait for prey. He smiled at her. "May I help you?"

Meg gave him a measuring look. Who was he? How to repel him? "I was just complimenting the band." The slender black girl in red stared harder at Meg now.

"I'm happy you're pleased, Miss." He turned to the musicians. "You boys, finish those drinks. Your break is up."

"Yes, sir, Mr. Corelli," Pete, the thinnest of the three musicians, spoke for the first time. The others obeyed the man.

Meg hid her irritation under a coy smile. "Yes, I'm ready to hear some more great jazz." Trying to look unconcerned, she sauntered toward her table.

"Miss Wagstaff," Corelli called after her.

He knew her name? Or had he just overhead her say it to the band? Uncertain, she ignored him and sat down at her table again.

"Miss Wagstaff," he repeated.

She looked up at him. Who was he? And why did she interest him? "Were you speaking to me?"

"Yes."

"I didn't know anyone here knew my name." She fixed him with an unwavering gaze. What explanation would he give?

He gave her a reassuring smile like a French merchant about to cheat her. "A lady as beautiful as you"—he kissed his finger tips—"can't remain anonymous long."

She nodded coolly, but his manner sent a zigzag of gooseflesh up her spine. What did he want? The black girl in the red dress was still eyeing Meg warily. Corelli sat at Meg's table.

She bit back, "Who invited you to sit down?" She needed information and to keep this man from thinking she was a threat. She'd simper like a helpless female and see what developed. Her timing lagged a bit, but she managed to give him a sweeter-than-sugar smile. "How kind of you to join me." *Do you know anything important, Mr. Smooth-as-Snake-Skin?* His presence made her nerves jump. "You know who I am, then?"

"You're that Yankee woman who came to hire a lawyer for Del DuBois."

His knowing this proved he hadn't merely overheard her giving her name. Evidently she'd been under observation. By whom? What would a helpless female say to this? She sobered her face. "You must be upset over losing Mitch Kennedy," she made her voice sympathetic. He frowned at her. Good. She'd thrown him a curve ball. She ran her finger tip around the smooth rim of her bourbon glass. "Del was saddened by Mr. Kennedy's death as well."

"His murder, don't you mean?" He lifted one eyebrow.

Meg went on in a sensitive tone, "How long had you and Mr. Kennedy been partners?"

Corelli surged forward on his chair. "Kennedy and I were never partners."

She'd nicked him. "Oh? You're only the manager, then?"

He glared, his chin jutting forward. "I am the *new* owner."

She let her mouth open. "I hadn't realized probate moved that swiftly in Louisiana."

"I didn't have to bother with probate." Something else had caught his notice, distracted him. "Mitch sold to me before he died."

"That made everything so much . . . easier for you, didn't it?" Meg slipped in.

"You've got that right." Corelli shot his cuffs and straightened his black tie. Someone at the bar had his attention now. Corelli rose. "You'll excuse me please."

Toying with her glass of Bourbon, Meg observed her unwanted companion speaking to a short bald man at the bar. The short man lifted his hand. Even in low light, the diamond solitaire on his pinkie finger flashed. Both he and Corelli glanced in her direction. As though unaware, she kept her attention on the band, now playing, "Bunch O Blues."

Out of the corner of her eye, Meg observed the young woman in the red dress pause again along the nearby wall. Meg wondered if she should make some motion toward the woman. Who was she and why did she seem to want to talk to Meg? The black girl's face widened with shock. She turned swiftly away—

A hand clamped hard on Meg's shoulder.

Meg jumped and reached into her purse.

"You are a complete idiot." Gabriel, still in evening attire, sat in the chair opposite her.

Jolted quickly from fear to anger, Meg felt ill. "What are you doing here?"

"I came to ask you the same question," he snapped belligerently.

She sent him a withering glare. This was just what she didn't need—to be seen with the parish attorney. "I'm not accountable to you. Go away. You're spoiling my enjoyment of the jazz."

"You spoiled my enjoyment of the opera. At the intermission, Belle asked me where Penny Candy was—that you had gone there instead of the opera—"

"I was in the mood for jazz, not opera." Surreptitiously Meg watched Corelli. Gabriel's elegant appearance contrasted with Corelli, who'd obviously attempted to cut a figure like St. Clair but came across as a cheap imitation.

St. Clair glared at her. "This is no place for a lady. Chivalry demanded I protect you from your own folly."

"Folly? What a delightfully old-fashioned word. It suits you." Nothing more could be accomplished tonight—thanks to St. Clair. She stood up. "Let's leave."

Startled, he rose also. "You mean you are not going to argue with me and insist on staying?"

"You've completely ruined my evening." *And my plans*. Having a parish prosecutor sitting at her table would scare away everyone, innocent or guilty. The woman in red had disappeared.

"Then we're even." He trailed Meg through the maze of tables. Behind them, LaVerne was squeezing off high notes on his horn in a haunting solo. The melody put her own frustration and worry into sound. Outside the door, Meg paused. The young black woman now stood across the street under a streetlamp.

Meg tightened her grip on her bag, its beads prickling her palms. With St. Clair at her elbow, she didn't dare make contact with the girl. Meg raised her voice, "Did you bring your car or do we need a taxi? I'm staying at the Monteleone."

"I know where you're staying," St. Clair growled. "I took you home last night—if you remember." With the wave of an arm, he hailed a taxi.

Just as she slid into the cab, she snapped, "I can go home alone."

He shoved in beside her, his solid form forcing her to make room for him. "I'm going to make sure . . . *very* sure you go to your room and stay there for the night." He gave the hotel name to the cabby.

St. Clair sitting so close made her intensely aware of him—his clean scent, broad shoulders—along with male strength and arrogance under the mask of evening attire. "How are you going to make sure I stay there?" Meg goaded him. "Going to sit outside my door all night?"

"No, I'm going to remind you that your behavior in New Orleans reflects on Emilie and her cousin, Fleur Fourchette Bower. I don't care if you're bent on social ruin, but I do care about Emilie and the Fourchette family."

Meg bit her lower lip. She hadn't thought of that tonight.

"You probably didn't know," he admitted grudgingly. "Penny Candy is one of the most notorious, dangerous clubs in Storyville. *Anything* could have happened to you there."

Did he think her a complete fool? "I don't think so." She slid her ivory-handled derringer from her purse. The gun weighed heavy and cold in her hand.

In the faint light, St. Clair looked shocked. "Put that away. You're beyond anything."

Slipping the gun back into her black bag, she chuckled. She'd gotten the exact response she'd wanted. Oh-so-proper Gabriel St. Clair invited her to be audacious. "Is that the best you can do?"

"It's obvious that you have no common sense or any sense of decorum—"

"I'm not interested in being decorous. I'm interested in finding out the truth about why Del has been falsely arrested. I'll do anything, go anywhere necessary to see him free again."

"Delman's guilty. And you're out of your depth."

Blistering words smoldered inside her, but why waste words on this museum relic? They reached her hotel; he escorted her inside. Striding ahead of him, she did her best to ignore him. But his powerful presence made this impossible.

The night desk clerk handed her a key and a yellow envelope. "This telegram came for you earlier in the evening."

She accepted it with a serenity she didn't feel. "Thank you." She'd already received a reply to her first telegram to her father. Had something happened to her stepmother or Kai Lin's baby? "Good night, Mr. St. Clair." Without a backward glance, she hurried to the staircase glad to be free of him.

"Don't mention it, Miss Wagstaff." His voice dripped with sarcasm. "See you in court."

Meg gritted her teeth. His reminding her that tomorrow she had to go to court without a lawyer to represent Del was just what she would expect from St. Clair. She would best the man if it was the last thing she did.

Chapter 5

"Good morning, Father, Gabe." With thin morning light behind her, Belle sat in her usual place at the breakfast table.

Gabe wondered why Belle was dressed in a red cashmere sweater and plaid wool skirt, an outfit she had formerly reserved for school. Gabe swallowed coffee, hoping it would brace him for the day. "You were out until two A.M. at that post-opera party. Why aren't you still in bed?

Belle lifted a cup of coffee. "I need a ride to school." Her chin quivered with the final two words.

Gabe set down his cup. Coffee splashed over the rim onto the white tablecloth.

Before Gabe could, his father inquired, "You're going to school today, Belle?"

She lowered her puffy eyes and in a subdued voice, said, "Yes, father, I'd like to."

"But you quit school before Christmas," Gabe objected. "This is your season, your Carnival. You can't go out all night every night and go to school every day."

"Why don't you tell us what you're thinking, my dear? I know I'm interested." Father's tone remained gentle.

Belle's gaze flickered from her father to Gabe, then back. "I decided I want to reenter school and graduate in spring." Belle faced them, her expression defiant. "Then I want to enter Newcomb in the fall."

"What?" Gabe gasped.

"This is very sudden," Father commented.

"No, it isn't." Belle's jawline and tone firmed. "I've wanted this for a long time."

"But what do you need a college education for?" Gabe asked dismissively. "You're just going to be a wife and mother."

Bridling, Belle threw him a disgusted look.

"What do you plan to do after college, Belle?" Father asked, still calm.

Belle drew herself up and took a deep breath. "I'd like to train as a nurse."

Gabe couldn't believe his ears. "My sister will not be a nurse. No lady becomes a nurse."

"What about that French nurse who helped you recover after you were shot down in the south of France?" Belle objected. "You said *she* was a lady."

"That was in the middle of a war. She had no choice, but to come to the aid of her country." Speaking of Lenore cost him. When would he get a chance to call Paul again?

Father cleared his throat. "Son, this is really between Belle and me."

"You can't mean you're going to listen to this . . . this nonsense." Gabe couldn't imagine his sister going to college. In a world run mad, venerable New Orleans, where nothing ever changed, had become his anchor.

Father ignored him. "Belle, your mother has her heart set on your taking part in this year's Carnival as a debutante. You've had dresses made—"

"But do I have to go out every night? Couldn't I just attend a few each week? I've wanted to attend Newcomb College ever since I visited there with my freshman class." Belle's expression begged for understanding.

"Why didn't you say something then?" Father asked.

Belle's eyes flashed. "I *did*. Mother said it was out of the question."

"I see." Father looked grim. "What caused you to decide to talk to me now?"

Though addressing their father, Belle's gaze met Gabe's. "Last night I felt so miserable that I went to Emilie's powder room and broke down into tears."

This surprised Gabe. His sister didn't cry easily.

"Miss Wagstaff came in." His sister's voice softened.

Gabe's temper flared. *I might have known.*

"She took me to the den and helped me stop crying."

"What did Miss Wagstaff suggest?" father asked.

Gabe didn't have to ask. Rebellion was that woman's middle name.

"She told me I should talk to you, that you seemed to be a reasonable man, and intelligent, too."

Gabe could just imagine Miss Wagstaff's opinion of him.

"I'm flattered." Father grinned.

"She didn't have a season at all." Belle rushed on, "She went to Europe instead."

"I'm not surprised," Gabe bit out.

"That's not fair, Gabe!" Belle exclaimed. "You wrote about the American girls who worked at the YMCA canteens, how brave and good they were. Miss Wagstaff was even wounded. How can you forget so easily?"

Gabe grimaced, disgusted with himself. "You're right. I did forget. It's just . . ." He passed a hand over his forehead. He didn't want to shatter Belle's innocent illusions. But out of that ghastly nightmare he'd gotten Marie, Lenore. *I must call Paul.* Glancing at his watch, he rose. "I've got to be off."

Half rising, Belle cast a worried glance to her brother, then her father. "Will you give me a ride to school, Gabe? May I go, father?"

"Yes, I've decided to go into town today. I'll drop you at school and explain to the principal that you'll be reentering—"

"Oh, father, thank you." Belle jumped up and hugged his neck.

Gabe didn't like the idea of that Wagstaff woman abetting his sister in flouting their mother. But it wasn't for him to correct his father. Belle, a nurse? What next? But he only said, "I'll see you this evening, then."

"I may see you downtown later, son."

Gabe paused. His father didn't venture downtown often. Gabe thought since his father could no longer practice law, being around the courthouse depressed him. "Did you want to meet for lunch?

I won't be free today." With any luck, he'd be talking to Paul in Paris.

"Just go about your business, son. If our paths cross, they cross."

Gabe left as Belle began serving herself a generous breakfast of scrambled eggs, sausage, and grits. If he didn't reach Paul at lunch, he'd try again after the afternoon recess. If he kept trying, he'd get a Paris telephone operator eventually and Paul would have to show up at the hospital sometime.

After a hasty, too-spicy breakfast, Meg dragged her feet up the marble steps of the courthouse, the sensation of doom permeating her. Last night's telegram said her stepmother was on complete bed rest and of course Del still had no lawyer.

God, why is this happening? Del's been through so much. We both have. Why didn't the faith learned from her father feel real after France? Meg forced back tears of frustration. She had to show Del a brave face. They'd survived an earthquake together; now just the two of them would be confronting this. Somehow, some way, she'd get Del set free. Clinging to this vow, she entered the formidable courthouse where her best friend in the world was held for a crime he'd never commit.

Inside, she made her way to the front row of the viewing section. St. Clair sat facing forward. His meddling still irked her. Now, sitting right behind where Del would sit alone, without counsel, she briefly entertained the idea of putting up bail and helping Del flee the county. *Am I coming unglued?*

Out of the corner of his eye, Gabe watched Meg Wagstaff take a seat on the defendant's side of the room. Carrying herself tall and confident, she looked neither triumphant nor downcast. The small ruby studs in her ear lobes called his attention to her pale cheek and creamy neck. Though not beautiful, she was the kind of woman one couldn't ignore. Had she actually found someone to represent Delman?

"All rise."

The judge in his black robes, stark against the pasty white of his face, entered. A group of rumpled prisoners, their eyes downcast, were herded in and slumped down on a low backless bench along the wall.

Gabe covertly studied Delman. Still swollen, one of his eyes resembled a mere slit. But he no longer wore a bandage to cover the crudely stitched gash on his forehead. Unlike the others, he sat stiffly looking like a man nursing broken ribs. Silently, Gabe cursed Rooney's clumsy brutality. If the policeman didn't stop this, he'd be forced to speak to the chief of police. This wasn't Bolshevik Russia. Even blacks had some rights in America.

Gabe watched Delman glance at the judge, then scan the rest of those in the courtroom. For a fraction of a second Del and Gabe's gazes met. The contempt in the prisoner's eyes sent a shock wave through Gabe. Then Delman looked to Meg. He didn't appear surprised that she sat alone. Had Delman accepted that he'd have no counsel?

The judge tapped his gavel, silencing murmurs around the room. Everyone sat down with much shuffling of feet and creaking of the old wooden benches. "The court will now entertain a discussion of bail for Delman Caleb Dubois."

The businesslike bailiff called Delman to the bar. Delman hobbled in his shackles to the defendant's table, his back to Meg.

"Delman, have you secured counsel?" the judge asked.

Delman cleared his throat. "I have counsel, Your Honor, but—"

The double oak doors at the rear of the courtroom pushed open with a bump and a swish of air. Gabe turned to see his family chauffeur pushing his father inside. "Dad?" Caught off guard, Gabe stepped into the aisle. "What are you doing here?"

"I'm here to represent my client." His father gave an unruffled smile.

Gabe gaped at him.

The chauffeur settled Sands beside Del. In deference to the court, he pulled off his own cap and retired to the rear of the courtroom.

Sands thanked the bailiff, then turned his attention to the judge.

"Please forgive my tardiness, Simon. Getting me up all those stairs took my man a little longer than we expected."

The old judge's thin, deeply lined face lifted into a brief smile. "Sands, you're a sight for sore eyes. But don't be late again."

Sands bowed his pepper-and-salt head as though accepting his scold. "I assure you, it won't happen again."

"I take it that this means you have taken Delman as your client." The judge sent a sharp glance at the two of them.

"I have, Your Honor." Sands nodded.

The Wagstaff woman gave a little gasp.

Gabe clenched his jaw. His father wasn't well enough to be in court. Over his shoulder, he glared at the Yankee woman. This had to be her doing.

"I'm confronted for the first time by two lawyers with the same last name." The judge regarded them with a stern expression. "Since I have known both of you for years, I will simplify matters by calling you—respectfully—by your given names."

Sands nodded.

"Your honor, the parish asks that bail be denied." Gabe's words came out harsher than he intended. "Delman Dubois has no family or other strong ties to New Orleans. There is the possibility of flight."

Judge LeGrand nodded. "Sands?"

"Your honor, my client has never been in trouble before. He is an honorably discharged soldier. He has no desire to leave New Orleans until his honest name has been absolutely cleared of all wrongdoing."

"That sounds very good," the judge replied. "But this is murder in the first degree. The prosecutor is correct. Bail denied." The judge tapped his gavel once. "Next case, bailiff?"

Gabe had no time to question his father. This morning he'd asked himself—what next? Now he'd gotten his answer.

Listening to the bailiff call another name as his father rolled his squeaking wheelchair to the back of the courtroom, Gabe muttered a few choice words with which he'd like to favor Miss Wagstaff. He was beginning to think Meg would be a good name for a hurricane. He'd have to do something to counter her effect on his family.

Meg stepped into the aisle and hurried to catch up to Mr. Sands. She knew what she'd seen. She just didn't believe it. How? What? Why? Questions, surprise, gratitude danced through her. She slipped out the door.

Sands awaited her, his chauffeur at his side. "Miss Wagstaff, are you free for a brief consultation?"

"Yes." Meg nodded, trying to catch her breath. Sands taking the case was like an answer to prayer.

"Then come with me. We'll discuss this at my office at home."

Chapter 6

Gabe sensed the ominous hush like a suffocating mist around his parents, his sister, and himself. After serving the chocolate-rum mousse, the St. Clair butler signaled the footman to leave with him. Despite the rich aromas of chocolate and rum, no one picked up a dessert spoon. Dinner had been a stilted meal full of pregnant pauses and reproachful glances. Who would open the discussion? Gabe's own taut nerves revved like a motor racing.

"I would be pleased, Sands, if you would tell me why our daughter returned to high school this morning." His mother's low voice vibrated with outrage.

The ragged edges of Gabe's own discontent goaded him to speak. "And I'd be interested in knowing why you were in *my* court today?"

"Your court?" Father gave him a quizzing glance. "I thought it was Simon LeGrand's court."

Gabe flushed.

"Is that where you went this morning?" his mother exclaimed. "Why was that Yankee girl in your office today?"

Father sipped coffee. "This family has been operating on two disastrously incorrect assumptions."

"What assumptions?" Mother stared at her husband.

Father stirred his coffee. "The first assumption was that Belle wanted to quit school and get married this year."

Mother's soft chin went up. "I've waited all my life to see Belle have her season—"

"I'm having a season, Mother," Belle put in.

Color flooded mother's face. "Belle—"

"Celestia," Father stopped her. "Why didn't you tell me Belle wanted to go to Newcomb?"

Mother waved her delicate hands. "That was just a girl's foolishness. A woman doesn't need an education. It could ruin her chances to make a match. Do you want people to think Belle is bookish?"

"That wouldn't bother me," Father returned.

Mother looked nonplussed.

"Belle, tell your mother your plans," Father continued.

Belle drew herself up. "During Carnival, I'll attend a couple of balls each week. I plan to graduate from high school in the spring."

Mother pressed a napkin to her lips to suppress a moan.

Belle eyed her mother. "Then in the fall, I'll enter Newcomb. If I do well there, I plan to go on to nurse's training."

"Over my lifeless body!" Tears sprung to her mother's eyes. "Ladies don't become nurses"—her voice quavered—"only poor, ugly women who can't find husbands—"

"Celestia, please let our daughter finish."

Mother visibly grappled with her upset. "I can't believe this."

Belle said in a coaxing tone, "I can marry after nurse's training, mother."

Mother's lips quivered. "And what true gentleman wants a nurse for a wife, may I ask? I was only seventeen when I married your father. Why is that wrong for my daughter?"

Father placed a hand on hers. "That was in another century, *mon cher*."

"It was only twenty-eight years ago," Mother declared.

"And that means you're too young to be a grandmother. You're more lovely now than you were at seventeen."

This flattery obviously disconcerted his mother. Father never said such things in front of them.

Father spoke gently, "My *cher*, it is unreasonable to think that Belle's life would imitate yours exactly. Too much has altered in our world. I courted you in a horse and buggy. Our son grew up to fly in the air. There are dirigibles, movies, phonographs—"

"Those are just things. People are the same," Mother interrupted.

"Are they? Belle was born in this century. She's better in tune with her generation. How do we know the changes she will face in the coming years?"

"Father!" Belle gazed at him with wide eyes. "You do understand!"

"Au petite." He sipped his coffee.

Mother hid behind her napkin. "How will I face our friends? I can't tell them my daughter is going to college."

"If you say it with pride, you may be surprised, *cher*." Father gave her one of his twinkling smiles, which Gabe hadn't seen in ages.

The smiled acted on his mother also, but she still looked dubious. "I can't believe this."

Gabe agreed. His sister, a college girl—a nurse. What had been going through his sister's mind? When he'd returned from war, she'd been all grown up. *Maybe I should have talked to her more since I came home.*

"Father, what was the second wrong assumption?" Belle asked. "I have double homework tonight because I don't want to miss the Jupiter Ball tomorrow night."

Mother gave a little moan.

"Mother, Martine Leon and Nadine Roberts are applying to

Newcomb, too." Belle turned to father. "Does the second assumption have to do with your going to court today?"

Looking grave, father nodded. "We all assumed my injury had ended my law career. It hasn't."

Gabe objected, "You're not well enough—"

"Are you my doctor?" Father's tone stiffened.

"Dr. Sankey said you are able to go back to work?"

Father picked up his spoon. "He's been suggesting it for months."

Mother looked startled.

"I'll never walk again. I'll continue having my headaches. But nothing has impaired my reason or my memory." Father took a spoonful of the mousse.

After his riding accident, his father had been bedridden for months. At first, just seeing him in a wheelchair had been a joy. "What if a headache incapacitates you when you're due in court?" Gabe asked.

"If that occurs, most judges in Orleans Parish would give me a continuance, don't you agree?"

Gabe nodded grudgingly. Knowing his father would never use his headaches as a ploy, most judges would grant him a continuance.

Father caught his eye. "And since you decided not to come into practice with me, I may take in another young lawyer. Then I would have someone to cover for me, if necessary."

Gabe stared at him. For over two years, Gabe had given up hope of practicing law with his father and taken the position with the parish. "I see."

"I realize it will be peculiar to face each other on opposite sides at court—"

"What?" Mother demanded.

"I'm defending Miss Wagstaff's friend, Del DuBois—"

"Hey, that's Jake!" Belle leaped up and kissed her father.

Mother shook her head. "Belle, please watch your language. A lady doesn't use slang."

Gabe still couldn't accept the changes. His father wasn't well enough to practice law. Belle was too young to make such momentous decisions. That Wagstaff woman's influence was changing, hurting his family.

Mother gave a sour expression. "I might have known that wild San Francisco flapper would be at the bottom of all this."

My thoughts exactly.

Later, Gabe sat alone in his home office. Only the desk lamp shone in the dark room. He'd tried three more times to get a telephone connection to the Paris hospital where Paul now worked. His call to the still-ravaged city hadn't been important enough to get through. Official government calls had priority, relief organizations . . .

He rubbed his forehead. Then taking out a sheet of onionskin paper, he wrote.

Dear Paul,

Your news took me by surprise. Please do all you can to bring Marie to Paris to you. Yes, I want her. With all my heart. I would never have left France if I'd known she'd survived the bombardment.

By wire, I'll set up an account at the Bank St. George with funds sufficient to bring Marie with a companion from Paris to New Orleans. Please wire me as soon as you know anything. I have tried to call your hospital without success. Merci, mon ami.

Yours,
Gabriel

He sealed the envelope and slipped it into his briefcase. He would send a duplicate as a telegram tomorrow. One or both would reach Paul. The agony of loss plunged its sharp, poisoned claws into him. "God, help him find her. She's so sweet, an innocent. Bring her safe to

me. I have no right to ask you anything. But for her sake. Please . . ." A
sob forced its way through him. "Oh, God . . . God . . ."

From the Clairborne home for the Jupiter Ball, strains of jazz,
"High Society Blues," floated through the cool evening air. The day
had been unusual—crisp and clear—and stars gleamed around the
full moon.

Belle on Gabe's arm murmured, "What a luscious moon." Ahead
of them, their mother in a wispy gray gown walked beside their
father, being pushed by the chauffeur.

Gabe squeezed his sister's arm in response. All day long, he'd
thought about Belle's plans, the letter and telegram he'd written,
Del's battered face, and Meg Wagstaff's tart words at Penny Candy.
How had life suddenly become so messy? He had to convince Miss
Meg Wagstaff to stop interfering with his family.

Inside the airy foyer, they were relieved of their wraps, then
they drifted into the luxurious wine red and gold ballroom. Gabe
scanned the large, filled room for Meg. He spotted her across the
room chatting within a circle of gentlemen.

His sister teased close to his ear, "She does know how to catch a
man's interest."

He made a face at his sister.

A young man approached. "Belle, you're a regular baby vamp
tonight."

Belle giggled. "Oh, Corby, you're the cat's pajamas yourself." She
drifted away with Corby toward the younger set.

Though amused, Gabe didn't think he'd call anyone a "baby
vamp" tonight. But Belle was right. Miss Wagstaff's black beaded
evening dress with its elegant high neckline and long form-fitting sleeves flowed over her slender form to her ankles. When she
turned, however, her backless evening gown was less than demure.
All over the ballroom, heads turned to catch a glimpse of her elegant spine, then away. Gabe hoped this shocking display would be
a lesson to his father. Was this Yankee woman someone he wanted
his innocent daughter imitating?

The band stopped for one of their breaks. "Good evening, Gabriel. I see you were taking in the view," Dulcine murmured.

He didn't pretend to misunderstand her. "Evidently, we're not quite up to the new Parisienne styles."

She gave a mirthless laugh. "My cousin Maisy mimics Miss Wagstaff's every move."

Gabe said, "I'm sorry to hear that." The band began a waltz. Gabe lifted Dulcine's wrist to read her dance card, which dangled from a golden cord there. "I see that I'm down for this waltz."

"Are you? Did you write with invisible ink?"

Laughing, he drew her to the dance floor and into his arms. Dulcine's rapt gaze soothed his ruffled nerves. Her form was soft and pliant in his arms. For a second, behind Dulcine, he caught a glimpse of his mother's beaming face. He knew she approved of Dulcine as his potential bride.

Inside, he faltered, then gathered his composure. He had no plan to marry again. And if Paul didn't locate Marie, he'd be going back to France himself.

Dulcine chuckled, "Corby looks as though he's won a horse race."

As Corby Ferrand whirled Meg around floor, Corby's hand pressed the bare skin at the small of the woman's back. For an instant, Gabe felt Meg's warm flesh under his own palm. The sensation enveloped him like fire. Immodest flapper. With the knightly courtesy he'd been raised to show a lady, Gabe danced the rest of the waltz with Dulcine. But his unruly eyes kept tracking the shocking brunette and the creamy skin down her slender spine. Vixen. Unfortunately, when the waltz ended, Gabe and Dulcine found themselves beside Corby and Meg.

"Dulcine," Corby said, "is there any room left for me on your dance card?"

Dulcine pouted prettily. "You shouldn't wait so long to ask." She glanced at her card. "I still have the two-step open."

"Fill in my name." Corby grinned.

While this exchange took place, Gabe locked gazes with Meg. The band began playing the lively new fox-trot.

"Thank you for a lovely waltz, Gabriel." Dulcine touched his arm.

"I beg your pardon?" Gabe glanced at her. "My pleasure." His gaze drifted back to Meg. Gabe was vaguely aware that couples formed around him and Meg. His thoughts scattered as he breathed in her French perfume.

Meg put her hand on Gabe's shoulder and took his other hand in hers. "Start dancing. People are beginning to stare."

Gabe's face burned, but he took her into his embrace and began to dance. What had just happened?

"It's my elemental appeal." She made her voice sultry and low. "I can't help myself. In an evening gown—I'm a siren."

"Pardon me," he said stiffly embarrassed, "I think you left half your gown at home."

"Which half would that be?" She mimicked his southern drawl.

He ignored her comment. "Evidently the gentlemen here haven't fallen for your elemental appeal. You had space on your dance card."

"What dance card?" She wiggled her wrist. "Are you seeing things now?"

"Why not?"

"Do you mean, why shouldn't you see things? Or why don't I have a dance card?"

He glared at her.

Meg shrugged. "I'm not a debutante, so I don't need a dance card."

"That's right." Her nonchalant dismissal of custom angered him. "You so kindly told my sister you went to Europe instead of having your debut."

Her expressive face slid into melancholy. "It's not something I would recommend to her."

This brought him up short. "Those are the first sensible words I've heard from your mouth."

"You should know."

And those three words formed a bond between them. He pulled

her tighter to him. Her skin against his palm warmed him. Her fragrance took him back to Paris, to crowded cafés where he had grabbed a few moments of relief from the war. He'd read deep loneliness in her eyes. The same loneliness he carried. He wanted to ask her, "When did the despair hit you? When did you realize you'd forgotten why you came? Who did you lose in France?"

Though she spoke no word, he sensed her understanding. A flicker of warmth flared in his heart. If he spoke to her of Marie and Lenore, she would understand, not judge him. The fox-trot ended. Shaken, he couldn't pull himself together or release her. Slipping out of his embrace, she linked her arm in his. "We're going to get refreshments. We need them."

He let her direct his steps to a love seat beside a lush potted palm, where they sipped tangy punch. Slowly, he surfaced. "Sorry," he muttered. "I've been under a great deal of pressure."

She nodded. "Me too."

This brought all his grievances to a quick boil again. His lips straightened into a line. "How did you persuade my father to represent Delman?"

"I had nothing to do with it. Don't you think you should discuss that with your father anyway?"

"I can't. We are representing the opposing sides in a murder case."

"I think I heard that," she said with a flippant lift in her voice.

"You've had quite an effect on my family. You've inspired my sister to become a nurse—of all things."

She smiled thinly. "When you were seventeen, did your mother tell you to get married and outline what you should do for the rest of your life?"

"Of course not—"

"Then why don't you think your sister has a right to her own decisions, her own life?"

"It's not the same. She is a woman."

"Yes, she's a woman. And she deserves the same freedom as you."

He glared at her.

She sipped her punch. "Your sister has depths you haven't even begun to comprehend. I think that must be the way between older and younger siblings. When I left for France, my brother was just a boy. I came home and found him on the threshold of manhood. I didn't know how to talk to him." She sighed.

Again, her mood touched a similar wound deep inside him. Since the war, he'd felt separated from his family, even as he sat among them. Still, he resisted her. "Your brother starting high school is natural, but Belle may fail to make a good match because she won't make as big a splash at Carnival as mother intended." He ignored Meg's attempt to speak. "And my father's health will suffer because of his taking Delman's case."

For an instant, Meg contemplated slapping him for his stubbornness. Had he learned no wisdom in France? Then she decided on a better punishment.

His impetuous words flowed on, "And your friend will—"

"Oh, Gabriel! The things you say!" she teased. She let a deliciously outrageous laugh ripple out of her. Then she kissed him on his parted lips.

He wanted to kill her. She read it from his expression. To keep others from reading it also, she kept her face just in front of his. "If you keep spewing nonsense, I'll only behave more shockingly."

He seethed visibly. "No southern lady would behave as you have."

"If being a lady means behaving as though I agree with all the nonsense you spout, I don't want to be one. You are quite sure you know exactly the lives your sister and father should lead. But you wouldn't, *haven't*, submitted to anyone telling you what life *you* should lead, have you?"

"The cases are not the same," he bit out.

"Oh?" She gave him a scathing glance. "I suppose you've never heard—'Do unto others as you would have them do unto you?'"

He scowled at her.

"Don't worry. Dulcine is on her way to rescue you from this notorious Yankee. I wonder if she will deign to kiss lips I've kissed. Oh, dear. I may have ruined all your chances." She sprang up to greet Dulcine and her escort who eyed Meg uncertainly. "Dulcine! Thank you for bringing me another dance partner." She took the startled gentlemen's arm and sauntered off with him in tow.

Fuming, Gabe stood.

"Gabriel," Dulcine's voice had lost its usual liquid charm, "it's time you took me to the buffet."

Then something caught his eye. A uniformed police officer entering the ballroom approached his father. "Dulcine, I'm sorry. I must see what's happened."

"Of course." Worry in her voice, Dulcine released his arm.

He slid between the dancers to reach his father across the room. "Father, what is it?" Gabe murmured, aware all eyes must be on them.

"Gabe, an attempt has been made on my client's life."

Gabe stared at his father in disbelief.

"Get Miss Wagstaff." His father glanced at the officer. "All three of us will come down—"

"Rooney said that wasn't neces—"

Gabe cut him off, "We're coming."

Chapter 7

Gabe, with Meg Wagstaff at his side, pushed his father's wheelchair down the stark stone hallway to the jail infirmary. Leaving the Jupiter Ball where laughter and music reigned for this dark, sad place . . . At the doorway, he let the lady, as out of place in her black evening gown as he was in a tux, precede him into the cell-like room. The family chauffeur waited outside, hat in hand. The smell of pine cleaner overpowered the room and made Gabe queasy. Rooney leaned negligently against the rear wall. The doctor blocked Gabe's view of the patient, who lay in the middle cot.

Out of the corner of his eye, Gabe watched Miss Wagstaff. She'd frozen just inside the door, staring at what she could see of Del beyond the doctor.

Gabe moved closer to see for himself. Delman was his responsibility and he'd failed to keep him safe.

Meg approached the doctor. "May I see him please?"

"Meg?" Delman's thin voice whispered.

The doctor stepped back. Meg took Del's black hand in hers. "How did it happen?"

"Jumped me," Del muttered.

Meg looked up at the physician. "What have you done?"

"I sewed up his shoulder. He lost blood and he'll be laid up for a week or two."

Gabe's sense of responsibility weighed him down even more. "Where is his cellmate?"

"Delman knocked him unconscious," the doctor continued. "Fortunately, the guard heard the fracas. He separated them and confiscated the homemade knife."

Meg looked faint. "How did he get into jail with a knife?"

Rooney scowled. "Who knows? These people knife each other. They don't know any better—"

In a flash, Meg faced him. *"Who are you?"*

Rooney smirked. "I'm Rooney. Deputy to the chief police."

"You?" The unbelieving tone she used made Rooney flush. He took a step toward her. Gabe moved to step between them. With a look, he warned Rooney back.

The lady stepped to Gabe's side, her hands balled into fists. "Let me give you a piece of advice, Mr. Rooney. My parents have a combined fortune of nearly fifteen million dollars. If anything further happens to Del, my family will turn all that loose on you."

Rooney gave her an ugly look. "Don't threaten me—"

"Rooney!" Father called out. "Don't think this wheelchair makes a difference. The only part of me that is crippled is my legs."

Gabe glared at Rooney and recalled that his first impression of Rooney had been never to turn his back to the man.

Father rolled closer to Rooney. "Don't think just because I've been out of commission for a few years that I can't shake things up. You know my contacts reach to the state house and all the way to Washington, D.C."

Rooney opened his mouth, then shut it.

Father fixed the man with a hard stare. "Now this is what I am going to do to insure my client's safety. After tonight in the infirmary, I want him moved to a cell by himself and I'll be hiring an around-the-clock, private guard—"

"You can't do that!" Rooney shouted.

Father held up his hand. In an ominously quiet voice, he warned, "Rooney, you know I can."

Relief trickled through Gabe. He'd rarely witnessed his father wield his influence to such an extent. Had Rooney forgotten what a stickler his father was about his clients, their rights and protection?

Rooney's jaw worked, but he said nothing.

"Now show me to the nearest phone." Father turned the chair himself. "Son, please stay with Miss Wagstaff while I contact the man I want to stay the night with Del."

Gabe nodded. He didn't want this case tainted further. Rooney barrelled out, cursing softly. Father and the doctor departed.

Gabe withdrew nearer the door. Meg drew closer to Del, then stroked his cheek. "Oh, Del . . ." Her voice trembled with tears. "If I could only take you home . . ." A sob stopped her voice.

"I'll . . . be—"

"No, you won't be all right." She dropped to her knees, her elegant gown pooling on the stone floor. Tears spilled down her cheeks. She bent her head and laid it on the cot beside Del's. "I can't stand to see you here . . . like this."

The woman's grief and tenderness toward the colored man jarred Gabe. It spoke of an intimacy he'd never seen between a young white woman and a young black man.

With effort, Delman lifted his hand and patted her shoulder. "Meg, Meggie, don't cry."

Then Gabe recognized the tone in Delman's voice, the same he'd use to comfort Belle. Miss Wagstaff had said she'd been raised by Delman's grandmother. Evidently, they had grown up relating as closely as brother and sister, a situation that shouldn't have been allowed to continue. The distance between the races, between them, should have increased as they grew into adults.

Delman rumbled, "Mr. St. Clair knows what he's doing."

Meg wiped her moist cheek with her hand.

"Now," Delman continued, "Meg, I want you to do what Mr. St. Clair says. He knows this city. We don't."

"I will, Del."

The woman's easy acceptance of Delman's instructions aggravated Gabe. Why couldn't she heed him when he tried to talk sense into her?

"How is Cecy's pregnancy going?" Delman asked in a comforting tone.

"She's on bed rest, but the doctor is still hopeful she'll deliver safely."

"I wish . . . I wish I could see them again."

The tone Delman used told Gabe clearly that the man thought he wouldn't see them again in this life.

"You will." Meg smoothed the covers around Delman's shoulders. "It won't be long and we'll be away from this dreadful place."

Gabe's father reentered the room. "Will you drive Miss Wagstaff home, son?"

"No! I —" she objected, rising.

Father held up a hand to halt her. "I'm staying to give definite instructions to the man I have called. Del will be quite safe with me and my man until then."

"Meg," Del murmured, obviously reminding her of her promise. She bent to kiss his forehead, then stood.

Shocked, Gabe said, stiffening, "I'll take Miss Wagstaff to her hotel, then return to help you."

Father shook his head. "No, I'll manage. I want Miss Wagstaff safely in her hotel."

"Certainly." Gabe stepped forward. "Come, Miss Wagstaff."

She made one final adjustment to Delman's blankets.

Turning the situation over in his mind, Gabe led her to his car and drove away. Gabe didn't know what to say to this woman, now reclining like a sleek cat on the car seat. At first glance, her backless evening gown appeared to be what had drawn men to her. But if Meg Wagstaff had worn a drab dowdy gown, she'd still have garnered admirers. No one would call her beautiful or even pretty. The only term that came close was "striking." Her attraction wasn't in her features. So much of Meg Wagstaff lay beneath the surface, a vibrant personality wrapped in an elegant form. This was her allure.

And it wasn't the first time he'd experienced this in a woman. Lenore had been the first. He recalled that awful dawn when he'd become aware of Lenore in her nursing uniform beside his cot. In that moment of acute awareness, the force of her personality had overwhelmed him, drawing him to her once and forever.

At the memory, Gabe's pulse quickened. A peculiar mix of discontent and awareness keyed him up. Moonlight illuminated dozens of the glossy beads on her gown. Meg turned toward him, her pale skin glowing against the night. She'd teased him with a kiss earlier. What would her lips taste of now?

But the image of her stroking the black man's cheek had burned itself on to his brain. It bothered him. Why? Was it just the crossing of the color line or more personal? Had he wished it had been his cheek?

Meg broke the silence. "That Rooney isn't to be trusted." Gabe longed to disagree, but words of denial caught in his throat.

"I see." Her tone pronounced her understanding of Gabe's dilemma. "Doesn't it strike you as ominous that Del was attacked?"

"These things happen," he said tightly.

"Especially around a man like Rooney."

Gabe didn't want to be separated from this woman—just why this was so eluded him. And he knew his destination, a spot he'd become familiar with while a student at Tulane. "I can't go back to the ball. But I don't want to go home."

Meg instantly agreed with him. Tears still so close and her nerves jumped in her hollow stomach . . . Facing all the fashionable people was unthinkable. Going back to her solitary hotel room to watch the hours inch by till morning . . . She covered her burning eyes with her hands. "Where did you want to go?"

"Alice's. It's a little café on Tchoupitoulas Street."

Exhausted, she simply spoke her thoughts, "I haven't eaten all day. I still don't have an appetite, but I can't go back to the hotel."

Meg watched the light from the full moon flicker over St. Clair's somber face. Gabriel St. Clair possessed that born-to-privilege arrogance that never failed to irritate her. She'd grown up in a mansion on Nob Hill but when she was thirteen, she had picked melons with migrant workers in preparation for her first article in her father's muckraking journal. All her life, she had moved in two separate worlds, San Francisco society and the regular world where people weren't born with silver spoons in their *houses*, much less their mouths.

Tonight St. Clair had revealed something she hadn't thought possible. "I've heard you were in France?"

"Why talk about France? It's over and war stories bore people."

Like Del, Gabriel had served, suffered in France. Not even a hero like Sergeant York could return from the Great War without dragging sacks of pain along home. Did that explain why Gabe was so adverse to change? Had so much altered inside him, that the outside world must stay the same or his world might career out of control? She'd experienced that feeling three times in her life: her mother's death, the 1906 earthquake, and the day . . . Her mind stuttered on this thought. The third shattering loss still throbbed too fresh, too raw.

She glanced at St. Clair. A question to ask him popped into her mind. Would she, could she ask it?

He parked the car on the narrow street across from a brightly lit café. Inside, the restaurant was long and narrow with rough brown-red brick walls on two sides, and a counter with round, red-leather-covered stools. The other wall had a half-dozen booths. The café's cozy atmosphere smoothed Meg's frayed nerves. St. Clair led her to a booth at the rear. "Shall I help you with your wrap?"

Inwardly, she grinned at his proper tone. His disapproval of her backless gown made him hesitate to "expose" her here. "You may help me off with it, then drape it over my shoulders." Then they sat down opposite each other in the oak-paneled, high-backed booth. A tall, slender black woman came up with menus.

"Alice's biscuits and red-eye gravy is excellent," Gabe suggested.

The thought of red-eye gravy nearly wiped out Meg's already-touchy appetite. "I think I might be able to eat some dry toast and poached eggs."

"You should eat more."

"I lost my appetite in France."

He grunted and ordered biscuits and gravy.

What are you hiding, Gabriel St. Clair? Or who?

Holding the warm, white china mug in her hands made Meg realize how chilled she had become by the cold. Looking up, she found her companion gazing at her. She grinned. "After earlier events, I didn't expect that you and I would be breaking bread together tonight." As soon as the words escaped her mouth, she regretted them. "Sorry. Can you think of a neutral topic?"

"What you are interested in?"

"I'm interested in buying a car."

In the act of lifting his coffee cup to his lips, he paused. "A car?"

She grinned. "Is this another touchy subject?"

"No." He sipped his coffee. "You might try Abbott Automobile on Baronne Street. They advertise that they are the oldest automobile dealer in the South."

"Thank you." *A straightforward answer from St. Clair. Progress.*

He frowned. "There is one thing tonight I wish you hadn't said."

"What's that?" Would he say something to spoil their truce?

"The part about your parents' wealth. Was it true?"

She nodded. "What's your concern?"

"Possibility of kidnapping. That amount of wealth is . . . unusual here. Many people have genteel fortunes in New Orleans—"

"Like your family?"

"Like my family," he agreed. "But fifteen million dollars plus the fact you don't have any family ties here might make you a prized target."

"I wasn't really thinking just then," she admitted. "Rooney is a bully and I wanted to intimidate him. I suppose subconsciously I chose my family's wealth as the biggest club I could shake in his face."

"I don't think . . . I don't know . . ." his voice petered out. "I'm tired."

For the first time, she noticed the gray shadows under his eyes. *Do you sleep at night, Gabriel? Or do you dream of the whine of falling shells?* If she asked the question she longed to, would he answer?

The waitress brought St. Clair his biscuits and gravy and Meg's dry toast and poached eggs. The white plate with the yellow yolks with firm whites and golden toast looked like an advertisement in a magazine. Meg sighed deeply. "Just what my stomach ordered. Thank you." A pleasant hum of voices and clinking of china filled the air around her. Meg felt as though her stomach had earlier collapsed in on itself and now began to expand.

Swallowing a bite of toast, she relaxed against the cool, high back of the booth. Her eyes drank in St. Clair; their booth became an island of peace. The simple food satisfied her, a sensation she hadn't experienced for months. But finally at her nod, he rose, helped her into her wrap again. She wondered how it would feel to have Gabriel St. Clair's arms around her for more than a fox-trot.

Out in the darkness of the frosty January night, she clung to his arm and leaned into his strength. For a few moments, she allowed herself the illusion that she was protected and loved. Again. And who was he thinking of, remembering?

A short drive passed. He helped her out at the entrance of her hotel. At the curb, she paused beside him and asked the question that had been on her mind all through their meal, "What was her name?"

"What?" He scowled at her.

She walked past him, then turned back. "His name was Colin."

Chapter 8

Wrapped up in her thick cardigan, Meg wandered through the open-air stalls at the French Market. Only a mission of importance to Del's case would have dragged her here. A hundred voices called out their wares, "Chicken! *Poulet*! Sweet ham! *Jambon*! Turtle! Turtle eggs! Grouper!" The pushing and shoving of the shoppers, the loud voices, the odor of fish. Over tiny stoves standing on tripods, black women cooked fried oysters and fish. They looked tempting, but her empty stomach felt like a tightly knotted drawstring purse.

Last night, in spite of what had happened to Del, she'd been able to eat and slept soundly until morning. When Meg had gone down for a late brunch, she'd received a note from the desk clerk. The note had said simply: "Meet me at the French Market near the fish stalls after lunch." No signature. Was this some trick? Gabe had mentioned kidnapping last night, so Meg had slipped her derringer into her sweater's large pocket, within easy reach. If she stayed in plain sight and in the midst of so many witnesses, no one could lure her out of the market to the nearby river's edge. Still she glanced suspiciously over her shoulder. *Stop that.*

Over an hour later by her watch, she wondered if the note had merely been a prank or a ruse. "Meg," a low voice spoke beside her ear.

Meg halted, turning her head. Standing beside her was the pretty girl who'd worn a red dress at Penny Candy. "You know my name?" she asked amid the raucous voices all around.

"You're Meg. Del showed me your photograph once. I'm LaRae. Del and me . . . was close. He was gone take me to Chicago with him. I can sing . . . a little."

"Del didn't tell me—"

"He wouldn't say nothin'. He'd try to protec' me."

"Protect you from what?"

LaRae shook her head. "Can't tell. It would only get you in more danger than you're already in."

"I'm in danger?"

"Don't never come to the Penny Candy again. That's what I come to say." Her large, dark eyes scanning the market, the girl edged away.

Meg caught her arm. "Please, won't you tell me what you know?"

"I can't . . . I mean, I don't known nothin' more than Del. Leave New Orleans."

Meg tried to hold on to her, but LaRae pulled away and disappeared between two stalls, heading toward the riverside. Meg began to follow her, then froze in place. This girl could be the bait in a kidnapping attempt. Her heart pounding in her ears, Meg couldn't breathe in the crush of people. She pressed her folded hands against her lips. Jostled from behind, Meg spun around, thrusting her hand into her pocket.

"Pardon, Miss." A shopper bowed his head in apology.

Grasping the cold metal in her pocket, Meg shivered. She pushed her way through the throng, then out onto the banquette. Unfamiliar indecision paralyzed her where she stood. Across Jackson Square, gray and brooding St. Louis Cathedral and the historic Spanish government building, the Cabildo, loomed up on the opposite side of the grassy park surrounded by the black wrought-iron fence.

A tall, well-dressed man with his profile to her stood just inside the entrance to the park. Was that Corelli? No, it couldn't be. *My mind is running wild.* The idea that she was being watched sent icy tentacles up her spine.

A cab pulled up. "Taxi, Miss?"

Reacting to the request, Meg moved toward the taxi, then halted. What if this taxi driver had been paid to whisk her away from the French Market? She shook her head at him and stumbled backward.

Seeking cover in the jammed marketplace, she pushed back inside. She leaned against a rough wooden post while she tried to pull herself together. She trembled and it disgusted her. *Dear God, guide me. I'm all alone.*

When she could, she threaded her way back out to the curb. Walking to the corner, she hailed a cabby. She slipped into the rear seat and gave the driver the name of her hotel. As it pulled away from the curb, she thought she glimpsed Pete Brown, the piano player at the Penny Candy. He was staring at her. Did he want to talk to her, too? She waved. The man turned away pulling up his shabby collar. Was his being here just coincidence? Was it really Pete Brown? Was her mind beginning to let her down? How long could a person go barely sleeping, barely eating before one caved in, fell apart?

At half-past eleven that evening at Antoine's, a distinguished French restaurant which had opened in the 1840s, Gabe watched Meg enter, wearing a flowing costume of fine white linen, sandals, and under one arm a small box of ornately carved wood. The irony of her costume was not wasted on him. When she arrived in New Orleans, she'd opened Pandora's box.

This took him back to this morning when he'd been six minutes late for Simon LeGrand's court. Wiring money to France had proved more complicated and time-consuming than he'd anticipated. The judge's displeasure had irritated him, but wondering how to interpret last night's attack on Del was more upsetting. Since the advent of Miss Wagstaff into his life and Paul's letter, reality had tilted off-center.

"That isn't true," Gabe confessed silently. Reality, his old reality, had vanished soon after he'd arrived in France and hadn't yet returned. He kept telling himself it was just a matter of time. But was it? Would things here ever be the same? Not if he was able to find Marie.

Last night at Alice's, he'd almost spilled everything about Lenore and Marie to Meg Wagstaff. But he'd known her for such a brief time and she remained unpredictable. Why hadn't he just taken her home? Resisting the pull to go to her, now he turned away and went outside to wait for his parents' arrival.

Meg saw Gabriel walk away. And was glad. She had too much on her mind to fence with him now. LaRae's assignation today had prompted Meg to reexamine every minute she'd spent at the Penny Candy. Del's three friends had looked at her with ill-concealed alarm. Corelli who'd already known her name had been at pains to unnerve her. LaRae knew something dangerous about why Del had been framed for murder. Or why would she warn Meg to leave New Orleans?

With these thoughts buzzing in her mind, Meg greeted her hostess. Pandora's Ball was already in full swing. The restaurant had been decorated in amber and green with silk and fresh garlands of glossy green smilax. Along the walls garden benches nestled among a profusion of potted palms. Also the rich scents of French cooking took her back to the outdoor cafés along the Champs-Élysées.

Finding an empty bench by the wall, Meg sat back to let the colorful costumes distract her. Spanish dancers in flamenco costumes, eighteenth century French nobles—ladies in wide brocade skirts and white powdered wigs with towering curls and men in pastel silk stockings and satin knee breeches. Meg noticed that Corby Ferrand wore a black-and-white-striped prison costume. Where was Belle?

"Good evening, Miss Wagstaff," a cloying voice sounded beside her.

Meg turned to see Dulcine. "Miss Fourchette, what a lovely costume."

The blonde wore a blue antebellum dress with a hooped skirt and a white picture hat, tied with a wide blue ribbon. "This dress belonged to my great-grandmother, the first Dulcine."

Dulcine settled cautiously on the edge of the bench. A hoop skirt could be tricky. If Dulcine weren't careful, her dress could fly up in front—no doubt revealing ruffled pantaloons, probably also worn by the first Dulcine. Imagining Dulcine in that fix managed to amuse Meg, but she suppressed her grin.

"I hear that you persuaded Mr. St. Clair to allow his daughter to return to high school—"

What business is that of yours? "I must protest," Meg imitated Dulcine's oh-so-proper, sickeningly sweet tone. "I did nothing but soothe Belle's nerves and suggest she discuss the matter with her father."

Dulcine pursed her mouth. "Be that as it may, your influence has encouraged my cousin, Maisy, to also reenter high school—"

"Now, that is shockin'." Meg added Dulcine's southern accent to her imitation of the blonde's overbred speaking style. "What will New Orleans do with so many fair and educated ladies?"

Dulcine glared at her. "I might have expected you to behave in this way—"

"You expected me to behave just like this, didn't you? So you can tell everyone—behind my back—how unmannerly I am?"

"What an unpleasant remark." Dulcine stood up abruptly, causing her skirt to sway and billow precariously.

"Be careful or you'll embarrass yourself."

Without a backward glance, Dulcine sashayed away, her pretty little nose in the air.

Meg chuckled. But her amusement was shortlived. Worry over Del pressed down on her. In the early hours at Alice's, she'd felt the relentless pressure crushing her heart, loosen. But her sorrow over losing her first love also would not release her. *"My sweet Meg,"* *Colin whispered, his tender lips grazing her ear. "Let us be happy while* *we can."* Meg closed her eyes and leaned back against the wall. *Our* *time together was too brief.*

"Good evening, Miss Wagstaff."

Meg opened her eyes and gasped. "Belle, what a delightful costume."

Belle blushed. The debutante had come dressed as a powder puff in sheered pink satin. A hoop high around her shoulders continued down and all around, stretching the pink satin in a full circle. Belle wore pink silk stockings and pink gloves up the length of her arms. On her head, she wore a tight matching silk cap which covered her hair completely.

"It's the most imaginative costume here."

"I agree." Corby Ferrand in prison stripes and a flamboyant mustache appeared at Belle's elbow. The friendly convict puffed his chest out and offered Belle his arm. "May I escort you to the punch bowl?"

Beaming, Belle nodded and Corby led her away.

Meg saw Gabriel St. Clair observe this from across the room where he stood beside his parents. Picking up her box, she rose and went to join him. After his sharing Alice's with her, she'd glimpsed the man under his facade. But she must keep her distance. Gabriel St. Clair was the prosecution. She must not forget this fact merely because she'd eaten a late-night supper with him in blessed peace.

He exchanged polite greetings with her. "Your costume suits you."

Meg nodded but refused to pick up that gauntlet. Gabriel had come dressed as a gentleman at the time of the Louisiana Purchase. He wore a high white collar, a short fitted black coat with tails, and form-fitting, buff-colored knit breeches. The outfit showed off his athletic form and broad shoulders. Awareness of him skittered through her. She recalled leaning close to him last night, feeling his warmth and strength.

"Yours suits you, too." Before he could reply, she turned to his father. "I've received your message at my hotel. I'm glad Del's continuance was granted."

"Simon LeGrand is a stickler in court, but he is a reasonable man. I told you I didn't doubt I could get the continuance." Sands had come dressed in regular evening dress.

She stepped close to him and bent to whisper into his ear, "I need to tell you something."

"After dinner," he replied.

Dressed all in lavender with a tall pointed hat, like a lady in a fairy tale book, Mrs. St. Clair frowned. "I don't like Belle's outfit."

No doubt Mrs. St. Clair yearned to tell Meg to stay away from Belle, that she exerted a bad influence on her daughter. For a moment, a longing to be with Cecy welled up inside Meg. When Meg had been home in San Francisco, she had avoided being alone with her young, beautiful stepmother. Now Meg regretted this. Cecy would have been so kind, so understanding.

With a coy smile and a come-hither expression, Dulcine floated by in her antebellum gown. Meg expected Gabriel to follow her. The thought brought a distinct tug to her midsection. But he stayed at Meg's side. Why? She glanced at him. Had he begun to take Dulcine's true measure?

"Doesn't Dulcine look lovely?" Mrs. St. Clair cooed.

"Yes, she does," Gabriel agreed. "Miss Wagstaff, may I escort you to dinner?"

Meg stared at him. "If you wish." _But why?_

Taking his arm, Meg let herself escape into this moment of nearness. His short hair still showed a tendency to wave around his ears. Meg imagined her fingers tracing the patterns of those close-cropped curls.

When they were far enough away from Gabriel's mother, Meg teased him. "I'm certain your mother would prefer you escort Miss Fourchette."

"I'm old enough to make my own decisions."

Looking up at him, she studied his gray eyes, so soulful. Then she tilted her head, inquiring. "I agree. But are you escorting me to point this out to your mother?"

Meg located her name card on the table and sat down, greeting Emilie and her son-in-law, one on either side of her. After helping her with her chair, Gabriel bowed to Meg and drifted away to find his place. After dinner, Meg danced with Belle's young beau, then Emilie's son-in-law. Finally, she gravitated toward Sands and sat down beside him under a palm and the abundant glossy green smilax garland. "Alone at last," Meg murmured.

For a change of pace, the band began to play the rollicking Virginia reel and one of the musicians took the role of caller. Dulcine and Belle had switched places. Corby partnered Dulcine while Gabe went through the lively steps with his sister.

Sands grinned. "What do you have to tell me?"

"When I went to Penny Candy, I noticed a pretty young black woman who looked as though she wanted to talk to me. When your son escorted me outside to take me back to my hotel, I purposely said my hotel's name loudly, so she would know where to find me."

"How did she know who you were?"

"Del had shown her a photograph of me."

"I see. Did she find you?" Sands glanced toward the musicians.

On the dance floor, the dancers laughed and called encouragement to each other as they tried to follow the caller. With her eyes, Meg followed the twists and turns of the dance. The flamboyant costumes and smaller-than-usual dance floor put the wall decorations at risk. One garland hung askew already.

Meg brought her mind back to Sands. "She got a note to me early today, asking me to meet her at the fish stalls at the French Market after lunch. So I went."

"I wish you would have consulted me—"

"I woke late and you were due in court." Meg paused. In the dance, Belle shook her head good-naturedly at Gabriel. "Besides I took my derringer in my pocket."

"Heavens." Sands grimaced ruefully. "Modern women. Did she come?"

Meg nodded. "She told me I was in danger and to leave New Orleans."

"What kind of danger? From whom?" Sands demanded in an undertone.

"That's all she would say."

"Think back. Tell me everything she said."

Meg closed her eyes, concentrating against the rollicking tune of the Virginia reel. "She told me her name, LaRae. That she was a close friend of Del and that I should never go to Penny Candy, that I should leave New Orleans."

"That's all?"

"Essentially." The dancers began to swing their partners round and round.

Sands frowned. "Did you see anyone else you knew?"

"I thought I saw one of the musicians from Penny Candy and maybe Corelli, the new manager."

Sands's brows drew together, making him look grim. "I don't want you taking *any more* chances like this in the future. We don't know what slime we'll be digging into with Del's case yet. Understand me. You're not to run this kind of risk again." Sands's stern tone reminded her of her own father.

She nodded. "I won't."

In the country dance, Corby Ferrand miscalculated swinging Dulcine a little too wide. The back of her oversized hoop skirt rocked up and caught on the tail of a green garland. Instead of giving way, the garland didn't budge. Off balance, Dulcine stumbled, tried to catch herself, but down she went on her bottom. The garland released its hold. Her hoop skirt flew up in front, hiding the damsel's face, but revealing modern underwear.

The music cut off. The dance halted. Shocked gasps and laughter burst out. Meg pressed her hand over her own mouth, fighting laughter.

"*Oh! Oh!*" Dulcine's voice proclaimed her outrage.

Corby tried to help her up, and Belle rushed over, too. Gabriel finally succeeded in lifting Dulcine to her feet.

The blonde's face, flushed hot-red, twisted in an ugly expression. "How dare you?" she shouted at Corby. "Why didn't you watch what you were doing?"

Corby, glassy-eyed, tried to answer, but his mouth opened and closed wordlessly.

Belle stepped forward. "Dulcine, it was just an accident. I'm sure Corby's very sorry—"

Dulcine gave a fierce growl, silencing Belle. Reaching over, she snatched the pink satin cap off Belle's head. A collective gasp went through the room.

Dulcine, you're a fool. Then Meg realized Belle looked different. "She's bobbed her hair!"

Sands grunted. "The fat's in the fire now."

Chapter 9

Arriving at home, Gabe, his parents, and sister filed into Father's first-floor office. Orange-gold flames flickered in the hearth, a few low electric lights glowed against the dark wood and brown leather of this masculine sanctuary. They'd come here to thrash out the unpleasantness over Belle's haircut.

Still in costume, Gabe as a Creole gentleman, his mother as the medieval lady, and his sister as a pink powder puff arranged themselves as if the office were a courtroom. His mother took the lone armchair to the right, as prosecutor facing his father, who rolled behind his desk as judge. Since Belle had settled down next to Gabe on the short sofa at the other side of the desk, she had evidently chosen him as her defense lawyer. If this had been a moment for humor, Gabe would have chuckled at the almost theatrical scene, complete with costume.

"Mother?" The judge prompted the prosecution.

Tears seeped through Mother's words. "How could you cut your beautiful hair without one word?"

Dulcine's "uncapping" of Belle had been farce. Gabe wondered if Belle felt ridiculous dressed as a powder puff for this confrontation.

Belle sat hunched, her pink-gloved arms crossed. "It's *my* hair."

"That attitude won't work here," Father replied. "You're our daughter who is not yet an adult. Now, I want you to explain to your mother why you cut your hair when you knew this would displease her."

Belle glanced at Gabe as though asking counsel if she should plead the Fifth Amendment. Gabe shook his head. Belle sighed theatrically, "My cap didn't fit over my long hair. It ruined the whole look of the costume. So I crossed the street to Gray's Beauty Salon and had my hair cut and marcelled."

As a defense, it didn't have much to recommend it other than it proved lack of premeditation. Gabe knew this matter was very serious to his mother, but he couldn't help feeling it was much ado about nothing.

"Belle," Father began, "I understand that you think differently than we do, but as a young woman, no longer a child, you must consider how your *every action* will affect others."

Belle hung her head. "I'm sorry, Father, Mother," she said in a contrite voice.

"Now, Belle, no more surprises. Promise us." Father stared at Belle.

"I promise."

Gabe couldn't make the same commitment. Right now, he hoped Marie would be on her way to New Orleans in a matter of weeks, at most a month. How, when, could he break this news to his parents?

Mother sighed. "Well, after all it's only hair. It was just the shock."

"I think it was mean of Dulcine to embarrass me that way," Belle grumbled. "She knew my hair had been cut because she was at Gray's Salon at the same time."

This piece of information didn't set well with Gabe. He'd thought Dulcine had pulled off Belle's cap in innocent retribution, but if she'd known . . .

Father said, "Celestia, will you take Belle up with you? I'll come up in a few minutes." Mother gave both Gabe and his father assessing looks as she and Belle left. Gabe wondered what it meant.

Father turned his gaze to Gabe.

It penetrated Gabe like the rays of a hot summer sun. "What is it, sir?"

Father lifted his shoulder muscles, trying to loosen them. "What's bothering you, son?"

Gabe opened his mouth, but couldn't bring out any words.

"You haven't been yourself since you got home. At first, I thought it would just take time for you to get over your experience in France. But lately, I say something and you don't hear me . . ."

Father's questions sank beneath Gabe's surface like a barbed hook, catching him by surprise. Gabe locked up inside.

"Son, I've heard you call out in your sleep."

Gabe swallowed, but his mouth was dry. He'd thought he'd done such a good job of hiding his ragged nerves and ghoulish memories.

Father's gentle voice continued, "I didn't see much action in the Spanish American War, but I did go. That's why I wouldn't let your mother say anything when you enlisted."

Gabe managed to nod. A buzzing sounded in his ears.

Father turned his chair to stare into the glowing embers on the hearth. "Your grandfather lost a leg at Chickamauga. The day after I turned fourteen, he took me away on a hunting trip. But instead we sat and he told me about the war. I'll never forget that day.

"It demolished my illusions about the glory of war." Father gripped the armrests of his chair. "But it made it more difficult when it came time for me to leave for Cuba in ninety-eight. So . . ." Father looked Gabe directly in the eye: "I didn't tell you about your grandfather's or about my war experience. Did I do wrong?"

Gabe shook his head no.

Father propped his elbows on the arms of his chair, then his chin on his hands. "What is it, son?" Father's caring voice was low, barely a whisper.

Gabe's chest constricted. He couldn't take a deep breath. Too much bottled up inside.

"I read enough to know this war, your war, differed greatly from any before. Tanks, trench warfare, bombing from the air, mustard gas . . ." Father's voice faded. "Just remember I'm always ready to listen."

"I know." The words scraped Gabe's throat.

Father closed his eyes. In the ensuing silence, Gabe found comfort in his father's understanding. Not everything had changed. His father, an honest man, still loved him. Maybe the God his father had taught him about would hear Gabe's prayers and bring Marie safe to this home. Soon he would muster the courage to tell his father.

Opening his eyes, father broke the quiet, "You're upset by Miss Wagstaff's influence on Belle."

"I was."

"The world is changing. I think the war, your war, changed everything."

Whether we wanted it to or not. Gabe nodded.

"I want Belle to be ready to be a part of these new times."

"And Meg Wagstaff is the woman of the future?"

"Yes, women may have the vote for this year's presidential election. If so, in four years Belle will be old enough to vote in the next presidential election."

Gabe tried to imagine Belle walking into a voting booth. A different vision came instead. "I can see Meg Wagstaff voting." *Meg is equal to anything.* Gabe wished now he had given an honest answer to Meg's question, "What was her name?"

A smile burst over his father's face. "Exactly. I want Belle to learn from her." Father grimaced suddenly.

Gabe wondered if this evening had brought on one of his father's headaches, which might put him in bed for a day or two.

Father smiled ruefully at Gabe. "I've loved your mother since she was fourteen. But many times I have wished I could discuss my law cases and politics with her." Father sounded as if the final words he spoke pained him.

This thought struck Gabe as revolutionary. "Do you think that will ever happen?"

Father shook his head. "She's always insisted she couldn't understand the law or politics." Father sighed with audible weariness. "These social evenings take more out of me than a day in court."

"I'll get your man to help you to bed." Gabe went into the hallway and froze.

His mother stood just a few paces from the doorway. He didn't have to ask her if she'd overheard father. Fresh tears sparkled in her eyelashes. Her hands covered her mouth. His father would be grieved to know his words had been overheard by his wife and had wounded her. Gabe tried to think of something soothing to say.

She shook her head, then turned and slipped away, making no sound.

"Is there anything wrong?" Father's voice came from behind Gabe.

Gabe couldn't tell the truth. His mother had signified that plainly. But he couldn't lie either. "Sorry. I'll get your man." *Mother, oh, mother.*

Gabe allowed Meg's heavy, sweet fragrance to envelop him. Her French perfume made the gloomy parish jail less depressing.

"It's very kind of you to arrange this for me." Meg walked beside Gabe down the gray scuffed corridor to the cells.

"I knew you'd want to see your friend once he was moved out of the infirmary." His guilt over the attack on Del had prompted him. Plus he couldn't get the sensation of her leaning close to him on the street in front of Alice's out of his mind.

"What did the doctor say?"

"Delman will make a full recovery." *In time to hang.*

Meg glanced up at him as if she heard Gabe's harsh thought. He recalled, as he had countless times, her parting question to him after their supper, "What was her name?" He didn't believe in voodoo, so her needle-sharp insight must be because of their shared experience. *Who was Colin and what happened to him?*

Gabe nodded at the grizzled jailer who with a huge, old-fashioned key unlocked the last door before the cells. The man's circle of keys clanked as the lock turned, a chilling noise.

Meg passed through ahead of Gabe. He recognized a tall burly man his father had often employed as bodyguard sitting outside a cell. He murmured close to her ear, "That must be Delman's guard."

As they walked down the cement floor toward the man, prisoners stood up in the cells and eyed them. A low wolf whistle came from a prisoner to Gabe's right. Gabe glared at the man.

Meg looked neither right nor left.

He couldn't help but admire her aplomb. Not many women could look as cool, as composed in this hellhole. His father had been more than correct in his assessment of Meg Wagstaff.

Del's hired bodyguard stood up.

Gabe nodded to the man. "Miss Wagstaff, this is Mortimer Smith."

Meg startled Mortimer by shaking his hand. "Thank you for taking this job. I'm sure you're bored sitting here."

The ex-prize fighter grinned, showing two broken teeth. "Always like to work for Mr. Sands. He's a gent."

This pleased Gabe. His father's reputation had always been a shining example. If only he might not be a disappointment to his father. Rooney's recent behavior had caused Gabe, for the first time, to doubt his wisdom in taking a public position. "I'll leave now, but will be back in ten minutes to walk you out, Miss Wagstaff."

Meg nodded her assent. The man seemed almost human today. Mortimer motioned her to take his chair, then leaned back against the bars, staring at the other prisoners. The oppressive atmosphere of the bleak, damp jail cells settled over her. She sat down sideways on the straight-back chair, so she would be closer to Del as she faced him. Then stiffening her courage, she allowed herself to peer at him through the iron bars separating them. "How are you?" The phrase sounded pathetic in her ears.

His face looked drawn and ashen. He held himself stiffly. "I'm alive." Del's voice came out low. He cradled one of his arms in his lap.

"Is there anything you need or want?"

He stared at her, his expression stating clearly that she couldn't give him what he wanted—his freedom. She reached between the bars.

Del leaned away from her hand. "Don't touch me," he whispered.

"Can't keep your hands off him, can you?" One of the white prisoners taunted her with a vulgar name.

Meg turned to look at the man. Now she understood Del's warning. Her relationship to Del could only bring him abuse here.

And Meg had come because she needed information about LaRae. She whispered, "LaRae met me at the French market."

Del's head jerked up. "Where'd you meet her?" He hissed.

Meg kept her voice so low. "I went to Penny Candy."

"I'd like to shake you." Del's face contorted with frustration. "Don't you ever go there again."

When they were children, he'd always tried to protect her, too. She whispered, "I couldn't just sit here and let you wait for the noose. I will go wherever I need to and do whatever I need to."

"Leave it to Mr. Sands."

"Let me tell you what LaRae said. She wanted me to leave New Orleans. Why?"

"Because you should."

"Is Corelli the man LaRae's afraid of?"

"You met Corelli?" Del looked appalled.

"He introduced himself to me when I was at the Penny Candy."

"Don't you ever go there again."

"You're repeating yourself," Meg snapped. "How did Corelli get ownership of the nightclub after Mitch Kennedy was killed? Did Corelli kill—"

"Corelli is a poisonous snake. I told you to let Mr. Sands handle this."

Meg shut her mouth down tight and glared at Del. Why did men—even Del—have to be so stubborn? Should she ask Del about Pete Brown? No, he'd just tell her to stay away from him. A thought occurred to her. "Is LaRae in danger?"

Del gave her a troubled look. "I hope not."

"Del, how close were you and LaRae?"

His mouth straightened into a line. "That's not for you to ask."

"If she's dear to you, should I get her out of town? I could send her to my father."

Frowning, Del looked uneasy. "She thinks she's in love with me. I was letting her sing a song or two with us so she could get off the street."

That sounded like her Del. Always looking out for others. "Then should I send her to San Francisco?"

"You might put her in danger just by trying to contact her."

A cold stone dropped in the middle of Meg's stomach. "What if someone saw her talking to me?" Had Corelli, Pete Brown been there? Meg stared at Del. "If she's in danger, I think—"

Del shifted his position and pain crinkled up his face.

"Where can we get in touch with her?" Her oldest and dearest friend had been snatched beyond her control. She couldn't even bring him a cup of water here.

"I'll tell my lawyer to handle LaRae. I don't want you getting in any deeper."

"Del, I'm not a girl just out of school." Meg fought tears. "This is life and death for you. Do you think this is the first time I've faced death?"

A strange expression passed over Del's face. He stared back at her, then bent his head. "Do you ever think of my grandmother?"

Meg knew he was remembering the day they lost her . . . Aunt Susan, the day they'd faced death together.

"Meg, do you ever pray anymore?"

The question had startled her, but she had to admit the truth, "Yes." New Orleans had forced her to her knees. But her prayers had no power in them. She poured out her anguish and anger to God. Hadn't she and Del suffered enough?

Del stared at the floor. "I've been praying. I know my grandmother's offering prayers for me at the throne of God. I know God doesn't judge us here for what we do, but I think sometimes he tries to get our attention. Well, he's got mine now." His glance asked for her understanding.

She nodded, moved by his confiding in her.

"Would you find a church and ask for prayer for me?"

The question startled Meg. Del hadn't attended church since a few years before France. But she replied, "Yes."

Chapter 10

Gabe walked into the breakfast room, shadowy in bleak morning light, and sat down near his father. "What does the *Times Picayune* say today?"

"Prohibition is coming in days."

"I know. We're invited to the Demon Rum Ball."

Father made a face. "The *Picayune* barely mentions it. This Eighteenth Amendment should never have been passed. It will create an enforcement nightmare. New Orleans is a world port. Liquor will be shipped in illegally—by the fleet. The city should be hiring new officers right and left."

Gabe shook his head. "I don't see that happening what with the post-war depression we're in. Nobody would dare raise taxes to hire more police and that's what it would take."

Frowning, Father lowered the paper, his eyes pools of worry. "The body of an unidentified young black woman has been found in an alley behind Mitch Kennedy's club. She was shot in the back of the head."

Gabe put his coffee cup down. "An unfortunate coincidence."

"I don't believe in coincidences." Father tossed the paper onto the table. "Miss Wagstaff must go see that body."

Gabe came up out of his chair. "No!"

Without a backward glance, Father rolled out of the room with one wheel squeaking as though mocking Gabe.

Two hours later, between Meg and Gabe, Father pushed his chair the few yards to the imposing brick building. Gold-leaf lettering read, "Morgue." They entered and the coroner in a white lab coat glanced up over gold-wire glasses. Gabe hoped this ordeal wouldn't be too much for Meg. She seemed all skin and nerves. A tenseness grew in him, keying him up. He tried to shake it off.

The bleak, unadorned room was making Meg's heart skip in funny little jerks. *Please, Lord, don't let this be LaRae.*

"Shall we get this over with, then?" Sands asked.

His heels tapping on the cement floor, the coroner led them over to a high metal table, which had been covered with a dingy white sheet. He folded back the sheet enough to expose the woman's head.

Meg forced herself to look. Dark, bloodless skin against white cloth. LaRae lay silent on the cold, metal table. Black spots wavered and danced before Meg's eyes.

Gabe caught her. She didn't push him away. The side of her slender body pressed against him, her perfume overriding the clinical odor.

"Miss Wagstaff, I take it you are able to identify this unfortunate young woman," the corner asked her.

"Her name is . . . was LaRae."

"Her surname name?"

She shook her head. "Del . . ."

"Del would know?" Sands supplied, looking stern.

She nodded.

"Just because they knew each other," Gabe objected, "that doesn't mean the two deaths are related. It's just a coincidence."

Father looked to Gabe. "Not deaths, murders. I told you, Gabriel, I don't believe in coincidence. I'll go over to see Del now. If he and this young woman were more than mere acquaintances, I think it would be better if he heard the news from me. Would you take Meg Wagstaff back to her hotel?"

Though Gabe nodded, he expected Meg to insist on going with his father. Instead, she remained leaning against him. Outside once more in the mist, Gabe sat in his car, his nerves spinning like a propeller. Beside him, Meg sat huddled next to the passenger door. Where had his sleek cat gone? *I can't leave her like this*. Or did he need her, too?

He started the engine and headed away. How much more could happen before Mardi Gras 1920?

"I saw her just days ago. So lovely," Meg murmured.

Death had made a mockery of the young black woman's beauty. No sweet words could rub away what they'd seen today.

"I'm so afraid I caused her death."

He sent her a sharp glance. "Why do you think that?"

She rubbed her forehead. "I spoke to her . . . about Del. Maybe someone saw us together."

"Why would that have caused her death?"

"I can't speak about this anymore. Not to you."

Gabe understood. Meg believed someone other than her friend, Del, had killed Kennedy and now she believed that same mysterious someone had killed Del's friend. Why?

"Don't you have to be at your office or court?" she asked, sounding half asleep, so unlike the decisive Meg Wagstaff he'd come to know.

"It's Saturday."

Closing her eyes, she leaned back. "Saturday. My days have all lost their identity. I don't have a life here."

Her sentence put into words what he had been feeling since he returned from France. Gabe glanced ahead. "Do you want to go back your hotel?

"No."

He drove west. The reason he wanted to keep her with him still fluttered vague, insubstantial in his consciousness. Somehow this woman had become key, but to what? "I'm taking you to Over the Rhine, a restaurant. It will take us out of, away from—"

"From this place of death?"

He refused to respond. Death happened everywhere, not just in France. Pushing away thoughts of Lenore in her lonely grave, he drove on. He parked his car to the rear of the restaurant, a one-story building in the Louisiana style—many chimneys and a low porch across the front of the white restaurant.

Gabe gripped her arm and drew her inside. Seated at a table for two beside a cozy fireplace, Gabe ordered coffee for him and tea for her. He waited for their drinks to come before he spoke to her again. He didn't know what he wanted to say to her yet, but she drew him irresistibly.

Meg sipped her tea and, finally, looked up into his face. "Thank you."

He nodded. Did he want to speak to her about Lenore, Marie? Words floated just beyond his reach. Instead of opening this painful topic, he reached for her. She let him fold his fingers around her black kid-gloved hand. Touching her took the edge off his need. "You're cold."

"How is Belle?"

The question caught him off-guard.

"Is your mother still angry over Belle's haircut?"

He said honestly, "I thought the whole fuss was ridiculous. Belle's bob is not world-shattering news."

She smiled at him.

This was the first true smile she had ever given him—not mocking, not teasing. It warmed through his heart down to his toes. He yearned to draw her fingers to his lips. With his thumb, Gabe traced the soft flesh beneath Meg's thumb.

Meg slipped her fingers between his, weaving their two hands together. This took his breath away. She craved his touch, too.

She leaned back in her chair. "Do you know of a Negro church? Del wanted me to find him a church and to ask for prayer."

With his fingertips, he traced her knuckles in circles, the kid leather like butter. "I believe the largest black church in New Orleans is the Mount Zion A.M.E. I believe that's where our servants worship."

The waiter brought their generous bowls of rich creamy soup and a basket of warm hard-crusted rolls, white and pumpernickel. "You seem to know all the best places to eat," she teased.

"I was hungry." More words, intimate ones ribboned through his mind. Finally, the reason he'd wanted her with him stood out in his thoughts. She drew her hand from his. He felt the loss of her touch. He watched her draw off her gloves, finger by finger. For the first time, he recognized how intimate this simple act could be. He asked, "Who was Colin?"

Chapter 11

Shocked, Meg searched Gabriel's intense gray eyes.

"I asked you a question that evening."

"You asked, 'What was her name?'"

"And?" Meg prompted, hoping he'd be candid.

"You won't tell me who Colin was, then?"

All right. I'll go first. "Colin Deveril was a son of Viscount Lynton of Derbyshire."

Lenore Moreau was from Versailles near Paris. "Did he make promises to you he didn't keep?"

Her heart skipped a beat. Had Gabriel made promises he hadn't kept? "Gabriel, talking about Colin is too deep for casual conversation over lunch."

He nodded. "I apologize. Eat. My mother says a light breeze could blow you away."

"For once, I agree with her." Meg closed her eyes, savoring the chicken soup with its celery and sprinkle of nutmeg. Maybe after lunch, she'd be able to think about how to help Del, how to judge what was evolving between her and Gabriel, Del's adversary.

Only a few other couples had driven out on the soggy Saturday. Meg watched a young couple sitting at a table behind Gabriel's left shoulder. Their hesitating movements and forced chatter broadcast their uncertainty about themselves and each other. She'd been a better actress. Colin had thought her older and experienced in flirtation. At present, the boldly handsome, but secretive man across from her wanted to know her secrets, but would he divulge his?

Soon he helped her on with her black coat. Lingering with her back to Gabriel, she didn't want him to remove his strong hands from her shoulders, but Del stood between them. And Gabriel's secrets.

Outside in the sodden cold, she walked close beside him again. He glanced down at her. "Are you still interested in buying your own vehicle?"

She couldn't believe her ears. "Do you mean it?"

"Yes."

She nodded. Soon they were driving back into town. Gabriel parked near a classy car dealership. Inside the windowed showroom, she walked beside him down a line of three shiny black new automobiles.

"What can we do for you today, sir?" a well-dressed salesman with his hair slicked back with Brilliantine asked Gabriel.

"Miss Wagstaff would like to buy a runabout for town use." Gabriel nodded to her.

"Well . . . well, how about that?" The salesman firmed his square jaw, evidently ready to sell his first car to a lady. "How about a Cadillac? It's reliable and easy to drive."

Meg said, "I'd like to take it for a drive first."

This also seemed to throw the salesman off-stride. "Of course," he recovered. "The gentleman would be accompanyin' you, wouldn't he?"

Meg grinned. "Gabriel, do you trust me to drive you around the block?"

Gabriel grinned back at her. "That depends, Miss Meg. How long have you been driving?"

Meg recognized the subtle teasing in his tone. "My father began teaching me when I was fourteen and I drove a YMCA truck all over France."

"Then, I'll be happy to accompany you."

The salesman goggled at them.

Meg bought the Cadillac. Outside, as she and Gabriel walked back to his car, she said, "I'll have to ask the hotel manager where I can park my new car."

"I think you should hire a driver, then he could park it near his residence and pick you up in the mornings."

"I can drive myself."

He smiled. "You drive excellently. But just think how hard it is to find a parking place in New Orleans."

"I hadn't thought of that." She studied him, trying to judge his motives. She was sure it was about more than finding a parking spot.

The evening of the Demon Rum Ball had come. In her newest black evening gown purchased at Maison Blanche, New Orleans's foremost department store, Meg dragged herself through the country club entrance. She was nearly two hours late; she'd not been the same after LaRae's funeral that afternoon. And to make her feel even worse, when she had asked for her key, the hotel clerk had presented her with her first poison pen note—anonymous, of course. The note had warned her about staying where she wasn't welcome. Who'd sent it?

The ballroom had been strung with black crepe paper streamers and red-gold silk draped along the walls and overhead like a canopy. Walking inside felt like stepping inside a blazing sunset with the cool, risky fingers of night just closing around her throat. The unusual decorations tightened Meg's already raw nerves.

As she gave the hat-check girl her wrap, Meg noticed Dulcine in a demure cornflower blue dress approaching. Miss Dulcine's scheming sweet-butter-wouldn't-melt-in-my-mouth mask was beginning to wear thin. Meg was starting to think Gabriel didn't deserve such a conniving woman as his wife.

"Miss Wagstaff," Dulcine greeted her with a prim smile.

Meg's frustration bubbled up and loosened her reckless tongue. "Call me Meg—please. After viewing your unmentionables, I don't think we need stand on ceremony."

Dulcine's eyes narrowed, but her evening-gala smile stayed tacked in place.

Meg started away, her silken gown rippling around her as she moved. A Frenchman had advised her—in order to catch a man's eye—always to judge a dress in motion. Would Gabriel prefer chaste cornflower blue or sinuous black silk?

Dulcine followed along beside Meg.

"Is there something you wanted to ask me?" Meg paused. LaRae's funeral had left Meg edgy, moody.

Dulcine's pretty eyes widened. "Oh, my mother is giving a tea party in two weeks. If you'd still be in New Orleans, she wants to send you an invitation."

"Well done." Meg gave Dulcine a measured look. "You veiled your curiosity about my departure perfectly." Meg began walking again. "Thank your mother. I may still be in town, but everything depends on my friend Del's case—"

Dulcine pulled her face down into a moue. "I don't know if you realize—"

The insinuating tone Dulcine used made Meg halt. "What don't I realize, Dulcine?"

"Your involvement with that jazz musician, a Negro charged with murder, is affecting how people view the Fourchette and St. Clair families."

"You're making that up."

"I know what I'm talking about."

Meg longed to wipe the sanctimonious, pseudo-sympathetic expression off Dulcine's face. "You know." Meg leaned close to the blonde. "I was going to say, 'Take him. I don't want him.' But this is too much. You don't deserve Gabriel St. Clair."

Dulcine's pouty, pretty face burned fiery red.

Meg sauntered away, churning with unspoken insults. The fanfare of a trumpet stopped Meg, along with everyone else in the ballroom, and she turned to view the entrance.

With an empty liquor bottle in his hand Corby entered, dressed all in black except for a crimson sash across his chest that read "Demon Rum." Was Prohibition something to laugh about?

The band began to play, "When the Saints Go Marchin' In." Corby swaggered around waving his bottle. Other young men dressed as policemen with nightsticks, bartenders, obvious drunks, and one man in an old-fashioned dress and bonnet with a hatchet impersonating Carry Nation, pushed in behind him. All converged on

Corby either to protect or attack him. People laughed and shouted encouragement to the broad slapstick.

The scene from LaRae's funeral came back to Meg full force. After the funeral service, she stepped out on the top step of Mount Zion church. Gabriel had appeared at her side. He had walked beside her the whole way to the peculiar above-ground cemetery. As the funeral procession made its way to the cemetery, a New Orleans band had played jazz, ragtime, and spirituals she learned as a child.

"Miss Wagstaff."

Interrupted, she looked up into Gabriel's unwavering eyes. "I was just thinking of you," she murmured. Why had he come to LaRae's interment? Had he come as her friend or as the parish attorney?

Gabe could tell from the haunted look in Meg's eyes that she was recalling the funeral. After LaRae's funeral, he had found a telegram from Paul waiting for him at his office. He needed someone to talk to. In his mind, Gabe practiced an opening, "Meg, I have a problem. I need some advice . . ." But no matter how he told the story, it made him sound like a shirker. *I wouldn't have left if I'd known. Will Meg believe that?* "I don't think we're in the right mood tonight for this."

Meg pressed a hand to her forehead. "Doesn't anyone here understand that this is real life?"

Could he speak to her of Lenore and Marie tonight? The telegram sat in his pocket, a stick of dynamite to his life. "I don't think anyone here believes that there will really be no more liquor after tonight."

Squeals of laughter exploded behind them. "Don't they realize that this means alcohol will . . . become more expensive, dangerous?"

Gabriel had gone to France looking for danger. He understood its lure for Corby and the other young men here. "Let's go out onto the terrace. Fresh air might help—" *Let me tell you about Lenore.*

Gabriel eased her through the clusters of people laughing over Corby's antics. Outside, she stood beside Gabriel. "I shouldn't have come tonight, but I couldn't just sit at the hotel."

"I'm glad you came." Knowing Meg would be here had made him come. If anyone in New Orleans could understand about Lenore and Marie, she could.

"I'm glad, so grateful you came this afternoon to the funeral." Meg touched his sleeve. "But why did you come?"

He put a hand over hers, keeping her near. *To protect you.* "I was curious to see who would show up for the funeral."

Meg frowned at him. The glow of electric light from inside illuminated his tense face. Pete Brown and LaVerne Mason had come. LaVerne had watched her from afar with the same fascination one would concentrate on a cobra being piped from its basket by a charmer. Both had steered clear of her until . . .

"I have someone in mind to take on the job of driver for you. Have you given my advice any thought?"

She stared at him. When she had come to New Orleans her mission had been simple, she would get things cleared up and take Del home. How had matters gotten so complicated? She no longer felt equal to the task. "Yes."

"Yes, you want a driver?" he asked tartly. "Or, yes, you thought about it?"

"Both." Was she doing more harm than good in New Orleans? Had she triggered someone to kill LaRae or was it just a coincidence? She must to talk to Sands about what she'd been told at the funeral, and something she'd noticed.

"Good. I'll have Jack Bishop report to your hotel tomorrow morning."

Meg saw again LaRae's coffin being slid headfirst into a stone mausoleum in the above-ground crypt. The mourners around her had sung, "Crossing over Jordan, what did I see, comin' for me for to carry me home? A band of angels comin' for me—coming for to carry me home. Swing low, sweet chariot . . ." A cheer rang out from inside the ballroom. Meg's eyes flew open. Demon Rum, Corby, had been shoved into the coffin. The policeman lowered the lid.

"No," Meg gasped. *I don't want anyone else to die.* "I'm so frightened."

"I know," Gabe whispered. *I must tell her, she'll help*. His impossible desire to hold Lenore gripped him.

He pulled Meg to him. Holding the back of her silken head in his hand, he bound her to him with an arm tight around her tiny waist. He gently brushed her soft lips. Tears he hadn't shed for Lenore in France trickled down his cheeks.

She pressed closer to him.

His arms felt how frail, how delicate she was. This took the edge from his need. His hold on her gentled to a sheltering embrace. "Lenore," he whispered.

"Gabriel?" Belle's voice came from behind him, shocking him back to the present and to what he'd just let slip from his lips.

Meg looked up at him with startled eyes. Still, with her gloved hands, she wiped away the evidence of his tears.

He let her go and turned to see his sister blushing in the doorway. "What is it, Belle?" His voice sounded funny in his ears.

"Dulcine says mother wants you."

Gabe excused himself and, without meeting anyone's eyes, went back in through the French doors.

"I'm so sorry," Belle stuttered. "I would never have come out if I had known Gabe was kissing you."

Meg stalked past Belle. "He wasn't really kissing *me*."

Chapter 12

Ready to spit fire, Meg followed Gabe inside the ballroom. When he reached his mother—surprise, surprise—Dulcine just happened to appear beside Gabe. The band struck up a lively two-step. Did

Dulcine deem her such a weak sister? Meg strolled up boldly. "Gabriel, this is the dance I promised you."

Dulcine tried to hide her chagrin and failed.

Looking puzzled, Mrs. St. Clair smiled. "Of course, son."

As stiff as a tin man, Gabriel bowed and led Meg to the couples pairing up and beginning to dance.

"Don't I get a thank-you for getting you away from the persistent Dulcine?" Meg demanded as she bounced in time to the rhythm.

He grimaced. "Didn't your stepmother teach you any society manners?"

"Yes, and in addition to learning which fork to use for which course, she taught me to be honest. It's time you were honest with me and with yourself."

"Who gave you the right to lecture me?"

"You did."

His neck turned red. "You mean when I kissed you on the terrace?"

"Did you kiss *me* on the terrace?" Meg raised one eyebrow.

"What do you mean? Of course, I kissed you on the terrace. Who else?"

"Her name was—"

He tightened his hold on her. "Don't pry."

"Don't lie."

They finished the dance in silence. In the early morning hours, the Demon Rum Ball began to limp toward its end. Meg sat alone against the red-orange silk wall and slipped into the pervading ennui she'd felt since her first year in France. She hadn't talked privately with Sands yet. All evening, people had monopolized him. A swirl of white silk sat down beside her.

"Meg, may I have a word with you?" Belle said. Meg nodded. Belle wouldn't meet Meg's eyes. "Corby told me he thinks he's falling for me."

Meg didn't feel capable of dealing with this right now, but what choice did she have? "What about you? Are you falling for him?"

"He's such a sheik, what if someone else decides to steal him away? What if he won't wait for me?" Belle's words came out in a rush.

Had Belle's burst of independence already failed with so little cause? Meg stood up. Mrs. St. Clair had left her husband's side and headed toward the hat check.

Belle jumped up, too. "What if Corby doesn't want to marry a woman with a career?"

"I must speak to your father now, then go home." She smiled at Belle. "Being an adult means making difficult choices on your own." I *better take my own advice. Sands needs to know what I heard at LaRae's funeral.* Meg made her way to Sands. "I'm worried."

"About Del?"

Mrs. St. Clair came with her dark sable evening wrap around her shoulders. "Oh! Miss Wagstaff, we were just leaving."

"Celestia, Miss Wagstaff will come home with us. I want a few moments alone with her in my office."

His wife hiding her surprise, the three of them started away. Soon, Meg sat beside the chauffeur. "What about Belle?"

Mrs. St. Clair replied, "Gabriel offered to bring her home soon."

At the St. Clair home, Meg perched in the wing-back dark leather chair in front of Sands's desk. One green-shaded desk lamp lit the room, casting deep shadows. "Today has been dreadful."

"I take it that you are referring to the funeral?"

Meg let out a dejected sigh and lowered her chin. "I went to pay my respects and Del's, but I also wanted to see who else came to the funeral."

"Tell me, who came to LaRae's funeral you know?"

"Two other musicians who played with Del—Pete Brown and LaVerne Mason."

"Did they speak you?"

A shiver shook Meg. "Pete passed by me and said, 'This is all your fault.'"

Sands stared at her over his folded hands. "Go on."

"LaVerne told me, 'Leave town before you get us all killed.'"

"Interesting."

Meg's temper cracked wide open. "Interesting? Now LaRae's death is on my conscience."

"Why? You didn't put a bullet in the back of her head. Did you think this was going to be a Sunday-school picnic?"

This question shocked her. "I expected to get Del out of this and back home without more people dying."

"Murder begets murder. Someone murdered Mitch Kennedy. Why? Someone killed LaRae. Why? I think the killer is the same or connected to both. But how?"

Sands's harsh voice unnerved her, but his words had proven true. "What should I do?"

"I don't want you going to Storyville by yourself again." Sands's calm voice enumerated the dangers she faced. "If someone contacts you, I want you to come to me first—no matter what. I'm going to see about hiring a car and driver for you—"

She dug her nails into her palms. "Gabriel . . . your son, helped me buy a Cadillac and he's hired a driver."

Sands's eyebrows lifted. "Who?"

"Jack Bishop. Have you heard of him?"

"Of course. He's one of the men I hire as a bodyguard for my clients."

Meg recoiled as though she'd been slapped. "Why do you need bodyguards for your clients?"

"Because I sometimes represent unpopular people or ones other people wish to silence."

"Like Del?" *Like me?* She swallowed and found her mouth dry.

He nodded. "I'm not afraid of standing out in the crowd. I have the feeling you aren't either."

Numbly, Meg nodded. "You think that I may be a target, then?" She had rejected this before, but now she forced herself to believe it.

"I think it is safer if we assume that."

Safer? She'd felt safer on the Western Front.

Mrs. St. Clair tapped on the door, then opened it. "Sands, it's really time you were resting. I'm sure Miss Wagstaff—"

"You're right, Celestia, but I'm inviting Miss Wagstaff to spend tonight in our guest room. I don't want her out in a car this late."

Celestia nodded. "Of course, she's most welcome. Sands, I will send your man in. Miss Wagstaff, if you will follow me, I will take you to a guest room."

The lady's easy agreement helped Meg accept. She wanted to refuse, but the thought that both Gabriel and his father believed she needed a bodyguard had sobered her.

As Meg followed Mrs. St. Clair upstairs, she turned this fact over in her mind—even though Gabriel was the prosecution, he had decided she needed a bodyguard. Did he know something that she didn't?

Outside home, Gabe noted the light on in his father's office. Was Meg in there now? "Here you are, sis. See you in the morning." Belle pouted. He reached across and pushed open her door.

She got out and closed the door behind herself. "Don't do anything I wouldn't do," she teased him.

"This younger generation," he answered in kind. Sliding the car into gear, he headed back to town. He'd seen Meg leave the ball with his parents, so she should be safe. And in the morning, Jack Bishop would be on the job.

Tonight, Gabe wanted to have a look at Storyville for himself and do a little fishing. He'd recognized one unwelcome face at the funeral. Had the man merely been an acquaintance of the dead girl or more? Gabe needed new information. And maybe some Basin Street jazz would settle his nerves.

He parked his car on Canal under a streetlamp. From under his seat, he drew out a pistol, cool and heavy in his palm, and slipped it into his evening jacket pocket. Stepping out of his car, he set his shiny black top hat on his head at a jaunty angle. Unless someone recognized him as the parish attorney, he'd just be another *bon vivant* ending a Carnival evening with jazz. He only walked a half block before he was approached by a young black woman wearing a very short purple dress.

"Want some comp'ny, gent?"

He wanted to say no, but experience had taught him that if he didn't have a woman on his arm, he would have to turn down many more such offers. "I'm in the mood for jazz. What about you?"

"It's your nickel," she replied.

They walked down the way to Rampart Street into one of the clubs and he seated her at a table by the back wall. A six-piece jazz band played "Tiger Rag." Gabe ordered gin for two. "What's your name?"

"Philly." She downed her drink in one swallow.

Deciding to take a chance on finding what he really needed, Gabe pushed his glass toward her. "Philly, you look like a smart gal."

She looked at him, puzzled. "You need a smart gal?"

He nodded. "Less than a week and it's prohibition. Who's going to have liquor? That's what I need to know."

"You and everybody else." She set her elbows on the table, which wobbled at her touch.

"Mario Vincent?" Gabe named one of the notorious powers behind much of the crime in Storyville.

Philly eyed him nervously. "I don't know him, sir."

Gabe leaned forward, so he wouldn't be overheard. "Maybe you know someone who knows him."

"Maybe. How much you be willin' to pay?" She sized him up with her eyes.

Gabe took a ten dollar bill out of his pocket. Philly reached for it. Gabe held on to it. "Come back with a man who knows Mario and I'll give you the ten."

"What if he busy?"

"Then you won't get this bill."

Philly downed the second gin and left him.

Gabe settled his chair back against the wall and listened to "Canal Street Blues." Tonight, he might gain nothing new or he might get lucky. He rested his hand on the gun in his pocket and remembered that Paul's telegram still remained there, too. *I should have told Meg.*

* * *

The next morning at nine before anyone else had come down, Meg left the St. Clair home without breakfast. It was broad daylight and she couldn't face trying to make small talk. The St. Clair chauffeur drove her to her hotel.

At the desk, Meg picked up her key and mail and walked upstairs in the quiet hotel to her room. Halfway up the steps, she heard heart-stopping shrieks coming from above. Her heart racing, she hurried up the last few steps and found a black maid outside the door to Meg's room screaming, "*Gris-gris, Gris-gris!*"

Doors on both sides of the hall were thrown open. People leaned out to see what was happening. The desk clerk rushed up behind Meg. "Stop this screaming at once, or you'll lose your job!"

The screaming stopped, but she pointed her finger to the floor in front of the doorway to Meg's room. "*Gris-gris.*"

On the floor, white salt had been spilled to make the sign of a cross. In the center of the cross sat a short white candle on a dish which obviously had burned out hours before. At the end of each point of the cross lay a nickel. Meg stooped to brush the salt away.

"Don't!" The clerk pulled her back.

"Voodoo!" The black maid shook her head. "Voodoo!"

Chapter 13

Stunned, Meg repeated, "Voodoo? What are you talking about?"

"Black magic," the desk clerk replied. "Our colored people believe in it."

Meg pulled herself from his tight grip. She noted that he—the white desk clerk—also didn't want her to disturb the *gris-gris*.

The maid warned, "You cross *gris-gris* you get real bad luck."

Casting about in her memory for an adequate reply to this demented assault, she stared down at the salt cross, the stubby white candle. Leave it to evil to use religious symbols and pervert them. A quiet voice, her father's, began reciting the truths she'd been taught as a child—*You are the salt of the earth. If salt loses its saltiness, can it be made salty again? No, it is good for nothing but to be thrown out and trampled under foot. If any man loves me, he must take up his cross and follow me.* And a candle, an ancient symbol of prayer. How dare someone corrupt that which drew one closer to the divine? She grappled with her outrage, trying to find a course of action.

No one went back in his room. No one spoke. Everyone stared at Meg and the voodoo symbol.

Meg closed her eyes. *Father, what should I do?* She couldn't differentiate in her own heart—was she praying to God or appealing to her own father. In this moment, they'd become entwined in her heart. A battle raged around her. She could almost hear demons shrieking.

Meg voiced the words that had come: "As the archangel Michael said to Satan, the Lord rebuke you." Meg stooped and picked up the candle and dish, the four nickels, then with one wave of her arm swept aside the salt, obliterating the sign of the cross. The black maid gasped and crossed herself.

Rising, Meg unlocked her door, stepped across the scattered salt, entering her room. Then she turned and faced the horrified witnesses. "Greater is He who is in me than he that is in the world." She closed her door. The murmur of disturbed voices filtered in from the hallway.

She walked to her bed and let herself down. She'd heard of voodoo long ago from Fleur Bower. People paid a voodoo priestess for these powerful hexes against enemies. Who had paid for her *gris-gris*?

A polite tapping on her door roused Meg from her thoughts. "Meg? This is Gabe. Will you come out?"

She shook herself, rose, and opened the door. "Gabriel?" The foolish desire to throw herself into his arms surprised her. Gabriel's gaze searched her eyes. Their acquaintance so fresh, so conflicted had led somehow into a special intimacy. Gabriel was enemy, friend, the man who last night had bruised her lips with a kiss.

She shifted her attention to a black man with a barrel chest standing behind Gabriel. "Is this Mr. Bishop?"

Jack gave her a wide smile. "Please call me Jack, Miss Wagstaff."

"Very well, Jack." She struggled to keep her voice light. "I understand you're going to be my driver." She paused to give Gabriel a significant look. "And my bodyguard."

"So my father told you?" Gabriel said.

Jack let out a sudden wordless exclamation, then pointed down to the rug. "Is that salt?"

"Yes, someone had a *gris-gris* waiting for me when I came home this morning." Her pulse jerked awake, but Meg watched for Gabriel's reaction.

"That is bad," Jack pronounced.

"Someone is taking pains to make me feel distinctly unwelcome," Meg pressed Gabriel.

Gabriel couldn't seem to stop glaring and frowning at the remains of the *gris-gris*. Finally, he shook his head. "I never expected anything like this."

What would you expect, Gabriel? A knife blade in my back like Del or a bullet in the head like LaRae?

"Who got rid of the *gris-gris* for you?" Jack asked.

"I did." Meg answered.

Looking impressed, Jack studied her. "I hear from Mr. Gabriel that you got a lot of bad luck already, Miss."

Meg shrugged.

Gabriel cleared his throat. "You should call my father. He'll want to know right away."

And my own father, too. Meg passed a hand over her forehead, disturbing her bangs. "I was just so shocked. I couldn't think straight."

She went to the phone at her bedside and asked the operator to dial the St. Clair home.

Mr. Sands had been driven into town.

"Then Jack and I will take you over to pick up your Cadillac," Gabriel offered briskly.

She scanned his face. His jaw had hardened and a vein along his neck bulged.

"Can you wait downstairs?" Motioning to herself, she continued in a humorous tone, "I don't usually pick up a car in evening dress." She wouldn't give in to the flutter in her pulse. She'd faced an earthquake, then a war. Now New Orleans, even with its voodoo, wouldn't conquer Del or her.

"We'll wait downstairs." Gabriel closed the door.

Within the hour, Meg walked outside and joined Jack and Gabriel at the curb. The dark St. Clair family sedan was parked there as well.

Sands rolled down his window. "Are you all right, my dear?"

"Certainly. *That* for black magic." Meg snapped her fingers.

Sands motioned to Jack. "Miss Wagstaff has an appointment at one thirty P.M. today at the jail. Stay with her at all times."

With mixed emotions, Meg wanted to see Del and reassure him, but she didn't want to have to answer any questions about LaRae. She was glad to have Jack's protection, but his presence announced her inability to protect herself.

Gabriel took her hand. "Jack will take excellent care of you."

Her skin tingled at his touch—disturbing. *We have business to settle between us, Gabriel. I haven't forgotten last night.*

She released his hand, wishing she could bind him to her. Sooner than she wished, they would sit on opposing sides in a courtroom. She had no hold on Gabriel St. Clair, but as he strode away, the strand that connected her to him pulled taut and strained.

Later, Meg walked beside Jack down the corridor to the visiting room at the jail, footsteps echoing in the heavy silence. She couldn't believe all that had happened since her arrival in this town. Who was friend? Who was foe? At the end of this, would she and Del crawl out of the pitiless New Orleans maze into the daylight—safe once again?

The police officer unlocked the door of the almost empty visitor's room. Meg sat down across from Dell. She folded her own hands in her lap to keep herself from reaching for Del's.

With arms folded, Jack waited just inside the door. She forced herself to say, "I'm sorry LaRae is dead."

"The same could happen to you."

She pressed a hand to her trembling lips while inside she collapsed in a heap, moaning her guilt and regret. "I'm afraid it's all my fault."

"Your fault? *I'm* the one who came to New Orleans. *I'm* the one who fought with Kennedy. *I'm* the one who made her a target—and you." So thin and drawn, he fidgeted in his chair, still moving stiffly.

What solace could she give him? Had they endured France for this?

Del stared down at the scarred tabletop. "I want you to leave New Orleans—"

"No. Your trial begins in days."

"Do you want me to have your death on my conscience, too?" he growled.

"I have my own car and bodyguard now. I have my gun. I will not leave you."

Del folded his hands and pressed his fist to his mouth, masking how close he was to breaking down.

She lowered her voice, "We made a promise once. Do you remember?"

Del stared into her eyes. "I release you from your promise."

Love for Del and faith in his love for her propelled her toward tears. Her voice came out gruffly: "That's not possible. The promises we made that day were for life."

* * *

The first floor of Hotel Grunenwald had been reserved for the gala celebration of the election of the new governor, John M. Parker. Standing in the hotel's lobby, Meg let Jack take her wrap to the hat-check. She waited until he returned, then she, dressed in one of her raven black Parisienne designs topped with a lavish red fox collar, sauntered into the packed room.

A band on the right of a stage blasted an ear-ringing arrangement of "Dixie." Overhead, red, white, and blue streamers looped and crisscrossed between the chandeliers.

Standing amid laughter and boisterous shouting, backslapping, Meg didn't feel festive. Behind her, Jack took a place against one wall, his hands folded. His constant presence plucked her tense nerves. All day Meg had looked over her shoulder, hunted.

On the Western Front, she had lived in danger from bombardment, pestilence, fear, and despair. But this present sense of pervading, active evil weighed her down, stretched her nerves. Underlying all this, her unfinished conversation with Gabriel St. Clair at the Demon Rum party nipped at the edges of her mind. Though adversaries, the two of them had drawn closer and dearer. Gabriel sought to convict her dearest friend. But she needed Gabriel to push away the emptiness that lingered in her after France, threatening to drain the life from her. With Gabriel, she could talk about what was central in her mind, her heart.

And he needed her. He denied it, but that didn't change his need.

The band halted midnote, then sped up the tempo to double time. Everyone around Meg began applauding and whistling. The noise of the crowd and the band deafened her. Finally, broad gestures from men on the stage quieted the gathering. The winning candidate stepped to the front and began to address his supporters.

Meg scanned the crowd for Gabriel. At last, she glimpsed him slipping through the crowd toward her. This realization uncapped a delirious joy. *I shouldn't feel this way.* She moved forward, her eyes tracking his erratic, but steady progress toward her. Acquaintances interrupted him as he made his way to her. Tonight, perhaps he would tell her what had happened to him, to his heart in France. Tonight, perhaps he would kiss *her* and not a memory. Just a yard from her, a man tugged Gabriel back toward the stage.

Frustration shredding her, Meg balled her fists. *Gabe, no.* But Gabriel stood talking to Parker. With a sigh, Meg wended her way to one of the tables and sat down. Mrs. St. Clair walked up. "May I join you, Miss Wagstaff?"

Meg's heart sank.

Sitting down, Mrs. St. Clair worried her lower lip. "I hope you won't think me forward, but I would like to discuss my son with you."

Meg was dumbfounded. "Do you think you should?"

"Yes, I overheard something a few days ago that has given me much food for thought." The woman pursed her lips. "I have not liked your modern ways, but I am trying to understand why you have had such a startling effect on my family."

"I wasn't aware that I have had any effect—" Meg stopped. Perhaps Mrs. St. Clair had a point. Meg hadn't intended to have any effect, but . . . She frowned.

"I am sorry if you feel I have purposely tried to change your daughter's direction in life—" Meg halted, then conceded, "Very well. What do you want to tell me about Gabriel?"

"I've wanted Gabriel to marry Dulcine." The lady stirred her tea silently.

The image of Gabriel waltzing with Dulcine the night before stung once more. Meg flared. "All New Orleans knows that."

Mrs. St. Clair looked tempted to snap back, but she merely took a deep breath. "When Gabriel returned from the war, I could tell he'd suffered terribly there, not just from his wounds, but from some deep emotional . . . shock."

"Is that why you told him not to talk about the war?" Meg couldn't seem to stop herself from attacking this woman.

"I never said that." The woman looked honestly surprised. "What are you talking about?"

Meg smothered her irritation. She had been judgmental and evidently wrong, too. "I'm sorry. Go on please."

"I thought if he would marry, a wife would be able to help him heal. She could . . . comfort him in a way I couldn't."

Meg hadn't been able to see past this woman's very obvious matchmaking ploys to the motivation behind them.

"Anyway, I knew Dulcine was interested in Gabriel even before the war. Gabriel showed a preference for her . . ." Mrs. St. Clair fell silent.

"I didn't come to New Orleans to fall in love and marry, Mrs. St. Clair."

"Love rarely comes when we plan for it."

These unexpected words kicked Meg in the stomach.

"Meg, I never thought to find love at a Y-canteen." Colin cradled her head in both his hands. *"Marry me."*

"What do you want from me?" Meg whispered.

"I don't want you to tempt Gabriel and destroy Dulcine's chances, only to leave him—"

"Be at ease." Meg rose and walked away. She couldn't take any more. *I just want to get out alive with Del.*

On her way out, Gabriel met her. "Why were you talking with my mother?"

"She was just being polite." His gaze on her brought an awareness of him, an aching to nestle close.

"I need to talk to you—alone." Gabe took her arm, hustling her toward the exit. From the corner of her eye, she glimpsed Dulcine glaring at her. "Gabriel, do you think—"

"Don't stop now. We're going."

His urgent tone sliced through her. "Where? What's happened?"

Chapter 14

Outside the hotel with the sounds of giddy laughter and the syncopated jazz band still around them, Meg pulled against Gabriel. The cool night air and her fear made gooseflesh zip up her arms. "Where are we going?"

He hustled her into his car. "I told Jack I'd see you home."

Meg studied him, a sick feeling tightening her stomach. "Is it Del?"

"Sorry." He gripped the steering wheel with both hands. "This has *nothing* to do with Del. I received a telegram today from France." She touched his sleeve to comfort him, to urge him to trust her. His words came out in a thick, edgy voice, "Her name *was* Lenore. But I was kissing you."

He trusts me. Clenched in the wintry fingers of loneliness and loss, Meg slid across the seat close against him.

"Stay close," he murmured roughly.

"I will."

Soon Gabe led Meg to his father's home office. There, he switched on the green-shaded desk lamp. Meg curled up on the sofa.

Unable to hit on a graceful way of bringing up Marie, Gabriel knelt in front of the green-marble hearth and busied himself making a fire.

Meg asked, "How did you meet her?"

"A surveillance flight over Argonne." His voice sounded wooden in his own ears. "I was hit but still managed to land the plane in a field. It put me in a hospital. Lenore was a French nurse there."

He began building a tiny pyramid of sticks and wadded newspaper to ignite the charcoal. "Her husband, a doctor, died of pneumonia." He breathed easier with each word—each weight deducted.

He struck a match and touched its flames to the paper.

"I'm glad you found her. I'm sorry you lost her."

The fire lit, crinkling up the paper into orange flame. He rose, staring down at her. Her white skin contrasted against the black of her dress and her short brown hair. She held out a hand to him. Crossing to her, he took it, nestled down beside her.

"Tell me."

Her two words acted like a cork drawing from a bottle. Lifting her hand to his lips, he branded it with a kiss of appreciation. "I loved her, still love her."

She squeezed his hand. "I knew."

"Yes," he acknowledged. He recalled her question, "What was her name?" Words began to flow from him, "She was like you . . . strong, passionate . . . a woman who understood things without having to be told."

His words played in her aching heart, evoking memories, linking him to her. Meg shifted her weight on the sofa, leaning into him. "It was the war. Such naked inhuman suffering. . . ." A remembered image—a field a day after battle, an up-flung hand frozen in entreaty. She shut her eyes; the image remained. She'd whispered, "Heaven, help him, help us all."

"I knew I would be expected to kill people. I thought I understood that. But knowing and doing are poles apart. Firing a machine gun at an enemy flyer—in the air." He pursed his lips. "We had to fly so close. I always tried to shoot the pilot, not the plane. A bullet in the gas tank turned a plane into a blazing coffin. The screams—I could hear them even over the engine noise—"

Meg wrapped her arms tightly around him. *Comfort ye. Comfort ye, my people.*

"I loved to fly, but I grew to hate it," his vehement voice shook. "The Germans, English, and French pilots had parachutes—not the Americans. Our brass said if we had them, we would bail out too quickly and wreck too many planes," he railed at the injustice. "Easier to train more fliers, than to build more planes."

She wiped away one lone tear on his cheek, then drew off her sheer, black gloves. She pressed her face into the crook of his neck. "I know," she whispered. "What did Lenore look like?" Meg tilted her head back to watch emotion play across his finely chiseled features.

"Tall, a Gallic brunette. Her beauty came more from who she was, what she did." He groped for words. "Undaunted . . . smiling . . . she knew my heart."

Bracing her hands on each side of his head, Meg bent his head forward and pressed her brow against his. "I felt the same with Colin. When we met, it was like we had known each other all our lives."

Words exploded from deep inside him, "We didn't have time to waste—"

"On getting acquainted," she finished for him. "We went from 'Hello' to 'I-love-you' in one evening."

"Facing death alters perspective, strips away—"

"Everything but the essential."

The white pillar of Meg's neck arched within a fraction of his lips. Unable to resist, he pressed his lips to her soft skin.

His touch made her breath catch; she kissed the lobe of his ear.

The touch of her lips suspended his faculties—as though she had released him from the constraints of time and space. Their intimacy made his pulse pound at his temples. Cradling her silken hair in both hands, he bestowed a kiss to each of her closed eyes, and with his lips, pushed back her bangs.

A red welt crossed her forehead—her shrapnel scar. "Meg, my poor sweet girl—"

"No, don't." She put up a hand to prevent him from touching the wound.

He captured her hand and held it. Her resistance gave way. Along the angled red crease, he pressed one kiss, two, three kisses. He rested his forehead against hers, warm skin against warm skin. "Colin died?"

Trembling, she rubbed her forehead against his. "Shot by a sniper two months before armistice." She swallowed tears. "Lenore?"

He forced out the words, "The field hospital bombed . . . an accident." He folded her into his arms against the past and its agonies.

She whispered a sigh into his ear, then relaxed against him, trusting. The charcoal fire glowed on the hearth. His father's mantel clock ticked-ticked. He drew in a deep breath. "Thank you," he whispered. "I haven't had anyone to share this with."

She pulled from his embrace yet stayed curled beside him on the sofa—his sleek cat had returned.

With his index finger, Gabe traced the line of her cheekbone. Then, exhaling, he reclined against the soft leather back of the sofa and stretched his legs toward the fire, crossing his ankles. The clock chimed the hour.

Meg looked to him. "Your parents will return home soon. You need to drive me to my hotel."

He hadn't come to the main point yet. Gabriel sat up. "I need to ask you for advice . . . for your help." He rubbed the back of his neck.

What more did he have to reveal? "What do you need?"

Gabriel stood and walked to the mantel. "Lenore had a little daughter, Marie—only three years old from her first marriage. I adopted her."

The desire to weep squeezed her breast. Another child in that war that had spawned so many tattered waifs. "Where is she?"

"I thought she was with Lenore during the bombardment," he railed at himself. "Lenore's grandmother, her only blood relative, often brought the child to eat lunch with Lenore at the hospital."

She understood his sudden anger. Children shouldn't be in danger of bombs. She clung to the hope his words offered. "But Marie wasn't there?"

Gabe had been right to talk to Meg. "No, Lenore and the grandmother died. Marie's body wasn't found, but she was so small . . ."

Gabriel didn't have to explain. A German shell could obliterate a little girl. Meg folded her arms around herself. "Where is Marie now?"

"A neighbor, another old woman, had Marie in her care that day when the bombardment came. When this old woman died a few months later, Marie was sent to an orphanage. I would never have known she was still alive except that Lenore's first husband's brother, Paul, kept searching for Marie just in case a mistake had been made. He couldn't give up on the chance that his only brother's only child had been spared."

"Is Marie with him?"

"Only briefly. France is so depleted because of the war, Paul is sending Marie to me. In fact, he telegraphed me that she is on her way to New Orleans with a nurse now."

Meg sat up straighter. "How soon will her boat arrive?"

"Three weeks."

"But your mother said nothing to me." She stared at him.

"She doesn't know." His eyes wouldn't meet hers.

Meg gasped. "But why? Surely she'll be delighted to have Marie—"

"I never told my parents about my marriage to Lenore. We married so quickly. I meant to tell them . . ." He stirred the fire with the poker.

"Why didn't you?"

Gabriel began pacing. "Did you tell your parents about Colin?"

"No." Suddenly restless, she rose and walked over to stand by the desk. "The loss . . . cut too deep." Each word stabbed her.

He nodded, resting a hand on the mantel. "How could we explain how it was in France?"

"And why?" she agreed, stepping nearer him. "They would only ask questions we wouldn't want to answer." Meg drew in a ragged breath, recalling her father's worried expression whenever he had looked at her. "But it makes it harder now . . . on every one of your family."

"You're telling me?" he asked with a dry twist. "How do I tell them about Lenore when Mother wants me to marry Dulcine?"

In her mind, Meg went over her recent conversation with Mrs. St. Clair. "Do you plan to marry Dulcine? What will she think about your having a child from a previous marriage—indeed, a child, not your own blood, one you adopted? Some people won't accept adopted children."

He stared at her, then down into the lambent flames. "I thought I could marry Dulcine, but no. Talking to her is like talking to a . . . moving picture."

Meg took hold of his sleeve. "You shouldn't lead her on."

"I know." He grimaced. "You're right. But how do I tell my parents, especially my mother about Lenore and Marie? It's my mother. I'm not worried about my father—"

"Your mother might surprise you." Meg gazed down at the sisal carpet on the floor. "Don't delay. You must give them time to adjust and prepare. Little Marie has lost so much. She must feel welcome right away. She'll sense it if she isn't."

He sucked in breath. "I panicked today when I got Paul's telegram. How will I manage to care for a daughter?"

"Your family will help you. Tell them tonight."

Drawing up both her hands, he kissed the soft palm of each, then drew her nearer. She came without demur. Holding her so close somehow wrapped him in warm contentment. Though as frail as a feather, Meg Wagstaff was a strong woman, admirable. For the first time in many months, he experienced peace . . . desire.

His mouth became dry. *I want to kiss Meg—not out of need or affection, but passion.* "Meg," he murmured, then he was kissing her as though her lips would give him life and hope. He deepened his kiss; she responded in kind, whispering his name against his mouth, pressing closer to him.

"Gabe!" Belle's shocked voice shattered their privacy.

Meg stumbled backward and would have fallen if Gabe hadn't kept his hold on her.

Meg took a deep breath. "It's all right, Belle." She tried to make her voice sound natural. "Corby brought you home? Did you have your talk with him?"

Belle came in, closing the door behind her. "That's why I wanted to see you. Corby is impressed that I'm going on to Newcomb," she announced with a defiant glance at her brother.

Gabe replied, "He seems to have good sense."

"Belle," Meg cut in, "where are your parents?"

"They said they'd be home soon."

"Gabriel"—Meg touched his arm—"I think you should take me home before they return."

He nodded. "Belle, would you tell our parents that I've taken Meg home and will be back very soon. I'd like them and you to wait up for me here in the office. I have something important to tell the family."

"Important? What?" Belle stared at them in obvious bafflement. When she received no reply, she agreed, "Okay."

"Come, Meg, I'll get you back to your hotel."

He whisked her outside into his car. She didn't speak, but watched the play of street-lamp light over his face as he drove her to the hotel. After their first standoff in his law office, who would have thought that she and Gabriel St. Clair would share such similar experiences? Gabe parked across the street from her hotel. "Thank you . . . for everything tonight. I had no right to involve you in my affairs, but—"

She pressed her hand to his lips stopping his words. "I was happy to listen." She lowered her eyes. "You helped me, too. Now, don't get out, just go home and tell your parents everything." Quickly, she got out of the car without his assistance, and began to cross the dark street.

From behind Gabe's car, another car squealed away from the curb and curved around Gabe. A volley of gunshots exploded the silence.

Meg screamed.

Gabe bellowed, "No!"

Chapter 15

The strange car roared away. *"Meg!"* Gabe sprinted to her. She lay facedown on the street. "Dear God . . . no." Kneeling, he lifted her limp shoulders. She moaned.

"Were you hit?" He slid his panicky hands over her body, feeling for wet blood.

"No." She threw frantic arms around his neck and clung to him. "Hold me."

He crushed her to him—shock making him both fierce and weak. *I nearly lost her.*

People at the hotel threw wide their windows and called down questions. Men burst from the hotel and surrounded them, shouting questions, yelling, "Police!"

Gabe lifted Meg. Pushing through the crowd, he carried her into the lobby. His heart hammering his ribs, he laid her on the nearest sofa and knelt beside her. The bright lights hurting his eyes, he swiftly examined her. She'd come through with only scraped elbows and ripped black silk stockings.

Meg clutched his lapels, but her words were calm. "I'm fine."

He framed her face with his hands. Her head trembled within his grasp. "Someone tried to kill you." *And I was helpless.*

She bit her lower lip. People flocked around them. Rising, Gabe urged Meg to remain lying down. "Where's the phone?" At the desk, he dialed police headquarters. Gabe didn't want to connect this attempt on Meg's life with Del's case, but he knew Meg would. In her position, he would too. But could it be a coincidence? But why here? Why now—if this shooting weren't connected to Del's case? This wasn't Storyville or Basin Street at two A.M. And the intent to harm or frighten Meg was monstrously clear. Rage flamed through him. He wouldn't let anyone sweep this attack under a rug just because Meg was a Yankee who'd attached herself to an unpopular suspect.

The lobby clock chimed three o'clock. He returned to Meg and leaned forward so only she could hear his words. "You're coming home with me." When she tried to object, he said, "I'm not leaving you here. Go up and pack an overnight bag." He wouldn't expose her to any further danger or terror. He nudged her toward the staircase and saw her safely to her room, which he examined carefully—looking under the bed, behind the curtains, and in the bath, the closet. Leaving her alone long enough to pack, he stepped outside, and leaned against her door to wait. The memory of Meg in his arms made Gabe ache to hold her close again. But did he have the right?

He walked to the bottom of the staircase, but remained vigilant. His mind replayed the sound of the bullets slamming and ricocheting off the street around Meg. *I nearly lost her. I just found her.*

Two days after the attempt on Meg's life, Judge Simon LeGrand sat down in the seat of judgment and began coughing into a white handkerchief held in his clawlike hands. Gabe stood, waiting for the first day of Del's trial to begin.

Gabe wondered where Meg was. Along with his father, he'd spent yesterday selecting the jury. Afterward, he attended a meeting with the chief of police about the attempted shooting of Meg, and then the ensuing evening had been filled with an unavoidable political dinner that stretched until the early hours of this morning.

He had also suggested that the chief review Rooney's competence. Gabe made the point that Rooney's behavior shouted untrustworthiness. The chief had seemed impressed with Gabe's argument.

But in all those hours, he'd only seen Meg in passing at his home. His mother, who had welcomed Meg, no longer pushed him toward Dulcine, and didn't appear to resent Meg. And he still hadn't had time to sit down and reveal that he had a daughter to his parents. His life was spinning out of his grasp. And Gabe was beginning to wonder whether Del was guilty or innocent.

Judge LeGrand put away his white handkerchief, staring down at Gabe. "Counselor, are you prepared to begin the prosecution of this case?"

"Yes, your Honor." Gabe glanced over his shoulder. Meg and Jack still hadn't appeared in court. Why? Had something else happened? He'd ordered Jack not to let Meg out of his sight except when she was in Gabe's own home. Gabe would let no one hurt Meg. No one.

The judge barked, "Well, Gabriel, the court is waiting."

"Your honor, the prosecution calls Patrick Rooney, the deputy chief of police, as its first witness."

Rooney, in a tight-fitting suit, swaggered to the witness stand, was sworn in, and sat down.

Revulsion washed over Gabe. In a vague way, he'd never liked or trusted Rooney. Now without question, he disliked him and distrusted him. His voice colorless, Gabe asked, "Mr. Rooney, would you please recount for the court your official activities early on the morning of January second, nineteen twenty?"

"Me and two other officers were called to the scene of a murder around three o'clock. The body of Mitchell Kennedy had been found behind a Storyville club, name of Penny Candy."

"How did Mr. Kennedy meet his death?"

"He had been shot twice in his chest." Rooney shifted in his chair.

To Gabe's right, his father and Del sat stone quiet. Facing his father in court made him feel like a first-year law student. He cleared his throat. "What evidence did you find at the scene?"

"We questioned a couple of Kennedy's employees, and they told us—"

"Objection," Sands said. "Hearsay."

"Sustained." LeGrand stared at Gabe. "You know better than that."

Acknowledging his fault, Gabe felt his neck warm. "Mr. Rooney, did you find any other physical evidence at the scene?"

"Physical evidence?" Rooney looked surprised. "No. Just a dead body in an alley."

122 Lyn Cote

"What did you do next?" Gabe felt the judge's disapproving gaze burn into him.

Rooney grimaced at the judge. "Following a lead, we—officers Bergman and Destry and me—obtained a search warrant for Delman DuBois's room at eighty-three Canal Street, a colored rooming house."

"Why did you go there?" Gabe proceeded with a growing uneasiness.

"To question Delman Dubois, who'd worked for Kennedy."

"And what did you find there?"

"We found Delman—sound asleep. We found over two hundred dollars under the mattress—the amount of money subsequently reported stolen from Penny Candy's office—and a gun under his pillow." Rooney spoke as though he'd memorized his testimony.

Who coached you, Rooney? I didn't. Gabe grimaced. For the gun and money, Gabe followed the appropriate procedures for identifying and admitting evidence. "What did you do next?"

"We arrested Delman for robbing and murdering his boss. I called it a neat arrest and a good night." Rooney grinned.

"This is no occasion for levity, Mr. Rooney." Judge LeGrand glared at the deputy.

"Sorry, Your Honor." Rooney looked unrepentant.

Judge LeGrand gave Gabe a brooding look as though he found him wanting, too. "Is that all for this witness, Gabriel?"

The door at the back of the courtroom opened, the barest swish of air alerting Gabe. He glanced over his shoulder and observed Meg and—his mother? She walked in beside Meg and sat down on the defendant side of the courtroom. *What is my mother doing in a courtroom?*

"Gabriel, is that all the questions you have for this witness?" the judge asked in an aggrieved tone.

"Yes, Your Honor." Gabe sat down.

His father rolled around his table and approached the witness stand. "You found money and a gun in Mr. Dubois's room?"

"Yes," Rooney sneered.

"How do you know this gun belonged to my client?"

"It was in his room, under his pillow," Rooney declared. "If it wasn't his gun, why'd he have it?"

"Did Mr. Dubois claim ownership?"

"No." Rooney gave a look of disgust.

"How did you connect the gun to this murder?" Sands asked.

"It's the right caliber," Rooney snapped. "Everybody knew this Negro had it in for—"

Father cut him off, "By that you mean, it matched the bullets found in the deceased man's body?"

"Yeah." Rooney's eyes bulged.

Unperturbed, Sands rolled his chair over to the evidence table. "How about the money? Had there been any record of serial numbers kept by Mr. Kennedy by which we can connect this cash to him?"

"No, nightclub owners don't keep lists like bankers."

"So what you're really saying is this: Mr. Kennedy was shot two times with a gun of the same caliber as this gun found in Mr. Dubois's room?"

"Yeah," Rooney growled.

Sands nodded. "And some money was missing from Mr. Kennedy's office and that you found some money in Dubois's room? That is your evidence?"

Rooney glared at Gabe's father. "It's enough. Down in Storyville some colors will kill you for two bits—"

"Some maybe. But not Delman Caleb Dubois—a graduate of Howard University. And a man who served his country bravely in France. Do you expect this jury to believe that Delman Dubois—who has enjoyed the patronage of the multimillionaire family who raised him—would kill a man for a few hundred dollars? Why would my client—who has several thousands of dollars of his own in a San Francisco bank account—commit murder for two hundred dollars?"

Every word his father leveled at Rooney stung Gabe like a lash. But each word also slit the veil that had separated Gabe from the

truth. He'd been blinded by prejudice. A black jazz musician in Storyville—that's how he'd seen Del. He'd spent no time checking into
the facts of the case, even when he knew the kind of man Rooney
was. *God forgive me. What can I do now?*

Judge LeGrand stung Gabe with a contemptuous glance.

Gabe couldn't disagree. His witness, this entire case, was worthy
of contempt. Why had the chief of police chosen someone so biased, so inept, as Rooney for his deputy, and who had really killed
Mitch Kennedy?

Dinner that evening at home was agony for Gabe. Belle had invited three friends, Nadine, Maisy, and Portia, over for dinner and
an evening of . . . giggling. And Meg remained aloof from him. After
dinner, Gabe escaped with his parents into his father's snug office.
Finally he had a moment to tell his parents about Marie. His father sat behind his orderly desk, his mother on the chair, and Gabe
on the old sofa opposite. Gabe fleetingly recalled the intoxicating
sensation of holding Meg in his arms on the sofa two nights ago.
He rubbed his forehead trying to erase that thought. The time had
come for truth telling regardless of the cost. Marie was counting on
him, her "Papa."

"This isn't about Del's case, is it?" his father asked.

Gabe folded his hands and looked down. "No, it's about France
. . . about the war."

His parents' combined attention daunted Gabe, but he took a
deep breath. "Things happened in the war that I never wrote you
about." His father nodded. His mother sat like carved marble. Gabe
continued, "I regret keeping them from you."

"What things, son?" Sands folded his hands under his chin.

"I married a French woman." *I married for love, passion in the
midst of carnage.*

His mother gasped. "Where is she?"

"She was killed in a bombardment near the end of the war." His
heart twisted. A gale of giggling filtered in from the other room
making his grief more stark.

"Why didn't you tell us? I knew something horrible had hurt you." His mother's voice resonated with pain.

"She was Lenore Moreau, a nurse at the hospital I was taken to when I was shot down." He reached into his pocket and pulled out his wallet, drawing out the one small photograph Lenore had given him. "She was a widow. With a small daughter." Gabe handed his mother the picture.

Jazz music from the Victrola tinkled in the background. A girl began singing along. His mother stared at the photograph, then up at him. "The child—you didn't leave her in France, did you?"

"I was told she was killed with her mother."

"But she wasn't," his father concluded.

"I've received a telegram from Marie's uncle in Paris that he had continued to search for Lenore's daughter just in case she'd escaped." Gabe turned to his mother. "So many children just got lost or misplaced. And Marie's body was never found—"

"So the uncle found her? Is it what you're telling us?" Father received the photograph and studied it.

Gabe lowered his eyes. "Marie never knew her father. He died before she was born, so I adopted her. Four days ago, her uncle put Marie on a boat with a nurse. She's only four and due here within three weeks."

"Oh, a child. My first grandchild." His mother popped up from her seat.

Gabe stared at her. "You're not upset?"

"I'm sad you didn't tell us about Lenore." Mother sat down beside him on the sofa and touched his arm. "Gabriel, I didn't know how to help you. I could see you were grieving, but I didn't know over what, over whom . . . dear, did you really think you couldn't tell us?"

Why didn't I trust them? "I couldn't seem to put the news of my marriage into a letter. Then Lenore died, and telling you seemed futile. I thought it best to close the book and spare you my grief." Both his parents gazed at him with sad faces. It cut Gabe to his heart.

"But you didn't." Father spoke at last. "Both your mother and I sensed your sorrow and didn't know how to comfort you. Don't do this again. This is what your family is for. You are a grown man. You don't need us for everyday things, but for matters like this, you do."

Gabe nodded gravely. "It won't happen again."

Mother sprang up again. "Let's tell Belle. She'll be thrilled." The jazz song had ended, but no more giggling could be heard.

Gabe objected, "But she has friends over—"

"Excellent," his father observed. "That will save us deciding who to tell about Marie first. We'll let the grapevine take care of that."

Gabe appreciated his grim humor. His parents led him down the hall toward the parlor where the four debs and Meg had been chatting. Before his mother preceded them into the suddenly quiet room, Nadine's hesitant voice stopped them, "But I don't understand, Miss Wagstaff. Why do you interest yourself so deeply with the son of a servant? I mean, we've all heard that the colored accused of murder was the grandson of your old nurse, but—"

"Ordinarily I wouldn't try to explain because you may not understand even after I do, but in these circumstances, in light of what you've heard, I'll try." Meg paused. "Del and I were children when we moved to San Francisco only a few months before the nineteen-o-six earthquake. My father had gone away that horrible day, so I was home alone with Del and his grandmother Susan."

Meg's voice took on a distant quality as though she were removed from them. "The quake hit at sunrise and Susan got us out of the house. She started to take us to the Golden Gate Park. On the way, she had a heart attack and died. No one would stop to help us," Meg's voice faltered. "No one acted normally."

Gabe watched Meg, his heart touched by her lost expression.

"An aftershock hit us. I thought we were going to die. When it finally ended, we promised to stick together. And we always have." She looked up at them and her voice hardened. "Is that a good enough explanation of why I will stick with Del no matter what? Do you choose to believe that nasty gossip or me?"

"What gossip?" Gabe demanded.

Chapter 16

Meg watched Gabe as Nadine, who obviously had a taste for melo-drama, said in a hushed tone, "Someone started a rumor that Miss Wagstaff isn't a friend to Del, but his . . . his paramour." The girl blushed a fiery red.

"I pay no attention to rumors." Meg forced a relaxed smile. "My family has never lived like everyone else and this isn't the first ru-mor—"

Mrs. St. Clair spoke up, "Gossip is the hallmark of small minds. That's what my grandmother always said."

"When did you first hear this rumor?" Gabriel's question sound-ed as though Nadine sat in the witness chair.

Nadine frowned. "The first time I heard it was at the celebration for the new mayor."

Meg watched the wheels turn in Gabriel's head. She had a sus-picion of who had started this rumor, but it didn't really matter. She would be in New Orleans only as long as it took to get Del out of jail. Somehow this thought didn't relieve her as much as it had previously. She found herself studying Gabriel's stern profile. She shook herself mentally. "Don't let it worry you—"

Belle declared, "If anyone says it within my hearing, they'll get a piece of my mind."

"That is very loyal of you," Sands said, "but remember Shake-speare, 'Methinks thou dost protest too much.'"

"Exactly so." Mrs. St. Clair sniffed. "Treat it with sublime con-tempt."

Sands nodded. "Exactly so, my dear."

Meg read the ill-concealed worry in Gabriel and his parents' ex-pressions. She knew just what kind of reaction this rumor could bring. The KKK held sway in the South and was spreading north. Whoever had begun this rumor had done it to drive her from the state. But Del stood in the greatest peril. A black man accused of killing a white man stood almost no chance of acquittal. If the jury heard of this rumor and believed it, Del was a dead man. Shaken, she stood up.

Gabriel moved to her side.

Nadine glanced at the clock. "Oh, it's eight! Time for us to get on our costumes for the Momus Parade."

While the girls hurried out giggling, Belle paused at the door. "You'll still go see us in the parade?"

Meg nodded. "We wouldn't miss it," Gabe added.

Belle grinned, then hurried out with Mrs. St. Clair close at her heels. Sands looked at them. "I'll be in my office. Gabe, if you don't want to escort the ladies, I'm sure we could manage to get me through the crowd some way—"

"Leave it to me," Gabe insisted. Sands nodded once, then left. Gabe looked down at Meg. "Tomorrow is Mardi Gras. I'll have to take you to the French Quarter." Trying to speak normally, he said, "How are you? I was worried when you didn't come to court. . . ." He stopped.

"I wanted to be on time, but it took me so long to fall asleep after . . . ." Meg braced herself. "Your mother didn't want to disturb me. You and Sands were long gone before I woke."

"I was surprised that my mother accompanied you to court."

"She insisted. She said she'd never had time to attend court to see your father represent a client and she wanted to see you at work as well."

Meg's explanation sounded like pure fiction to Gabe, but he'd seen his mother in court—with his own eyes and for the first time in her life. Had his mother come to court to see his father or was it out of concern for Meg?

Meg asked, "You told your parents tonight?"

He nodded, his eyes devouring her, always elegant, always in black. Now he understood. She was in mourning for Colin. But her black silk dress with its sleek lines—he couldn't look away.

"How did they take it?"

Belle's small Victrola upstairs began with a sudden burst of song, "I Wish I Could Shimmy Like My Sister Kate."

Gabe concentrated on Meg despite the loud music. "Mother is excited over Marie—her first grandchild." He forced a wry grin. "I felt guilty for not telling them sooner."

Recalling her own father's drawn expression the morning she'd left San Francisco for New Orleans, Meg wrapped her arms around herself, wishing Gabe would draw nearer. *Father, why didn't I tell you about France?*

Gabe shoved his hands in his pockets. "I don't feel like the same man who traveled home from France over four months ago."

"I know. I lost Colin in September. I came home for Thanksgiving. I wanted to tell my parents, but I felt like I was drowning in sensations and images from the trenches—"

He looked into Meg's warm brown eyes. "I took the job as parish attorney to give me a life, a reason to get up in the morning and get dressed. I thought I could forget by keeping busy." His voice came out rough.

"I was so frightened. I thought I'd never feel like myself again," Meg said.

Am I falling in love with this woman? Is that why I can't hold back? Or is this just shared experience and sorrow? "I know. But I don't think we'll ever be exactly as we were."

"If I were, it would mean that Colin had no effect on me." She lowered her eyes. "My poor father—he has me to worry about, my stepmother's difficult pregnancy, and Del being arrested . . ." Meg didn't raise her gaze. "Did it feel peculiar to face your father in court?"

Gabe took her gloveless hand in his. In his pocket, he held information . . . possibly helpful information. Should he give it to her? Would it help her? He kissed her hand and wished circumstances were different. They couldn't talk about what separated them, but the barriers between them had tumbled down two nights ago in his father's study. He shuddered with awareness of her.

Meg spoke in a low, desperate tone, "What are we going to do?

I can't discuss Del's case with you. But something dreadful is happening in this city."

The four girls clattered down the stairs and burst in on Meg and Gabe. Meg pulled away from him again. Gabe's frustration level spiked. *We need to be alone.* He swallowed his anger.

The girls posed in the doorway. "How do we look?" they chorused, then giggled at themselves.

Meg made herself smile though the muscles of her face and neck were taut like steel cords.

Belle was dressed as the Statue of Liberty—the other three were a black cat, a veiled harem girl, and a Japanese geisha with a powdered white face.

Meg kept her smiled in place. "What inventive costumes."

"You girls, get your wraps now. The cars are in the porte cochere," Mrs. St. Clair instructed from the hall.

Soon they all crowded into two cars. Mrs. St. Clair and three debutantes in the family sedan and Belle in the backseat of the Franklin behind Meg and Gabe.

In the darkness, Gabe slid his hand over the front seat till he touched Meg's hand. He clasped it in his. The agony of their situation twisted his gut.

What am I going to do? Gabe asked himself. *I care about Meg. How can I prosecute her dearest friend with a flawed case?* What did a prosecutor do if he became convinced that the defendant was not guilty? It was the kind of question he would automatically want to put to his father, but how could he? His father was the defense lawyer.

The chauffeur drove to the corner of Canal and Rampart streets near the edge of the Quarter. The debs flocked out of the family car into the throng. "The parade is gathering here," Gabe explained to Meg.

She nodded.

Squeezing out of the sedan, his mother pushed her way back through the crowd to Gabe's window. She had to shout to be heard over the noise of the crowd. "A spot has been reserved for you on Felicity Street, you remember where?"

Gabe nodded.

His mother motioned broadly. "Our place in the pied-a-terre is on Rampart right over there!"

"I remember," Gabe shouted back. "Meg and I will walk back and join you!" His mother nodded and turned away to push her way to the nearby pied-a-terre.

Gabe threaded the Franklin through the packed streets and found his spot at a friend's home and parked. He helped Meg out of the car. Only blocks separated them from the riotous celebration in the Quarter. But Felicity Street looked deserted. The night breeze rustled through the tall live oaks, the Spanish moss fluttering over their heads like tattered sleeves on an ancient shroud.

Meg looked up at him, her eyes pleading for . . . what? What could he give her? The piece of paper in his pocket weighed him down. It might put her in danger.

"I want you to hold me," she murmured into his ear.

Pulling her against him, he closed his arms around her. With his forefinger, he tilted her quivering chin up. He kissed her. Again, the pain of the past fell away in the joy of Meg's kiss, the coming together of their lips.

Meg swayed in his arms. Gabriel's kiss shoved back the pain of losing Colin, the horror that she might lose Del. She pushed away from him. "We must go. Your mother will worry if we don't come soon."

Gabe allowed her to draw him along. The tap of their heels on the paved banquette gave sound to their hurried pace, a counter-point to the cacophony of human laughter and jazz trumpets in the distance. Gabe wanted to pull Meg into his arms again and forget about the parade, his mother . . .

Soon Rampart Street was in sight. Gabe drew Meg closer to him. Sometimes, a young man will try to steal a lady from her companion. No one was stealing Meg from him tonight. They had too much left to discuss. Finally, he led her past the wrought iron double gate and inside the apartment, up the curved staircase to the noisy crowded second floor.

At the top of the flight, Dulcine gazed down at them. "Gabriel's here!" She ignored Meg pointedly and reached for Gabe's hand. "I've been waiting for you!"

Gabe evaded her hands as he bowed to her. "Good evening. Did my mother arrive safely?"

Dulcine looked disgruntled. "Yes, she's on the balcony."

Gabe nodded his thanks. Taking Meg's arm, he led her to the balcony. He greeted his mother, then drew Meg to the end of the balcony where they could be more private.

Meg leaned close to his ear again. "It's fairly obvious Dulcine isn't thrilled to see me. Go back inside—"

A gin-flushed male voice came loudly from inside, "Did Gabe bring that Yankee with him? Doesn't he know the truth about her yet?"

Meg gripped Gabe's arm. "Go sit beside your mother. I don't want a scene."

He whispered back fiercely. "No one will tell me who I may or may not escort—"

His mother rose majestically from her nearby wicker chair and reentered the room. "Charles DuPuy"—a hush fell over the festivity inside. Mrs. St. Clair proceeded—"You are, what we called in my youth, foxed. Please take yourself away until you've recovered your proper sense." Then she returned and sat back down calmly.

"Bravo, mother," Gabe whispered beside Meg's ear.

"You should still go inside. Dulcine might . . ." Meg drew in a dismayed breath. She hadn't meant to reveal she suspected Dulcine of starting the rumor Belle's friends had overheard.

"I'm to blame for encouraging her. I was so broken up I thought my mother was right and I should court Dulcine."

Meg tucked her chin low. "Perhaps it would be advisable for you not to make a clean break with her just yet."

"Why?"

"I believe—though I could be misjudging Dulcine—that if she thought we were romantically attached, she would spread more rumors."

Meg's every word rang true. How could his mother have wanted him to marry such a pedestrian and spiteful woman?

The evening inched on. After his mother's attack, no one dared slight Meg. Gabe argued back and forth inside himself over whether or not to give her the piece of paper, the name he'd been given. At last, he and Meg stood, alone, back home in front of his parents' fireplace.

"I should go up," Meg said with a weary sigh. She didn't move. "But there are things I want to say to you."

"Say them."

Meg drew in a ragged breath. "I feel such a presence of evil. Not just because of Del being wrongly accused."

Gabe pulled her closer. "Two nights ago when they shot at you, it was too fresh—"

Meg's voice went on, steady and calm. "I think if they had wanted me dead, I'd be lying in the morgue today. I was too easy a target. Someone wants me to leave New Orleans and wants Del convicted."

Gabe could say nothing. Frustration burned in his stomach.

Tears collected in her throat. "I feel like crying and I don't know why." Meg buried her face in his stiffly-pressed cotton shirt. She breathed in Gabriel's distinctive scented shaving soap, so reassuringly masculine. Gabe kissed her hair. She fingered one of the round buttons of his coat. "I don't want you to suffer because of my friendship."

He circled her tiny waist with his hands, drawing her against him. *Friendship? Meg, what I feel for you is much more than that. But how do I reconcile our relationship with my conscience over Lenore, over Del's case?* "I think my only course is to resign from the parish staff of prosecutors."

"No!" She stepped back, out of his hold.

He gripped her shoulders and drew her closer again. "Now

I would much prefer to enter into practice with my father. That wasn't a possibility before . . . before you came."

"I don't want you to resign." She pulled from his grasp. "Don't you see? Resigning from the case could put you in danger."

"Danger?"

"Mitch Kennedy was killed—by whom and why? Del was stabbed by his cellmate, but why? LaRae was killed probably because of her talking to me. Someone ordered that attempt the other night—"

"I'm not frightened!" Gabe's hands balled into fists.

"Of course you're not! You faced death in France! But what about your parents? You once warned me about kidnapping. Would your family be safe? What about Marie? She needs you. She needs to come to a calm, a happy home, not one filled with mourning—"

"Stop!" He wrenched her to him. "I refuse to be frightened by evil. I will do what is right. I will serve justice."

She threw her arms around his neck and kissed him.

He reveled in the abandon of her kiss and swayed with her in his embrace. Her kiss shouted her trust in him, the possibility of a future. He deepened and prolonged the kiss. Finally, breathing hard, he drew back a fraction from her lips. "I will resign. We won't be afraid of the future. And I will give you and father a chance to prove Del's innocence."

Meg stopped breathing. "What are you saying?"

His decision made at last, he pulled a slip of folded paper from his pocket. "I visited Storyville not long ago to try to find a new informant. This man may be able to help you or he might be worthless. I haven't spoken to him about Del's case, so I don't feel that it is dishonorable for me to give you his name. I pray he will help you."

She accepted the paper, gratitude swelling inside her. "Thank you. I want to ask you many questions, but I won't ask you to do anything against your conscience."

"I'm frightened for you. Be sure to go in daylight and take Jack with you." He cupped her now unwavering chin in his hands. How could he have thought her less than beautiful when first they met?

He wouldn't let this woman go down into disaster or slip from his life. "Right now I can't say all I'm feeling, but know that you are dear to me."

The next morning, parked at the curb on a misleadingly quiet street in Storyville, Meg glanced at Jack beside her in the plush leather front seat of her Cadillac. "I'll be fine. I told you I got this man's name from a trustworthy source. You're armed. My derringer's in my purse. I've entrusted you with the cash, so he won't be able to get it unless he gives us some good information."

"I don't like you hobnobbin' with lowlife kind of people who live in this neighborhood," Jack grumbled. "Can't this wait? Court doesn't resume until tomorrow afternoon."

Meg opened her own door and got out. The warmer breeze spread a brackish odor from the nearby Mississippi River. "Wait for me!" Looking affronted, Jack scrambled out and hurried to Meg's side. "We should-a told Mr. Sands we were comin' here."

"I didn't want to bother him unless we actually get lucky. The person who gave me Asa Dent's name wasn't sure this man would have anything worth paying for." Meg tugged her black velvet hat more firmly in place.

"Storyville is no place for a lady." Jack grimaced. "But I can see I'm not going to change your mind. Give me that address—please."

Meg chuckled. "Here it is. It's broad daylight and you're with me. What harm could befall me?"

Jack grumbled wordlessly to himself, but studied the address and the doors along the dead-looking street where Penny Candy was. "Looks like he across the street at the far end." Jack led her to the corner.

As they waited to cross, Meg recognized an open car as it turned farther down on the street and pulled into a parking place in the next block. Shocked, she said, "Look there, Jack, that's Mr. Gabriel's Franklin, isn't it?"

Jack followed her gaze. "Yes." Then he whistled low.

"What is it?" Meg asked, staring as three men got out of the car along with Gabriel. All the men in suits gathered on the banquette beside the car and began talking.

"Mr. Gabriel keeps high company. That's the chief of police and the mayor with him."

"Really?" Meg's brow furrowed. "Why would he be with them here and now and who's the fourth man?"

Jack shook his head. "I don't have a clue why they'd be here. The fourth is probably a plainclothes cop. I think I seen him with Rooney. Here, let's cross now." He took her in hand and escorted her to the other side of the shabby street.

Meg hesitated looking down the street. Penny Candy, Kennedy's club, lay between Meg and Gabriel. *What had brought Gabriel to Storyville this morning and in such company?* Meg could think of no logical answer.

"Have you seen reason and changed your mind?" Jack asked in a hopeful tone.

"No, let's see if Mr. Dent is at home and awake." Meg started walking again. She felt as though she were being watched. She glanced around, but couldn't discern anyone interested in them— just a few drunks lying in doorways and closed cars driving through Storyville.

Jack followed her to the address, where Meg tapped the peeling green front door. An old black woman in a faded red house dress, the landlady, greeted them warily and sent them up her stairs to Dent's room. Meg sensed her suspicious black eyes following their every move.

The smell of stale smoke and coffee hung in the sour air. Being in such a rough boardinghouse made Meg uneasy, but she pushed her concerns to the back of her mind. She had to find more evidence to clear Del. Even after Rooney's biased testimony, Del's life still hung in the balance.

Jack knocked on Asa Dent's door hard enough to wake the dead. A careless, tobacco-rough voice called out, "Don't break it down. The old girl will take it out of my hide. Who's there?"

"Jack Bishop."

"I don't know any Jack Bishop."

"Well, you might know my friends, George Washington, Abraham Lincoln, even Andrew Jackson—"

The door swung open. "You got some friends I like."

The landlady called up querulously, "Remember rent's due today!"

"You'll get it, old lady!" Asa Dent in wrinkled trousers and a stained T-shirt looked to be in his thirties, thin, with yellowed brown eyes. "Come on in." Then he spotted Meg standing behind Jack and his eyes widened.

Jack stepped aside and let Meg enter first. She glanced around. The sparsely furnished room was tidy but dusty. A cigarette burned in an ash tray by the still-rumpled bed.

"What brought you to me?" Dent's eyes assessed them.

Pulling out his wallet, Jack slipped out a five-dollar bill. "We're looking for information."

"What kind?" Dent's gaze roved over them and back again, puzzled.

Meg turned her eyes on him. "Anything to do with Mitch Kennedy or Corelli."

"Mitch is dead. Corelli's the new owner. That's all I know." He folded arms over his thin chest.

Meg couldn't have told anyone how she knew he was lying. But Dent was. Why would Gabriel send her to someone who wouldn't cooperate?

Dent looked nervous, too. " I don't know nothin' about no whitey club owners."

Jack took out another crisp five-dollar bill and added it to the first.

"Can't tell you what I don't know," Dent said sullenly.

Jack flashed a twenty-dollar bill.

Dent snorted and glanced away.

"Mr. Dent, we need information for my friend, Del DuBois." A bad feeling grew inside her. Dent had knowledge, but he wasn't going to sell any to them.

"I can't tell what I don't know." He turned and picked up his cigarette.

"That's true," Jack replied in a quiet tone. "But I hate to put these presidents back in my wallet."

Dent's yellow eyes turned greedy. He took a step closer. "Maybe you're interested in bettin'. I can line up some action for you, hot wagering. Better odds than the on-track bookies."

Jack shook his head and folded the bills back in his wallet. "Sorry we can't do business."

"Maybe you know someone who could help us," Meg ventured, her hope shrinking fast, but grabbing at any chance that remained. "I'd pay you a finder's fee."

Dent shook his head. "No can do."

Jack took Meg's arm. "We'll be leaving you, then. Sorry we wasted your valuable time." He led her out.

Dent clicked the door closed behind them and turned the lock.

Meg's tender optimism of this morning hit the floorboards. Her insides started folding up, shutting down.

Jack and Meg walked down the steps, bid the landlady farewell, and stepped out into the balmy day. Numbly, Meg paused and looked up the street again where Penny Candy lay between them and Gabriel's car. Another hope dashed. Why couldn't anything turn out right for a change? Had Del been just a convenient party to pin a murder on? Or when he'd insisted on being paid, had he unknowingly stepped on someone's toes?

Back on the street again, a black newsboy neared them, shouting, "Extry! Extry! Read all about it! Deputy found dead in Storyville!" Across the way, Gabriel and his companions emerged from another doorway and vanished inside Penny Candy. Had Gabriel seen her? "What's going on here?"

"Paper, lady? Paper, gent? Deputy found dead in Storyville." The boy waved the single sheet special at her. Absently, she took it and handed the boy a nickel. Meg's eye caught the name, Rooney, in the headline. She cried out, "Jack, look here! That's why Gabriel's here!"

A soft curse. Jack fell to the banquette in a heap.

Meg gasped. Searing pain. Her head! She was falling . . .

Chapter 17

Stepping outside of the Penny Candy with his companions, Gabe glanced at his wrist watch. Half past eleven. Mardi Gras festivities would soon fill the nearby French Quarter.

"Mr. Gabriel!" Jack Bishop waved to him and charged across the street.

"Jack! Where's Meg?" Gabe froze, an awful premonition rising within.

"They took her! The paper boy distracted me!"

"Who took her?" Gabe gripped the large man's shoulders. "When?"

"Here! I can't have been out long." Jack struck the air with clenched fists. "How could I be so stupid? I told her we shouldn't have come here!"

Gabe knew why Meg had come. By giving her Dent's name, he'd set her in danger's path. *I'm a fool. How could I have exposed her like that?*

"Who's disappeared?" the chief of police demanded.

"Miss Meg Wagstaff." Gabe looked up and down the somnolent street, anger igniting in his belly.

"You mean that young woman whose name has been linked to that black boy who's on trial?" the mayor asked.

"That rumor, sir," Gabe spat out the words, "is scurrilous. His grandmother was her old nurse."

Lyn Cote

"I see." The mayor nodded, still eyeing him.

"Is Rooney really dead?" Jack asked.

"Yes, that's why we're down here," Gabe replied. "We wanted to question Corelli about it."

"What was *she* doing down here?" the chief demanded. "Storyville is no place for a lady . . . *if* she is a lady."

Burning, Gabe held himself in check, but it cost him. "Miss Wagstaff is every inch a lady. This must be connected with Rooney's death."

"How is Rooney's death connected to Miss Wagstaff's disappearance?" the mayor asked.

"They must be connected," Gabe insisted, his stomach rioting. "Why else would Rooney be found dead in Storyville and Miss Wagstaff kidnapped on the *same street* the next morning? Both of them are involved with Del's trial."

"Well, we can't argue with that," the mayor said.

The chief of police looked as though he'd like to, but he turned to the fourth man who'd remained silent. "O'Toole, you better call into the station and give them the particulars about this Yankee woman who's gone and gotten herself kidnapped."

Gabe bridled at the chief's belligerent tone. He couldn't reveal his feelings for Meg, so he used the only tack he thought they'd understand. He declared in a heated voice, "Miss Wagstaff is a guest in my family's home. The St. Clair honor is at stake. I'm going to advertise a reward for her quick return—five thousand dollars."

O'Toole, the plainclothes police officer, gave him a startled look. "Okay. I'll get right on it."

"Instead of calling, you may take the chief and Mayor Behrmann back to headquarters in my car. Just leave it in my assigned spot." Gabe handed the man his key. "I'll go with Jack in Miss Wagstaff's auto."

The police chief glared at him. "You should leave this investigation to the department, St. Clair."

Gabe fought the impulse to break the chief's jaw, but his voice came out stiffly polite, "I'm sorry, sir. The lady is a guest in my home.

Southern chivalry demands that I do all I can to find her and bring her home safely."

This left the three men nothing to say, which was exactly what Gabe had intended. He watched them retreat, then he turned to Jack. "Now, I want you to tell me exactly what happened—from the time you picked Meg up this morning until she was kidnapped."

Within minutes, Jack helped Gabe retrace Meg's movements, straight to the informant they'd come to question. Upstairs in Dent's boardinghouse, Gabe grabbed the front of Dent's shirt. "You'll tell me the truth, tell me what you know about the lady's disappearance or you will regret it."

"I told you I don't know nothin'. Getting rough won't change that." Dent clutched Gabe's hands to keep his balance.

From where he stood by Dent's window overlooking the street, Jack cleared his throat. "Corelli just walked into Penny Candy."

"Don't leave your room. I may be back." Gabe released him.

Dent stumbled backward.

Within minutes, Gabe stormed into the empty and hollow-feeling Penny Candy and confronted Corelli beside the bar. "All right. What do you know about the kidnapping of Miss Wagstaff?"

Corelli leaned against the bar smoking a cigarette. "I don't know what you're talkin' about. You called and told me to get here. I came over as soon as I was dressed."

Gabe's right hand clenching into a fist at his side, he pictured himself smashing the man's smug face. "Don't play dumb. Everyone in New Orleans knows who Meg Wagstaff and Del Dubois are."

"So?" Corelli flicked the ash off his cigarette.

"I'm putting up a five thousand dollar reward for her safe return."

Corelli gave a low wolf whistle. "That's a lot of money. Sorry I can't help you."

Gabe would have paid five thousand dollars for a legal excuse to drag Corelli down to police headquarters. Instead, he slammed his fist onto the bar. He turned on his heel and marched out. Jack followed him.

Outside, Gabe looked up and down the afternoon street. Most of Storyville still slept. "Where do we go from here?"

Jack rocked back and forth on his heels. "Well, I would go to Mr. Sands."

Why didn't I think of that? Maybe Del or Meg had told him something that would give them a lead. "You're right." They got into Meg's car and Gabe pulled out and took off with a squeal of tires.

Through the buzzing in her ears, Meg heard voices, men's voices, arguing. She tried to straighten up, but couldn't without making her head spin. She gave up and let her head loll weakly forward. She became aware that she was sitting on a chair, but held so tightly . . . *I'm bound.* She tried to speak but a cloth gag stopped her. Through the haze in her head, the voices intruded again.

"You're a fool!" An unseen man's sharp voice hurt her ears. "Did I tell you to kidnap anybody? Did I?"

A low voice that she thought she'd heard before tried to explain, "She was nosing around the club, then more showed up—the chief of police, the mayor—"

"So what?" the sharp voice demanded, sounding as though it were below her feet.

"I saw her go to Dent's, then go behind the club. He may have told her something," the familiar voice tried to sound reasonable.

"I got Dent in my hip pocket. He don't tell nobody anything I don't want him to. You've made a mess of things. Rooney made a mess and look what happened to him."

A silence. "You mean that was you—"

"Sure it was. Rooney messed this up from the beginnin'. But yesterday in court was the last straw—"

"You went to court?" the familiar voice asked.

"I got someone who did. Rooney picked the wrong fall guy. That jazz player is more than just a cheap Joe. He's got an education. He's got a family behind him worth millions. The guy who raised him runs a high-class magazine that blows the whistle on people who do things he don't like—one of those do-gooder muckrakers."

"Who knew?"

"*Rooney* should have known! He bungled this whole deal from the beginning. Now, don't you bungle this." The sharp voice sounded stern. "Even if she is a Yankee, the death of a white woman, a lady will cause big trouble. And her father's got enough money to make waves. I don't want to kill her unless I have to. "

"Don't worry."

"I'm not worried. *You're* the one who should be worried. I want this taken care of today. One way or the other! Don't forget what happened to Rooney."

"Sure, boss . . ."

The voices faded from her hearing and receding footsteps told Meg that they were leaving. She opened her eyes and scanned the room she was being held in. One small window let in the only light from high above. She could see no door, but it might be behind her. How long had she been unconscious? Lifting her aching head made her feel woozy. She lowered it fraction by fraction.

What happened to Jack? Did they kill him, too? Tears flowed down her cheeks. Kennedy, LaRae, Rooney had been murdered. Maybe Jack. Am I next?

Her heart beat so fast it hurt. She cried out against the gag. *Oh, God, I'm so frightened. What can separate us from the love of God? Can bombs, mustard gas, barbed wire?*

Colin's face came before her eyes. Pain cut her in two. Her wrists and ankles pounded with sluggish blood. Only her bindings held her up. Her grief dragged at her like poisoned nails. *Dear God, save Del. Save Gabe. Save me. Without you, we are lost.*

"Del?" Gabe stared in shock at his father who sat behind the desk in his office at home. "I need to question Del to find Meg? What could he know about this, he's been in jail under guard—"

"Yes, Del," Sands interrupted. "If you want the truth, son, you must go to him."

Gabe felt hot and cold. His fears for Meg's safety had shaken him to his core. He now knew the extent of his feelings for Meg. *I can't lose her. I can't face the future without her.* "You'll tell me nothing, then?"

"I can't tell you what I don't know. I think Del knows more than he's told me." Father picked up the newspaper, folded it, then handed it to his son. "Take him this. I think the headline will loosen his tongue."

Gabe took the paper and walked out.

Belle, with Dulcine at her side, accosted him at the front door. "Gabe, I need to know if you will take me to the Rex parade this evening—"

"Parade?" He stared at her.

"It's Mardi Gras today," Dulcine trilled. "Did you forget, Gabriel?"

Meg's kidnapping had driven everything else from his mind. "Meg has been kidnapped."

"What!" Belle exclaimed.

Dulcine looked startled.

"I'm on my way to try to get information from Del at the parish jail."

Belle clutched his sleeve. "Kidnapped? Why!"

"Isn't that a job for the police?" Dulcine asked in a brittle tone.

"No, Dulcine, it's my responsibility because I'm the one who put her in harm's way. Besides," he went on rashly, "I intend to ask Meg Wagstaff to be my wife."

Dulcine's face went white except for two spots of red, one flaming on each cheek.

"I'll be praying for her," Belle murmured.

Gabe touched his sister's shoulder, then left.

Gabe faced Del alone in the jail infirmary. The wall clock read quarter past three. Nearly four hours since Meg had been kidnapped. The clogged streets and a fruitless talk with the chief of police had gobbled up precious time. He'd had Del brought here so they couldn't be overheard. Del's bodyguard and Jack stood guard outside the locked door.

"Why did you want to see me alone here?" Del stared at him suspiciously.

"Meg was kidnapped this morning."

Del reared up out of his seat, cursing Gabe. "Mr. Sands said you hired a good bodyguard for her! What happened?"

"Jack Bishop is a good bodyguard, but they took him by surprise. You can't blame me more than I blame myself. I need you to tell me everything you know, so I can find her."

"She might already be dead." Del clenched and unclenched his hands as if he fought the urge to throttle Gabe.

"I hope, I pray not." Gabe pushed the paper into Del's hand. "My father told me to show you this. Read the headline."

Del took it reluctantly, but one glance at the headline and shock spread over his face. "Rooney's dead?"

Gabe nodded. "I saw Rooney's body at the morgue before breakfast."

Del slumped back into his chair.

Sitting down on a stool, Gabe bent over. Folding his hands together, he propped his elbows on his thighs. "Tell me anything you know that might help me to find her. Please."

Del glanced up. "Your father tells me that you and Meg are an item, is that true?"

"I have fallen in love with her." *Would Del be able to help?*

Del looked at the paper again. "You say you love Meg. Rooney's dead. Why does that mean I can trust you?"

"Because my father sent me. Because Meg trusts me. Because only the truth can free you and save Meg. Tell me. Please." *Dear Lord, make him confide in me.*

Del stared hard at Gabe. "All right. I can talk now with Rooney gone. It took me a while to sort everything out, but . . ." Del paused, staring at the ceiling, then he looked down. He talked slowly as though exhausted: "As I've figured it out, Rooney framed me. Late one night, I saw him with Corelli and the man who wears a flashy diamond ring on his little finger. At the time, I didn't even know who the three of them were."

Del shrugged. "I didn't put it together until after my arrest when I found out who Rooney was, then I asked other prisoners about the man with the ring. They told me his name is Mario Vincent."

Gabe tried to take in what he was hearing. *Kennedy, Rooney, Corelli, and Vincent?* "Vincent runs most of Storyville."

"That's what I've found out—*since* being jailed."

"When did you see them together?" The enormity of what Del was revealing shook Gabe.

"Two days before Mitch was killed, about an hour after closing. I think they thought everyone else in the club had gone home but Mitch. But I was in the back in what we called the dressing room. I heard raised voices—"

"They were arguing?"

Del nodded. "I didn't think anything about that. I came out, ready to leave. I just nodded at them and left. They were talking to Mitch. The thing is I don't think I would ever have put it altogether if they'd just let me go north."

"They needed someone to charge with Mitch's murder." Gabe burned with the injustice of Rooney's treachery. He'd betrayed the public trust. For how long? *Dear God.* Corruption this close to the chief of police.

Del nodded. "Yeah, you're right."

"Do you know why Mitch was murdered?" Gabe looked into Del's eyes.

"I pieced that together, too. I think someone is trying to challenge Vincent for control of the new gin trade."

Gabe repeated, "New gin trade?"

"There'll be more dirty money made than ever selling illegal liquor. Storyville will be a boomtown with cash rolling through it. What I've heard in jail is that someone from New York City wants in. Mitch must have decided to back Vincent's competition. I think they were trying to convince him not to when I saw the four of them together. Evidently Mitch went with the competition. That must be why he was killed—a warning to the other club owners—to remember who they paid protection to and why."

"I've been afraid of what Prohibition might bring." *God, how can something meant to do good, do so much harm?*

Del's jaw hardened. "Well, whatever you have imagined, the reality will be worse. Big money draws tough predators. It will be a bloody fight over the control of the smuggled liquor trade."

"It's already brought three murders and a kidnapping." Gabe stood up, suddenly restless. *Meg, where are you? How will I find you?*

"You've got to find Meg. She is one in a million." Del stood up, kicking his chair back. "You realize they killed LaRae just for talking to Meg. Probably a warning to me and Meg."

Dear Lord, help me find her alive. But Gabe asked, "Did you tell my father about Rooney and his criminal connections?"

"No, I didn't tell anyone." Del looked at Gabe as if he were insane. "What I knew had gotten me arrested for murder. Why would I sentence someone else to death?"

Gabe faced Del squarely. "My carelessness in regards to your case makes me as culpable as Rooney. I want you to know that I intend to resign my position as parish attorney. If I had taken the time to do any investigation of you, I would have known that evidence had been planted on you."

"You thought I was just another colored jazz player in Storyville," Del said bitterly. "But I was as foolish as you. I thought I could come home and bury myself in my music here and forget the Klan and Jim Crow. I was a fool to come home to face the same old bigotry. France was the first place I've ever lived where I wasn't judged by my color. That made coming back ten times worse. Meg told me I should have stayed in France. She was right."

Gabe could say nothing. Hearing Del's bitterness for the first time, Gabe felt ashamed. But Gabe could right no wrongs now except to free Del and find Meg. *The mystery is solved, but that doesn't help Meg.* Gabe shoved his hands into his pockets. "Who do you think kidnapped Meg?"

"Corelli. He may have panicked. Or Vincent himself. I don't see that anyone else has a motive, do you?"

"No, but I've missed so much of what is going on around me I don't trust myself. And how do I go after them?" Gabe slammed his fists onto a nearby cot. "I have no evidence against either of them. Even if I bring them in for questioning, that won't protect Meg! I could have them here in front of me and someone could . . ." He broke off unable to say "kill Meg." "What are we to do? Every minute lessens her chances."

"Well," Del let out a deep breath, "my grandmother always said there'd come a day when I would be pushed beyond what human flesh could bear. I know what she meant now. We're there. We can do nothing in our own strength."

"What did your grandmother tell you to do then?" Gabe ground the words out in a voice that didn't even sound like his own.

"You either give up and go down in defeat or . . ."

"Or?"

"Or you hand everything over to God and take whatever He decides."

"That doesn't sound . . . hopeful." Gabe stared into Del's eyes and saw his own fear and despair reflected there.

"We can always trust God—even in the face of death."

Del's last words froze Gabe inside. *I can't face losing her, God.*

"Are you ready to accept God's will?" Del stood up.

"Are you?" Gabe countered.

"I already have. I've been powerless since Rooney framed me six weeks ago. I'm still powerless—even though Rooney's dead."

Gabe rubbed his forehead. "I have no choice."

Del lowered his head, then raised his hands. "Oh, Lord, you know our sister, Meg, you have tried her like gold and found her pure and faithful. She's in your hands, Lord. Bring her safe through this testing. Please, Lord, please."

Gabe stared at the floor, pressing his fingers to his eyes, forcing back tears. "I know you have the power, Lord." He prayed silently, *I've buried my head in the sand too long, Lord. Please help me find Meg or let someone else find her before it's too late.*

* * *

Staring up toward the dimming light of day, Meg ached within her tight bounds. The blood in her wrists and ankles throbbed from the pressure of the ropes. The sensation of pins and needles prickled in her hands and feet. From outside came loud jazz, laughter, and shouting. Mardi Gras. New Orleans was celebrating while she waited alone to see if she would live or die. *Oh, God, help me. I don't want to die—not when I've just found hope again.*

You did not forsake me in the Quake or in France. Trust in the Lord and lean not on your own understanding—Father taught me that years ago. Why did it take a war, a death, a murder charge, a kidnapping to make me really know it? Trust in the Lord while he may be found. "I do trust you, Lord. Am I too late?" She hung her head and sobbed.

Gabe paced his office. Night had closed around him. The shouts and laughter of Mardi Gras reached him through closed windows. Jack sat, slumped in a chair, his head down in defeat. He and Jack had searched for Meg for hours—by car, then on foot. But Mardi Gras had clogged the streets and banquettes of the French Quarter and Storyville.

The police search for Meg, desultory at best, had given way to crowd control. When Gabe and Jack had returned to Penny Candy, they'd found Corelli gone and received evasive answers to their questions. "Come back tomorrow after Mardi Gras" and "We're too busy trying to keep up with business."

Mardi Gras had become Gabe's adversary and in the end, it had won.

Someone banged on the outer door of Gabe's office. Startled and wary, Gabe opened it.

Dent faced him. "Still offerin' five G's for information about the Yankee woman?"

Gabe's heart jerked; he hauled the man inside by the lapels of his coat. "Do you know where she is?"

"Sure do." Dent smirked. "What about the reward?"

"Tell me where she is and if I find her there alive, you'll have your money."

* * *

Because of the holiday, it took Gabe four excruciating hours to get a search warrant. It was nearly eleven at night when Jack Bishop, O'Toole, Asa Dent, and one uniformed policeman accompanied Gabe. They pushed their way on foot through the Mardi Gras revelers jamming the French Quarter. Dent had fingered Corelli as the kidnapper and had given Gabe an address of a house on Royal Street.

The Rex Parade was in full swing snaking its way through the Quarter. All around them people in shimmering and outrageous costumes and masks greeted one another and danced to the music which filled the air. Prohibition had been forgotten for the day. People openly shared bottles of liquor and toasted Mardi Gras.

Because of the din, Gabe pointed to the number that matched the one on the search warrant. The uniformed policeman pounded on the door. When no answer came, he tried it, found it locked, and kicked it in. Gabe rushed in first with his gun at the ready. The house had a musty, closed-up odor and no electricity. Fireworks burst over Royal Street and lit their way as Gabe led the search through the first floor. No one. "I hope you didn't bring us here for nothin', Dent," Gabe growled.

"She's here, just go on." Dent pointed to the next flight of stairs.

Gabe nodded and started up. Second floor. No one. Gabe turned to Dent, ready to rip his heart out.

Another rapid explosion of fireworks lit the sky. Jack pointed upward. Though the din from outside was muted, he still had to raise his voice, "An attic?"

Gabe caught a flickering glimpse of the outline of a hatch. Before Gabe could act, Jack dragged a chair underneath it, and pulled at the handle, drawing the hatch downward. Gabe grabbed a ladder that had been left propped against the wall. Jack stepped aside and Gabe placed it in the hatchway and climbed up the ladder into the attic.

He nearly collapsed with relief. In the dim light, he saw Meg on a chair. But her head hung low. Was she alive?

Rushing to her side, he tenderly lifted her head.

Meg's eyes flew open. She tried to shout but the gag prevented her.

With his pocket knife, he stripped away her bounds. He clasped her close to him—shaking with relief. "I thought I'd be too late! You're alive! Thank God!"

Trembling, Meg clung to him, gulping air. "I never thought . . . I'd see you . . ."

Sweeping her into his arms, he carried her to the hatch and lowered her to Jack's waiting arms, then scrambled down the ladder after her. "O'Toole, I think you should stay here and secure the crime scene. We might get some evidence to convict Corelli—"

"It was Corelli," Meg croaked with her dry throat. "I overheard him speaking . . . with a man."

"Dent here gave us a tip on Corelli. This house belongs to him, too. But why did he have you kidnapped?"

"He panicked . . . saw us around . . . Penny Candy." Meg leaned against him limply.

"We can take care of him later." With Meg in his arms, Gabe descended the narrow curved staircase, the noise of the celebration bombarded him. At the front door, Jack pushed and kicked aside the debris left of the splintered door. Gabe stepped out onto the street with Meg.

She screamed, "He's got a gun!"

Gabe dove for the cold pavement taking Meg down with him, his body covering hers. Gunshots roared above them. Screams, shrieks, bellows exploded. Dent fell, lifeless, on the banquette beside them.

Two days after Mardi Gras, Gabe sat behind the prosecutor's table in Judge LeGrand's full-to-bursting courtroom.

Judge LeGrand gaveled the court into session and everyone sat. "You newspapermen, no picture-taking. None!" He turned to the prosecutor, "Gabriel, are you prepared to resume the prosecution of Delman DuBois?"

"Your honor, the parish withdraws all charges against Mr. Du-Bois." Gabriel couldn't help grinning.

The judge turned his stringent attention to Delman. "Delman DuBois, please rise."

Del rose.

"Since all charges have now been dropped in the death of Mitchell Kennedy by the parish of Orleans in the state of Louisiana, Delman DuBois, you are free to go."

Del nodded gravely. "Thank you, Your Honor."

Judge LeGrand hit the gavel, then departed. As soon as the door closed behind him, the courtroom erupted into exclamations and excitement.

Meg flung herself in Gabe's arms. He hugged her close. Del stepped up and pumped Gabe's hand. "Thank you. I never expected to be cleared like this—even after all that's happened."

Gabe shook Del's hand. "The chief of police and Mayor Behrmann decided proceeding with such a flawed case would only bring disgrace on the city. After Rooney's murder and Corelli's disappearance, the chief decided a new investigation should be started. You wouldn't have killed Mitch for the reasons Rooney had concocted. The whole case had become too suspect, too flawed, too dangerous in light of public opinion to hazard."

"Do you think Corelli was killed, too?" Del asked.

"We haven't found a body."

Meg broke in, "I think Corelli fled out of fear of Vincent. And I think Vincent gave Dent my location and ordered Dent killed to make certain no one would be left to testify to anything." She shivered, thinking about ruthless men. "It's just fortunate that I didn't see anyone when I was kidnapped. My ignorance saved me."

Del squeezed Meg's shoulder. "You never gave up on me, Meg."

She turned to him. "Our promise stands."

Del blinked away tears. "I'm going back to France."

"Go to San Francisco first, Del. Little Leland William was born last night. I received the telegram first thing this morning."

"When are you leaving, Meg?"

Gabe smiled. "She has an engagement ring to pick out."

Nodding, she looked up at Gabe. "And I have a little girl to welcome."

March 3, 1920

In the warm spring sunshine, Meg and Gabe stood with his parents and Belle with Corby at her side at the New Orleans dock. Gabe's lips tickled Meg's ear. "I still don't know why the whole clan had to come. Marie is a shy little girl."

Looking up at him from under the brim of her jaunty new blue hat, Meg grinned and touched his arm. "When she arrives, just pick her up and don't let go of her." He nodded, but concern for his adopted daughter tightened the lines around his mouth.

Over an hour later, a woman wearing a nurse's white uniform and cap, holding a small child by the hand, stepped off the ramp.

"Marie!" Gabriel scooped the little girl with brown curls into his arms. "This is my daughter, Marie Lenore St. Clair!"

Gabriel's family called out *"Bon jour*, Marie!" The little girl hid her head in Gabriel's neck. Everyone laughed.

Gabriel's mother, the recent founder and president of New Orleans' first Ladies Political Discussion Society, came forward in a chic new purple dress and hat. "Gabriel, please tell her that I am her grandmother."

When he had, the little girl studied her new grandmother, then reached out for her. Mrs. St. Clair burst into tears as she hugged the little girl to her breast. "Oh, my sweet, sweet little baby girl. We are going to love you so much."

Meg smiled. After all that had happened, all the danger and all the deaths and disaster, God had brought them safely together.

In the Franklin driving home, Meg sat beside Gabriel with Marie in her lap. "I'm still sorry you couldn't go home to San Francisco right away," Gabriel apologized again as he tickled Marie under her chin.

"My parents understand and Cecy is fine. My new brother is

healthy and Del is with them and is recovering from his ordeal here. When Marie's settled in, I'll go home for a week or two."

"When does our wedding fit in that plan?" Gabe quizzed.

"As soon as Marie knows me and can enjoy the wedding." She chucked Marie's chin, making the little girl grin.

"What about our honeymoon?"

"You're very naughty," Meg replied in a prim tone, "but if you marry me, I'll consider a honeymoon."

"How very kind of you."

"Don't mention it." Meg fluffed Marie's soft brown curls.

"And you're still going to law school?" Gabe glanced at her sternly.

"Yes, but not this fall. I think a husband and babies will come before a law career in my life's agenda. I have plenty of time—"

"All right, but remember part of our marriage bargain is that you will practice law with me and father."

She chuckled. "I won't forget. I didn't know I would ever be this happy again."

"Neither did I. Probably neither did Marie."

Hearing her name, the little girl said, "Papa. *Je t'aime*, Papa."

"*Je t'aime*, Marie," Gabe replied. He traced Marie's cheek, then Meg's. Little Marie clapped her hands and clambered to her knees to study Meg more closely. Meg whispered back, "*Je t'aime*, Marie. *Je t'aime, Gabriel.*" *Thank you, Lord.*

Historical Note

The Great Chicago Fire, October 8–10, 1871, destroyed 17,000 buildings, left over 100,000 people homeless, and took the lives of between 200 and 300 people. There was never an actual body count. Many victims fleeing the flames drowned in either the Chicago River or Lake Michigan while many of the missing must have been literally burned to ash. An excellent resource is Robert Cromie's *The Great Chicago Fire*.

The San Francisco earthquake began at 5:12 A.M. on Wednesday, April 18th, 1906. Eyewitnesses described it as a violent shaking with jolts and a circular motion. Then the fires started. When they ended on Saturday, downtown 500 city blocks had been ravaged. Over 200,000 of 400,000 city population were left homeless. To read more, try *Three Fearful Days* by Malcolm E. Barker.

Prohibition, the Grand Experiment, only lasted from 1920–1933. But it made a mark on American society. For more information about the drastic changes in American life before and after 1920, pick up Fred Lewis's classic, *Only Yesterday*.

Dear Reader,

I hope you enjoyed reading the three stories of *Blessed Assurance* as much as I enjoyed writing them. I love writing about women and the men they fall in love with, but even more I enjoy unraveling the tales of how God challenges them to do more than fall in love. In each of these stories, the heroines and their heroes "took on" their times. They weren't satisfied with the way things were, but pushed against the inequities they saw.

As Christians, Americans often participated in horrible excesses of violence and cruelty. But at the same time, other Americans fought against the intolerance, ignorance, and poverty. I see our history as a long struggle between our Christian ideals and petty human greed and bigotry. Surely Jessie and Lee, Cecy and Linc, and Meg and Gabe portray countless nameless Americans who fought for what was right. And they were God's salt and light to those around them, examples to us all.

Lyn Cote

Discussion Questions

1. In each of these novels, the main characters faced "moments of truth."
   What was Jessie's? What was Lee's? What about Esther and Hiram? Did they come to realizations by the end of the book?

2. What was Cecy's moment of truth? Linc's? Gabe's? Meg's?

3. Which one meant the most to you and why?

4. Which heroine did you relate to the most? Why do you think that was?

5. Was there a hero you were particularly drawn to? Why?

6. How was Miss Wright different at the end of *Whispers of Love*? What changed her?

7. Alcohol abuse is rampant in our society. Why do you think Prohibition didn't work?

8. Mentors are very important in young lives. Name the mentors that were important in each of the stories and tell how they made a difference. Have you ever had a mentor in your life?

9. In each of these stories, some characters possessed wealth. How did this make life both easier and more difficult?

10. In each of these stories, the characters face an overwhelming challenge—fire, earthquake, social change. Which one struck you as the most difficult or most frightening? Why?

LYN COTE married her real-life hero and was blessed with a son and daughter. She loves game shows, knitting, cooking, and eating! She and her husband live on a beautiful lake in the northwoods of Wisconsin. Now that the children have moved out, she indulges three cats—V-8 (for the engine, not the juice), Sad ie, and Tricksey. In the summer, she writes using her laptop on her porch overlooking the lake. And in the winter, she sits by the fireplace her husband installed with the help of a good neighbor during their first winter at the lake.

Lyn's inspirational novels feature American women who step up to the challenges of their times and succeed in remaining true to the values of liberty and justice for all. The story of America is one of many nationalities and races coming together to forge our one nation under God and Lyn's novels reflect this with accurate historical detail, always providing the ring of authenticity. Strong Women, Brave Stories.

Lyn loves to hear from readers, so visit her website at *www.LynCote.net* or e-mail her at l.cote@juno.com.

Introducing

AVON
INSPIRE

Celebrate the grace and power of Love

Discover Avon Inspire, a new imprint from Avon Books. Avon Inspire is Avon's line of uplifting women's fiction that focuses on what matters most: family, community, faith, and love. These are entertaining novels Christian readers can trust, with storylines that will be welcome to readers of any faith background. Rest assured, each book will have enough excitement and intrigue to keep readers riveted to the end and breathlessly awaiting the next installment. Each title includes reader's guide questions, a letter from the author, and a preview from their next book.

Look for more riveting historical and contemporary fiction to come from beloved authors Lori Copeland, Kristin Billerbeck, Tracey Bateman, Linda Windsor, Lyn Cote, DiAnn Mills, and more!